Starlight Legend

Alana Lee

PRINTED BY KINDLE DIRECT PUBLISHING, AN AMAZON.COM COMPANY

This is a work of fiction. All events, establishments, names, and characters (living or dead) are likewise fictional, and any similarities are purely coincidental, except in the cases of Wayne and Rose who are named after my parents. Though this story takes place in some actual locations and establishments in Idaho, they are only used for fictional purposes.

Layout by Alana Lee

Cover design and lettering by Alana Lee

To my sweet husband, and to my daughters Mia, Courtney, and Lylah, who are my dreams come true.

CHAPTER ONE

Enlisted

IN HER REARVIEW MIRROR, she saw a police car racing towards her, lights flashing, siren screaming.

Elliana pulled to the curb and stopped. She never worried the siren was for her. She checked the dash clock and reached her hand into a bag of gummy fish, but it was empty. She wrinkled her nose.

When the police car passed by, Elliana resumed travel in the outside lane. She tapped her fingers on the steering wheel as she pulled to a stop behind a loud, red truck. She would never admit to being in a hurry to get to the library, of all places, on a Thursday afternoon. At least not out loud. But it was the escape she was looking forward to. She had finished the second book of a thrilling trilogy the night before and was on the hunt for Book 3, so she braved the afternoon rush.

In the cross traffic, she watched an old purple Beetle Bug, covered with no less than fifty bumper stickers, slow, putter, and stall near the crowded intersection of Ustick and Five Mile Road. Someone honked. A twenty-something girl jumped from driver's seat and began pushing her heap of metal out of the way by herself.

The driver's door of the red truck in front of her swung open and a young man burst out, running to push the dead car. Elliana wrestled with herself mentally for just a moment and then put her car in park to join them. By the time she got to the Beetle's bumper, two more people had appeared, and Red Truck Guy told Tattoo Girl to get back in and steer toward the gas station on the right past the intersection.

"Thanks guys!" Tattoo Girl said and hopped back into the driver's seat.

Elliana placed her hands over two bumper stickers that read: "Love all the humans" and "Kindness Matters."

A dip in the road made it hard to get the car moving at first, so they rocked it a few times to get momentum and then pushed until they were running through the intersection and into the parking lot of the gas station. Tattoo Girl's brake lights glowed red as she waved and yelled, "Thank you! You guys totally saved me!" Red Truck Guy fist-bumped Elliana and the other two helpers as they all sprinted back to their cars just after the light turned green.

Her heart pounded from the exertion, and a smile crept to her lips. She was proud of the good people who lived in the Boise, Idaho, vicinity. It also didn't hurt that Red Truck Guy improved the scenery. It made it worth going out of her way to get Book 3.

She walked into the library toward the young adult section, joining three other people searching the same aisle. She crossed her fingers in hopes that the third book was still on the shelf.

An arm clad in black stretched past Elliana's head towards the same trilogy she was scanning the shelves for. Just as her eyes locked on the very last copy of Book 3, the other female hand retrieved it. Curses.

The girl's black sleeve had pulled up slightly during the reach, revealing dozens of raised red lines and tight rows of long, thin scars, so the teenage stranger tugged at her sleeve and shifted backwards to walk away.

Elliana would have to drive to another library now. But, maybe she should still say something. She hesitated, contemplated, then decided.

She touched the stranger to prevent her from leaving and looked into her eyes, sensing the girl's fear and shame. Elliana whispered, "You are enough. The world needs you. And you are not alone." The girl's breath caught a few times before she crumpled into Elliana's arms and sobbed. Elliana put her arms around the girl and stroked her back. "It's true, I promise. You are enough. Don't hurt yourself anymore."

She had decided to say something because complete strangers offered their help to Tattoo Girl in her desperation, and it inspired Elliana to pass it on.

After they parted ways, Elliana walked empty-handed through the crowded parking lot and then drove in awed silence toward another library branch ten minutes away, obeying the speed limit the whole way.

After she found Book 3 and stopped for small bag of gummy fish, she turned on the main road back to her hometown of Star, a little more than a half-hour northwest of Boise. With the look of rush-hour traffic, it might take double that. She regretted not having tried to download the audiobook on the library's Wi-Fi for the drive home.

Now she had plenty of time to think. Elliana frowned as she mentally compared herself to the heroine in the trilogy. Where was her sense of adventure? Where was her persevering spirit? All she was good for was being nice, and being nice made people think she was weak.

Maybe she was.

Speaking those few words to the girl in the library had the power to uplift, and Elliana puzzled how she could believe so strongly that the words she had spoken to a complete stranger were true, but felt less sure about those same words towards herself.

The risk of talking to the girl in the library had worked out well. But the risk she was seriously considering for her future was a scarier proposition. If only someone would tell her the same reassuring things she had said to the troubled girl in the library.

She knew she shouldn't feel so out of place, because after all, she had good friends and a loving family. If she could believe that she truly belonged somewhere, that she could overcome her stupid mistakes, she could feel at peace. If she could only believe that an amazing life lay ahead of her, she would dare to dream. But for now, she found comfort in helping others feel what she sometimes lacked.

She remembered the exact day she started apologizing for things that weren't really her fault and letting people win no matter what. It was the same day she'd said five regrettable words to Bobby. The black, tarry slime of shame from having been too cruel still clung to her memory, dripping, drowning, asphyxiating the hope that she could ever rise above it and be a good person. Besides, rising up seemed to make one a target.

But that was in seventh grade.

Now that Elliana was a senior in high school, her method of safe living, of apologizing for everything, of living vicariously through the adventures of others, of refusing to take real risks for her dreams was getting old.

She grew bored of watching other people get exactly what they wanted out of life, while all she got were good grades and guy friends who laughed at her hilarious jokes and then hooked up with her girlfriends afterwards. Perhaps playing it safe was a recipe for regret.

Perhaps she could entice life to give her more by being strong enough to ask for more.

Or maybe that only worked for lucky jerks, and she was destined to be a spectator at the event called life.

No, today she wouldn't believe that because it felt like a lie, and after the library encounter with a stranger who was in pain from believing lies about herself, Elliana felt like kicking lies in the teeth.

Then she wondered how amazing it might feel to like a boy who also liked her back—an experience that was unfortunately foreign to her. She tried telling herself that she didn't need a boy to define her, or that maybe she hadn't met the right guy, but she wanted that to be a lie as well.

Her pulse raced at the thought of one boy.

That dark, starry night in the middle of April in Star, Idaho, Elliana sat cross-legged on Marlee's wrought-iron bed, tucking her long, brown hair behind her ears and flipping through a rough draft of Copernicus Charter High School's most recent yearbook.

She stopped on the first page of the "Senior Superlatives" and stared at one picture for too long. In the snapshot, she stood next to Burke Bradford, her best guy friend, with his arm resting around her shoulder, both looking at each other with questioning smiles. She read the caption like an obituary: "Cutest Couple that Never Was."

Marlee stood at her dresser, brushing her dark auburn waves into a high ponytail. "I voted for the both of you, and I saw the final tally. You guys won four-to-one." She twisted a thick rubber band around her mane and then sat down on her bed. "When are you going to tell him?"

Elliana shrugged and let her hair fall in front of her face to hide from the question.

"I know you hate dances, but you should ask him to Spring Formal now that he's single. I don't think he would ever say no to you, so this could be your big chance at moving past being just friends." Marlee's eyes closed slightly to be more persuasive.

Elliana didn't put a whole lot of stock in formal dances, because dances so far were disappointments masquerading in fancy dresses and suits. But maybe this time Spring Formal could be the means to the perfect end.

Or it could completely ruin things.

Just the thought of rejection made her ribs squeeze her lungs. "I don't know if I'm ready for the truth, Marlee. I've liked him for almost two years, but I don't want to ruin our friendship. And if I don't go to Spring Formal with him, I'd rather not go at all."

"Don't think like that. You worry too much—you need to learn how to live a little. At least walk to the edge where the view is better."

"Easy for you to say. You always get the guy you want, while I am permanently invisible to the male species, unless they need help with math or proofreading or something."

Marlee's ponytail swung back and forth as she shook her head. "Not true. What about Ross?"

Elliana's back stiffened; Marlee was being a rat by bringing up his name. "Thanks a lot. I'm still furious that I wasted my last homecoming on that guy. Don't even get me started!"

Marlee laughed. "Ross-Schmoss. He's a moron who will never come close to deserving you." She probably used this sour memory to get her friend riled up and to make her next statement more powerful. "That's all the more reason for you to end your high school experience with someone way better, someone special like Burke—even if you just go as best friends. Why don't you ask him tomorrow night at the cookout? Only three weeks left, and if you wait any longer, you'll for sure lose out."

Elliana looked up at her friend. "I have a better idea. Why don't you talk to him tomorrow night when no one is around, and just feel him out to see what he would think about going to Spring Formal with me." Elliana pleaded with her eyes. If Marlee could gather some information on her behalf, she'd be less likely to make a fool of herself. And the fear of looking like a fool was a big reason why she didn't do a lot of things. "Pretty please?"

"Of course, I'll ask him for you, scaredy chicken." Marlee clucked like a hen and then smiled. "By the way, tomorrow you should wear those designer jeans you just tried on. They look smokin' on you, and Burke would be an idiot not to notice."

"You'd let me borrow them even though you've hardly worn them?" Elliana closed the yearbook draft and set it aside. She had never owned a pair of designer jeans before, and she half-wondered if that's why she was invisible to guys.

"You can't borrow them. You can have them. It's my little way of helping my best friend get a hot date with her best guy friend."

"You're the best!" Elliana leaned forward and hugged Marlee. "By the way, who do you want to go to Spring Formal with? Jared?"

"I really hope so. Don't tell anyone, but after everyone left last weekend, we just stayed around the fire talking. He was sitting right next to me on the log and had his arm around me, and he whispered, 'If I had a nickel for every time I saw someone as beautiful as you, I'd have five cents.'"

"You told me that already." Like Elliana could forget that ridiculously cheesy line.

Marlee hesitated as though lost in thought. "But did I tell you that he came over last night?"

"And? Are you guys a thing now?" Elliana didn't know why Marlee hadn't said anything yet, because it wasn't like her to keep those kinds of things to herself for more than twelve seconds.

"Not officially, but I really like him, and I'm pretty sure he likes me, too. He makes me feel so...real."

Rather than feel jealous that Marlee always seemed to get the guy she wanted when she wanted, and seemed to be getting exactly what Elliana wanted for herself, she forced herself to be happy for her best friend. "It sounds like he likes you, which means he'll probably ask you to Spring Formal."

"I'm hoping." Marlee held up two sets of crossed fingers sporting red fingernail polish. "We had so much fun together yesterday—I can really see myself with him."

"Marlee Mooney, you'd better spill it. Tell me everything."

"Okay, and you can help me figure out if he really li–"

At that moment, Elliana glanced at her watch: 8:54 p.m. She leaped off the bed, grabbing her purse and new jeans from the floor. "I want to hear all the details, but I've only got six minutes before I'm grounded for missing curfew. I'm so sorry— please tell me everything tomorrow. And thanks for the bling

jeans!" She had to avoid getting grounded the night before her big chance.

CHAPTER TWO

Chasing

TIDBITS OF WHAT SEEMED LIKE A MEMORY had been teasing her for several years. Every so often, she would get glimpses of this and that and write them in her journal, but she could only vaguely remember the details. Today Elliana awoke with a partial remembrance of what felt like an actual memory and with a feeling in her heart that something important would happen. She decided right then that it was going to be a great day.

In this memory she entered a fantasy world where she felt an incredible sense of belonging, but she had no idea how she got there.

It had seemed so real, so believable. Admittedly, this place probably didn't even exist. But if it did, she wanted in—no regrets. If the fantasy land didn't really exist, then no harm done; if she didn't tell anyone her plans, no one could call her crazy for trying. She remembered how her dad said that *crazy* was a label that the average put on the exceptional, and she ran her fingers over her temples as if she could pull the answers from her head.

Tempted to just lie there with her eyes closed, reveling in the memory, but fearing her mind would quickly fog over, Elliana grabbed a pen from her nightstand and her journal, which was laying underneath Book 3, and wrote what she could remember.

As her pen scratched furiously on the paper's surface, a colorful prism of light rested on her right wrist, warming her skin faintly. She glanced downward, flipping her hand over several times, watching the prism float on her skin, and then traced the origin back to the crystal wind chime hanging just outside her second-story window which sent dozens of dazzling prisms throughout her room. Boy, her room needed cleaning.

Having an odd suspicion that she was being watched, she jerked her head toward the doorway and then looked around the rest of her room, but she was alone. Alone, except for a bird perched on the window, warbling and singing the arrival of morning.

Returning her gaze to the floating spark of light on her hand, she saw her diamond-sapphire ring was missing, the ring she inherited from the mother she hardly remembered. Elliana dismounted her bed and searched the nightstand and the floor but found nothing.

Frustration turned to fear. It couldn't have gotten far. A panic set in because the sentimental value of the ring made it irreplaceable.

She knelt on the floor and reached under the bed. As she swept her hands beneath the dust ruffle, hoping no spiders bit her, her fingers grazed the cool metal band of the missing ring. She put the ring back on her right ring finger and held up her hand to admire the stones glinting in the sunlight. She had probably knocked it off her nightstand when she had scrambled to hit the snooze button.

Her eyes wandered to the silvery, diagonal scar on the topside of her wrist that resembled the losing-side of a broken wishbone. This scar was a visual reminder that she had survived the same car accident that killed her parents. Surely it was strange to treasure a scar, but she did because it was her surest connection to her origins, which were largely entangled with the unknown.

Almost sixteen years to the day had passed since the horrific car accident stole her parents away and left her and Abbie orphaned. No one really knew what had happened on that lonely road, and Elliana had almost no recollection of it. Their small family sedan traded paint with a dark-colored vehicle before smashing head-on into a massive tree about twenty feet off the road, but that other vehicle was long gone by the time the accident was reported by a passerby.

Her parents' deaths had been swift. However, Elliana, who was almost three at the time, and her sister Abbie, who was hardly one, had been spared, holding hands in their car seats surrounded by shattered glass. Elliana had been told she was particularly distraught by a spider hanging from the flannel ceiling.

Though she dearly loved the Reinharts (her adoptive parents), and though she tried not to dwell on it, she still felt a measure of loss not knowing who her biological parents really were. She imagined that her first-parents must have been friendly, outgoing, well liked, smart, talented, and confident—like the heroes in Book 3. There were days she stared at their tattered driver's licenses and wondered if she looked more like her mother or her father. Abbie looked so much more like her mom, their first-mom.

Abbie was lucky to be tall and athletic with long blond hair and amber eyes—just how she imagined her first mom beyond the headshot from her license. Elliana wasn't sure if she envied

Abbie more because she looked like their first mom or because of her beautiful voice, but she was a tad jealous that her sister had features and gifts that she didn't.

Elliana wasn't as tall nor as fair-skinned; she claimed her blue eyes came from her first-father (because his license stated that he had blue eyes), and maybe her gift for words and wittiness came from him, too. She decided to credit an unknown great-great-great-grandmother for any unshared features. All she really knew was that she wanted so badly to believe she came from strong stock biologically. She had no real proof, so she relied on her vivid imagination, which reminded her she had been writing down her dream-memory before she got distracted.

"Breakfast!" her mom called up the stairs.

"Coming, Mom." A minute later Elliana closed her journal, jumped up, stretched her arms to the ceiling and then down to the floor for a few seconds, and walked briskly downstairs. Since it was hot-breakfast Friday, the aroma of fresh, buttery biscuits, sausage links, and eggs wafted from the kitchen.

"Morning, Mom." Elliana bent down, kissed her mother on the cheek, filled her plate, and took a seat beside her at the table.

"Good morning, darling," her mother said. "Burke called a little while ago."

Elliana jumped up and grabbed her phone out of the basket on the counter and checked for a missed call. "Did he call my cell? Oh, never mind. Looks like it shut off. It never charged." She grunted and wiggled the cord in the charging port.

"He said it went straight to voicemail. Anyways, he called to make sure you remembered that he was picking you up this morning at seven o'clock so you guys could study for your calculus test before school."

As if she could forget. "Is that all he said?" Her train of thought led to their plans that evening to drive to Eagle Island State Park on the Boise River to have a barbeque and play Frisbee with some friends in her new jeans, but she still had to clear it with her parents to make sure it didn't interfere with special family plans.

"He also made sure it was okay to pick you up after school to go to Eagle Island. He wanted to make sure we didn't have any family plans given the anniversary this weekend, you know, but I assured him you were free, and that you've had a crush on him since the tenth grade, and you would love an outing with him, preferably alone. I told him not to bring you home until curfew." Her mother looked very pleased with herself.

"MOM! You didn't dare say anything of the sort!" Elliana's eyes darkened and then brightened again as she sipped her cran-orange juice.

Her mother looked her in the eyes. "Ellie, you can't wait too long or you might lose your chance."

"What if he doesn't feel the same way? First of all, I don't want to be rejected. Second of all, I don't want to risk losing my best friend and make things all awkward and stupid between us. And third of all, I'm a total chicken when it comes to the business of boyfriends and stuff!" Elliana's face flushed. "Good thing I asked Marlee to talk to him tonight to see what he thinks of going to Spring Formal with me, and if he sounds positive, then I will ask him."

"It's puzzling. You guys have been friends since you met in middle school. You study for tests together, spend your free time together, and share secrets. And yet he seems completely blind to how you really feel about him."

"Do you really think he hasn't a clue that he's deeply, madly in love with me?" Elliana had a hard time not being hilarious around her family. She frequently joked about her crush on Burke, but only occasionally permitted it coming from others.

"I don't know. Sometimes I see the way he looks at you and it seems like you could be more than friends, and other times just friends. Either way there will likely come a day when you'll regret not having been upfront with him about your feelings," her mom said. "Maybe he just needs to know. Sometimes you can look at something and not realize that it could be different—it just takes a nudge in the right direction."

Elliana pushed her breath out slowly with puckered lips, as she usually did when deep in thought. "You're probably right. But I'm not going to say it for fear of it going straight to your head. And now I'm changing the subject. Where are Dad and Abbie?"

"Abbie's in the shower, and your dad is in his office writing. He got a stroke of inspiration."

Her mom's words were laden with hope. Her dad hadn't been able to write like he'd been able to before his stroke, and his current day-job didn't pay that well, so it was good that he was feeling inspired.

"Mom, do you ever have memories of something that never happened, almost like a dream, that seem like they're real? Like a clue you're supposed to learn something from? You know, besides learning that I might be a weirdo who can't get a date?"

Her mom shook her head. "I haven't, but I've heard other people do. I do think that the universe has a way of communicating important things through dreams, and that everything happens for a reason—my mom taught me that, and moms are pretty smart." Her mom pushed up the rim of her glasses and smoothed her gray hair into her bun, and then sipped from her glass.

Elliana didn't want to ruin her memory-like dream by finding out it was only a figment of her imagination, because there's something magical about a dream. Just like she didn't want to ruin her friendship with Burke by finding out there was nothing more. The worst thing would be finding out her dream-memory meant something all along, but that she was too scared to try. She wanted to believe that this exciting (and almost absurd) fantasy would change the course of her life. What if her biggest regret at the end of her life was not following it? Chasing this seemed less risky than chasing a boy. If it were meant to be, someday she would remember the whole dream-memory, and then she would seek it.

"I'd better go shower." Elliana stood up and took her plate to the sink.

Abbie came waltzing into the kitchen, her skin clean and pink, her wet hair pulled back into a messy bun by a jaw clip. "Burke just drove up. Is he picking you up for school today?"

Elliana gasped, looking down at her wrinkled t-shirt, pajama capris and bare feet. "Already? You'd better be joking!" She glared at her sister.

"I am. But you should have seen the look on your face. It was pretty classic." Abbie snorted. "He called and talked to Mom right before I went running and I couldn't resist. We think you need to confess your love to him. I can help if you want."

"Very funny. I'm going to take a shower, and if he happens to show up before I'm ready, I forbid you to say anything I wouldn't approve of." Elliana cast a stern glance at her mother and sister, hoping that would make them behave, and then she scurried down the hallway and bounded up the stairs, two at a time.

It was an average Friday at Copernicus High. Every teenager was full of pent-up energy now that the weather had warmed and the weekend had arrived. Maybe her mom and her sister were right, but she wasn't sure how to go about telling Burke that she liked him. *Burke, guess who's been in love with you since tenth grade? That's right! This hot mess! I played MASH and we end up married with fourteen kids.* Her mind ran through all the possibilities, and she decided she wouldn't tell him today unless she encountered some pretty convincing evidence that she wouldn't be making a fool of herself.

They had held hands a week ago, during a scary story night around Marlee's fire pit, but she wasn't sure she could contribute that to him like-liking her because he knew she was scared. Although, he did hand-feed her a marshmallow. She couldn't tell if any of it was flirting because they had been best friends for years.

They were comfortable around each other, and yes, they told each other most of their secrets—except for the one about her liking him. She had no idea if there was anything more than friendship, but if there was a sign today, any hint that he might reciprocate her feelings, anything that meant she should ask Burke to Junior-Senior Spring Formal, then she would gather her courage and ask him tonight.

The test took the entire class period of Calculus, and she felt she did well, but AP Spanish dragged on, and the outing to Eagle Island seemed too far away. She struggled to pay attention.

In English class, they discussed a writing assignment with the first draft due May 4, exactly two weeks away. She was supposed to be working on an outline, but she still hadn't chosen a topic. The only criterion was to write a research paper on any topic, and the top three essays would be entered into a local writing contest that awarded two scholarships. She really wanted a scholarship since money was a little tight.

She wasn't terrible at writing—she just didn't enjoy it because it was so time consuming for her, and some of her friends could whip out a better paper in a quarter of the time. When she brainstormed in class, all she could think of was sitting next to a certain cute guy friend during lunch, getting hand-fed marshmallows by him at Eagle Island, and then slow-dancing with him at the Spring Formal.

Lunch period arrived like a sloth on Benadryl. Burke and Elliana stood in the lunch line together, wrinkling their noses at the lima beans and laughing at inside jokes. Elliana caught some envious gazes from younger girls because of her friendship with Burke. But the way she saw it, that envy was misplaced because she definitely wasn't as involved with him as she wanted to be.

As they mazed through the cafeteria, Elliana said hi to almost every table she passed. She had many friends: the popular kids, the orchestra members, the honors students, the rebels, and the outcasts—not that she hung out with most of them outside of school, but they were friendly to each other in the lunch room.

The two took a table in the corner, near the back, sitting next to each other and beside several of their friends: Keisha, Marlee, Quintin, and Jared. Marlee was boisterous, shining in the spotlight, intent on gaining Jared's attention. But Jared looked checked-out; he kept gazing toward a table of giggling, kind of annoying, sophomore girls, who obviously craved just as much attention as the auburn-haired storyteller at his table.

Marlee held everyone else's attention with the tale of a six-foot rattle snake that her dad killed the day before with a well-aimed rock. He had been showing some property to the CEO of a large corporation and it became quickly apparent that the CEO was no fan of snakes. He yelped like a ninny child and leaped back the length of a man, which was quite a feat for the conceited, jowly-faced executive. The group laughed at Marlee's impersonation. The CEO was a powerful man who went to great lengths to cover up his mistakes and preserve a superior yet false image, so this was good dirt.

Burke leaned in toward Elliana until their shoulders met. "I wish I had that on video—it would've gone viral!" He rubbed his thumb against his first two fingers to indicate money.

"I'm sure if you just ask Marlee, she'd help you set that all up. Rattler, camera crew, and all. She's quite the event organizer—not a detail would be missing!" Her friend was eccentric—in a good way—and thrived on throwing parties, on organizing events, and on getting people to do what she wanted.

Burke nodded.

"Although Mr. CEO would probably put a hit on everyone involved and claim they all died of natural causes."

Burke nodded again, and as he looked at her, he squinted slightly.

She hoped he was noticing her, noticing that she was his dreamboat and they could sail off in the sunset to Spring Formal together, and hopefully noticing that she was almost the exact opposite of Marlee in a good way. Elliana was not overly concerned with name brands or fake nails; she had wavy brown hair instead of reddish-brown; she wasn't obsessed with each new release of a smart device; and she felt she had a heart as deep as the ocean if anyone cared enough to go scuba diving.

Maybe he was really seeing her, and maybe this was a good sign. *Yes, I'll marry you! Thanks for asking,* Elliana thought.

CHAPTER THREE

The Truth

Anxiety for the recon mission at Eagle Island caused her lungs to hiccup and her stomach to roll and thump like a tricycle with a flat-edged wheel. Elliana looked in the mirror and fidgeted with her freshly-ironed waves, sweeping them up into a pony tail, looking sideways at her reflection, and then releasing them in frustration. As badly as she wanted to hide, she also wanted to be noticed, so she pinned the sides of her hair back so that it was still down, but not in her face. She wore her lucky amethyst earrings her dad bought her for her sixteenth birthday.

She did not want to appear over eager nor overdressed, but she did want to look her best. She wore a light blue top to bring out her eyes, the jeans from Marlee, and four layers of plum lip gloss.

Hearing Burke's Tahoe pull up the driveway, she called out, "Bye, Mom and Dad. I'll be back by curfew, and I have my cell on me. Love you!" She grabbed her purse and was gone before anyone could protest or ask her to invite Burke in for some embarrassing chitchat.

Burke nodded a greeting to Elliana. She waved at him, shut the front door to her home, and ran down the driveway to his

SUV.

"Hey, Ellie. I brought your usual: orange soda and gummy fish. I stole the fish from the stash my mom keeps for you in our pantry."

"You're the best," she said as she leaned toward him to bump knuckles. He was so thoughtful and way more observant than a lot of other people she knew. Maybe this was the evidence she was looking for that he did like her deep down inside. Then a rotten thought wormed its way into her mind: maybe his mom was the one being thoughtful and she had reminded him to bring her favorite treats? Elliana slid her retro sunglasses onto her face to block the blinding afternoon sun and to hide the uncertainty in her eyes. "Is everyone still coming?"

Burke drove the silver Tahoe southeast toward the lake. "Jared and Quintin said they would meet us there. As for Marlee and Keisha, no idea."

"Keisha told me during PE that she was able to get out of babysitting and will be there. And Marlee was dead-set on going," said Elliana, remembering how Marlee said she would talk to Burke for her. "By the way, is Jared going to ask Marlee to Spring Formal?"

"Um, I don't think so."

"Oh," she said, wrinkling her nose. She didn't like the way he said *um* first, like it had been a stupid question because Marlee had seemed so sure that he liked her.

"At least he didn't make it sound that way when I talked to him yesterday. Why, does she like him now?"

"All I will say is that Marlee would probably say 'yes' if he asked her to the dance, but you never heard that from me." Marlee had a heart of pure gold—well perhaps eighteen-karat gold because she could hold a grudge when she needed to—but

Elliana was careful so that a grudge would never be leveled against her.

Who are you going to ask to Spring Formal? The words wouldn't come out. Instead she asked, "Do you have all the food for the barbeque?"

"I brought the hot buns," Burke said, with raised eyebrows and a devilish smirk.

He deserved a good slug in the arm, so she obliged him. She loved his dimples and the way his blond curls barely stuck out from underneath his baseball cap. He turned and gave that smile that made her insides bubble.

Elliana was better at flirting with other guys, but when it came to Burke, she clammed up and just played the comfortable role of best friend. Pretty soon they were both singing along with the radio, oblivious to the rest of the world, when Burke's cell phone rang. He leaned toward the window and pulled his phone out of his back pocket, glanced at the caller ID, and then answered it. "Hey, Quintin.... What's up? Yeah, we should have enough food.... What? That's interesting. When did this happen? Of course, who'd say no? Good for him, I guess.... I'll tell them. You guys on your way? 'Kay, we'll meet everyone at the Shady Acres gas station."

The other side of that conversation was obviously full of juicy details. The second he ended the call, Elliana burst out with: "What did he say?"

"Oh, nothing interesting."

Elliana's fist collided with Burke's right shoulder, but he was ready for it. He laughed so hard she thought he was going to drive off the road. "Seriously, what was that all about?"

He laughed a few seconds more, which just made her more anxious and irritated at not knowing what was going on, but she couldn't help but laugh along with him because that was their normal.

"Just that Quintin and Jared will meet us at the gas station." Burke was regaining control of himself at this point and wiped the back of his fist across his eyes.

Elliana rolled her eyes. "I heard that part! Come on! Out with it!"

"Okay, okay. He was calling to see if we had enough food to accommodate Jared's Spring Formal date, or if they needed to buy more."

"Jared's Spring Formal date? Who did he ask? Why are you holding out on me? You are being such a rat!" The words came out almost faster than she was thinking them. She gave Burke an impatient look and then swatted his shoulder, knowing he was thoroughly enjoying this.

"Quintin said that Jared asked Daisy to Spring Formal, and she said yes."

"He asked that new sophomore girl who hardly knows the meaning of clothing to our Spring Formal? Ooh, Marlee's going to be crushed."

"So she does like Jared." Burke grinned. "I'm telling."

"I'm going to punch you later when you're not expecting it."

"Again? Another light-as-a-feather punch? Promise?"

"Yep. That's a promise. And speaking of promises...." Elliana trailed off. "I think it's time you made me a promise."

"Yes, your majesty. What shall I promise you?" The mock in his tone was obvious.

She twisted forward and said, "Promise me you'll never go out with Veronica Curry."

"Before I make this promise official, tell me why I'm making it."

She hesitated. She looked down at her hands and fidgeted with the ring on her right hand and briefly considered telling him it was because she wanted him all to herself. "Because she's bad news. That's all I'm going to say. I don't like to gossip—unless it's about Jared, of course—but that girl is slightly eeevil." She drawled out the first syllable to the last word.

Skirting Elliana's request, Burke said, "I love the way you just said eeevil!" He mimicked her.

"I'm serious! Promise me you won't go out with her." Elliana looked straight into his eyes.

"Okay, okay. If it will make you happy, I won't."

"You won't what?" Elliana prodded.

"I won't go out with her."

"Really? You want to be my punching bag all night?"

He laughed before giving the expected full-sentence answer: "I promise I won't go out with Veronica Curry. Happy?"

"Yes, thank you, I am." Elliana smiled and batted her eyes in victory. "By the way, I heard Veronica likes you."

Burke pursed his lips like he was about to say something, and then relaxed his face.

"Trust me," Elliana said.

"That's just it. I'd trust you with my life."

By the time she and Burke pulled into the gas station, there were two cars waiting for them. She saw Jared's blue sedan, and in the other car she saw Keisha sitting next to a fuming, glaring, red-faced Marlee. She knew.

"If looks could kill," said Burke, pointing in the direction of Keisha's silver car. From their seats, they watched as Quintin leaned against the back of the blue car, and Daisy flirted gratuitously with Jared and ran her fingers through his hair pretending to style it. Elliana's heart sank for her friend—he definitely had led her on.

"This isn't going to be pretty," whispered Elliana.

Burke killed the engine. "Guess who's going to freeze tonight?"

She looked the younger girl over to see what the attraction was. Daisy's bleached blond hair was cut in a long bob, teased high, curled towards her jaw, and aqua-netted into place. She was only average, thanks to a half-dozen layers of makeup, but it was obvious several males were only noticing her skin, which she was showing way too much of—typical of a Californian transplanted in Idaho. Elliana watched Daisy swing her boyish hips from side to side as she walked with Jared into the mini-mart. That girl was way too skinny. "We brought dinner, she brought the show."

Burke laughed and opened his door, and Elliana jumped down and walked toward the silver car.

"Girl, you look hot in those jeans!" Keisha yelled from her car.

Elliana did a quick strut as she neared Keisha's car and leaned in the driver's window. "Hey, Marlee. Hey, Keisha." They both greeted her, but Marlee wouldn't make eye contact and her lower jaw jutted out beneath pressed lips.

Elliana got straight to the point. "I guess you heard about Jared's Spring Formal date. I just barely found out on the way here. I'm sorry."

"I figured as much when I saw him pull up with that stupid riffraff in the front seat. Did you see how she hangs all over him? Who cares. I don't even care," said Marlee, her voice toxic. Her face flushed and her eyes filled with water. She lifted her chin up a degree and tried to hide her emotions.

"I'm so sorry, Marlee," Elliana said again.

"Just keep Daisy away from her," said Keisha. "We don't want a cat fight. Actually, the guys might enjoy a cat fight, but we aren't interested in permanently marring the new girl's face, assuming one could break down her impenetrable shield of makeup."

Keisha Fox was a good friend of Elliana's, but they usually only hung out together in a group. She was the motherly-type of friend who made sure no one got out of hand—everyone respected her both for her sense of right and wrong and also for her muscles. It was rumored that her mother had made a living as a show girl in Las Vegas back in the day, but no one was stupid enough to ask Keisha if that was true.

"I'm going to buy some gum, do you guys wanna come?" Elliana figured some minty gum could come in handy.

Marlee stayed in the car.

Quintin was inside buying more ice for the coolers and lighter fluid for the charcoal. When they emerged, everyone was in their cars ready to go, so Elliana jogged back to Burke's Tahoe.

Within a few minutes, their tires hit the gravel road leading down to the Boise River. Burke took up two parking spots, as he usually did, because "My dad would kill me if I got a scratch on his SUV."

The boys grabbed the small charcoal grill and the cooler of food, and the girls grabbed the Frisbees and camping chairs, and all headed toward a spot near the water's edge. After helping Burke and Quintin get the grill started, Jared and Daisy selected a spot away from the group to flirt, or whatever. It was just as well. If Daisy had half a brain, she would realize that no one but Jared wanted her there anyway, and that it was too chilly to dress for the beach.

Quintin and Burke chose a stretch of lawn right in front of the ladies to flex their muscles as they tossed the Frisbee back and forth.

Elliana bent down to roll up her jeans, kicked off her shoes, and walked into the shallow water. The water was much higher this time of year with all of the runoff, which also meant it was icy cold. The water nipped and bit at her skin, and she watched a cloud of sand and dirt form and then dissipate. Keisha joined her in the cold water until the pain got too intense.

Marlee stayed in the car for nearly half an hour taking "an important phone call," as she said, and when they had walked back to the car and tried to entice her over to the water's edge, Marlee said she'd be along shortly.

"If you need to talk, we're your girls," Keisha said.

"Thanks, Keesh. Really, I'll be fine. I'm just talking to my mom."

They let Marlee have her space, which meant they were free to join in a game of Frisbee.

After thirty minutes, Elliana and Keisha returned to the picnic area to start grilling. Elliana worried that things weren't going as planned: Marlee wasn't in the right mood to talk to Burke for her, and she doubted that she had enough courage to ask him anything herself.

"Ellie, what are you doing for your birthday?" Keisha asked, rolling the hot dogs on the grill with a whittled stick since no one thought to bring tongs.

Elliana blinked and looked up. "I don't know. Still haven't decided, but I don't think I want to have a party. I don't like the stress of throwing parties. Or having a bunch of uninvited people show up." Elliana wasn't big on birthday parties because they were sometimes disappointing. Her last birthday party with just her family had been pretty close to perfect, but parties with friends rarely had been. As fun as a friend-party could be, she didn't want the hassle or the letdown. Better to play it safe.

"Marlee could plan it! Why don't you let her? It would be fun and your nineteenth is a big deal! It's the last one of your high school career. Maybe planning a party just might help Marlee take her mind off of Jared's jerkiness."

Keisha had a good point. "Good idea. I'll ask her," Elliana said and then changed the subject. "So, I'm thinking I might actually have the guts to ask Burke to Spring Formal—it's only three weeks away, and he hasn't asked anyone yet, you know, since he's single now."

"You're right—this is the perfect opp, girl! You should totally ask him. I think you guys would make an awesome couple." Keisha's smile created the perfect pink apples on her dark skin. "When are you going to ask?"

"I was thinking I would do it on the way home tonight, if all goes well. Marlee's supposed to talk to Burke tonight to see what he would say if I asked him." Looking around, she was suddenly aware that Marlee was nowhere to be found—not even in the car. And neither was Burke. And since they both stayed gone a long while, Elliana was confident that Marlee was getting a lot of good information, which freed her up to talk to Keisha about boys, books, graduation, and summer plans while enjoying the fading sun as much as possible.

ℒ

The minutes dragged on until Elliana could hardly stand not knowing. A full hour later, Marlee and Burke came walking from the asphalt path that led to the grass field.

Marlee threw her head back, laughed, and then gave him

a coy look. "You're so funny, Burke!" She wasn't being a sour puss anymore. Burke must have played the hero and cheered up the damsel in distress. Marlee's hand brushed her hair away from her eyes and said, "You are so sweet! Thanks for being such a great friend," and then gave him a hug.

Elliana's heart quickened with hope. He must have said yes. The excitement caused her to breathe more shallowly, and the anticipation welled up in her like a balloon blown up almost to the point of bursting.

Marlee traipsed over to where Keisha and Elliana were sitting, but the pace was too slow for Elliana's liking. Burke returned to playing Frisbee with the others, casting a strange grin at Elliana as he walked away, giving her his I'll-tell-you-about-it-later look as he readjusted his baseball cap.

"Guess wha-at?" Marlee asked.

Marlee's singsong voice must have meant she had really good news—otherwise, she probably would have been less chirpy. Elliana couldn't stop her heart from pounding as she pictured herself in a satin gown at Spring Formal with him, on his arm. It was going to happen! Her dream would come true thanks to her best friend Marlee.

"What did he say?" asked Elliana and Keisha at the same time, giving each other hopeful looks.

"He asked me to go to Spring Formal with him! Can you believe it? He is such a sweetheart, and he's exceptionally hot, too. I can't wait!"

"Wow." The disappointment imploded in her chest, as if it were sucking all hope from her. "I didn't see that coming," she said half under her breath, deflating. The moment of truth had arrived; Burke wasn't interested in her that way. Though the truth hurt, she was thankful she had spared herself some embarrassment by not asking him herself. What a heavy realization though. Her heart drooped and she scolded herself for getting her hopes up, willing herself to not cry.

"I hope you don't mind, Ellie. It seems he'd rather go with me, and it's not like you had the guts to ask him."

Elliana forced a smile.

"Anyways, I'm über excited! We will make such a dreamy couple. I have to figure out what I'm wearing so I can color-coordinate with him. Can you imagine if we get Spring Formal King and Queen together? Wouldn't that be the ultimate best?" Marlee sighed. "Let's go dress shopping, ladies!"

"Right now?" Keisha glanced sideways at Elliana, who did her best to appear calm and unaffected by her best friend's blatant insensitivity.

"Of course not! Tomorrow. I want to make sure no one has a dress like mine."

The combination of Marlee's irritability and exuberance made it difficult to be around her.

Elliana said, "I have my family thing tomorrow, so I'm going to have to take a raincheck. But text me pictures of the dresses you try on, 'kay?" She was trying to be pleasant, trying to be happy that Marlee was happy. But all she wanted was to get out of there fast. It was getting harder to breathe; she felt a painful hole in her chest growing larger that seemed to burn and sear and smother the happiness she normally felt.

Elliana should never have gotten her hopes up. She was a complete idiot to think she ever had a chance at dating Burke—that much was obvious now. She was just-friends material. After excusing herself, she walked to the restroom. She looked in the warped plexiglas mirror at her distorted face and blinked quickly to abate her tears, feeling ugly and out of place. She thought perhaps she was never meant to find love. She just didn't have the look guys wanted. The mis-shaped image in the mirror did not try to argue, and even validated every negative thought that came to her head. She asked herself the question that would probably be too painful to answer: *what is wrong with me?* How in the world she was going to keep up her happy-for-Marlee-act all evening? If only she could bail. She wished as hard as she knew how that something would happen to give her an out. *I can't do this, at least not tonight. Please, something happen*, she pleaded in her mind, not really knowing to whom or for what she was pleading.

A shrill crack of lightning streaked the sky and was followed by rolling, booming thunder a second later. Thunder sounded again. She breathed a huge sigh of relief to hear an impending storm gathering overhead and emerged from the restroom. Thank heavens! A storm meant they would have to leave early and it was barely 8 p.m.

She returned to her group of friends who were busy grabbing camping chairs and roasting sticks. Elliana grabbed some supplies and threw them in the back of Burke's SUV. The SUV she would have to ride home in. Alone, with him. Insides writhing like a den of angry snakes.

Storm

SHE WORE A PRETTY CALM facade, but Elliana's mind was reeling and she felt an unfamiliar ache in her chest. The group gathered around the cars, packing up, while Daisy stood there shivering. She resisted telling Daisy that she wouldn't get so cold if she simply wore more clothing—it would have been her pain talking, and would say more about herself than Daisy, and she had vowed in seventh grade never to purposefully stab with words again. She also resisted the urge to curl up in a ball and cry.

She mustered the strength to act normally when she said bye to her friends in the parking lot, and only Keisha suspected anything was wrong—but Marlee would have to be a moron not to realize that Elliana was hurting. That was the right word, hurting. Maybe she couldn't be mad at Marlee because he had asked her, but she could be sad that her dream was farther away than it ever was, receding quickly into a black hole in a corner of the galaxy, eternally out of reach. She might as well have wanted to climb Mount Kilimanjaro at this point. Love was never going to happen, but she would pretend everything was fine, just fine.

"Looks like a mean storm ahead," said Burke as they pulled out of the park.

"Yup. Came out of nowhere."

"Everyone is headed over to Marlee's house to hang out."

"Oh, that's always fun. And her house is always chock full of the best junk food," she said, pretending to care about junk food even though she had zero appetite.

Burke drove along the main road back toward Star as they listened to the radio for a few minutes. "I'm sure you heard."

Elliana didn't want to act strange and forced herself to speak. "Yeah, that was nice of you to cheer up Marlee and ask her to formal."

Burke eyed Elliana suspiciously. "What makes you think *I* asked *her*?"

"Um, because that's what she told us. She said *you* asked *her* to Spring Formal."

"Ellie, she asked me. She cried a lot and then told me that I was 'such a sweet guy and good-looking,' and to 'forget about Ellie' and go to Spring Formal with her already."

"What? She said all that?" Elliana fell silent again and felt a lump growing in her throat. Now it clearly seemed a premeditated duplicity. How could Marlee betray her like that? How many nights had they stayed up talking, and Marlee would assure her that one day Burke would notice Elliana in a romantic way, and to not give up? She wondered if Marlee ever asked Burke what she was supposed to ask.

She had rain in her eyes, thunder in her mind, painful burning in her heart, and the emotional storm threatened to blow her just-friends cover. This was not how she wanted it all to come out, so her emotions turned her mute, which never happened when she was with Burke. The ache in her chest burned hotly.

Burke tapped his hands on the steering wheel to the music and sang along to one of their favorite songs. When she didn't say anything for a few minutes, he said, "You're quiet, which is unusual. What's up?"

"Nothing." She worried her strained smile would give her lie away.

"Don't lie to me, Elliana Reinhart."

Elliana chewed her bottom lip, closed her eyes, and then, for once, decided to tell him what she had really been feeling for the past few years. "This is going to be hard for me to say, and it isn't how I wanted to do this, but...."

He prodded her on with an inquisitive look.

She sighed quietly to calm herself and give her time to think about what to say next. "Burke, I.... I like you. And Marlee knew that—she has known a long time—and she was well aware that I wanted to ask you to Spring Formal. Her mission tonight was recon—to find out how you'd react if I asked you. And then she asked you for herself instead. Did she even ask you what you'd say if I asked?" Her voice cracked. Her heart was beating wildly out of control, and her thoughts were jumping all over the place. She willed herself strong with a deep breath, realizing that the moment she most needed to express herself eloquently, she was at a loss for words.

"Wait. What do you mean? You...like me? Is that what she meant by that 'Forget about Ellie' comment? I just figured it was because we spend so much time together."

"Yes, I've liked you ever since the end of tenth grade. But I never wanted to risk our friendship, especially if you didn't feel the same. Our friendship means the world to me, and I don't know what I'd do without you."

Burke looked shocked at the confession—which meant that she had been a pretty good actress. "She never asked me what I'd say if you asked me. I'm not sure what to say, Ellie. I already told Marlee I would go with her, and I don't want to have to put up with her crying again, but—"

"Don't worry about it. You don't have to say anything. But now you know, for what it's worth." She turned to the window and let a teardrop fall and quickly swept the traitorous moisture away with her right hand.

He reached over and grabbed her left hand, gently squeezing it. "Ellie, look at me." He waited for her to look at him while keeping a careful watch on the road.

She blinked hard a few times and then turned to look at him.

"I wish you would have told me sooner. I had no idea. I totally would have taken you to the Spring Formal. You're my best friend."

Ellie breathed shallowly, still not knowing what to say. She loved the touch of his hand on hers, and let his rest there for a few minutes, until she felt unsure of what the hand-holding meant. She pretended to adjust her jeans, turned up the radio and smiled at Burke with a shyness he probably wasn't used to. Thunder boomed so loudly it rattled the car. She looked out the window and saw the gray clouds roiling overhead while the music filled the silence.

"Are you okay?" Burke asked.

"I'm fine. Can you please take me home though? I really should get started on my English paper—I'd hate to shame my father's good name by flunking out of English." She made a pathetic attempt at laughing.

"As if you'd ever flunk any class. Why don't you just come

hang out with us for a few hours. It won't be the same without you—we might not laugh even once. I'll stay by you so you don't feel awkward."

"Thanks, but I think I'd rather go home if you don't mind."

"You sure?" Burke asked.

"Yeah. I can't go to Marlee's house now. I just need some time to think. I'll be fine though, don't worry." She had to play it cool or he wouldn't leave, and she needed to be alone because she was running out of strength to hold back the tears.

"Do you want me to stay with you at your house?"

"No thanks, I don't think my parents are home yet, and you know their rule. But I'll be fine really. I just have lots of homework to do." She worried that this moment would change their friendship permanently, that it would never be as comfortable and fun as it was before.

The Tahoe turned onto Elliana's street, and Burke pulled slowly into the driveway. Of all the things that Elliana wanted to say to him at that moment, the only thing that passed her lips was, "If you don't want to call me anymore, I'll understand." And she opened the car door, half-wishing she hadn't just opened her mouth and said something that stupid.

"Nonsense, Ellie. You're still my best friend. You can't get rid of me that easily."

She forced a smile and nodded at him. "Thanks for the ride."

The gray clouds released their first raindrops as she shut the car door. She was walking up the front path, praying he wouldn't come chasing after her, hoping he would anyways. She opened her front door slightly, made like she was going in, and with her tears blinding her view, she waved off Burke. As he drove away, she stepped back onto the porch and shut the front door quietly. And then the rain came down all around her. How fitting because that's precisely how she felt inside.

She walked around the left side of the modest stucco home, through the wooden gate, past the strawberry patch, around the tulip garden, and over to the cement patio. But by the time she reached the edge of the patio, the rain was falling even faster. She stopped where she was and looked upward, closed her eyes, and let her own tears mix with the tears from the sky. She reached her arms out to the side in a gesture to question why. Why did her best friend betray her, and then lie about it? Why didn't she have the guts to ask Burke to Spring Formal herself? Why did she have to say such stupid things? Life seemed to be crumbling just when it was supposed to be getting better, and answers seemed non-existent. Her hands fell limply to her side in despair.

Staring into the gray sky, she muttered, "It's not raining hard enough. This doesn't even come close to how horrible I feel!" As if the sky obeyed her command, the rain came down in giant drops, bending the leaves and grass blades as they hit, splattering on the ground.

Throwing her head back, she dared the dark clouds to try a little harder, whispering, "Better, but still not hard enough." A moment later, a flash of lightning zipped through the sky and a thunderous clap polluted the serenity, with water pouring from the sky in a torrent of great dollops that could probably drown a bumblebee. The cool drops splashed against her warm skin and soaked her thoroughly, forming standing puddles on the patio. That was more like it—that was exactly how horrible she felt and how hard she wanted to cry.

She wanted to boom like the thunder which shared the sky with the powerful tears falling forcefully to earth, but she didn't dare yell because she didn't want to freak out the neighbors—no matter how badly her heart hurt. The last thing she needed was to become the laughing stock of the neighborhood, for she already felt like the laughing stock of love.

She wrapped her arms around herself and sobbed so hard that her shoulders shook, but she hardly made a sound above the storm; she knelt and bowed her head low, sinking down on the cool cement. Her insides were aching in a way she had never felt before. She held nothing back, and every painful emotion came dripping out like the flood in her yard. She could not recall a time when it rained so furiously and thought that this rain was her rain, having been stored up in a lost corner of the universe for years, and finally sent washing down through the atmosphere.

Elliana's wet brown hair clung to her neck and cheeks. She shifted and sat on the patio, in the showering rain for a full twenty minutes, letting it clear away the pain and confusion in the unlikely hope it would make room for something happy. The rain eased up and then ceased entirely almost as quickly as it had started, leaving her drained and waterlogged. She inhaled deeply to take in the clean, after-rain smell and studied the crispness and enhanced color of nature. Rain had a way of making things clearer, more defined; sometimes tears did the same thing.

She stood up, her clothing taut and binding from the water, clinging to her shape. She pulled her soggy hair behind her head, and ran her hands down her mane, expelling the excess water which splashed down on the patio. She wrung out her shirt and pant legs as best she could, kicked her shoes off outside the sliding glass door, and headed to her room, stepping carefully across the tile floor and leaving puddles in her wake. She was grateful no one was home to stop and ask questions, which was best, for she had no answers. She needed some time for all the clouds in her mind to clear.

In her room, she towel-dried her hair, changed into pajama pants and a t-shirt, and lay on her bed staring at the ceiling for what seemed like hours pondering how she could seek revenge on her best friend who double-crossed her so viciously. Her best friend disregarded her feelings completely, and instead of asking Burke what he would say to Elliana asking him to the Spring Formal, Marlee asked him for herself. A deliberate betrayal. It would have been so much easier to handle had Burke really done the asking, but Marlee flat out lied about how it happened.

Feeling unable to forgive this catty behavior, Elliana feared this betrayal could cause the end of a great friendship. Maybe even two—if she freaked Burke out with her awkward confession. She felt utterly stupid.

It would be difficult to act normal in front of Burke now... if he really still wanted to stay best friends after her sudden declaration of love. No, he probably was freaked out, and she couldn't blame him. Burke obviously didn't have feelings for her, which would make things uncomfortable now, and maybe this had ruined everything good between them.

Tears streaked her face again. She rolled over and buried her head in her pillow, banging her fists against her plush bed, feeling embarrassed, hurt, and lost all at the same time. If only her mind would cease thinking and her heart would stop caring.

Almost instinctively, Elliana walked to her window to see that the clouds had cleared. She peered out in the night sky at the Big Dipper, which always made her feel more at home, more grounded, which is why she frequently doodled it in her journal. The Big Dipper had been her favorite constellation as a young girl (it was the first one her mom taught her), and she insisted on looking out the window each night to find the Big Dipper before she could fall asleep, pretending it could scoop out sweet dreams from a magical part of the galaxy and pour them over her head. She recalled how regularly she counted on that constellation to bring her peace. She left a portion of her sadness at the windowsill and walked back to her bed.

She had known Marlee since the first grade, and she never took kindly to people trying to get close to Elliana, but her personality demanded the spotlight and attracted people to her. Sometimes she could be over-the-top, but Marlee had a good heart most of the time.

She recalled all those yearly summer camps with Marlee since they were twelve. They were inseparable and had more fun than anyone else. Marlee was spontaneous and helped Elliana overcome her somewhat reserved, cautious nature, teaching her to be more adventurous.

Most everyone wanted to be Marlee's friend, and she couldn't fault them for it. Marlee was magnetic and socially powerful—and Marlee had chosen Elliana's friendship as the most important one and taught Elliana how to have fun. It was Marlee's spontaneity that she most admired and now most despised. She figured that was true of everyone: their greatest strength was also their greatest weakness because it blinded them when they were most fallible.

There was no way that Marlee knew how she was feeling because Marlee got what Marlee wanted. As if her beautiful dark auburn hair and smile weren't enough, Marlee had long legs that everyone noticed and a sexy saunter that seemed to make up for what little she lacked in looks. Elliana felt so average when she compared herself to Marlee. Now she wanted to hate Marlee—hate her as much as she had loved her. Or, at the very least, Elliana wanted to call her friend out on what she had done so deceptively, to let everyone know how it really went down: Marlee, the back-stabber, did the asking and betrayed her best friend.

Anger felt like a more just reward for Marlee than forgiveness, until Elliana remembered she had once been fallible and despicable in seventh grade when she said something unforgivable. The incident was too painful to recall, and usually she refused to relive it in her mind, but that night she pushed herself to remember as she felt the weight of her seventh-grade guilt after the temptation to convict Marlee with a few words.

Seventh grade seemed to bring out the worst in everyone, and Elliana had been cruel to Bobby because he'd poked the bear one too many times.

Elliana wasn't necessarily good at sports, but thanks to her one-hundred-sit-ups routine every night and to the fact that most seventh-grade boys hadn't hit their growth spurts, she had just set the class record for the number of sit-ups in one minute in P.E.

Bobby had accused her of cheating, and so the whole class had gathered around to watch her second round: seventy-six sit-ups in sixty-seconds. Bobby was a sore loser.

"Look, here comes the tiny baby who looks younger than my fourth-grade sister!" Bobby taunted as Elliana brushed by him the next day. He taunted her every time he saw her. But she said nothing in return.

The daily ridicule went on for weeks, and she now walked the hall with her head down wondering what she had ever done to deserve his hate.

A month later, her desperation reached a new height when Bobby said, "Hey loser. Nobody likes you. Why don't you just go back to kindergarten where you belong?"

Tears stung her eyes.

"Oh what, is the little baby going to cry?" he said in a tone that felt like a bat to her bones.

She quickly brushed away the tears. Too weak to resist the temptation to pounce, too anxious to end his tirade of harassment, she spoke only half of a sentence before she regretted having spoken it at all: "At least my dad didn't—." She couldn't finish the sentence because it was too cruel, and she hated bullies and didn't want to become one. But it was too late. That half-sentence was all it took to defeat him. It wasn't Bobby's fault his dad was a low-down, dirty scumbag facing life in prison. And she'd hated herself intensely for losing her temper.

No one knew what she said to Bobby in the hall (she never told a soul), nor that her words likely exacerbated his depression from his family turmoil and extinguished his will to live. He had needed a friend, and all he got from Elliana was cruelty. But the crazy thing was that Bobby never outed Elliana even though he was hospitalized and gossiped about.

Elliana had wanted so badly to be a good person like her mom, but five words spoken in survival mode seemed to ruin that possibility, and she vowed never to speak so cruelly again. She vowed to sacrifice and swallow her words to prevent an additional wrecking ball of guilt on her conscience. She vowed that rather than make people cry, she wanted to use her words to make them smile. She started apologizing for things that weren't really her fault and letting people win if it meant she'd have to break that promise.

With that horrid memory clawing at her mind, Elliana decided then to stick to her seventh-grade vows. She forced herself to remember that though Marlee had her flaws, she had goodness too. She often brought extra money each day to school to buy more than she could eat, giving the extra food to less-fortunate kids, claiming she wasn't going to eat it and didn't want it to go to waste. She was generous with her money and enjoyed sharing with others, even if some motivation came from wanting to make herself look good. But underneath it all, she was a good person. Stabbing her best friend in the back was an uncharacteristic move for Marlee, and Elliana worried that if she reacted out of anger now, that it may cause Marlee to crumble like Bobby had.

She tried to reason that even really good people make mistakes and need forgiveness—a concept that she had been battling for over half a decade. Elliana hated to admit that even though it was painful, maybe Marlee wasn't one hundred percent to blame for this. Elliana was the one who was too scared to take risks, the one who begged her best friend to do some one-on-one investigating with Burke, the one who hid the truth about her feelings from Burke, the one who was too chicken to get what she wanted out of life. She was a coward. At that moment, her own weakness and former guilt disgusted her. Why would anyone want someone like her?

It wasn't worth it to pursue her romantic interest in Burke at the potential expense of two friendships. Marlee had won, but at a cost. Elliana had a fresh wound in her heart and was done with this business of love because all it did was complicate two of her closest relationships.

Hours later, most of her anger had transformed into a surreal awareness of humanity and the issues girls face.

Though she was sorely tempted, she decided not to let this one indiscretion poison her against her friends and against seeing the good—and certainly not six weeks away from graduating. She decided that she would not seek revenge, and not even gossip about Marlee, regardless of her fault in the matter—paying forward Bobby's favor—and that she would try to be happy for her best friend's scammed date. But Elliana would not go to Spring Formal, and she couldn't wait for high school to end and get out of dinky Star, Idaho.

When her mind slowed down enough for a pen to keep up with it, Elliana wrote until her fingers smarted from the grip, wrote until the ink spilled beautifully over many pages, wrote until she vented each last emotion. Then she picked up Book 3 and read until she eventually drifted off into a heavy and deep sleep.

CHAPTER FIVE

Memorable

IN ANOTHER REALM, a woman watched with a heavy heart and wished Elliana Reinhart understood that she was born an old soul in a new world for a very specific reason.

The woman knew that Elliana didn't just happen to live in the small, seemingly inconsequential city of Star, Idaho, since she was three years old. And Elliana needed to know that even though she had not chosen Star herself, Star needed her.

Yes, the city of Star needed Elliana, even though she was overly modest about her abilities. Star needed her even though she was eliminated from the fifth-grade spelling bee for misspelling the word pretentious. Star needed her even though she would never be any good at volleyball, physics, or public speaking. Star needed her even though she'd never forgiven herself for speaking five cruel words in seventh grade. But most importantly, it needed her because of who she had the potential to become if only she could learn to believe in and forgive herself.

Star, Idaho, was one of the strongest links to a realm that gave life to a dying star that protected the earth.

Elliana needed to remember the instructions from the

implanted memory that taught her about the Seeking Realm waiting for her.

The woman gave her the dream again.

For the first time since the recurring memory-dream had been nagging her, she awoke more determined than ever to find this fantasy realm, inspired by a possible answer from the unlikeliest of sources. Though she hadn't yet finished Book 3, she read that the protagonist was using an ordinary janitorial closet with a flawlessly hidden secret door that led to her underground room where she was organizing and training her team for their latest quest. In the book, an ordinary door disguised what hid behind it.

The crazy thing was that last night she dreamed she opened her eyes in the fantasy world standing next to a tree with silvery, heart-shaped leaves, and the initials "S.R." engraved in the bark of the trunk. The tree was the door that hid the beautiful new world where she met someone who had been waiting for her— someone who might hold the answers to her deepest questions about life and love (the latter of which she had very recently sworn off), and someone who hinted at the absurd notion that she was needed to accomplish something important.

In her dream, the tree she stood next to was the portal into the fantasy place. All she needed now was to find this magical tree portal and get the heck out of high school drama.

Sure, maybe she had snapped in the night, and maybe reading too much fiction was giving her crazy dreams. But the worst had already happened, and she was ready to be an adventurer. Time to live on the edge, to be the protagonist of her own life's story.

Really, what she most needed was a distraction and a goal

to help her heal and refocus. In the safest place she knew, she filled a half-dozen pages writing her craziest thoughts for escaping this world and what she would do once she got there.

That Saturday was a typical morning in April: the sun's rays working to evict the night chill, birds chirping happily, the air smelling new. But in another sense, it was a bittersweet day in the Reinhart's lives. April 21 was the sixteenth anniversary of the day that Elliana and Abbie lost their parents, Dylan and Madeline Upright, and survived to be adopted by Harrison and Tina Reinhart, who were almost old enough to be their grandparents. Tina Reinhart had been an EMT at the scene, and she and her husband visited the girls in the hospital that evening of the accident. They visited each day for weeks, forming a strong bond with the little sisters, and when no relatives were able to care for the two, the Reinharts jumped at the chance to adopt them.

Though the adoption didn't happen until a year after the accident, the Reinharts loved to celebrate the miraculous survival of their long-awaited and much-prayed-for angels; for them, it was a day of blessings that overwhelmed the tragedy. Miracle Day usually started with planting flowers in their tulip garden and concluded with family dinner at a local restaurant—just their little family.

Elliana was the first one downstairs. Two pots of tulips sat on the table: fiery pink and pastel blue with white tips.

Abbie clunked down the stairs in strappy high-heel sandals and a lime green dress. She stopped by the hall mirror to admire her blond mane and makeup.

Abbie turned and met the eyes of her sister. "Hey, Ellie."

"Hi, Abbs." Elliana was dressed more casually in khaki capris. Her blue eyes darted to the tulips, and her fingers tousled her freshly curled brown hair behind her ears before she quickly let her hair fall back in place to hide her puffy face.

"Good morning, my beautiful angels!" Her dad hugged his daughters and kissed each on her forehead.

"And Happy Miracle Day," her mom said as she joined the family hug. "Ellie, you were fast asleep when we got home last night. How did your outing go?"

Elliana's eyes softened. She wished that wasn't the first thing they would ask about because it hijacked her from her coping space, and she worried she would cry again.

Her dad cast her mom a cautious look, and then asked, "What happened?"

"Just a ridiculously difficult emotional situation." Elliana wiped her palms on her pants and walked around the counter and pulled out some waffle mix. "Waffles sound good, right? Mom, will you plug in the waffle iron right there?"

Abbie's eyes narrowed. "And...?"

Elliana measured the mix into a bowl and added water, eggs, a scoop of white cake mix, and flax seeds. "And I cried a lot last night, and I'm mostly better today."

Her mom frowned and turned on the waffle maker. "You cried?"

Elliana swirled the mix in the bowl like it was a meditation exercise and then looked up. "A lot. Jared asked Daisy to Spring Formal yesterday, which set Marlee off because she wanted to go with Jared. So instead of asking Burke if he would say yes to me, she asked him to go to Spring Formal with her, and then lied to me and told me Burke asked her. I only found out that she lied when I was talking to Burke on the way home last night. He asked me why I was upset, and so I told him I had a crush on him. My words fell out all wrong, and I felt like a horse's rear end. He felt badly about it all and said he would have taken me to the Spring Formal, but I wasn't much in the mood for talking, so I had him drop me off, and then I cried until there were no more tears left to cry."

Her parents both uttered apologies.

Abbie reacted with a dose of sisterly venom. "What the heck is her problem? Why would Marlee deliberately ask Burke when she knew that you have liked him for almost two years? That is so low! I hope she gets diarrhea and a big zit on her perfect nose."

Elliana almost smiled. "I don't know how to make sense of it all. But I've decided it wasn't meant to be, at least for right now—or that maybe it happened for a reason. So I'm going to try to be happy for Marlee. I don't want this to sour my relationship with her or Burke."

Silence.

"Um, NO! There is no being happy for the betrayer of all betrayers! It's not okay what she did to you. She needs to learn her lesson that she can't treat my sister that way. I say we put a dead skunk in her car! Or spill punch all over her fancy designer Spring Formal dress! Or toilet paper her house!"

Abbie was just trying to help her sister feel better and to feel loved, but Elliana had already decided not to go there and thought of her goal to find a magical tree portal instead.

"Let's not plot revenge right now," her dad said to Abbie. "But I know I can't control you."

"You're such a good old soul, Ellie. Most girls wouldn't be as nice as you're being." Her mom turned to Abbie. "And I know I wouldn't dare touch a dead skunk!"

Elliana smiled this time and poured a cup of mix into the hot Belgian waffle maker.

"I'm proud of you," her father said.

Abbie rolled her eyes. "Do I have to be nice to Marlee? I don't know how I can, seeing as she is bird crap—"

"Yes, for my sake, please do," Elliana said before Abbie could finish her tirade. "Maybe she's liked him all along and just never said anything to me because she didn't want to cause a fight. I'm the idiot who was too scared to ask, and this is what I get for being a chicken. It's not like I own Burke, or that he's interested in me in that way."

"Is that what he said last night?" her mom asked. "I thought you said he would have taken you?"

"Well, sort of. He basically said that he would have taken me since I was his best friend."

"Oh, honey. I'm so sorry this turned out the way it did." Her mom almost looked guilty. "Maybe we shouldn't have pressured you to open up to him. I am really sorry. Please forgive me."

"It's okay, Mom. It's not your fault. In fact, if I had acted a little sooner, this may have had a totally different ending. But it is what it is at this point. Not that it feels good, and not that I won't have a rancid taste in my mouth if I were to see them at Spring Formal together."

"Are you going to go to Spring Formal?" Abbie asked. "I'll man the punch bowl."

"Very funny. I'm not going at all."

"Or you could find something better to do. Senior Spring Formal isn't all that wonderful, no matter how fantastic everyone tries to make it seem. My prom was a total letdown," her mother said. "Maybe there is a reason for all of this. Somehow, something good will may come from it."

"Thanks, Mom. But for right now, my goal is to not feel bitter." Fresh tears appeared, and to keep them from falling Elliana batted her eyes. Her mom walked around the counter and embraced her, and Abbie did too.

Her dad stood and put his arms around all three of his girls. "Those guys in your school have no idea what they're missing, sweetie. You are a gem. Not only are you beautiful, you are smart and caring and a true friend. Any guy would be lucky to have you, but he's going to have to go through me first."

Her dad was totally biased, but it felt good to hear it. "Thanks, dad, but there's a very short line for that, so short it's kind of non-existent. In fact, I swore off love last night, so no need to worry."

❧

Each girl took a turn placing a pot where the sprinkler system could keep them watered, and then her dad would finish transplanting the tulips in the fall. The girls smiled at their beautiful garden.

"Where do you girls want to go tonight?" her dad asked while they walked back toward the sliding glass door.

"I'm in the mood for some mean Chinese," Abbie said while attempting a few laughable kung fu moves in a dress.

"I could go for some Chinese, too. How about Confucius take-out?" Elliana said. She suggested take-out for the obvious reason that she did not want to be seen in public just yet—her swollen eyes would scream her secrets. She couldn't face being seen.

They had never resorted to take-out as part of their celebration, but Elliana tried to sell them on the idea of a fun, cozy, low-key dinner at home with paper plates and plastic ware so no one would have to do dishes.

Abbie had the better argument about keeping with the tradition and enjoying being out together—which Abbie claimed would keep her from planning criminal revenge and ending up in the slammer.

Dinner was at Confucius in Boise at 5:30 p.m. Elliana offered to meet her family at the restaurant so she could spend the afternoon in the library, which her mother thought was odd, but they all conceded that Elliana could use some quiet space especially since she had to be seen in public that evening.

Her mom was right. Elliana was trying to pretend that her heart wasn't broken in two places, but there was something about academics that took her mind off her troubles. She had no control over Marlee, but she did over her grades, and she was good at school. An A on her paper would help her feel better about herself and may also win her a scholarship. She needed to focus today on what she could control instead of on the hurt, and getting good grades was her drug. So was thinking about her dream and the tree portal.

و

She sat in the library at a secluded desk in a corner at a computer, books spread around her, earphones in and music on, still brainstorming and thinking about a topic. She had searched the internet and the library catalog and found a few books that sounded interesting. She grabbed a book and skimmed the index. As she read, her mind ruminated on how stupid and vulnerable she felt last night; the memory brought hot tears to the corner of her eyes. It was frustrating enough to have acted like an idiot when she said goodbye to Burke, but to keep remembering it was torture. It was being replayed in slow-motion with every absurd word repeated in her head, and she would shake her head like she could shake the memory from her brain, but the incident continued to loop.

She leaned over a sheet of paper, adding another barely-interesting topic to her brainstorming list when a teardrop spattered on her paper. Not again, dang it.

Her eyes were obviously still swollen from a night of crying, and the fact that she was weeping again wasn't improving her fragile appearance, which tempted her to figure out how to weasel out of a public family dinner. But it was an important family dinner for her entire family, so she'd force herself to go, and hoped they'd be seated in a private booth in a far corner of the restaurant because she was fresh out of invisibility cloaks.

Even though she had thoroughly examined her emotions the night prior, it didn't remove the lingering pain. Being human felt rotten at times, but she'd do her best to not be a Debbie Downer at family dinner.

The topic wasn't coming and was adding to her frustration, and she thought of her dream, the beauty, the sense of belonging. She closed her English notebook and instead researched portals and how they were used in any book she could find. She recorded pages of research notes in her journal just after a short story she had written about the most beautiful tear ever shed.

She felt her cell phone buzz in her back pocket. *Burke? Great.* She had no idea what to say to him, but quickly exited the main part of the library and answered the phone.

"Hey, Burke. What's up?" She tried not to sound too friendly nor unfriendly.

"Ellie, how're you doing?"

"Fine, I guess. How are you?"

"Good. I just wanted to call and wish you a Happy Miracle Day. I know it's a family day, but I wanted to call and check on you. After last night, I wasn't sure you ever wanted to talk to me anymore."

"That's not it at all. I just feel like an idiot...." She couldn't think of anything else to say.

"Don't feel that way. You're my best friend, and I would hardly classify you as an idiot. In fact, I was wondering if you wanted to help me do calc homework Monday after school?"

Elliana knew that Burke was better at calculus than she was, but she agreed anyway. She said they could meet at her house, and her mom would probably have warm cookies ready for them, and he could even stay for dinner.

"It's a plan." He sounded just like he always did. Before he ended the call, he asked, "We're good, right?"

She felt pulled toward the familiar comfortableness they once shared. "Of course. Good as ever." A smile grew on her face. If she no longer had a chance with him, at least he was still her best friend.

Elliana usually silenced her phone before a family meal, because if she or her sister got caught calling or texting or playing on their phones at the table, they were tortured in the most brutal manner: they lost their phone for three days. Such was life with old-school parents. When she met her family at Confucius, she left her phone in her car under a jacket just to be on the safe side. Plus, she wasn't ready for any texts about Marlee's dress-shopping adventures.

Much to Elliana's dismay, the party of four was seated smack dab in the front of the restaurant by the giant golden Buddha, but not until each of the family of four had rubbed Buddha's belly—well, her mom didn't exactly rub the belly, she just barely touched it with her fingertips like she was afraid someone important would catch her in the act and then upload the video to the internet. Her dad had started rubbing Buddha's belly for good luck when he was in college, and it evolved into a family ritual. Elliana needed good luck.

After the waitress took their orders, Elliana mentally reviewed her dream notes and ideas to figure out where a tree portal could be located. Her eyes closed momentarily until her father interrupted her.

"How is your English paper coming along? That is what you were doing all afternoon, right?"

Elliana shrugged. "It's not coming along at all. I have tried a few different topics, found information, but nothing is coming together on paper. Nothing sounds good to write about. What did you do when you got stuck?"

Her dad, who loved to offer writing advice, said, "Sometimes I started by reading a few pages of one of my favorite books to get my mind in the mood, and then I just write. I wrote the first thing that came to my mind and I let my mind wander on the screen or page until it finds something worth sticking with."

"I haven't tried that yet," said Elliana, eying her leather journal that lay next to her purse on the booth's bench. Maybe the reason she didn't get very far on her paper was that her mind was preoccupied with her new goal or with the story of the most beautiful tear. She had never let anyone read anything she had written in her journal, and bringing it in the restaurant was a risk, but she was paranoid about leaving it in her car and having it stolen by some lunatic with internet skills. She placed her purse directly on top of her journal to hide it from view.

"Can Burke eat dinner with us on Monday? We're working on calculus."

"Of course," her parents said.

"On to weightier matters. What does my Ellie-bell want for her birthday? And please don't say a hairdryer or socks." Her dad's facial hair made a wire brush sound as he rubbed his hand over his mouth.

Her gift requests were usually too practical: books, pajama pants, a flat iron for her hair, more books, gel pens. Elliana thought about how the family finances were getting tighter. "I don't know. A new journal, or a sketch book, or maybe new paint and paint brushes."

"That's better than last year," her mom said.

"Yeah, well I'm going to start living on the edge now. I hear the view is better." Those last words came out a little sassier than she'd intended.

Abbie said, "Yeah, and the edge is great place to give betrayers a little push."

Elliana started to laugh, but air caught in her throat which made her hack a few times, and while she was thus being unattractive, her eye caught Red Truck Guy and two young women being seated together several tables away in another booth. Holy no way.

He was cute in a different kind of way, which made her hacking even more embarrassing. She liked looking at him.

She shook her head; she had evicted any notion of romance from her heart, so that ping of hope could take a hike.

It didn't.

Abbie nudged her sister under the table. "What are you staring at?"

Forcing her eyes back to Abbie, she said, "The universe is taunting me. That's Red Truck Guy from the intersection— remember I helped push a car through the intersection the other day? That's the cute boy."

Abbie started to turn around to gawk, but Elliana forbade her with her eyes, and scolded through clenched teeth. "Don't look yet! I don't want him to see us checking him out."

"Fine, I have to go to the bathroom anyways. Wanna come?" Abbie stood up with her purse in hand, hesitated only for a second, and walked in the direction of Red Truck Guy's table on the way to the restroom. Elliana was not usually the type for girlish games but knew Abbie would go with or without her, and she had nothing to lose at this point.

Their parents looked at each other with raised eyebrows and shook their heads, most likely thinking: *teenage girls.*

Abbie strutted and Elliana walked very respectably past the threesome. Elliana drew in her breath; his cologne smelled like the woods mixed with spice.

When they were safely inside the restroom, Elliana turned to the mirror and primped her wavy hair, reapplied her super-shiny lip plumper, and removed her eye makeup smudges. "He's cute, right?"

"Yes. He looks older though," said Abbie. "Definitely not in high school, which is perfect."

"Too bad I swore off boys last night, not that it would matter. At least he's fun to look at." Her smile faded. "But he's with two pretty girls, so he's probably taken."

"Maybe. But if he were, why would he be with two girls instead of one?"

"Because...the boyfriend always has to get in with the girl-friend's best friend? I don't know."

"Either way, he's hot. You should say hi or wink at him when we walk back."

Elliana's eyes grew huge. "No way! I'm a scaredy chicken. I've had enough rejection to last me a few years. And don't you dare say hi or wink at him, either."

"Fine." Abbie deflated. "But that's no fun. So much for living on the edge. When was that supposed to start again?"

"Tomorrow."

They headed back to join their parents, who eyed them both. "What are you two up to?" her mom asked.

"Does this have anything to do with the young man sitting in that booth over there?" her father teased, pointing with his chopsticks, his smile drawing up the corners of his goatee.

"Dad, stop pointing," Elliana yell-whispered and felt her face flush at being caught checking out a boy, which was weird because she told herself she didn't care.

Abbie informed their parents of their necessary trip to the restroom past the "dessert bar" to check out a "certain male patron" that Elliana had met in an intersection a few days ago, and who was making Elliana "swoon." Her parents nodded in comprehension.

"I wasn't swooning. I was merely admiring the scenery, like an artist." Her parents could probably see the truth written all over her face, so she added, "But I swore off love last night, so you really have nothing to worry about. Besides, I'm sure he doesn't even remember me or know I exist, which makes things super easy."

Luckily for Elliana, the waitress interrupted the uncomfortable conversation when she delivered their savory, steaming entrees.

⚘

Her dad handed the waitress his credit card, and they each opened their fortune cookie hoping for the best fortune of the batch.

Her dad's read, "In life, you only have yourself to blame."

Her mom's said, "Happiness eludes those imprisoned by comparisons."

Elliana wondered if maybe her mom's fortune was meant for her because her own fortune didn't tell her anything she didn't already know she had to do. "Look forward, not backward, and you will find what you seek." Blah, blah. Dumb fortune. Why didn't she get one about where to look for a tree portal?

Abbie leaned forward like she had the best fortune yet. "Before you embark on a journey of revenge, dig two graves," to which she added, "one for each of Marlee's two faces." Abbie laughed so hard she cried, but Elliana wavered between stifling laughter and giving her sister the look that she really ought to behave herself.

Before she got dragged into another public adventure, Elliana begged to go back to the library for a few hours, which also gave her an excuse to avoid any possibility of going dress shopping with Marlee. She could continue to work on writing her paper. Not only was the paper worth one-third of her final grade in English, she also needed the cash scholarship. Or maybe she really wanted to be alone to figure out how to access that fantasy world from her dream, but she couldn't tell her family about that or they'd really be worried about her sanity.

Elliana grabbed her purse and headed out the door with her family, stealthily taking one last mental picture of Red Truck Guy without getting caught. Once outside, she kissed her parents on the cheek and headed to her car. She fumbled for her keys for a moment, unlocked the car, and slid into the driver's seat, still thinking about the guy at the restaurant—the boy she would probably never see again—which was okay, because what could she possibly say to him that wouldn't be idiotic? *Hi, I drool.* Or *Hi, I'm awkward around cute boys and can't get a date.* It was so much less risky to crush on a guy who wasn't really a possibility, which meant she hadn't really broken her vow of swearing off romantic feelings.

When she finally checked her phone, she had a missed call and several texts from Keisha. Keisha had texted her at the library asking if she was okay, but she had forgotten to reply, mostly because she was trying not to think about the Marlee betrayal, and she wasn't sure how okay she really was. But she was feeling better now and returned Keisha's call. Elliana started her car and had just clicked her seatbelt when her friend answered.

Elliana blurted out, "Oh. My. Gosh. Listen to this! I was eating at Confucius with my family, and I just saw this cute guy I sort of met before! And it wasn't just that he was cute, but...I don't know; it gives me hope that I can get over Burke."

"You're okay after what happened last night? I texted you like ten times today because I've been so worried. Nevermind. Who is he? What does he look like? Did you talk to him?"

Elliana shifted into reverse and backed out of the parking stall, placing her cell between her left shoulder and chin. "His name is Red Truck Guy and of course I didn't talk to him. Other that, I have no idea who he is, but he is tall and hands—"

Just then she felt a soft thud immediately followed by a louder thud on the back of her car. "Oh, crap! I just hit something. I'll call you back!" She threw the phone onto the passenger seat and quickly re-parked the car as dread set in, like her body was being filled with molten lead. She had been so distracted that she didn't physically turn around before backing out. She was mentally slapping herself as her heart raced, wondering what or who she had hit, praying it wasn't a child or a dog, and hoping she wouldn't get sued.

She got out of her car and walked around the back. Sitting on the pavement a few feet away from her car was the Red Truck Guy from the restaurant, holding his knee in one hand. And her tattered journal in the other hand.

CHAPTER SIX

Fortune

"Ohmygosh, please tell me I didn't just run you over!" She reached out her hand.

"I'd like to," Red Truck Guy said as he took her hand and stood up, trying not to wince, "but that would be a lie."

"I am so, so sorry." She didn't know whether to smile or continue feeling like an elephant's enormous, hard-to-miss rear end. "I was talking on my phone and I—"

"I noticed. I was trying to wave you down, and I honestly thought you saw me or I wouldn't have gotten so close." He leaned down and rubbed his right knee.

"I'm really sorry. Are you hurt?"

"I think I'm okay. My knee is a little sore, but I managed to jump out of the way before you could finish running me over."

"I feel so stupid. I can't believe I just hit you." She hung on to that last word, giving it a little too much emphasis.

Red Truck Guy quickly caught her innuendo. "Why? Were you aiming for someone else?"

"No, I mean that I am a complete idiot. I am so sorry. Can I drive you to the hospital so you can get checked out? Or my mom could take a look at you. She's an EMT—"

"No, no, I'll be okay. I dropped your book though."

"My journal!" She almost scolded him. "I didn't even realize I'd left it."

"Well it looks pretty old and sentimental, so I thought you'd probably want it back. I promise I didn't read anything you wrote about me though."

Hopefully he hadn't seen her staring at him in the restaurant. She reached, more like grabbed for her journal, breathless, anxious, and horrified that he might have read anything. "What makes you think I wrote anything about you?"

"Were you not plotting my demise?" He teased her by holding onto her journal for a moment before releasing his grip.

Elliana forced a laugh as she seriously contemplated slugging him if he wasn't going to cough up her book of secrets. She hugged her journal close to her chest feeling baffled by the irony of it all. She was so distracted by the rugged good looks of Red Truck Guy that she called Keisha to tell her about him, and she ended up half-running over him with her car on the same day the car accident took her parents, coincidentally affording her the opportunity to meet the guy who made her broken heart start beating again just hours after she swore off love. She reached her hand out. "I'm Elliana, the stunt driver."

"Cai." He smiled and nodded once as he shook her hand. "We've met before, right?"

She almost said "You're Red Truck Guy," but caught herself in time. "In the intersection of Ustick and Five Mile Road?"

"Yeah, I thought that was you. Fancy meeting again like this. You're a lot more aggressive than the last time I saw you."

She smiled. "Are you sure I can't do anything for you?" Elliana fidgeted with her hair, chewing on the side of her bottom lip.

"I'll just let you owe me."

"What do I owe you? Target practice on me?" She grimaced.

"Don't know. Depends. Are you in a hurry?"

"Not really. I was just headed to the l i b r a r y." As she stuttered out the last word, she wished she could swallow it. She realized how dorky she sounded and wished she had said something more exciting, like going cliff diving or to the movies or even eating a gallon of ice cream—anything but the library.

"Why would you waste a perfectly good Saturday evening at the library? Are you grounded?"

"Nope, just a humongous nerd." She laughed.

Their conversation turned to her English paper; that, yes, she had in fact passed her driver's test on the first try, and how tasty Confucius' food was. He was easy to talk to and very charming.

Elliana suddenly remembered that he had two girls waiting for him in the restaurant. "I didn't mean to keep you from your dinner dates."

"We were mostly done eating, but I should go in and tell my sisters goodbye and pay the bill."

"Oh, those were your sisters." Elliana's comment sounded too much like relief.

"Yes, who did you think they were?"

"Um, girlfriends?"

"I'm a one-woman kind of guy," he said. He walked with an exaggerated limp toward the red doors and laughed. "Don't leave the scene of the crime. I'll be right back. "

She leaned against the trunk of her car while he went inside, trying to figure out if this was real. Could this be happening to her? Her heart was excited and was having a really hard time playing dead at this point. Elliana quickly glossed her lips and ran her fingers through her hair.

Cai approached her while replacing his wallet in his back pocket. "My sisters are dying to hear how the 'cute girl who forgot her journal' managed to run me over."

"It is rather incredible. Your jumping under my tire like that."

They both laughed.

A few minutes later, they walked a short distance to a neighborhood park, each sitting on a swing, digging their shoes into the sand, cocking their heads sideways to look at each other as they talked.

She studied his face as he talked about college and working on his commercial pilot's license. She liked that he wore his straight brown hair short and tousled on top, forming a small spike above his widow's peak because it reminded her a little of her first dad's picture.

Cai was intelligent and amusing and refreshing, which kept her hope growing and her insides fluttering like baby birds that just learned to fly. Compared to how defeated she felt the night before, this was the best feeling in the world. Somehow it was easier to be herself after last night.

They walked over to where the sand met the lawn and sat down. The sun began to set and glowed a pinkish-orange in the horizon, hovering for a while, and then disappearing all together, which sent a chill up Elliana's spine. She rubbed her arms to keep warm.

Cai lifted his sweatshirt off. "Here. It'll be a mite big on you though."

She thanked him and pulled the still-warm sweatshirt on, which smelled like her imagination of a Greek God.

Once the sky had darkened completely and the stars began to twinkle, Cai looked toward the heavens. "I'm taking an astronomy course right now, and I learned the neatest story this week. Do you see that group of stars over there, in the northwest, right at the horizon?"

She shook her head.

"Follow me." He lifted her by the hand and led her toward a sand volleyball pit that had a better view of the stars. They sat down on the sand and resumed their star gazing.

"Make a fist." Cai held her fist out away from her in the direction he was pointing. "If you hold up your fist right here, it will cover that group of stars. It's part of Taurus the Bull that sits next to Orion the Hunter."

"I see it now." She lowered her hand, loving that he liked to look at the stars as much as she did. The only difference was that she could only identify the Big Dipper and the Little Dipper.

"That group is one of the closest to Earth. It's what they call a nebular nursery, or a place where new stars are born. There are literally hundreds of confirmed stars just in that little group, but we can only see a half dozen or so with the naked eye." He pointed and then lowered his hand again. "They call that group The Pleiades or The Seven Sisters."

"I've heard of the Pleiades." She had read Homer's *Odyssey* in English last quarter.

Cai said, "The Greeks say that the Giant Orion was chasing seven nymphs, and to save them from him, Zeus turned them into doves and set them loose in the sky. Orion still chases them, but never gets any closer."

"Sounds like Orion can't take a hint."

"He was probably under some sort of nymph spell, the poor fool." Cai half-winked at her.

"Those spells are the worst." She was falling under one of

those spells. Perhaps he was a Greek God after all.

He nodded like he knew about those spells and held her gaze. "They say there are seven sisters, but we can only really see six of them because one went dim. Every culture throughout history seems to have an explanation of what happened to the Seventh Sister. The Greeks say she married a mortal and was cast down to Earth."

The side of his forearm brushed along hers as he shifted in the sand. She forced herself to pay attention to his words rather than the butterflies beating around in her stomach. "Tell me some of the legends."

"My favorite is the legend of the Western Mono Indians. They believed the Seven Sisters were the wives of seven husbands, and their wives loved to eat onions. The stench angered their husbands, and the husbands kicked the women out. Realizing how lonely they were, and probably after getting sick of cooking for themselves, the husbands sought out their wives to apologize, but the women had wandered forever into the sky."

"That one is funny, but that doesn't explain how one of them went dim," Elliana said.

"No, but it's still my favorite." He shifted again in the sand. "Maybe a crazy woman driver backed over one of the wives and that's why the star went dim."

Elliana laughed and playfully smacked his arm. "Very funny."

"I'm just trying to see more of that beautiful smile." Cai shrugged and grinned.

Her lips curved upward as she mentally scolded her heart to calm the freak down. "Okay, tell me a legend on why one star dimmed."

"Greek mythology holds that one of the Seven Sisters,

Electra, gave birth to a son who founded the city of Troy. When Troy was destroyed, she disappeared in grief. And that is why one star dimmed."

"The Greeks turn everything into a soap opera." While shaking her head, she added, "and I'm not sure I believe their story. There's got to be a better explanation. What's your theory?"

Cai looked toward the Pleiades while time ticked ticked ticked by, and then his gaze rested on Elliana. He leaned in as if to tell a secret. "I think Electra is the star of love. And its light is fueled by heartfelt kisses. There obviously aren't enough people in the universe kissing with their hearts involved, so the star is dying of a broken heart."

The idea actually intrigued her, but it was surely only a romantic idea from the lips of a Casanova. "Interesting theory."

"We could always do a scientific experiment to test it," he said, "and see if a heartfelt kiss won't make the star glow brighter." His smile curled up on one side.

Her stomach leapt. She was pretty sure he just asked to kiss her. Her. The girl who'd never kissed a boy. The girl who vowed never to entertain romantic thoughts again. Maybe he was just flirting, but his flirtatious ways were turning her into a silly, twitterpated vow-breaker.

She pursed her lips. "Yes, but if it were purely scientific, then it wouldn't be heartfelt, and the results would be muddled." She batted her eyelashes twice and then looked toward the group of stars she had seen earlier. "And besides, I can't even see the Pleiades anymore. They seem to have disappeared over the horizon."

Cai glanced toward the horizon and then returned his gaze. "Okay, smarty pants, you are right. But now I know what you owe me for your little game of bumper cars this evening: a heartfelt kiss—*if* and *when* kissing me would become heartfelt for you." Cai stuck out his right hand and said, "Deal?"

Elliana hesitated, gauging how serious he was. He looked serious indeed and was very persuasive, although she could hardly believe this was happening to her, just one day after she decided romance was too complicated. As much as she wanted to say no to this boy who could totally be playing her, her stomach fluttered again. "Deal." She offered her hand to shake on it. "Wait, doesn't it have to be heartfelt for both of us?"

He held on to her hand. "I'm already half-smitten, sweetheart."

"Not likely. This better not be some game you play with all the ladies." She pulled her hand loose from his.

"I promise I have never made this deal with any other female before. Of course, no other girl has cast a spell on me like you have."

She chuckled. "I'm not sure running you over with a Japanese car counts as a spell. But I promise to use more orthodox methods of spell-casting in the future."

He paused a moment, and Elliana wondered if she had said something wrong. Then he said, "What are you doing tomorrow? Can I take you out?"

She swallowed her excitement. "I should be free after four o'clock." She couldn't believe any of this was happening. She couldn't believe the irony.

"Great." He smiled. "I'll pick you up at five."

They exchanged numbers and she told him she'd text her address. She looked at the clock on her phone. "It's almost my curfew. Do you need a ride home?"

"No, it's okay. I met my sisters at the restaurant."

They walked back to the restaurant's parking lot. Elliana unlocked her car and Cai held open the driver's side door for her. Their hands brushed as she got into her car.

As much as she tried to resist, he was reviving her broken heart.

❧

Elliana arrived home right at eleven o'clock and hung her keys in the laundry room. Her family was sitting in the family room watching a movie with three popcorn bowls and three glasses of ice and soda arranged on the floor next to the couches.

"Hey, sweetie. How was the library?" her father asked.

"I don't know. I never went."

The three turned toward her, curious, and her mom paused the movie.

Elliana smiled.

Abbie raised her eyebrows and patted the seat next to her. "Spill it! Everyone else, shush!"

"My fortune came true."

Her family listened intently as she relayed the events of the evening, looking forward not backward and hitting the boy from the restaurant. Abbie could hardly contain herself. Elliana left out the part about the star and the heartfelt kiss deal but told them that she had plans to see him the next day.

"Leave it to my prudent, rational-thinking daughter to run over a guy and score a date!" Her dad shook his head. "I'm really glad he's not suing. And he'd better not be a serial killer."

Her mom said, "What a wonderful way to end the day! Do we get to meet him tomorrow? Will he stay for dinner?"

"No, we're going out. But you'll get to meet him when he comes to pick me up. And if all goes well, I promise I will invite him over for dinner soon—but let's not get carried away."

"I'll try not to scare him too badly when I meet him tomorrow," her dad said, "but go ahead and tell him I'm a human lie-detector."

❧

Cai pulled his truck into the semi-circle drive, put it in park, and before he had walked ten steps, he was met by two blonds in pajamas and fluffy slippers, who came bounding out of the front door, squealing like hot teapots, accosting him with important girl questions.

"What happened with the Confucius Girl? Where have you been all evening?" Lauren, the twenty-year old, asked as she looped her arm through his.

He turned toward the other and held out his free arm. Paige, the eighteen-year old, linked her arm with his, and said, "Yeah! And don't tell us to calm down. I can tell by the look on your face! Who is she? And what has she done with our brother?"

The trio ambled up the majestic steps and through the heavy wooden door. They settled down in the sitting room, sitting close to one another, and he enraptured his sisters with the tale of the evening.

When he got to the part about the dim star and the heartfelt kiss, both girls dropped their jaws in disbelief.

"Where did you come up with that?" Paige asked. "That's a good one!"

Cai shook his head slightly and said, "I can't reveal all my secrets. I looked at the star and then looked at her, and it came to me."

"And?" Lauren asked.

"She made the deal."

"Man, you are smooth!" Paige said.

"Listen, she was just as smooth as I was. She had me eating out of her hand. She was amazing and witty and perfectly wonderful. I told her I was already half-smitten."

"We need to meet her." Paige shook him by the shoulders for emphasis.

Lauren cast a wary glance. "Wait, does she know who you are?"

"She knows that my name is Cai, and that I am picking her up tomorrow at 5 p.m. And for right now, that's all that matters."

CHAPTER SEVEN

The Garden

ELLIANA FELT GUILTY for breaking her promise to call Keisha back, and it was way past a decent hour for phone calls, but she was happy when Abbie sneaked into her room hungry for more details because she wanted someone to talk to. Both sat cross-legged on Elliana's pink and white comforter talking about Cai, the deal, and her first mutually-interested date. They chatted like best friends, telling each other everything, listening, and making the other's life seem so much more exciting than their own.

"I have to be honest. I was so not jealous of you this morning with all the backstabbing and such, but I kind of am tonight. You really deserve someone good, especially since you won't let me seek revenge on a certain female betrayer," Abbie said.

"Yeah, well they say living a good life is sometimes the best revenge."

"But putting a skunk in her car or a mouse in her purse is way more fun."

They both laughed at the thought since both of them would never actually set fingers on any diseased roadkill or rodent.

Elliana yawned and then Abbie yawned.

"I'd better get some beauty sleep," Elliana said as she hugged Abbie and they said goodnight, leaving Elliana to her cart-wheeling thoughts.

Tomorrow she would find out if this fantasy realm really existed. Elliana struggled to find sleep that night as her mind reviewed her encounter with Cai. She couldn't stop remembering his face, the way he looked at her, and the way it felt when he touched her hand, the way their personalities clicked. She was too busy having fun to think about Burke or Marlee even once that night. As the scenes replayed in her head, she remembered clearly the thought she had the previous night that all things happen for a reason. And with that comforting thought, she slumbered.

✄

She awoke with a moving picture in her mind of a tree portal in the center of a grove, with a little orange-and-brown bird chirping from the lowest branch. It wasn't really a dream; maybe it was an epiphany?

She sketched the image and wrote down her thoughts on how to use the tree portal: a mixture of research, brainstorming, and fanciful guesses. If she could find the tree portal and enter the realm, hopefully she could say and do the right things, and not get trapped in a parallel universe or something, so she could get back for her hot date.

✄

She pondered where she could find this grove of trees. Groves in Southwest Idaho are usually located by bodies of running water or by farms. Great-grandpa Reinhart had planted trees near his farmland as windbreaks a few miles down the road. The land had eventually become her father's, and he mostly leased it to other farmers, but she could get away with wandering around. It was a starting point at least.

She showered, dressed, pulled her hair back into a low ponytail, and walked down the hall to Abbie's room. Abbie was reading in her bed and asked where Elliana was headed.

"Just in nature to journal and be alone." Elliana was really tempted to tell Abbie about her dream and what she was really going to do that day, but she figured that she'd just wait until after she knew whether or not she could even find this fantasy place. Her sister might think she was looney-birds. Maybe she was out of her mind, but she had nothing to lose in trying.

"Do you want to take a skunk trap with you, just in case?"

"You and your skunk plan. You crack me up. Like you'd ever actually get your hands near it."

"No, I'd use dad's barbeque tongs."

They both laughed at the devious thought.

"I love you, Abbs. I actually wanted to see if you'd be willing to help me do my hair for my date tonight."

"Absolutely."

After announcing that she was going on a solo nature walk, her mom packed her a bag of homemade chocolate chip cookies, two cold water bottles, and a few healthy snacks. She always did motherly things like that, even if it was to help Elliana pack supplies to run away.

When she was six, Elliana got mad for some molehill reason and announced that she was running away. Forever. Her mom helped her pack a hobo bag and began making homemade sugar cookies, Elliana's favorite. She had been anxious to run away, but her mom held her off with the promise of warm cookies.

By the time the cookies were ready, Elliana had started to cool off, but to save her pride she put the cookies into her already stuffed bag and stomped out the door and into the backyard. She walked to the edge of the yard, realized she didn't know where to go, then spread her blanket on the back lawn. She pulled out the bag of warm cookies and snacked while she read a book—or tried to read a book. The sun's reflection off the white pages made it very difficult to read, so she got bored very quickly. After she finished the last cookie, she figured she had taught her family a stern lesson and repacked her bag. When Elliana walked back into the kitchen, her mom hugged her and said, "I'm so glad you're back, sweetie. I was really worried!" It looked like her mom had been crying; she never ran away again after that.

After finishing breakfast, she kissed her parents goodbye, and skipped out the door to her boy-magnet car.

"Check your mirrors and don't run over any good-looking boys," her dad shouted from the front porch, as Elliana pulled out of the driveway. "Just invite them over instead!"

"Okay, Dad." She rolled her eyes playfully.

She drove west on the main road that led to the edge of town only a few minutes away. She wondered what she was getting herself into. Hopefully not a mental institution. This adventure would be just for kicks—no big deal, nothing to lose. If nothing panned out, she had brought her journal and Book 3 to devour. But deep down she hoped that it was real because of how amazing and whole she felt in her dream—which seemed to only make sense in her head.

It was ten o'clock in the morning, and she had plenty of time to pass before her date.

Within a few minutes, she was surrounded by freshly-sprouted fields of grain. In the distance, she could see the small grove of trees at the west end of her dad's leased-out alfalfa farm.

She drove down the dusty farm road and parked the car about twenty yards away from the grove of trees. After studying the trees for a minute and calling herself a "dork chocolate" out loud, she walked straight to the center of the grove looking for the large tree with silvery leaves. They all looked to be the same kind, same leaves, same size—none of them looked like the Tree Portal she saw in her dream. Discouragement barked and nipped at her like a rat dog.

She pondered the idea of entering a fantasy realm and how it was definitely something you wouldn't keep trying day after day—so today was it. She kicked a tree and closed her eyes; she needed to get her mind right. Maybe it was like how you had to believe in something first before it was real, like believing in miracles. If she was going to give this fantasy world a go, then she would make darn certain that she believed it could happen, or at least hoped it could, before she tried her various entrance methods. In her mind she repeated, *I hope it's real. I hope it's real.* If she had to explain any of this out loud, she would be so embarrassed.

As she turned around to see how far she had walked, she saw the tree with heart-shaped leaves towering over her. There on a branch about ten feet above her head perched an orange bird just like the one she saw in her dream. It said nothing, and did not remove its gaze from her, but she was certain the bird nodded its head. "Hi, pretty bird. Don't mind me—just trying to figure out if I'm looney-birds. Sorry, that wasn't very nice of me. I'll just get to it then."

Birds don't laugh, but this one warbled like it was laughing. Then she noticed two letters carved into the trunk about waist-high: S.R. This had to be the tree!

What did those initials mean anyway? Secrets Revealed?

Spock's Retreat? Spiders Reincarnated? Stay Rad? Super Route? Sucker's Remorse? Who knew.

She'd leave the best option for last, so she started with the zaniest way she concocted to get into the fantasy world. She looked at the initials and said, "Open Sesame." Nothing happened.

"Open the portal." Still nothing. It didn't work in Spanish either.

"Let me into the fantasy world! Transform into a portal." She looked upward and made Spock fingers by spreading her ring and middle fingers. "Let the door open once more. Magic tree, open for me. Roses are red, violets are blue, this tree is a portal, let me on through!" She pushed on the trunk with both hands with each phrase as if it would swing wide open, but no door turned on hinges. "Please?" She rested her forehead against the bark, but since it was scratchy she turned around and leaned her back against it while she pondered.

She thought of the number seven, from her research, and how it was the number that combined mortals and immortals—four symbolized earth and mankind; three symbolized divinity, harmony, and wisdom. Her goal was to move from earth to this place of harmony and wisdom. This was her last idea, but it clarified in her mind as she considered it, almost like another epiphany.

She pulled her shoulders back and placed her right hand on the special-looking tree believing it really was a portal that led to the fantasy world. Her right hand traced the trunk of the tree over the initials, and she counted her four clockwise steps, and then closed her eyes.

But before Elliana took her last three steps, she hoped. She hoped to find the beautiful world she often dreamed about.

She hoped to find answers about life. She hoped she wasn't just crazy in the head, nor in the heart. Hope started to feel more like belief the more she ignored the imaginary peer pressure she put on herself, the more she quit caring about what others might think, the more she relinquished the idea of being normal and ordinary and rational. She wanted more from her life. Her eyes were still clenched shut, and her heart thudded with a hunger to know, to face the truth of what she had the power to create. *I believe. I believe.* She had never wanted something so badly in her entire life. She took the last three steps.

Slowly she opened her eyes.

As her lashes parted, she saw sunlight streaking through the grove of trees.

Then she saw newness.

She stood in an enchanting forest within arm's reach of a bird who had morphed into an extraordinary winged creature that was more beautiful than any bird she'd ever seen. The bird's tail feathers were long and curly, with sprouts of copper feathers sticking into the air like a royal crown—its orange feathers incredibly vivid.

This was exactly like her dream, only real. She bit her pinky to make sure. Although she was astounded to find herself in the fantasy forest, she also expected to find it in a way. A peaceful feeling swelled within her chest, and the worries of her old world weakened and waned.

Her gaze followed the tall trees reaching toward the sky, and instead of just greens and browns, the colors were intensified into a gamut of scintillating colors she had never seen, and the leaves shimmered like specks of metallic dust in the sunlight. The little wildflower blooms and the entire forest boasted more intense colors than normal, glowing with an aura of sun glinting off metal—almost like she could see the light or life of trees, bushes, and earth. Everything emitted brilliance, some things more brightly than others, which made her surroundings the most magnificent scene she had ever experienced.

The trees and plants were translucent on the surface, and she could see the inside membranes flowing with life and energy. She watched with delight as a flock of winged, glowing insects fluttered up from the ground and flitted about the twinkling forest.

Somehow this was more beautiful than her dream. It was surreal. Standing on the same patch of ground where she had entered, her right arm still rested on the trunk as if keeping one hand in her old territory, so she dropped her arm and took a strong step forward.

As soon as she moved, a cloaked man on a dark horse appeared in a spot to her right that she was sure had been vacant nanoseconds before. The horse was breathtakingly beautiful, a navy sheen of black, opalescent like black oil floating on lake water. It stood higher than most horses she had seen. The man's right hand held the reins, and his other hand rested on the golden hilt of a sword sporting a long clear blade.

"What are you seeking?" The man's voice was polite, though she couldn't tell if he was smiling because his face was hidden behind a scarf—only his eyes were visible.

The horse dipped her head and jerked it upright, her mane a cascade of silvery waves so striking that its beauty distracted Elliana from feeling fear. She stuttered out her answer from her dream-memory. "I'm seeking my Soul's Purpose."

His eyes softened a bit and blinked a few times. "That is good. Welcome to the Seeking Realm, a refuge for the hopeful."

Seeking Realm. That's what the initials stood for.

He continued, "If you proceed, I have to warn you that you will be required to make great sacrifices, your life may be put in danger, and things will not be easy for you. But you will be given power and strength to overcome obstacles in your path. If you succeed, you will meet the rulers of this realm and be given instructions to help your earth friends and aid a dying star. If you fail, you will be worse off than if you had never embarked on this quest in the Seeking Realm. Do you still wish to proceed?"

Dang it. The dream never warned of danger. But she was already there in the beautiful, peaceful forest and felt there was no turning back—there was so much she wanted to see. Besides, being in this new realm made her mind and heart work differently—the most hopeful and fearless she had ever felt—and seeking came more naturally. Summoning her courage, she looked the figure straight into his eyes, the only part of his face not covered by a black scarf, and said, "Yes."

He pulled down his scarf, and a charming smile transformed him into a friend. He appeared handsome for being middle aged. "Elliana, I am Wayne, the Guardian of the Portal."

He knew her name.

"We've been waiting for you," the bird chirped, its voice almost a whistle, yet easy to understand. "I'm Orly, the Instrument of the Portal. Remember to learn something from each person you meet. Please leave your shoes at the foot of the tree and Wayne will take you where you need to go," the bird warbled as it pointed its wing.

"Thank you." Elliana nodded her head at the bird, and the bird bobbed its head in reply. She set her shoes at the base of the Tree Portal and wriggled her toes in the soft, spongy earth.

Elliana turned toward Wayne. "What is the Seeking Realm...and where am I exactly?" Feeling she ought to speak more formally to a man with a sword, she added, "Sir" at the end.

"This is a place where you can learn to make the most of your life and to find answers to the big questions. You are standing in Star, Idaho, but on the Seeking Realm side." Wayne dismounted and led his mare by the reins. "Follow me, dear."

Inhaling deeply and exhaling slowly, she took her first steps into the new world that stunned her with its beauty. "Yes, sir."

Though Wayne was unusually tall, his mare dwarfed him, and Elliana thought how easily it would be for the horse to squash her like a fly—though she didn't fear it happening. They walked toward a break in the forest ahead. "Sir, how do you know my name and why were you waiting for me?"

"You belong here and we know you, sweetheart—you'll understand that better in time. The Seeking Realm needs your help, so we've been waiting until you proved your strength." Wayne raised his eyebrows and said, "You're different in a good way—in a useful way."

Elliana shrugged and gave a half grin, thinking of how many times that very idea made her feel like a misfit. But this awesome misfit figured out how to access the Seeking Realm. Still, she had to ask, "How did I figure out how to get here?"

"Some things are given to you. Others you must work for, through asking questions, seeking knowledge, and standing tall through difficulties. And your being raised in Star is not happenstance. It was meant for you to grow up there because it is the birthplace of the Seeking Realm, and it has the strongest connection to this realm, which gives life to a star, which in turn gives life and love to the Earth Realm. We knew that if you grew up in Star, you'd find us. Up ahead we'll come to our cottage where you'll meet my sweet wife, Rose."

She walked on the soft earth on the opposite side of the horse as Wayne. The further she walked, the more a deep calm settled in her heart and the more her senses were overcome with awe.

"My mare's name is Serenada. Best horse I've ever had." He nodded to invite Elliana to pet the horse.

Elliana ran her hand along Serenada's shoulder and marveled at the silkiness of her hide. Without thinking, she twined her fingers into the horse's chrome mane.

As they neared the edge of the forest, Wayne stopped and motioned toward the little cottage ahead. "Rose will be happy to see you've arrived. Go on up to the cottage, dear. I must return to guard the Portal."

Her hands brushed through Serenada's mane when she let go. She stepped into the full sunlight, no longer canopied by the trees of the forest, and padded down the soft tawny path to the cottage which lie only a stone's throw away. Wayne said a quick "goodbye" and patted Elliana's shoulder, and then swiftly mounted his horse and retreated back into the forest.

She was instantly greeted by a beautiful woman wearing a strand of pearls, her brown wavy hair hanging down to the middle of her back with the sides secured by wooden clips. "Elliana, my darling!"

She was quickly enveloped by the arms of the woman who squeezed her like they were parted friends. "Please come in, and please call me Rose." Kindness radiated from her sky-blue eyes and her rosy, welcoming smile. Rose's gracefulness of younger years still accompanied her, making it hard to tell her age. She adjusted the blue flower in her hair and led Elliana by the hand into the front room of the cottage where they sat on cushioned armchairs. Elliana marveled at how at home she felt.

The cottage had a thatched roof, not of straw, but of green vines and vivid flowers that intertwined with curling tendrils. The windows were glass-less, and instead of a door, the cottage had a wide arched opening.

Elliana still wondered what she was doing there, what all of this meant.

"I know you have many questions. This is what you must know to fulfill your Soul's Purpose: You are needed to warm Earth's hearts and teach them pure love." Rose nodded slightly as she spoke.

"Earth's hearts?"

"That's what we say here, but you'd probably say human hearts."

Elliana let that sink in before responding. Hopefully Rose didn't mean ALL humans. The idea that Elliana could teach anyone anything, especially about love, was almost funny, but that thought made her feel more like crying than laughing. She wondered how exactly she qualified for the job because she couldn't understand why anyone would want a girl like her to teach others about love—a girl who had never kissed a boy or even had a real boyfriend, and who seemed to make better best-friend material than girlfriend material. She was the most unlikely of rescuers for that particular task. She wanted to ask who decided they needed her in the first place, and what had happened for them to run out of all viable options before landing their sights on her?

"You are not the only one we need. Everyone is needed, but you are the first one to successfully open the portal in decades. We've needed Seekers direly, and you have no idea how incredibly overjoyed we are right now." Water welled up in Rose's eyes and she blotted the tears with a lace-edged handkerchief. "Make yourself comfortable. I've got something for you."

Wide-eyed and sitting on the edge of the padded armchair, Elliana examined the room. The floor was hand-scraped hardwood. Beautiful paintings of nature and scenery and starscapes adorned the sky-blue plaster walls, as well as a few child-like drawings, one of which was a colored picture of the Big Dipper that resembled one Elliana had painted in elementary school. How curious.

Rose returned and handed Elliana a wrapped gift. "The Seeking Realm is to aid you in discovering your Soul's Purpose by reminding you daily of where you belong. This will help you remember who you are. Please, open it."

Elliana's fingers examined the small rectangular package. It was wrapped in homemade pulpy paper and tied with a ribbon. She pulled the ribbon and the wrapping fell open—almost as if its contents were bursting to be known—to expose a white-gold chain necklace with a rounded sapphire pendant that reflected a six-ray star on its surface.

"Wear it at all times and visit the Seeking Realm often to gain wisdom and direction for your journey, and your heart and mind will be strengthened."

"It's beautiful. Thank you." She had meant to ask Rose about the Big Dipper picture, but it completely skipped her mind as she dropped the necklace over her head and around her neck. "If someone asks where I got it, what should I tell them?"

"No one else will be able to see it, but you can tell them you got it from your friend named Rose. Keep it near your heart always."

Elliana toyed with the pendant in thought. "I'm still not

sure exactly why I'm needed and what I have to do, but I hope I can."

"You have come to the right place to gain wisdom and understanding. We all feel unsure or lost at times, my dear, but we always find truth when we seek it earnestly. And even doing the right thing only for the sake of curiosity or hope is still better than not doing it at all."

Elliana had to ponder that later, for it seemed deeper than her mind was willing to go just then. "Can you please tell me more about Orly and the Portal. How does it work?"

"Orly is your bird. She is an orange-crowned warbler known for her singing. She serves as the eyes and ears of the Portal on both sides of the Seeking Realm and will watch for danger and make a way for you to escape—even if circumstances seem life-threatening—by creating a Portal. Now that you know about her, you will notice her constancy, for she has always stayed near you throughout your life."

Her mind reflected back to Friday morning when an orange bird was perched at her window, and she thought about how a bird could fly most anywhere without anyone thinking anything of it. Elliana's mind was filling with questions faster than she could ask them. She asked more about the Seeking Realm.

"The Earth Realm and Seeking Realm do not coincide in terms of our five senses, though they both occupy the same space, so you are not far from home." Rose patted Elliana on the knee. "Come now. I can see that you have many more questions, for there is much to learn, but first I will give you a tour of your Garden."

"What do you mean, *my* Garden?"

"Outside the door is your Garden, and I am the Matron.

When you were born, I planted and cultivated your garden to beautify the Seeking Realm, to make it an inspiring place worth visiting so that you could accomplish your Soul's Purpose. I have been working in your Garden for nearly nineteen years preparing for the day that you would find me, and I could help you grow in mind and heart." Rose's eyes watered again. "I'm always here any time you want help finding answers, or even if you just want someone to talk to. Remember that in the Seeking Realm you are expected to seek by asking questions, and asking the right questions is crucial."

Rose led them out to the back of the cottage, out the door-less arch, down a narrow path, and then it was right in front of her. It was the most beautiful garden she had ever seen: lush, colorful, and full of fantastic colors of glowing light—even more so than the forest.

She heard a faint whisper of harmonious music in the background, like thousands of trained tones that blended into a trill. She didn't really know where the music was coming from, but she imagined that each plant played in a symphony of soothing and comforting music. Every thought and emotion felt purer and more acute, and she felt an irrevocable sense of belonging.

The Garden was extra beautiful; Elliana wondered if she was somehow transformed into a more beautiful version of herself while in it, but she didn't have a mirror handy to check.

Seeing the rapture on Elliana's face, Rose said, "Yes, dear, it is beautiful. Thanks to you, and a little bit of me. I plant a seed for each of your good intentions and uplifting thoughts. Each seed sprouts and grows as you do the right things, and the seedlings are nourished by the beauty of your life—a very beautiful life indeed. In the Garden, we get to celebrate with you for the goodness you help create on Earth. Do you see that tree over there between the chartreuse and orange-fire rose bushes?"

"Yes." Elliana puzzled whether Rose was able to read her thoughts, because Rose seemed to know Elliana's questions before they were asked. She had been looking at that same tree: lime green leaves with gorgeous violet and indigo flowers covered the tree—more flowers than leaves—and it exuded a brilliant aura of gold. The leaves and flower petals had a fluorescent, sparkly glow about them as if infused with a glimmery serum. "What does it mean?"

"This tree has a story you will recognize. The flowers on this tree blossomed overnight, on the night of the Great Rain, the night you decided to remain true to your character in the face of betrayal. Before that, it had only the green foliage."

She remembered clearly the night her so-called best friend heartlessly betrayed her and how heavily it had rained, almost upon her request. "You know about that? And why do you call it the Great Rain?"

"Yes, I am in your heart and thoughts—that is the best way I can explain it. And the Great Rain accompanies a broken heart, for it is only through a broken heart that one can transcend to a higher goodness."

"So that Great Rain, as you call it, was for me?"

"Truly. You may not have noticed, but the storm followed you and the heaviest rain fell only in your yard. The Great Rain was yours and yours alone. And it worked, didn't it? Did it not clear your mind and open it for something new?"

She remembered how it started raining only once she was in her driveway, how things became much clearer, and it felt more than plausible. "This is mind-boggling!"

"There is so much more to tell you, but it would be too overwhelming to try to learn it all at once—maybe even irresponsible to give you too much too soon. You will learn day by day until eventually you have all the knowledge and wisdom to fulfill your purpose," Rose said. "Anyone can be a Seeker, but few today have the desire, and of those, most lack the stamina and willingness to persevere in the search of answers to their questions. Being a Seeker will be an arduous adventure of greatness—mediocrity will not do. But in time you will look back and see that it was worth the toil and struggle."

"Can you tell me about the dying star Wayne mentioned?"

"Of course. The dying star is called Electra."

"The same Electra in the Pleiades? The Electra star that practically every civilization in the history of man has a legend about why it went dim?"

"Yes. Only to Earth Friends those are just stories, not truth."

How coincidental was it that Cai had just taught her about Electra? Now she could learn the truth about the star; although the legends were entertaining, she was sure none of those could be the real story.

"Electra has always been an important star for Earth and all her peoples—although no one in the Earth Realm knows that anymore because the knowledge has been lost. Although she appears to be an ordinary star, Electra is a Reflecting Star, meaning she reflects light depending on the values of those who dwell on Earth—or more specifically, she reflects the light generated by the Seeking Realm, and that light is magnified when a Garden is visited often."

Elliana's eyes widened. "How?"

"There is a supernatural connection between Earth and Electra; you could call it a conduit. The Star's life depends on the choices of her Earth Friends, and her Earth Friends' hearts are growing cold. There is an enemy, the Shadow Realm, which competes with our realm for control over Electra—if their dark power surpasses our light power, they can control Earth's hearts and will use their power to destroy the will and humanity of Earth friends. Electra has suffered greatly, and now her time is growing short. If Electra dies, the emotion of love will languish and die itself, which would result in a world of Shadows and misery, so we must do everything possible to prevent that from happening. You have an urgent purpose that affects the happiness of each Earth Friend."

Elliana tried to feel incredulous because this all seemed so unreal and fantastical, but it was hard to not believe while in the Seeking Realm because believing came naturally there. "Are you saying that the reason Electra dimmed was because the people on Earth don't love enough?"

"Yes."

Her mind jumped to the conversation she had with Cai about the dim star and the heartfelt kiss. Maybe he wasn't just a smooth talker; maybe there was some truth to his theory. "So, if I do something good, something heartfelt for someone else, the star will shine brighter?"

Rose smiled. "Yes, but so much damage has been done that it will take more than the noble actions of one person. But one person can make all the difference by becoming a catalyst for positive change."

"Wait, doesn't it take hundreds of light-years for light to travel from a star to Earth?"

"Not for a reflecting star. The change in light is almost immediate. Just as your good actions cause flowers of light to bloom in your garden, the good actions of many cause more light to bloom in the Seeking Realm, which means more light is reflected on Electra."

Rose and Elliana ambled through the glowing garden, admiring the beauty of the hues and shapes of the various plants, flowers, and trees, talking for hours. At one point, Elliana reached down to touch a blue tulip that looked exactly like the ones she had planted the day before, and as her finger grazed the petal, the end of her finger began to tingle. The sensation was warm and cool at the same time, like mint oil on her skin. She quickly retracted her hand, and the sensation gradually faded away as she rubbed her fingertips together.

Rose taught her that goodness is contagious, and that goodness and kindness and love all feed her Garden plants. She turned and pointed toward the most magnificent tree with neon blooms whose branches reached more than twenty feet in the air. "This is the Ambrosia Tree, the first tree I planted in your Garden, named for the amber-colored nectar that you can see running through its veins and into the blossoms. This tree produces living nectar you can drink and fruit you can eat for nourishment." The Ambrosia Tree was ever-bearing with a seven-hour cycle, taking about seven hours for the nectar in the tree to turn a flower bud into a fruit.

The tree was a perfect sphere of deep green foliage adorned with amber-colored blossoms and gold-skinned fruit. The blossoms favored both lilies and tulips, with long, shapely petals forming a floral cup that pointed skyward. Perfectly round fruits hung from the tree. Elliana plucked a blossom from the tree and carefully lowered it to look inside, where a tablespoon of amber-colored liquid pooled in the bottom.

"Drink it, dear. It will make you stronger in body. The fruit, however, will make you stronger in heart, so have as much as you wish for it will aid you in your quest. Surely you hunger by now."

Elliana did feel a hunger pang of a different sort. She tipped her head back slightly and the warm liquid slowly oozed onto her lips, which tasted of honey and almond oil. She was told to drop the blossom, and it shriveled and dissolved into golden speckles that were quickly absorbed into the soil. She plucked and drank until her mouth and soul tingled.

Next, she tugged a golden fruit from a low branch and examined it. It was about an inch in diameter and had a slight dimple where it was attached to the stem. She looked at Rose, who nodded for her to continue, and then sank her teeth into its soft, sweet flesh.

The fruit tasted so differently than the nectar, the taste reminding her of peach with a splash of strawberry and a flavor she didn't recognize. As she examined the half-bitten fruit, she could tell there was no pit or seed, and she finished the rest in one bite. The flavor made it easy to eat a dozen fruits, and her hunger pangs evaporated like raindrops on a hot rock. Afterwards, she felt drawn to return to regular old Earth Realm.

"I hope you'll come back often, my dear. You have no idea how I've waited for you." Rose embraced Elliana. "Your life is as beautiful as this garden. Please keep in the right way and remember your task. Many have tried and failed because of discouragement, so take courage and know that we believe in your goodness."

"Rose, thank you so much for the Garden, for your kindness, for teaching me. I'd better head back because I've been gone for several hours—I don't want my family to think I was eaten by a bear or kidnapped or something."

Rose smiled as if withholding another secret and escorted Elliana back to the edge of the forest. "This is as far as I go, darling. You exit the Realm the same way you entered. Be watchful."

Although she had only just met Rose, she felt a deep connection to her—like they had known each other once. With a hug, and a kiss on the cheek, Elliana was stepping lightly through the woods toward the Tree Portal. Orly was sitting on the lowest branch, warbling a melodic tune. She waved to Wayne nearby. "Bye. Thank you for everything."

Tracing the tree with her right hand, Elliana looked up at the bird. "Shall we?" She counted her first four steps; then in darkness, one, two, three.

She reentered the Earth Realm anxious for her first real date, which she did not want to miss. Hopefully Abbie would still have enough time to play hairdresser after her delayed return from the miraculous Seeking Realm. Those were the most awe-inspiring hours of her life—a life which she now knew had real purpose.

She glanced at her watch and tapped it. It must have stopped. It read 10:16 a.m. Porting to another realm must have nuked her watch or run down the battery, and she panicked about being too late for her date. Maybe she needed a new watch for her birthday.

CHAPTER EIGHT

First Date

ELLIANA SPRINTED to check the clock in her car and the time on her cell phone, and they all agreed: she had only been gone maybe a minute.

There was zero chance she could confuse several hours with a minute. She shook her head, afraid her mind was playing tricks on her.

She heard a chirpy laugh coming from a tree nearby, but when she looked up, the bird only bobbed its head.

Elliana retrieved her journal from the car and leaned against the car in confusion as she puzzled through what had just happened. Then she slid to the ground, opened her journal, and began to weave the tale of the Seeking Realm: the horseman, the matron, her Garden, the Shadow Realm, the dying Star and her quest to save it, the Great Rain, and the Ambrosia Tree. She thought it strange that the journaling took several hours for an experience that supposedly only lasted a minute.

Yes, the whole experience was very far-fetched. No normal person would believe she visited a fantasy realm, and she felt like one of those dingbats that believed in time travel or getting beamed up. No one would believe it unless they personally witnessed her disappearing and reappearing in a grove of trees. But it really had happened. The experience was real and wonderful, and rather than share it with people who might try to cheapen her experience, or have her committed, she treasured it and decided to tell no one. Not even Abbie.

After she finished journaling, Elliana had enough time and presence of mind to make some phone calls. Thinking to get the hardest conversation over with first, she dialed Marlee, though anxiety about talking to her after Friday night's betrayal made her hesitate a full minute before connecting the call. Her gut clenched on the first ring. To her great relief, it went to voicemail. "Hi, Marlee. It's Ellie. Just calling to see how your dress shopping went. Call me back. Bye."

Next, she called Keisha to explain each exciting little detail from her encounter with Cai, especially since Elliana had left her hanging so abruptly that night.

She was met with friendly scolding. "Ellie, you never called back! I've left you a ton of messages! What did you hit?"

"I actually backed into that cute boy I call Red Truck Guy, but fortunately he only got knocked down and wasn't hurt too badly—or so he claims." She explained how it happened, how she had been so twitterpated that she wasn't paying attention when she was backing out. "I felt like a total moron, but he was so sweet and charming, and we ended up talking for a few hours, and...listen to this: I'm going on a date with him today at five!"

"That is crazy! Who is he?"

"His name is Cai and I don't know a whole lot about him, except that looks older than me, has two sisters, and is intelligent and funny and easy to talk to. And...you're never going to believe the deal I made with him."

"Keep talking," Keisha said.

Elliana divulged the story of the Pleiades, Electra, and the heartfelt kiss.

"And?"

"I made the deal. At first, I thought he was trying to play me, but I'm pretty sure he was serious. He makes me forget about liking Burke and all the things that seemed to be going wrong a day or two ago. It's amazing."

"Well, good! I hope he's real. You deserve someone wonderful in your life, even if he doesn't have a brother for you to hook me up with."

Elliana laughed. "I knew you'd be happy for me. I know we need to talk more, but I have to go get ready for my date. Abbie is going to help me curl my hair and find something cute to wear." Elliana's voice squeaked with excitement.

"Okay, call me as soon as you get home tonight, if you have time! I want to hear everything!"

Elliana was glad that her friendship with Keisha was blossoming more than it had before. She needed a good girlfriend that she could trust. The more she got to know Keisha, the more she felt she was indeed a true friend who shared her sorrows and celebrated her happy moments, and who wasn't trying to compete with her.

Abbie insisted that Elliana wear something feminine for her date. She handed her sister a dressy outfit, but Elliana opted to go more casual. Elliana was nervous so Abbie offered advice as she curled her sister's hair and pinned the top in an up-do.

At five o'clock on the dot, the doorbell rang. Elliana clamored for the door, beating the rest of her family to the handle, and paused a second before opening it so she didn't appear too eager. "Hi, Cai."

"Hello, Elliana." He handed her a long-stemmed white rose, noticing her family eying him, and whispered, "I just wanted to show this rose how beautiful you are."

She thanked him, inhaled the fragrance briefly, and then invited him in to introduce her family. "This is my dad, Harrison Reinhart."

"Wait, not The Harrison Reinhart?" Cai asked while shaking Harrison's hand.

"One and the same," Harrison conceded.

"I am a big fan, sir. Your first book is the reason I wanted to become a pilot."

"Glad to hear it. It seems that my book might not be the only thing of mine you're a big fan of," he said, winking at Elliana.

Elliana blushed and continued. "This is my mom, Tina Reinhart."

"Hello, Mrs. Reinhart." Cai grasped her hand with both hands and shook it warmly.

Cai nodded and then reached out his hand to Abbie. "You must be Abbie, the pretty little sister."

"Yes, nice to meet you."

"Well, we are certainly glad to see you are all in one piece, and that you're not pressing charges," her dad said. "We had no idea Ellie was so reckless behind the wheel."

Cai laughed.

"Would you like to come sit down for a minute?" her mom asked.

"I'd love to, Mrs. Reinhart."

They stepped inside and parked themselves in the living room. Elliana offered to get drinks, disappeared momentarily, and returned with a tray holding five tall glasses of ice water. She mock-curtsied as she offered her guest the first water.

"Tell us a little bit about yourself," her dad said.

"I'm from Boise—Northeast Boise to be exact, and I live with my parents and two sisters. I'm attending Boise State for a bachelor's in Geoscience and expect to graduate a year from now."

"That will be quite an accomplishment," her mom said. She smiled because she always wanted her daughters to marry a man who pursued a formal education.

"I take my semester finals the second week of May, and then I'm done for most of the summer, but I'll be TA-ing two classes and logging hours in the pilot's seat so I can get my commercial certificate. I've had my Private Pilot's certificate since I was nineteen," Cai said.

Abbie replied, "So it seems you have a thing for the sky. I wonder, does that also include stars?" The smirk on her face made it obvious that she knew about the deal.

He glanced sideways at Elliana and then back to Abbie, his smile betraying his understanding. "Naturally. I have a thing for beauty. And besides, the more you know about the universe, the more you know about life. And maybe some time I'll let you tag along for a flight so you can understand why."

Abbie nodded.

"With your permission, Mr. and Mrs. Reinhart, I'd like to take Elliana on a picnic date."

"Where are you two headed tonight?" Her dad's demeanor got serious.

Cai said he was taking her to the park near Confucius, and her dad nodded in approval.

"I hope you're driving." Her dad laughed gruffly as they all stood and walked to the door.

"Yes, of course. What time should I bring her home?"

"It's a school night, so by ten o'clock."

"I'll have her home on time. It was nice meeting you all. You have such a nice family."

Cai walked Elliana to the passenger side of his crew-cab Silverado truck and opened the door for her, holding her elbow as she jumped up into the seat. They headed out of the little town of Star toward the park where they made the Starlight deal.

"Hope you're hungry," Cai said.

"I am."

"Good. I packed us a pick-a-nic basket."

The park was old enough to boast huge, mature trees. It was under one of these lofty trees that Elliana and Cai chose to have dinner, but they didn't sit in the shade as April was still a little too chilly without direct sunlight. They relaxed near a duck pond with the "pick-a-nic" basket between them, on a denim quilt that his grandmother had sewn. He opened the basket and withdrew two heavy-bottomed glasses, ceramic plates, sandwiches on hoagie buns, fabric napkins with little yellow birds embroidered on each corner, bright green granny smith apples, salt and pepper, and some sparkling cider. He left some items in the basket and set it to the side.

"Looks delicious."

"It should. I made the sandwiches myself." He smiled and placed a wax-paper wrapped sandwich on each plate and set a napkin underneath it. He handed her a glass and filled it half full of the bubbly cider, and then poured some into his glass. "To what shall we toast?"

"How about to my sweet driving skills?"

"I'll toast to that. To your sweet driving." He clinked his glass against hers and took a sip.

He grabbed one of the apples, fished a sharp knife out of the basket, and sliced two sides off the apple before shaking a dash of salt on each.

"Try it. My grandma taught me the salt trick."

Elliana took a bite and chewed, reaching up to wipe away a splash of apple juice from her chin. "This is good. I would have never put these two together." She realized the same could be said about her and Cai and hoped she was meant to nearly run him over.

"I've been meaning to ask you how old you are."

She swallowed and hoped her answer to his question wasn't a deal breaker. "I'll be nineteen on Friday. Just a senior in high school. And, no, I didn't flunk. People always ask when they find out my grade and age. My mom kept me home until I was six so she could spend more time with me. Same with my sister." She lifted another salted apple slice to her mouth and asked, "How old are you?"

"I turned twenty-one a few months ago." He looked like he expected her to say something.

"I could tell you were older than me."

He smiled. "I'm okay with a two-year difference if you are."

"Me, too. I'm used to hanging out with old people, so it's no big deal for me."

"Old people? Are you referring to your parents?" Cai asked.

"Yeah. You did notice that they look almost old enough to be my grandparents, right?" Elliana smiled so that he wouldn't feel like he was prying.

"Yeah, but they aren't your grandparents, are they?"

"Nope, they're my adoptive parents. They weren't able to

have children of their own for many years, so they adopted me and Abbie after our first parents were killed in a car accident."

He looked pained. "Oh, I'm so sorry."

"It's okay. I was three so I don't remember them very well." She twisted the diamond-sapphire ring on her right hand, and then said, "See this ring? This was my first mom's. She was wearing it in the accident. Each year we celebrate our survival by planting tulips in the garden and going out to eat, which is why we were at Confucius yesterday."

Cai asked if both her and Abbie were in the accident, and she said, "Yes. My mom, Tina, was one of the EMTs at the scene. She says guardian angels and excellent medical care is what saved us. I have some cool scars, too." She offered her wrist to show him the scar.

He held her hand, turning it to get a better look at the scar, examining her wrist a few seconds before letting go. "So the anniversary of the accident was yesterday?"

"Sixteen years ago, yesterday. It's not really a sad thing for us though. My mom calls it 'Miracle Day,' and that's how we celebrate it. Tina and Harrison are the only parents I can remember. They have rules and can be strict, but they are good to me and Abbie. I love my parents."

"A teenager that likes her parents?"

"I know." She shrugged her shoulders and smiled.

"Your parents did seem nice."

"Until it comes to boys. You're lucky my dad didn't happen to be cleaning his twelve-gauge shotgun when you came to pick me up."

"Has he done that before?"

"Once, last fall when a guy he didn't like came to pick me up for a dance. I was kind of glad he did it because I didn't really like the guy," she said. "He was a show-off with an ego. I would have liked to back my car into him."

Cai studied her.

Elliana pressed his leg. "I'm totally kidding."

"Now I'm wondering why you backed into me. You didn't even wait to see if I was a show-off with an ego."

"Are you?"

"To a degree."

"That must have been why my car was attracted to you." She laughed and shrugged.

"But I can also be charming."

"Yeah, I noticed. But seriously, how did you see my journal, and how did you know it was mine?"

A smirk traveled across his face. "You think I didn't see you and your sister saunter past me? My sisters pointed out that it was some sort of girl code."

"Well, that's just a little embarrassing," she said. "Abbie made me do it."

"Okay, I'll share something embarrassing, too. I was hoping I could meet you somehow. I wasn't about to go hit on you while you were with your family, and especially not in front of your dad. I saw you sitting with your family, and when you left, I noticed your journal on the seat, and it was my chance."

"I think I'm the one who ended up doing the 'hitting on.'"

"Like I could forget." Cai pulled out a clear plastic baggie containing a few slices of bread, and stood up, holding his hand out to Elliana. "Let's feed the ducks." He pulled her to her feet, and they walked to the water's edge, brushing into each other several times.

He handed her two slices of bread. She tore off bits of bread and tossed them to the ducks and geese, inciting a frenzy. The more dominant geese flapped their wings and pecked angrily at the others who were vying for the same morsels. Cai walked a few feet over and threw some bread to the weaker birds, but the mean ones were fighting for the new food in a matter of seconds.

"Greedy little buggers," Cai said, tossing the last of his bread as hard as he could. His face looked triumphant when a few of the smaller ducks were able to get to the bread first.

Just before she ran out of her bread, a loud quack rang out from behind, and she wondered if she was under attack. She turned around to see a mallard duck following her, bobbing its head as if begging. She tossed the last bit of bread to the duck in her shadow and continued walking around the park with Cai.

Elliana nudged him with her elbow. "Do you always root for the underdog?"

"For the most part."

She paused and puzzled if that's why he was interested in her and then shooed away the thought by changing the subject. "Tell me about your parents."

"My parents are kind of opposites, and they help balance the other one out. My dad is more the serious business type, and my mom is the spontaneous, fun one."

Elliana asked how his parents met.

"They'd known each other as young children in the same elementary school. My dad always picked on her doing typical boy things: pulling her pony tails, kicking the back of her chair, chasing her on the playground. He drove her nuts. And the summer after fourth grade, my mom's family moved to a different Air Force base, and they never saw each other again until, of course, my mom walked into his ballroom dance class in college."

"And the rest is ancient history?"

"No, not yet. My mom had no idea who my dad was—she claims she didn't recognize him. Of course, my dad knew exactly who she was and says that she was the most beautiful thing on campus. With a little finagling on his part, he became her dancing partner, and during a dance they were learning, my dad pulled her hair and asked if she remembered him from elementary school. Then it dawned on my mom, and she threatened to get switched to a different dance partner. He promised to behave himself, so she stayed. And by the end of the semester, they were falling in love."

"That's so cute."

"Yeah, you should hear them both tell different versions of the same story—they are funny. Right now, they're celebrating their twenty-fifth wedding anniversary in Europe. I talked to them earlier and they are gorging themselves on Belgian waffles, which apparently aren't breakfast waffles—they're rich, sugary pastries."

"I want to go to Europe someday, but the farthest I've ever been is a few states away. My best friend and I were supposed to go camping on the beach in Washington after graduation, but I think that's out of the question now." She had to explain the situation, talking about her crush on Burke and how Marlee asked him to Spring Formal the night that she wanted to. Though she still liked Marlee, and though a few other girls were planning to go also, the debacle at Eagle Island was too fresh to think about spending a week in close quarters with her.

"That's a pretty sucky situation. But I must admit I'm not sad that you didn't end up with him, because it worked out really nicely for me—except for the knee part." He winked. "Maybe it happened that way for a reason. But I still think you should do something to celebrate your graduation."

"Probably so, but I don't have a back-up plan. And after last weekend, let's just say being done with high school drama can be my graduation reward."

The conversation meandered to Spring Formal, and Cai asked her if she was going.

"No. The student council advisor says that all senior reps should go because we helped plan it and raise money, but I don't want to go." She asked him if he thought she'd be missing out.

"I went to Spring Formal with a girl that I thought I liked, but looking back, it wasn't anything spectacular. It was an expensive tux rental, corsage, limo, and dinner with the wrong girl. For a lot of my classmates, it was an excuse to get liquored up and try to get a hotel room. But that's not my style. I'm a pretty clean-cut guy, and I avoid those scenes. So if you're not into that, you won't miss anything at all."

"I'm definitely not into that," she said emphatically to make sure he understood her standards. "You really don't think I'll regret not going?"

"Nah, but I'll tell you what. If you feel like you're going to be missing out by not going to your last Spring Formal, I'll take you—only if you want. Or I'll take you out somewhere nice for dinner and we can dance to music blaring from my truck radio on the bluffs outside of Boise."

She chewed on her bottom lip, a little excited that he was interested in another date, and then asked if he wouldn't be super embarrassed to go to a high school dance.

"It's hard to get embarrassed when you quit caring what

other people think of you, especially when their opinions are irrelevant and ignorant."

His argument sounded reasonable. Going with Cai could be fun, but she wasn't sure she was ready to watch Burke swaying with Marlee all night long, and she wouldn't have to if she went on a date somewhere else with Cai. "Maybe I'll take you up on option two."

After walking the park, they arrived back to their picnic spot when the sun was beginning to set. They reached down, each grabbing a corner of the blanket, and pulled it back into the fading sunlight. They sat facing each other.

"What are you doing for your nineteenth birthday? It's on Friday, right?"

She nodded and then shrugged. "Don't know. I always have cake and ice cream with my family, but I don't have anything beyond that planned. My friend Keisha thought I should ask Marlee to plan my party because she's so good at entertaining, but it's too weird right now."

His hands fidgeted with a yarn tie on the quilt. "Can I take you out? Before your family party?"

She nodded.

"I'd like to take you flying in my small plane, if your parents don't mind. I am an excellent pilot." Cai squared his shoulders.

Her face brightened. "Sounds awesome!" Wasn't excitement and adventure just what she needed?

"Am I allowed to get you anything?" he asked.

"Of course not. The plane ride will count."

Cai cast her a look that told her she wasn't going to win this one.

"Can I stop you?" she asked.

"No, not really. I am very determined."

"Okay, fine, but nothing big."

He agreed. They exchanged stories for another hour while munching on caramel corn that was stashed in the bottom of the picnic basket, flirting with each other, and making the other laugh.

When she twirled a yarn tie on the blanket with her right hand, he traced the scar on her wrist with his thumb. They locked eyes for a long moment, and then Elliana cast her gaze downwards.

Cai apologized. "Sorry, I didn't mean to make you uncomfortable."

"Oh, it's not that. I was just thinking." She knew she had turned suddenly shy from the unfamiliar situation and didn't want to send him a keep-away message because she liked him. "I'm glad my car was attracted to your knee."

He relaxed. "Me, too. But do you know how hard it is to study when you can't get a certain girl off your mind? There's something about you."

"I'm glad I have that effect on someone. I thought I must be invisible to the male species. No boy has really paid much attention to me, except a few who are totally not my type."

"And by not your type, you mean?"

"Idiots or bad boys. Actually, there was this one guy who was stupid smart—one of the smartest kids in my grade, but didn't get it when it came to girls and friends. Nice enough for someone else, I guess, but no chemistry whatsoever."

"You mean he wasn't easy on the eyes, right?" he prodded.

"I was trying to be nice about it." She pursed her lips. "But yes—he thought much more of atoms and science than he did people. Maybe I'm just too picky, but probably it was his lack of social skills."

"You're easy on the eyes, so I can't believe that he's the only one who has shown any interest." Cai put his hands out to defend himself and said, "I'm not trying to be a schmoozer."

"You're sweet." She smiled. "My parents say that all the boys in my school must be stupid, but parents are very biased. It's their job."

"It's certainly a good thing for me that so many stupid boys attend your high school. And because it's a school night," he said glancing at his watch, "I'd better get you home so your dad doesn't happen to be cleaning his shotgun next time I show up."

Her heart fluttered again at the suggestion of a *next time*.

"Which means I'll see you Friday for your birthday flight, unless I can come up with a better excuse to see you before then."

They gathered their picnic items and headed home. When he parked in her driveway, Cai opened Elliana's door and helped her down and walked her to the front doorstep.

He pivoted to face her and thanked her for a wonderful evening.

"I had a great time, too. Thanks."

After gazing briefly at the starry cope above, Cai took a step toward her.

CHAPTER NINE

Just Friends

CAI RAISED HER HAND to his lips, kissed it, and bid farewell.

"Bye," she said, flitting into her house, watching him leave as she pressed the door closed and breathed deeply. Before she could even replay the hand-kiss in her mind, her mom's voice rang through the hall asking how her date went.

Elliana swished toward the family room and plopped down on the couch.

"We had so much fun. We had a picnic at the same park we went to last night, fed the ducks, and just talked and talked. He was so sweet, and funny, and respectful, too. Much different than the guys at my school."

"He seemed like a very nice boy," her mother said.

"Did he behave himself?" her dad asked.

"Yes, Daddy. He was a perfect gentleman."

"Good. He brought you home happy and on time," said her father, "which means my shotgun doesn't need cleaning just yet."

After talking to her family, she headed up stairs. A deluge of dread and guilt set in as she lounged on her bed and made sure her alarm was set. She had broken her promise to call Keisha back again, and it was too late according to house rules. She would have to apologize profusely at school tomorrow.

At the beginning of fifth period painting class on Monday, Elliana noticed a new kid.

When the bell rang, the teacher appeared. A few seconds into describing the next painting project, Mrs. Pratt noticed the new boy sitting at the table to the left of Elliana. "Are you new?"

"Yes, ma'am. Here is a note from the office." The boy handed the teacher a yellow slip of paper.

"I'm Mrs. Pratt. Go ahead and introduce yourself to the rest of the class."

"Of course, Mrs. Pratt. My name is Granger, last name Lamme. L-a-m-m-e, not spelled like the fuzzy animal. You can call me Gray. I'm a junior from Nevada, but I'm living with my uncle here in Star."

That kid didn't miss a beat. He must've taken the spot of a junior that had just gotten expelled for cheating. She noted that Granger was unusually muscular, but everything else about him was average: average height, average looking, average-length wiry dark hair that sprouted from his head.

After welcoming him to class, the teacher continued describing the painting requirements: color mixing, contrast, and texture.

Granger caught Elliana looking at him. He briefly, but skillfully, raised his eyebrows and nodded toward an empty chair at his table, like he was inviting her to come over and talk to him. But she didn't have to, because as soon as Mrs. Pratt walked to the back of the room to her desk with the yellow paper, he slid into the chair across the table from her. "You're

Elliana, right?"

Her forehead wrinkled. "How do you know my name?"

"In my math class this morning, I heard several people talking about you—you know, about wanting to vote for you for Spring Formal Queen, but that you didn't have a date yet. I asked a pretty dark-skinned girl who they were talking about—I think her name was Keisha—and she described you: brown hair with long waves, bright blue eyes, kinda short, and then I saw you walk in and figured it had to be you."

"Yep, that's me."

The new kid looked her over and nodded slightly. "Actually, I think you and I went to the same elementary school for a year when I was in kindergarten and you were in first grade." He paused for her to respond, but she didn't. "I also heard that you're the one I need to talk to if I need help in art, which I probably will."

He didn't look familiar to her, but then again it had been almost a dozen years since she had been in first grade, and there was no sense in being rude. "Nice to meet you, Granger. You like to paint?"

"It's okay. Let me put it this way: I'm a better admirer of art than creator of it myself. I guess I'm the worst of the best... when it comes to painting."

"Mrs. Pratt's a good teacher. You'll like her."

"I'm sure I will. I have already met several people who are worth liking." His smile was friendly and it drew her attention to the slightest soul patch below his bottom lip, which was borderline unacceptable at her school.

He interrupted her assessment of his looks. "Why aren't you going to Spring Formal?"

Elliana tucked her hair behind her ears. "I have an

engagement that evening."

"Come on. Everybody wants to go to their last formal. What if they make you Spring Formal Queen?"

"I guarantee they won't, but why do you care?" Elliana asked.

"I don't really care all that much about high school dances; I'm just trying to make friends." His smile made him more charming and personable. "And I heard a leggy redhead campaigning for herself this morning, which I find absolutely repulsive, so I'm going to sway the results and tell everyone to vote for you instead."

She rolled her eyes slightly. "Please don't. You don't even know me well enough. Besides, I already know who I'm voting for, and it's not myself. In fact, maybe you could help me." She thought it odd that she wanted to confide in this new kid, but he needed friends and was extra personable, and she didn't really have much to lose, so she told him who she thought deserved to be voted as king and queen.

"More painting, less talking," Mrs. Pratt chided.

Elliana grabbed a pencil and a few sheets of sketching paper and started a rough drawing of a barn next to a field of flowers. As she worked, she chatted quietly with the new kid, who was very talkative—a good trait for a kid who had just moved to a new school. They seemed to connect and be instant friends. If in his shoes, she would have felt so lonely moving to a new place, so she asked him why he moved so close to the end of the year instead of waiting until the next school year.

He had been on the waiting list for Copernicus Charter High since the beginning of the school year, and a slot had just opened up. Rather than risk losing the admission lottery again in the fall, he took the spot that guaranteed he was in. That made sense, and her school was a great school, especially for science and math and for anyone who wanted to be an engineer—like Granger. The kid seemed to be a real go-getter.

The bell rang and they exited the class together. She turned toward him and said, "I hope you like it here in Star, Granger. If you need anything, just ask."

"Thanks, Elliana. The people are so nice that I'm sure I'll love it here. Oh, and all my friends call me Gray."

Lunch was the first time that Elliana had seen or talked to Marlee since the previous Friday. But somehow Marlee wasn't the same. Burke sat next to Elliana, bumping her playfully with his elbow. Marlee quickly snatched up the seat to the other side of Burke like a possessive fifth-grader.

"Hey, Marlee," Elliana began, "I tried calling you last weekend—"

"I know, but I was so busy with dress shopping, and we had this big birthday party for my grandpa yesterday. I've just been super busy. Please forgive."

The lack of sincerity in Marlee's response grated against Elliana's resolve to be kind. "I bet the party was awesome."

"Honestly, Ellie, do I ever throw a party that isn't awesome?" Marlee turned to Burke and started yacking about Spring Formal. Ugh!

Keisha approached the table, and Elliana motioned for her to sit in the seat next to her. "Hey, Keesh."

"Well if it isn't Miss Keep-Me-Hanging! You never called me last night to tell me how it went with Mr. Amazing!" Keisha leaned toward Elliana, hoping to learn the juicy details of her date.

Marlee overheard Keisha's comment and glanced up with a strange look on her face, but then busied herself again with conversation.

Elliana apologized several times. "I'm so sorry I didn't call back. It was perfect. He is so dreamy," Elliana whispered. "He took me to the same park for a picnic where we made the deal, and then we walked around the pond and fed the ducks. He was so sweet—a total gentleman, no red flags."

"When do I get to meet this guy?" Keisha asked.

Burke raised an eyebrow. "Wait, what guy?"

"Ellie met a hot guy over the weekend, and they went on a hot date last night." It was rather obvious Keisha wanted both him and Marlee to hear the news.

Perhaps Burke didn't look stunned, but he didn't look thrilled either. "You'll have to tell me all about it over cookies and dinner tonight."

Marlee barged into the conversation. "Wait, you're going over to her house for dinner tonight?"

Burke bent his head toward Elliana. "Yes, we are studying for our calc test, and we'd invite you, but you're not in Calculus II...or even Calculus I. So please forgive."

Marlee looked pained for a second, and then wore a fake smile for the rest of lunch.

When the bell rang, Burke nudged Elliana. "See you after school, Ellie."

Marlee's fake smile got even faker, if that were possible. If Marlee assumed that she and Burke were automatically becoming a thing because they were going to Spring Formal together, she clearly underestimated his friendship with Elliana, and perhaps resented it now more than ever.

After lunch, Elliana and Keisha walked down the hall together. Elliana said, "I sensed some hostility coming from Marlee."

"Yeah, well, I'd be feeling guilty if I were her. She knew you wanted to go with him!"

"Keesh, I'm just going to let it go. Don't tell anyone please— it will just give her more reason to dislike me, if that's what she's after." And if Keisha knew the truth, that Marlee did the asking, that could unravel the next few weeks and make things even worse.

As they walked to their next class, both girls decided that they had done nothing wrong to earn her wrath, and although it stung, they wouldn't get sucked into her drama.

"By the way, did you meet that new kid today?" Keisha asked.

"Yeah, he's in my painting class."

"He's kind of nice, don't you think?"

"Yeah. Definitely not a shy one though."

"I know what you mean. He overheard a few of us talking this morning and just joined in the conversation, asking who we were talking about. We were talking about you, but we weren't saying anything negative, I promise. Just that we thought you should be Spring Formal Queen, since you have too much decency to campaign for yourself. And I think it would help prove—"

"First of all, I don't want to be the dumb Spring Formal Queen," Elliana said. "In other news, did I tell you Cai is taking me out instead of Spring Formal?"

Elliana had been home for about ten minutes when Burke pulled into the driveway. She heard his music blaring all the way inside and chuckled to herself. Silly boy. She pushed the glass storm door open and invited him inside. The aroma of fresh chocolate chip cookies greeted him.

"Hi, Burke," her mom called from the kitchen.

"Hey, Mrs. Reinhart. Smells good in here!"

Her mom had just finished setting down a large plate of gooey cookies, two tall glasses, and a jug of milk on the kitchen table when Burke entered. She patted each of them on the shoulder, walked into the family room, and picked up a book to read.

Elliana and Burke sat opposite each other, spreading their textbooks open on the kitchen table. He flipped through a few pages and asked, "Who is this guy I heard you and Keisha talking about?"

"His name is Cai. When my family was eating at Confucius on Saturday, I kind of rammed him with my car in the parking lot, and we ended up talking for a long while. Then he asked me to marry him, and I obliged."

"What?" His face contorted until he saw her laughing.

She had to catch her breath after belly-laughing at her own joke. "Your face was priceless. He only asked me out on a date and then a second date."

"How old is he?"

"Thirty-something," she said studying a page in her calculus book. "Just kidding, he's only twenty-one."

He stole her pencil to get her attention. "Twenty-one? Don't you think he's a little old for you, Ellie?"

"No. We're okay with the age difference." She grabbed her pencil back.

"You hardly know the guy. How do you know you can trust him?"

"Don't worry so much. He met my parents on Sunday and he took me to a public park for our date. I felt safe. I really don't think he's the shady type—he seems clean cut. He doesn't smoke or drink or sleep around or kill people."

"According to what he told you, right?"

"Burke!" she said with mild exasperation.

"Ellie, you know I have to ask only because I care. That's what best friends do. I've told you that a guy will say anything to get what he wants, and he can fool the best of them. I'll try to be happy for you, but I'm not diving in head first yet."

"Thanks, Mr. Overprotective." She batted her eye lashes in false appreciation and flipped to the homework assignment that reviewed the two chapters the test would cover.

Halfway through, Burke noticed that she kept glancing at her phone, sometimes picking it up and staring at the screen. "Ellie, what's with the phone?"

"I'm expecting a text."

"From whom? Lover boy?"

"No. I texted Marlee after school asking if she was okay, because to tell you the truth she has been acting really strange today, and she still hasn't texted me back. Did you notice the way she pounced on Keisha and me today?"

"Yeah, I don't know what her deal is. Maybe she's just having an unusually bad day."

"Maybe. Are you and Marlee a thing now?"

"We are just friends." After seeing the prodding look on her face, he continued, "To speak in girl language, I don't like-like her, if that's what you mean."

"Oh, just checking. Because that's what best friends do." She kicked his shoe under the table.

They studied until dinnertime, and then Burke ate hot bean soup and fresh baked wheat bread with the Reinharts—just like old times. Elliana was glad that they were still able to be best friends after her awkward confession of like-like just a few days before. Just friends was fine with her.

Granger took a seat across from Elliana before painting class and fist-bumped her. He was pretty easy to talk to. As she painted, she told him that in addition to art, she loved to read, and laugh, and go on hikes in the foothills of Boise, noting her favorite spot that was usually pretty quiet.

Halfway through the class Elliana realized that he was learning a lot about her, but she still didn't know much about him.

"Your turn. Tell me about yourself." Elliana said.

"I love running and mountain biking."

"My sister, Abbie, loves running, too. Are you in track?"

"I was in my other school. I want to talk to the coach today to see if I can compete in the last few meets."

She looked up. "There's a meet on Thursday, and three weeks after that is district championships. Are you any good?"

"I set a few records at my last high school in the one-hundred-meter and the hurdles, so if that's good, I guess I am." Granger smirked like he didn't know how to be humble.

"My sister is running the sixteen hundred, so I'll be watching from the stands on Thursday."

At lunch she was dismayed that Marlee's attitude wasn't much improved, but Elliana tolerated her and tried to be friendly, though it was getting harder. They each sat on one side of Burke, who seemed conflicted by the tension. Elliana didn't make a big deal about it publicly, but inside she struggled with resentment and trying to maintain the forgiveness she thought she had already granted Marlee. This forgiveness business was like playing whack-a-mole: each time she thought she had forgiven Marlee, another stinking mole would pop up to remind her she still had more heart-work to do.

Out of nowhere, Granger showed up with a lunch tray and asked Elliana if he could sit with her.

She scooted her chair and made room on the other side of her. "Sure."

Granger pulled a chair from another table and sat between Elliana and Keisha, gave them both fist bumps, and flashed them a charming smile that improved his looks.

"Has everyone met Gray?" Elliana asked.

Her friends nodded and greeted him, which meant he hadn't wasted any time making friends. He was so outgoing that he probably wouldn't shy away from striking up a conversation with an A-list movie star either.

He spent lunch telling tales of exciting (yet gory) mountain biking accidents, revealing a plethora of scars on his elbows, knees, and one on his chin. A total adrenaline junkie. The kids at the table seemed riveted by his misadventures because of the suspenseful way he told the story. He had instant friends because of his outgoing personality—even Marlee seemed to appreciate him, though he was her competition when it came to storytelling.

As Elliana got up from the table to return her lunch tray, she noticed a brown bird with orange head feathers perched on a skinny tree just outside the cafeteria—a bird that looked an awful lot like Orly.

After school, Elliana ran up to her room and grabbed her journal, thumbing through until she landed on the page that talked about Orly. She knew that Orly was her bird, and Orly followed her throughout the day, watching. Orly was the Instrument of the Portal, which must mean that Orly made that tree in the forest into a portal. If Elliana was right, all she had to do was perform the steps while holding onto any tree Orly landed on, and she would enter the Seeking Realm.

Elliana ran down the hall, down the stairs, and out the front door—searching for her bird. Orly wasn't difficult to find; she was sitting on a branch of the blooming cherry tree in the front yard. The bird bobbed her head at Elliana.

Next, she ran to the backyard, near the edge of the property that was lined with white-barked Aspen trees. She stopped and spun around only to see Orly landing on a branch just above her head. Again, the bird bobbed her head.

She walked about ten feet down the line of trees and watched as Orly faithfully followed her and landed on the tree that was closest to her. She was instantly grateful she had a magical bird rather than a grody bug or nasty varmint following her around to open magic portals. And she was grateful that she never shot at any birds with her cousin's bb gun.

After making sure that no one was watching, Elliana placed her right hand on the nearest tree, feeling its rough, papery bark beneath her hand, and counted her seven steps. She opened her eyes, hopeful.

She found herself standing on the soft, spongy ground in the forest of the Seeking Realm, surrounded by light and beauty.

She greeted the cloaked equestrian and ran her fingers through Serenada's silky mane. "Wayne, I've been wondering about the time difference. How does time work here?"

He chuckled. "One hour in the Seeking Realm was equal to one second in earthly time, and because of the time difference, the nectar and fruit from the Ambrosia tree give stamina to the body and heart." He said, "It could take a lifetime to learn all about the Ambrosia tree and the Seeking Realm."

"Sounds like how much time I have left," she replied. "Can you remind me what my quest is?" It had been a lot to take in, and she wanted the comfort of hearing it repeated from someone who knew.

"The Seeking Realm needs you to complete quests, which if you succeed, will grant you power and lead you to the knowledge of saving the reflecting star Electra, whose dimming starlight indicates hearts growing cold and relationships suffering in the Earth Realm. There is too much hate and division, so your first quest is to understand the human heart and pure, healthy relationships. Discovering your origins will help with your first quest."

She made a mental note to record that in her journal when she got home and reached up and touched her pendant necklace. After saying bye to Wayne, she jogged past the fluttery, glowing insects through the trees to the cottage and knocked gently on the door jamb just as Rose was exiting.

"Hi, darling. I'm glad to see you. Would you like to take a walk?"

She nodded and they walked side by side into the Garden, with Rose gently stooping to smell some of the freshly blooming flowers. "Smell these ones," Rose said.

Elliana bent forward, gently grasping the large white bloom and inhaled deeply. "That smells ten times better than anything I've smelled in any other garden!" And the strong scent didn't give her a headache.

"Yes, the Earth Realm doesn't grow flowers this aromatic. Try those blue clusters over there." Rose pointed to a spot a few feet away.

Elliana inhaled the pepperminty scent. "That flavor would make the best gum." Elliana walked a few more feet into the vast Garden and sat on the velvety green grass.

"Rose, I was thinking today about everything I learned from my last visit and figured out that Orly creates portals. I tried it out in my backyard instead of my dad's farm land, and voilà, here I am."

"That's the beauty of it. You can get here from anywhere, and it doesn't cost you more than a few seconds of your time. And once you've felt the beauty and power of the Seeking Realm in your soul, you'll be drawn back."

Elliana nodded in agreement. "I saw Orly outside of my school today, and that's what got me thinking about what you said the other day, about how Orly would watch for danger and provide a way for me to escape."

After Rose explained the shortcut method for porting to the Seeking Realm, Elliana said, "That's way easier. Why did I see the more complicated way to use a portal in my dream then?"

"Using the portal needs to be somewhat accessible so that you can always find an escape, but the way you were shown in your dream required more effort—a test of your will. Counting your steps required concentration; you had to hope and believe. If it was too easy at first, would you have appreciated it as much as you do now, having had to find the grove of trees and counting your steps? Would it have seemed as important?"

Elliana shook her head.

"It was the first test of your readiness. And you must realize that finding the Seeking Realm was not an easy task by any means. You're nearly nineteen years old and you've been seeing portions of the same recollection, or dream-memory as you call it, for many years. What you might not realize is that you've been working toward this your whole life and have had to suffer many losses, as well as the recent pain of betrayal inflicted by your best friend. Only after you showed your intent to remain honorable under very sensitive and hurtful circumstances did your recollection give you the final steps."

Rose talked more about Electra, and things made more sense. Elliana's mind ignited and zoomed like a rocket into outer space.

Elliana found it odd that Electra's starlight had been dimming for millennia, so Rose explained that reflecting stars have an invisible connection, a symbiotic relationship with Earth where the starlight is completely dependent upon Earth. The fallout of the star dying meant the Shadow Realm could control the way humans felt and acted, rather than the Seeking Realm. "For there is no life without love," Rose said.

As they walked toward the end of the garden, Elliana saw something glint behind the foliage and asked Rose about it.

"That's the gate for the next portion of your quest. It's a special gate, and you'll know when it's time to travel beyond it."

Elliana walked toward it and caught a narrow glimpse of a white stone wall with a wrought-iron gate and crystalline pickets and narrow view of a cobblestone path.

Three seconds after she walked around that tree in her backyard, Elliana reappeared at that same tree, facing the back side of her home with a cheerful expression, happy to be seeing the positive amidst all the negatives.

She wondered if she could ever talk about the Seeking Realm without being laughed to scorn. That surely would be a difficult conversation to have: *Hey, I can travel to a different realm where magical flowers grow from my good deeds. I'm pretty special, huh?* Any sane person would dismiss it as utter hogwash. As she thought of explaining it, she knew others would seriously question her sanity. Fear of how others would react almost made her doubt the veracity of her experience, like maybe she'd been hallucinating—but in her heart, she knew it was real.

Abbie might believe it, that was possible, but how to tell her? *Hey sis, I'm so cool and special that I have my very own garden of good deeds and a quest to spread love. Jealous much?* Of course, she wouldn't really say it like that, but would Abbie feel happy for her or jealous, or even believe her?

Elliana was hesitant to tell her younger sister about her Garden for fear it would cause Abbie to feel less important, or maybe even envious—and envy had caused her enough grief lately.

Then she began to doubt if this errand was even possible, but thought she could make a little difference in the lives of people she knew, like her family. She believed she could make a little difference in the community by being kind and volunteering. But how could she, who was just one person without fame or fortune or experience, possibly have any effect on people, love as a whole, and the outcome of a star?

Perhaps she didn't want this gig at all now. Self-doubt crept over her like a chill from a north wind.

But the Seeking Realm needed her. They needed everyone. If only she knew how to find those ready to help. How would she figure out everything she had to do to save Electra? She struggled to think anyone would believe her if she told them, *Hey, this one star in the sky is a living thing, but is dying because you're being a jerk, so be nice to people and it will shine brighter again.*

She had to laugh at the thought because it sounded pretty ridiculous. Of anyone, her family and close friends would be the most likely to believe her. But even that was a stretch.

She had been given the solution to a suffering world, but she was alone with her secret. And she wanted to explore beyond that gate.

CHAPTER TEN

Nineteen

THE WEEK HAD flown by. It was Thursday, and tomorrow she would finally be nineteen. What no one would really understand is that she mostly dreaded her birthdays and kept her expectations low just to be safe. She asked her mom for white cupcakes with pink cream cheese frosting, and mint chocolate chip ice cream—not the kind with big chocolaty chunks, but the kind ribboned with delicate flecks of dark chocolate. She didn't mess around when it came to ice cream because good ice cream could fix almost everything.

Elliana hadn't heard from Cai since their date on Sunday and was beginning to wonder if she had had more fun than he did. But he was studying, so she tried not to worry about that and instead worried about the continual bad mood Marlee seemed to be in. It both annoyed and frustrated her. Earlier that day she had entertained a few wicked thoughts, hoping Marlee got a big zit on her nose for Spring Formal, or giving her a taste of her own poison, or being extra flirtatious with Burke just to make her mad. Things between the two girls were getting worse, driving the wedge deeper, but also bringing Keisha and Elliana closer than before.

Elliana sat at the kitchen table painting her fingernails bubblegum pink as her cell phone started ringing in her back pocket. She immediately realized her blasted dilemma, not wanting to smudge her nails or ruin her jeans, and she could tell from the ringtone that it was Cai. Curses! There was no one to help her. Her parents had taken Abbie to her track meet, which she was supposed to be going to as well but was still waiting for Burke to pick her up. She thought of rubbing her hind end against the edge of the table to try dislodge her phone. But three seconds into her panic, the doorbell rang. She flitted to the front door, swung it open, and commanded her guest to grab her phone out of her back pocket since her nails were wet.

Burke fumbled for the phone, being careful not to touch anything but the ringing apparatus, clicked the answer button and held it to Elliana's ear.

"Cai! How are you?"

At hearing his name, Burke rolled his eyes and puckered his lips, kissing the air.

Elliana slapped him in the arm with an open palm and glared at him to knock it off. Deftly, she squeezed the phone between her jaw and shoulder and turned her back on Burke.

"Sure, what time did you want to come by?" Elliana knew she was smiling. "Okay, see you tomorrow at four. Bye."

Burke leaned his shoulder against the door jamb. "Mr. Amazing is coming over tomorrow?"

"After school. To give me my birthday present." She motioned to Burke to pick up her purse so she wouldn't smudge her nails.

Burke picked up the purse and slung it over his shoulder, holding the door open for Elliana. As they headed to his car, he asked: "Why is he getting you a present? You just met—not even a week ago."

"I told him he wasn't allowed to get me anything big. But he told me he has to give me the first half of my present when it's light out, and the other when it's dark."

"How romantic," he said with heavy sarcasm. "He's going to try and make out with you."

They walked around opposite sides of his Tahoe and hopped in. Burke acting like her best-friend from a few weeks ago was comforting, and having a new love interest helped erase any awkwardness she had created the previous weekend.

"No, I know for a fact he's not. We have a deal." She clicked the seat belt.

"Oh, really." He furrowed his brows and started the car. "What kind of a deal?"

"We're not going to kiss until it would be heartfelt for both of us...so no pressure."

"Ellie, you are a piece of work. Only you could get a guy to make a deal like that while nearly every other guy is off kissing girls just for the thrill of it." He thought for a moment and looked at her, closely, before backing out of the driveway. "I hope this guy is all he seems to be. Because if he hurts you, I'll throat-punch him. And worse."

"If he turns out to be a jerk, I give you full permission to beat the crap out of him, but I really think this guy is sweet, and I'm hoping it's not an act. The good guys aren't all gone, are they?"

He laughed and deepened his voice. "I'm right here, Ellie."

"Haha, very funny."

Burke looked at Elliana and then turned his eyes back to the road and headed toward the track meet in the neighboring city.

"What are you thinking?" Elliana asked.

"Nothing."

Elliana rolled her eyes.

"Your mind can't be that blank."

Burke cleared his throat. "Just thinking about this Cai character. He's a lucky guy."

"I've known that from the start."

He smiled. "That's not what I meant. It's just that if you start spending all your time with him, then I'll never get to see you anymore. And I might go through Ellie-withdrawal and have to be institutionalized, and then you'll have to come visit me and bring me sports magazines and tell me jokes and feed me your mom's chocolate chip cookies."

She played along. "Whoa! That's a drastic way to get my mom's cookies." But she had to wonder. "We'll still see each other. And we'll still hang out, right? Is it bad if I still hang out with you if I have a boy...friend?" She seemed to trip over that last word.

"Don't know. You'll have to ask loverboy. He might not like it. I mean, if I had a pretty girlfriend, I don't think I'd want her hanging out with some other super-hot guy, even if they claimed to just be friends."

She belly-laughed and then it hit her. "Did you just call me pretty?" She meant it as a joke, but it verged on serious.

"I've always thought you were pretty, Ellie."

"Oh." She felt her face flush, feeling sheepish for asking.

"I'm not the only one." He shook his head. "You have no idea the crap I've had to listen to."

Her eyebrows gathered. "What do you mean?"

"I heard some guys debating a few weeks ago about who could be the first to kiss you, which one of them you'd rather go to Spring Formal with, et cetera, but I told them to knock it off and that you already had a date, and that you wouldn't go with anyone of them anyways because you're not their type." He saw the look on her face, and his face softened. "Please, please, don't get mad at me, Ellie. I just couldn't bear to see you go with any of them knowing that they were the type that moves from one girl to the next. You're too good for that. I decided that if a decent guy didn't ask you to the Spring Formal, I would have, but then Marlee asked me. I wasn't going to say anything, but I guess you know now, and it's probably better you do."

Elliana inhaled slowly. That explained a lot about the lack of boy attention, which made her feel as cute as a blobfish, or a baboon in a bonnet. It wasn't clear if he was confessing anything more than friendship, but that enough implied how much he cared about her at the expense of her getting dates, so she tried to blow it off with a little humor. "So, everyone knows I'm a card-carrying member of the Virgin Lip Club, huh?"

"I think they assume because none of them has kissed you. Are you mad at me?"

Being noticed is one thing; being used is a wicked game, and he was trying to spare her. She shook her head. "I'm just really surprised. All along I thought I was some homely looking girl.... No, I'm not mad at you. I think that's sweet of you to—"

"It's not that you need protecting because you can hold your own, but I couldn't listen to that about you. And they won't mess with me."

"I didn't realize."

"It was just a few of the guys. They're conceited idiots. Most everyone else only has good things to say and would never try anything." He smirked like he had just thought of something entertaining. "You know, my mom has been telling me for the past year that you're the marrying type."

"What's the marrying type?" She fidgeted with her purse strap.

"The kind of girl that is worth the wait, but sometimes doesn't get asked out because guys aren't ready to commit or settle down. The kind of girl you want to spend the rest of your life with because she's funny, and pretty, and smart. The kind of girl that you someday dream of proudly introducing to your parents as your fiancée."

"Phew. I thought you were going to say the marrying type had great hips for birthing or something awkward like that."

They both burst out laughing.

Burke pulled into the school parking lot, weaving around to a patch of dirt and grass on the far side by the tennis courts. They paid their fee and walked toward the stands for the away team. It wasn't hard to spot Elliana's parents, not with her dad's bright green shirt and oversized foam hand with a tall index finger announcing "#1." Her parents waved at them and scooted over to make room. They arrived just in time to see the one-hundred-meter dash.

Burke and Elliana sat down to talk to her parents. Her mom asked, "Who is that dark-haired boy at the starting line? I don't think I've seen him before."

"Oh, that's a new kid, Granger. He just moved to Star. I met him on Monday—or he thinks we met when I was in first grade."

"What's his last name?"

"Lamme. I guess he's living here with his uncle?"

"I don't think I know anyone by that last name. Is he a nice boy?" her mom asked.

"I think. Tells lots of exciting stories, like the other day he was bragging about having set a school record in the one

hundred and hurdles, so I'm anxious to see if he's really that good."

The sprinters took their mark, and when the gun sounded, Granger immediately pulled away from the competition. He was lightning fast—at least two to three paces ahead of the next fastest guy—and the more he ran, the more distance he put between himself and his competitors. He passed the finish line a full three seconds before anyone else. He might be an average painter, but it was looking like he might be one of the best sprinters her high school had ever seen. Whatever it was that brought him to Star was working out well for their track team.

Elliana looked over at Burke, and his eyes were wide with disbelief.

"That dude really is fast," Burke said.

"I guess he was telling the truth, which is good, because some of his stories seem so—"

"Insane?"

She nodded.

Elliana watched as Granger wiped his face with a neon green hand towel and threw it over his shoulder. He walked right over to where Abbie was stretching her legs, and they started talking. Both looked over to where Elliana and her family were sitting and waved. She envied Granger for his outgoing and fearless nature.

Strutting in her short track shorts, the shameless, leggy Veronica Curry approached the stands. "Hello, Elliana." Her tone was nasally and her expression flat, but she had hardly finished her greeting when she turned to Burke and smiled devilishly. "Hey, Burkie. Are you going to watch me in the sixteen hundred?"

Burke shifted on the bench, perhaps remembering Elliana's

warning about her. "I'm watching Abbie run the sixteen hundred, so...."

"Good, I'm going to win it just for you." She winked and then strutted back to the field.

Elliana stifled a laugh. "Burkie?"

"I don't know where that came from."

"You got a sweet pet name, and all I got was a curt hello from that little demon. And then right in front of me, she flat out says she's going to win the race she's running against my sister!" Elliana ended with a cackle like a green-skinned witch.

"Don't worry about her, Ellie. We both know that she doesn't have a chance against your sister, or with me."

By the time it was Abbie's turn to run the 1600, Granger had finished first in three different events. He was the fastest sprinter on either team. And when he ran hurdles, he reminded her of a deer bounding through a field.

The female athletes lined up at the starting line for the 1600 with Abbie in the outside lane. Abbie gave two thumbs up to her parents just before she situated her feet for the starting signal. She reacted like black powder when the gun went off and kept just ahead of Veronica. During the fourth lap, Veronica began to gain on her, slamming her feet down right behind Abbie's heels. Elliana's dad jumped from his seat and yelled, "Go, Abbs! Get those legs in gear, you've almost won! You can do it!" Her mom cheered, and Elliana and Burke were about ready to jump from their seats to celebrate the victory when Abbie went down. She stumbled and tumbled across the finish line with Veronica.

It had happened so fast that she wasn't sure who crossed the finish line first. The coach ran to them. Abbie's left wrist was swelling, a cut on her forehead was bleeding profusely, and her knees were stained with road rash. Veronica ignored her scraped knees and elbows and scanned the score board to see who won.

It must have been so disappointing to Veronica, a senior one month away from graduation, to have been beaten by a sophomore who fell over the finish line a fraction of a second before her, winning first place in the girls' 1600.

Within a few seconds, Abbie's family gathered around. Granger hurried over to the growing crowd and stood next to Elliana and Burke, and few noticed Veronica limp away.

Her mom asked, "On a scale of one to ten, how is your pain?"

"I don't know, a seven or eight?" Abbie's eyes were taut with pain, and she kept one eye closed to keep the blood out. "Did I win?"

Granger nodded. "You beat her by .03 seconds, blondie."

Abbie mustered a "Yay" and then lost the struggle to hold back tears.

"I'm calling an ambulance," the coach said. "It doesn't look like she can move that left hand, and she's going to need stitches on her head."

Her mom said, "We will take her to the ER. Hold off on calling the bus." She grabbed the first aid kit from the coach and skillfully wrapped gauze around the wounds.

Since Granger was done with his events, he tagged along in the car ride to the ER with Burke and Elliana. They talked about the fall and decided it wasn't much of an accident at all—Veronica was a rat.

"I've heard that Veronica has her eyes on you, Burke." Granger purr-growled like a cougar. "She told half the team that you came to watch her run the sixteen hundred. But I knew why you were here, so I promptly clarified that you were here with Ellie to watch Abbie's race. Her face got all red, she called me a 'stupid bastard,' to which I replied that she was mistaken on both accounts because I have an above-average IQ and I was conceived in wedlock. She said 'whatever' and then stomped off."

Everyone laughed.

"Attracting the unstable, jealous ones is what I seem to do best," Burke sneered.

Elliana hit him in the chest with the back of her hand, a little harder than she had meant to. She did not want to be compared to that cold-hearted tripper.

"You know I didn't mean that about you, Ellie."

"Good."

The emergency room was moderately busy, but the group was able to find enough open seats near each other. Abbie added a few details to the story while balancing an ice pack on her left wrist and holding an ice pack over her forehead bandage with her good hand.

"During the last lap, when Veronica was right on my heels, she said, 'You're going down, wench!' And then she tripped me. I think her cleat hit my forehead."

Elliana's parents barely tried to calm Abbie's lust for revenge.

Three long hours later, Abbie received twelve stitches on her forehead right below her hairline, a temporary splint on her left arm, and bandages on her knees. Although Abbie's wrist was broken, she was so glad it wasn't her writing hand nor one of her legs. Her doctor told her she shouldn't race for at least four weeks, but Abbie hoped to compete in the district champion-ships in three weeks.

&

The next morning greeted Elliana with bright sunshine and

singing birds. Just as expected, Orly was perched just outside her window on a leafy branch, and she wondered how long Orly had been with her in life and never noticed because of her ordinary appearance. She walked downstairs for breakfast after she reminded herself not to get her hopes up.

"Happy Birthday, Ellie-bell." Elliana's dad looked up from the table. A large boxed gift sat in the center of the table, flaunting a pale pink ribbon and bow.

Her mom looked at everyone and gave the signal to start singing, "Happy Birthday." Elliana loved listening to Abbie's raspy, soulful voice.

As the song ended, Tina placed a platter of steaming eggs, sausage links, hash browns, two pancakes smeared with peanut butter and syrup, and one burning candle in front of Elliana. Elliana blew out the candle, plucked it out of her pancakes, and set it aside. She thanked her mom and grabbed a forkful of hash browns.

"Anything for my Ellie," her mom said.

"Does that mean I get to open my present before school?"

"No, not until this evening, as usual," her dad said.

She agreed. "By the way, remember how we talked about me going flying with Cai? He wants to take me today after school. Is that still okay?"

"Sure, but only if he stays for dinner and dessert," her mom said. "I think your dad has a few questions for him."

"I'd like to see his license first," her dad said.

After school, Abbie watched Elliana curl her hair and freshen her make up. If it weren't for the broken wrist, Abbie would have been the one handling the curling iron and the lip liner.

The doorbell rang a few minutes early. Elliana ran downstairs and opened the door to find Burke standing there with a square flat envelope wrapped in purple wrapping paper, topped with a curly bow.

"Burke! What are you doing here?"

"I had to bring you your present, silly, and I didn't want to do it at school."

Elliana gave Burke a firm hug. "Thanks, but you know you didn't have to do that. Do you want me to open it right now?"

"No, open it later."

Elliana set the gift inside the front door on a table just as Abbie appeared with a curious smile.

He nodded to Abbie and then refocused on Elliana. "I hope you have fun on your date."

"Thanks. It should be fun." Elliana was giving Burke another side hug when she saw the red Silverado pull into the driveway. "Look, Cai's here! I want you to meet him and tell me what you think."

Elliana bounded off the front steps and walked to meet Cai as he got out of his truck. "Hey."

"This is for the sweet birthday girl." Cai pulled a single long-stemmed pink rose from behind his back. "Happy birthday."

"Thanks, it's so pretty." Elliana smelled the bud, but it didn't compare to the flowers she smelled in her Garden. "I want you to meet my best friend. Cai, this is Burke."

The two guys shook hands. Cai said, "Nice to meet you, man." Then he sized up the younger male. "So, you're my competition."

Burke looked puzzled for just a moment, and then grinned. "I guess you could say that. I'd still like to hang out with her more than every once in a while. Besides, most institutions could use a little healthy competition, you know, to hinder the formation of any monopolies."

"Probably so, but I don't give up easily."

"I don't think you have anything to worry about; Ellie won't stop talking about you."

"Burke!" Elliana scolded.

"It's okay, I haven't stopped talking about her yet either. My family is anxious to meet her."

Burke fidgeted with the keys in his pocket, turned to Elliana and said, "Well, I'll let you get to your date. I just wanted to bring your present by."

She thanked Burke and invited him to come by later for cake and ice cream around seven, and he said he might.

Burke drove off. Elliana ran in the house to put the rose in a vase and to grab her purse, and her mom appeared at the door.

Cai greeted her mom and asked how she was.

"Good, Cai. Nice to see you."

After proving to her dad that he was legal, Cai said, "I'll have her back by six, Mr. Reinhart."

"Have fun you two and please be safe."

Cai walked Elliana around his truck and helped her into her seat. Her mom and Abbie waved them off from the front door.

Cai got in the driver's side and asked if she was ready to fly because they were headed to the Caldwell airport. He glanced down at a flat rectangular box. "That's your present. As promised, it's not very big, but you don't get to open it until later."

Elliana had grabbed the seat belt on the passenger side of the bench seat, when Cai interrupted. "Scooch over here by me. I don't bite. It's just a lap belt, but I promise I'll drive safely."

Elliana scooted toward him, her left arm brushing against

his as she latched the lap belt. As they pulled onto the main road and headed west toward Caldwell he asked about Abbie's arm.

Elliana told about a mean girl tripping Abbie, with all the details, and then added the new detail that Veronica got kicked off the team. "We still can't figure out why her own teammate would trip her and risk getting booted from the team."

"Jealousy," Cai said. "People do all kinds of stupid things when they are jealous."

"I guess you're right. I've been jealous of Abbie at times. She's taller and very pretty and more talented, and sometimes it gets to me, but I would never do anything to hurt her."

"She may be taller, but I prefer your look. I think you're beautiful."

She smiled, and butterflies began beating around in her stomach. She wasn't used to that compliment.

As they headed west out of Star on Highway 44, Cai asked about her plans after graduation.

"I've been accepted to a few out-of-state universities, but I will probably just stick around and go to Boise State. My parents said I could get an apartment near the campus if I wanted to, but I might just live at home to save money." She instantly recognized that her decision didn't reflect living on the edge. And when he asked her about her major, she felt even less sure when she said, "maybe accounting?"

Elliana redirected with, "Does your family own a plane?"

"No, it belongs to a close friend of my dad's. But my goal is to have my own someday."

Within a few minutes, they arrived at the Caldwell Industrial Airport sandwiched between the highway, an irrigation ditch, and several acres of farmland.

He parked his red truck outside a hangar and helped Elliana out from the driver's side. "Come on. I'll show you how to do a pre-flight checklist."

∽

Soon the four-seater Cessna with red and blue stripes was soaring high above the city of Caldwell. The small plane turned to the left and lowered in the sky. "Look down there and tell me if you see anything."

Below she could make out tiny houses, tinier cars, and lots of green and brown farmland. As she was staring at the little black dots that must have been cows grazing in a green field, it dawned on her what she was really seeing: a faint design cut into the grass. She strained her eyes and could see a set of swirls and circles.

"Is that a crop circle?" she asked.

"Yes. That's the last place I ever saw my brother."

"You don't have a brother."

"Not anymore. He was abducted by aliens."

Elliana threw her head back and laughed.

"Pretty funny, huh?" Cai jerked his head sideways. "Not the abduction; that was very traumatizing. I meant the crop circle. A guy who cuts corn mazes did it with his tractor as a joke."

"That's hilarious." She straightened her expression and added, "The crop circle, not the abduction. Please forgive my insensitivity."

"Only since it's your birthday."

After she had taken a few pictures of the crop circle and one selfie with her pilot, the four-seater plane flew over the Boise River, over her dad's land, over her parent's home and back to the hangar in Caldwell. It was easy to have a different perspective on life when looking at it from a couple thousand feet above the earth. With Red Truck Guy.

As they walked from the hangar back to his truck, Elliana's hair blew wildly in the wind, obstructing her view. Cai stopped and stood directly facing her, gently tucking a strand of hair behind her ear. "What are your plans tomorrow? Can you squeeze in another date with me?"

"I'm free. What do you want to do?" Hopefully being so available didn't make her sound desperate.

"I'll take you all day, if that's okay with you. You know, a picnic, hiking, showing you some of my favorite spots, and keeping you gone until your curfew."

She thought that if he tried to hold her hand, she would totally let him, because that just might be the best birthday present in the world.

CHAPTER ELEVEN

Unexpected

HE DIDN'T TRY. Not on the drive back to her house at least. She was doing the very thing she scolded herself not to do: getting her hopes up. She knew her dad would play twenty questions with her date, and she hoped he wouldn't scare Cai away.

Elliana and Cai arrived several minutes before six to find her dad and Abbie setting the table with dinnerware reserved for special occasions. Her mom was in the kitchen sprinkling sugar over a bowl of freshly cut strawberries, while her dad sneaked a taste.

Elliana and Cai walked toward the kitchen, and after Cai set his gift down on an end table in the hallway and greeted the Reinharts, he offered to help.

Elliana's mom looked up, relieved. "Would you mind pouring lemonade into all of the glasses? It's in the fridge, sweetie."

"Not at all, Mrs. Reinhart." He looked at Elliana and mouthed: "She called me 'sweetie.'"

Elliana chuckled. She walked around the table where her father was folding the last napkin and examined the cluster of Mylar helium balloons in the middle of the table. There was a large, heart-shaped one that said: "Happy Birthday, Princess."

She playfully flicked each balloon with her fingers, but only one balloon actually hit her target, bouncing lightly off her father's graying head. "Hey, Daddy."

He smiled.

Elliana held up the glasses for Cai to fill, and then placed them back on the white table cloth. When the meal was ready, Cai took a seat next to the birthday girl on the long side of the table.

Her dad looked at her. "This feast is fit for a queen. Happy birthday. We are fortunate to have you in our family, Elliebell." He reached out his hands and everyone at the table joined hands and then blessed the food. They passed the food around the table until everyone had been served.

Cai glanced at his stack of steaming cream-cheese stuffed French toast, fresh strawberries in a glaze, apricot syrup, and whipped cream. "Looks divine."

Her dad looked at Cai, and Elliana felt the knot tighten in her stomach. And as she expected, he asked Cai the first of many questions. The questions about his family seemed safe enough; what she thought she should be worried about was any questions about dating, marriage intentions, or anything else that would make her want to crawl under a rock.

Cai was pleasant and didn't seem to mind sharing that his dad grew up in Mountain Home, Idaho, nor that his mom's dad was in the military and had been stationed in the same town for a few years, nor about how they met and then settled down in Boise. He seemed happy to talk about his two sisters as well, Paige who would graduate from high school this month, and Lauren who went to Boise State with him.

Elliana really wanted to add, "He had a brother, too, but he got abducted by aliens," but knowing only Cai would get it, she said instead, "They were the two girls he was with at Confucius last Saturday, if any of us had been looking, that is."

Her dad asked what Cai's dad did for a living. Cai had been taking a drink of lemonade when the question was asked and choked a little. "Excuse me," he said as he cleared his throat. "My father is an attorney."

"What's his specialty?"

"Personal injury mostly, but he does some pro bono work that isn't always related to injury claims. Like custody, adoptions, estates, and the like."

"That's great. What's his name?"

The irony struck her that she nearly ran over the son of a personal injury attorney and managed not to get sued. Elliana could feel Cai's knee start bouncing next to hers and hoped her dad wasn't ruining a good thing by asking too many questions, though sharing his father's name surely couldn't do any harm.

"Leo Wittington."

The few seconds of silence slowed down long enough to create an awkward feeling.

"You mean the Leo Wittington on all the billboards and commercials? And on the cover of the phone book?" Abbie asked.

Wiping his mouth with his napkin, Cai said, "Yup. That's him."

"So that's your last name. I kept forgetting to ask," Elliana said. She filled her mouth with food and her mind filled with thoughts of what-ifs.

His smile calmed her, and he said, "I never offered it. I like people to get to know me first before they find out my parentage and jump to conclusions about my socioeconomic status and whatnot."

Leo's face was sort of famous in the Boise area, and now that she looked at Cai, she could see that his chiseled jaw and slightly pointy nose resembled his father's. She had to wonder if she was good enough to go out with his son, if her manners were good enough, even if her life goals were ambitious enough. Then again, why else would he be interested in dating her if he wasn't actually interested in a nineteen-year old senior in high school. Thank heavens she hadn't known his last name before—or she'd have been nervous and may have fumbled it.

She was relieved when her dad said, "I see nothing wrong with your father's occupation. Becoming a lawyer takes a lot of hard work and schooling."

"Believe me, I know. My dad's worked very hard to get where he is today, but I caught a lot of flak from kids at school who loved to refer to my dad as an ambulance chaser. It got annoying, so I quit telling people—at least right off the bat."

She made a mental note to never call anyone an ambulance chaser again and hoped she'd never said it in front of Cai. She didn't know what to say in response, only that she should say something. "I promise not to judge you by your dad's success if you promise not to judge me by my dad's."

Everyone laughed, especially her dad. Thankfully, the conversation steered toward easier subjects and they continued talking well after the food had disappeared from their plates. At the first lull, her dad suggested dessert. Forks and knives clanged against the glass plates, and Elliana's mom rose to take them all to the kitchen sink.

"No, Mrs. Reinhart. You sit down. You've done enough to make a wonderful dinner. Just let Abbie and I clear the table for you." Cai smirked at Abbie. "You still have one good arm."

"Oh, you dears!" her mom said. "That's so sweet."

Abbie used her good hand to help load the dishwasher after Cai rinsed the dishes. Elliana watched her restless mother twiddle her thumbs, shift in her seat, and then finally stand up and enter the kitchen. "I promise I won't help with the dishes. I'm just going to get dessert ready."

Just then the doorbell rang. Elliana jumped up to answer the door, noticing Burk's still-wrapped present on the hall table, hoping it wouldn't hurt his feelings that she hadn't opened it yet. When she swung the door open, she was surprised to see Burke with Marlee, Keisha, and nine other friends from school singing happy birthday. She blushed the color of gummy fish.

It took about ten seconds for the rest of the house to gather at the door. Cai stood directly behind her, and she noticed Keisha and Marlee checking him out and tried to ignore the extra-friendly look Marlee shot at Cai.

"You guys are just in time for cake and ice cream. Come on in." Elliana motioned for them to enter.

Twelve friends shuffled past her, kicking off their shoes just inside the front door, and then bustled down the hall.

Keisha hugged her. "Sorry to crash your party. Burke told us he was coming back, and we invited ourselves to come along. I hope you don't mind."

Nonsense. She was glad they came. She had been wrong to not invite her friends over.

Her dad started moving kitchen chairs into the family room to accommodate the extra guests, and Cai and Burke joined him. Keisha led the group in and sat down on the end of the long leather sofa. Burke sat down next to her, and Elliana thought she saw Marlee try to sit on his lap, but Burke deftly moved her to the side before she had a chance to sit all the way down. The rest of the crowd took up the remaining seats, and a few sat on the floor, leaning their backs against the couch.

Having her friends stop by on her birthday was the gummy fish to the fluffy white icing of her birthday cupcakes, one of which Cai handed to Elliana on a plate with one lit candle.

"You guys will have to sing again so she can make a wish." Abbie stood up. "On the count of three."

Elliana hesitated a few seconds after the song ended before blowing out her little candle. Cai and the rest of Elliana's family handed out dessert to all the guests. When he was finished, Cai sat down and nudged Elliana with his knee and whispered, "Are you going to tell me what you wished for?"

Elliana nudged him back, savored a spoonful of cold ice cream, and let her silence communicate that she would not divulge her secret wish. Although she curled up the edges of her mouth to make him think it was about him. "I wished that you could find your abducted brother."

He smiled. "So, your wish did include me." Cai picked the red candy fish off his cupcake and popped it in his mouth. "I'll take that as a good sign."

After everyone finished their cupcakes and ice cream, her mom and dad stood up and gathered the small plates and took them into the kitchen and returned with the present that had been on the kitchen table that morning. Elliana hefted the box and was puzzled by the weight because it was larger and heavier than a sketchbook or paints and brushes. She carefully removed the ribbon and began peeling off the wrapping paper to reveal a heavy-duty cardboard box with a picture of a laptop.

Her eyes went wide with surprise, and she jumped up and hugged her mom and dad, kissing them both on the cheek and thanking them. "This will be so great to have for college, and it's good to have now because my English paper is due next

Friday!"

He patted her on the back and said, "I'm glad you like it."

Elliana thanked her parents again and ran her hands over the box, relishing it, but secretly hoped this gift didn't put her parents in a financial bind.

Abbie handed her a box. Inside was a new journal with a daisy on the front cover. "It's for when you fill the other one up. A girl like you always needs to have a backup."

The teenagers hung out and played a dance video game for a few hours, with Quintin and Granger getting the highest scores. The girls gravitated toward Cai and Elliana and asked him what seemed like a hundred questions. Several of her friends played with her new laptop once she got it set up.

Just before eleven o'clock, the three vehicles parked on the street were full of boisterous teenagers ready to head home.

Elliana turned to Cai. "You've had me in suspense long enough. Now it's your turn."

Cai handed her the flat box, but before he relinquished his grip, he said, "Be warned that this isn't nearly as exciting as a laptop. But at least pretend it is, for my ego's sake." Then he flashed that charming smile that made her insides feel gooey.

She tugged gently on the box until he let go, and then unwrapped the present to find several documents and a booklet. She was a bit confused about receiving loose papers in a box. The one on top was printed on a large piece of parchment and decorated with star-speckled snapshots of the night sky nestled in between bold lettering which read: "Map of the Incredible Universe. Created by Cai."

The next document was a folded chart that labeled the stars and constellations. Cai reached down and pointed to a star on the chart and said, "Here are the Pleiades; I know how much you like them. Then over here is a star I took the liberty of re-naming Elliana, you know, because it only had a really sad, boring name like K-Five or C-Two-Thirteen or something like that."

"Hopefully stealing a star isn't a crime."

"It's a risk I'm willing to take."

"I always knew I'd become a star." Elliana laughed at her own joke.

"I tried to get a star that was close to the Pleiades. I thought you might like to enjoy the company of the infamous onion eaters, but you're still far enough away that you won't have to deal with any of their insufferable Greek drama."

Her parents gave each other questioning looks. Abbie understood a lot more than her parents did but didn't say a word, fortunately.

"There's a constellation book in there for you, too, underneath the star charts." Cai lifted the other document to reveal the book. "Now whenever you feel lonely or lost, you can look into the sky, and make a wish on yourself."

"I'll try it out tonight." Not only was his gift thoughtful, but it was practical, which was totally her.

Elliana's parents stood up to leave, claiming they were up way past their bedtime and were ready to turn into pumpkins. He looked at Cai and said, "Time to say goodnight."

"Yes, sir." Cai nodded.

"Good night, sweetie," her mom said. "I'm so glad you came tonight. You're welcome any time." Her mom patted Cai on her way out of the room.

"Thank you, Mrs. Reinhart. Dinner was wonderful."

Abbie faked a yawn and trotted off to bed after her parents.

Cai stood up. "Well, I'd better get going if I'm going to stay on your dad's good list. Happy birthday, and thanks for letting me celebrate with you." He reached his hand down to pull Elliana up off the couch.

CHAPTER TWELVE

Encounters

"I THINK THIS IS my favorite birthday yet." Elliana said as they stood on the front porch.

"I'll pick you up tomorrow at noon, 'kay? Wear something comfortable." He reached down and took her left hand, lifted it to his mouth, and kissed it. "Sweet dreams, birthday girl."

She waved and watched him pull out of the driveway. It was a clear night with a full moon that cast shadows on the driveway, and the bright stars pulled her gaze upward. As she scanned the skies for the Big Dipper, Orly flapped her wings on a high branch of the cherry tree that stood beside her home near the gate. She had never been to the Seeking Realm at night and it made her wonder if it would be sunny or starry, or something else entirely. She walked toward the tree on the side of her house, eying the neighborhood to make sure no one was watching.

Elliana used the shortcut that Rose taught her during her last visit by placing her right hand on the tree trunk, closing her eyes, and whispering, "Port to Seeking Realm," while taking a step forward.

Wayne and the more beautiful Orly welcomed her to the

darkened Seeking Realm with a "Happy Birthday." Elliana thanked them and reached up and patted Serenada on the neck as she chatted with Wayne. He told her what a special girl she was and to not get discouraged. "Remember to focus on the good in life, but don't ignore the bad, because it will teach you wisdom and help you make decisions." He smiled. "Rose is anxious to see you. Go on ahead, sweetheart." He pulled on the reins and bid her farewell before heading back to the portal.

Elliana waved and looked upward through the trees to get a glimpse of the night sky, but found the foliage was too thick for her to see much overhead. Once she was no longer under the canopy of trees, she cast her eyes skyward. The full, apple-flesh colored moon seemed so close that she reached up her hand instinctively to see if she couldn't touch it. The stars were more brilliant than any other night sky she had seen, and happy feelings swelled within her while she admired the millions, or billions of glowing stars twinkling overhead. And this time one of them was hers, sort of.

Still admiring the bejeweled heavens above, she walked toward the cottage where Rose greeted Elliana with an embrace.

"Happy birthday, my dear."

"Is it too late to visit?"

"Not at all. I don't sleep like you do, so you can come any time of the day or night, and I mean that."

The thought puzzled her briefly until she remembered why she had come. "Rose, I had the most incredible day, today! I just had to come and tell you what happened."

"I'd love to hear all about it. Come, let's go sit by the Singing Stream that runs on the side of your Garden." Rose led her through the cottage and then along a spongy path that brought them near the trickling brook where the water poured off of green and blue and red rocks, swirling around and trailing off in the distance. Instead of a metaphorical babbling brook, it really did sing like it contained the soft voices of angels. This must have been where the music had been coming from the whole time. The beauty of the singing was that it was soft enough not to distract, but noticeable enough to be soothing.

"I've never seen this part of the garden," Elliana said.

"There is much to see, and you will probably see something new each time you come." Rose motioned for Elliana to sit on one of the rocks nearby, and Elliana chose a translucent rock that had green around the edges and a pinkish flare in the middle, like a watermelon. "Please tell me about your day."

Elliana told Rose about their most recent date, and Rose nodded like she understood.

"Did you know that already?"

"I love to hear about your life from your own lips. Do continue."

Elliana continued to describe their date, dinner, her surprise guests, and Cai's gift. Rose was a gracious listener, nodding her head in understanding, and raising her eyebrows at the exciting parts. She smiled when Elliana told her about the star chart and Cai re-naming a (stolen) star after her.

"Rose, I like this boy a lot and I've only known him a week. Is that weird?"

"Not necessarily. Have you ever thought that maybe you two knew each other before, in a different realm?"

Elliana shook her head, silenced by her thoughts for a few seconds, and then continued on. "I think he might like me, too. I found myself hoping he'd hold my hand, but he hasn't yet."

Rose just smiled like she knew more than she was letting on.

"Oh, and yesterday Burke and I went to Abbie's track meet, and in the car ride, Burke tells me that he has been warding off other boys from asking me to Spring Formal because he thought I deserved better. And then he told me that I was the marrying type! I'm not sure if that means he likes me, but I'm even less sure what to think of it all now. The truth is that I like them both, but differently, if you know what I mean. What should I do?"

"It's your choice, Elliana. But let me give you a little hint. Don't kiss either one of them until you've made your choice. Otherwise your kiss will choose for you."

"What do you mean?"

"The human heart was meant to be sincere. You should only kiss a boy if you feel something strong in your heart for him and are willing to focus on building a relationship with him. If you kiss someone before you have chosen him with your heart, your heart will choose him for you anyway over a boy you haven't kissed in a subconscious effort to keep your heart sincere. If you were to kiss many boys without liking them, your heart's ability to truly love would be impaired, even damaged, because hearts are delicate things. Any attempt to leave the heart out of the matter will make the heart central to the matter."

"I've never thought of that before, but it makes sense." Elliana gazed downward at the rushing water, deep in thought. She rubbed the soles of her feet on the shimmery grass; it was refreshing. "How will I know when I feel strongly enough to kiss a boy?"

"You will know when you are only able to think of one boy all the time. He will occupy your thoughts, your time, and eventually your dreams. You will feel your emotions for all other boys fade, and your feelings for the one boy will grow stronger, and you will want to spend more time with him because he makes your heart sing. And if he also makes you a better person, and treats you with dignity and respect, then you'll know you can trust your emotions. It takes time though."

Elliana contemplated where she was on that spectrum and then thought of Marlee. "Why would Marlee treat me like we were never best friends after she betrayed me? It really hurts."

"Most likely, she is mistreating you because she knows what she did was wrong, and she feels guilty. In a misguided attempt to assuage the guilt, she is treating you like you weren't a friend, which makes her feel less guilty about going behind your back to get a Spring Formal date with Burke."

"Okay, that makes a little more sense. I try not to let it get to me when she treats me so callously, but to be honest, it's sometimes unbearable."

Rose patted her knee. "I'm sorry she has hurt you, but the truth is that if you feel pain when someone you care for hurts you, it is natural, and it is a good sign. Many people might feel vengeful or vindictive on top of their pain—and those feelings leach poison into your heart."

"I know, I can feel the poison each time she is mean to me because I start thinking mean things about her, and one mean thought usually leads to another. I thought I had forgiven her, but forgiveness doesn't seem to be as permanent as I thought—it's like every day, and sometimes every hour, I have to work on forgiving her. I guess the good thing is that I'm not outright rude to her, but I am in my head. But that's not good either, is it?"

Rose helped her explore her feelings and emotions and the power of thoughts in changing our actions, either for better or worse. Each thought moves a person in one of two directions: either up or down. There really was no such thing as a neutral thought, which meant even if she didn't behave rudely, it wasn't good for her soul to harbor ill feelings towards Marlee because it was pulling her down, and it was an obstacle she would have to work to overcome for her quest. Elliana feared she wasn't strong enough to overcome this—it had been eating at her even though she decided she wasn't going to be mean, bitter, or hateful. This business of forgiving was tougher than she thought. Yes, Earth Realm had a heart problem, and she was part of it.

Rose advised her to be kind to Marlee and she wouldn't have any regrets, and it was possible that Marlee had her own hidden struggles that Elliana wasn't privy to.

Her mind jumped back to seventh grade for a split second before she beckoned it back to the present. Elliana couldn't deny that Marlee had not been acting herself in the least, and said, "I'll still be nice to her and I'll try harder not to entertain negative thoughts."

Rose asked Elliana to dip her toes into the clear water. It gave her a sensation that was difficult to describe—like pulling out every negative emotion from her head down to her toes and washing them downstream. The longer her toes were in the water, the less hurt she felt about Marlee's betrayal. She glanced up to see Rose studying her.

"How do you feel now?" Rose's eyes twinkled.

"Better. Was it the water? I felt a pulling sensation that took away my sadness and anger."

"Yes, but it only works when you're ready to give the pain away."

"That was the most incredible feeling." She dipped her toes

again in the water.

Rose then promised that if Elliana would spread kindness, visit the Garden often, wash her feet in the stream, eat from the Ambrosia Tree, and wear the pendant, she would become stronger and would have more power to overcome those weaknesses that plagued her. And she would be able to accomplish her quest. Life wasn't meant to be lived solely relying on one's own abilities: her Garden was intended to provide support for her daily struggles and fulfilling her soul's purpose; Rose and Wayne imparted knowledge; the Singing Stream provided healing, cleansing, and strengthening; the Ambrosia Tree was nourishing to both mind and heart; and the pendant was a reminder.

Elliana pulled her feet toward her, stood up, and mentioned she was hungry.

They walked toward the Ambrosia Tree where Elliana plucked a blossom from the tree and sipped the nectar. She couldn't get over how fulfilling and delicious the juice was—it was better than gummy fish and orange soda. After drinking from several blossoms and watching the discarded petals dissolve into golden specks and seep into the ground, she plucked a fruit and bit down. She reached up to wipe away the juice that dripped down her chin. Elliana picked another fruit from the Ambrosia Tree. "I could eat these every day and never get tired of them."

"That is the idea, my dear. You can eat as many as you want—you only have to visit." Rose looped her right arm around Elliana's arm and walked her toward the Tree Portal as if she could sense that Elliana felt ready to return home.

When Elliana saw Wayne, she said, "I'm spending most of tomorrow with Cai. Any advice?"

"Be patient and be yourself, dear. Dating is about having fun and developing a friendship. It's best to go slowly. You have to get to know him before you can decide how seriously you want to date him, before you can decide eventually whether you want to marry him. Don't worry too much about acting out on attraction—get to know his heart first, and your heart as well." Wayne reached down and rested his hand on her head. "A word of caution: beware of so-called friends who allow themselves to be influenced by the power of the Shadows and who will hurt you when they find the opportunity."

That sounded exactly like Marlee, but Rose had just told her to be nice to Marlee, so Elliana would have to think about that later.

"Your quest is a threat to their goals." Wayne smiled. "Thanks for coming to visit on your birthday. You have no idea how much we love your visits."

Elliana wondered if Wayne and Rose had contact with anyone else, or if it was only with each other, which could get lonely. "I'll come by tomorrow." She put her hand on the tree and disappeared from view. Only two minutes after she had vanished while walking around her tree in the dark side yard, she reappeared with a beaming glow, and ran inside and up to her room. She needed sleep for her all-day date the following day—at least that's what she had been thinking before she realized she forgot to open Burke's present that still sat on table near the front door.

She tore off the purple wrapping paper to find a cd in a slim case with this note written on striped stationary:

Ellie,
I made this cd with songs that remind me of you and

all the fun times we've had. I'm lucky to have you as my best friend, and I'm sorry about Spring Formal. If you go, maybe you can save me a dance if you hear one of these songs. I'm sure you'll have fun blaring these tunes in your boy magnet of a car. Happy birthday!

Love, Burke

Funny boy. CDs were a little old school. She read through the list of ten songs he had included, which brought back a lot of memories of spending time with him. One song was from the soundtrack to their favorite movie. Another song reminded her of the time they had stayed after school working on signs for a pep rally last year. One song was about a blue-eyed girl. Another was about two best friends on a road trip. One song she had never heard of. Two were songs she knew were his favorites, which they usually sang along with when they came on the radio. She laughed out loud to see he had included a funny song that parodied her least favorite music artist. It gave her one more reason to smile on the birthday she feared would be a flop; she planned to listen to it in the morning while she played on her new laptop.

Before closing her eyes, she rubbed her pendant and pondered on the task of understanding the human heart and discovering her origins.

In her last visit, Rose had said that throughout history origins are known and recorded somewhere, and chances would be placed in her path where she would feel guided towards them, as long as she opened her mind to possibilities, was willing to have hope—an exertion of the heart and mind—and had courage to seek.

As she rubbed her sapphire star again, she hoped for an

answer to her task, and then sleep overcame her.

৵

After they enjoyed their picnic, Cai took Elliana along the Greenbelt—the paved path along the Boise River—and then along a secret trail. The trail led to a spot behind a large evergreen bush next to other large bushes that grew near the water's edge, which created a little cove where Cai frequently hid as a child. It was not a well-known location, which made it a perfect place to sit and talk, uninterrupted, watching the water flow by. The water level was high from the run-off, and the noise of the rushing water kept their conversation private.

They sat facing each other next to the flowing river. The wind blew gently from the west, the chill from the run-off giving her goosebumps, so she untied the sweatshirt from around her waist and put it on.

"I think you should let me take you to your Spring Formal," Cai said.

"Won't you be too embarrassed since you're in college?"

"There's no way I could feel embarrassed being with you, Ellie. I don't want you to ever regret not going and not knowing what you missed."

Elliana chewed on the side of her bottom lip. "Okay, you can take me to Spring Formal, on one condition...."

He raised his eyebrows.

"No fancy restaurants. No other couples. No limos." She figured the less of a big deal it was, the less pressure, the lower her expectations, and hopefully she would be able to enjoy it, because she was sure that it would still be hard to see Burke and Marlee together on that dance floor.

"Deal." Cai's smile widened. "I mean deal number two. I'd love to cook you dinner that night and take you to your dance."

Elliana playfully flicked her hand against his knee. Cai reached out and grabbed the flicking hand and traced nine letters onto her palm: "I-C-A-N-T-W-A-I-T." Their eyes met again, but she looked down after a few seconds.

"Don't worry, I promise I'm not going to try to kiss you until you give me permission, and I don't expect your permission for a little while yet. I want us to feel comfortable getting to know each other without any pressure, which means I'll wait as long as you want me to, and I'm positive that if and when it happens, the wait will have been worth it."

Her inexperience and uncertainty knocked around inside her. "What makes you say that?"

"Because I like you, and because things are always better if you have to wait for them. But no pressure, seriously. I'm not going anywhere."

At that moment, Elliana almost wished he would try to kiss her. But it wasn't the right time, and she knew she needed to let her heart, not a kiss, do the choosing—and they technically hadn't even held hands yet. She was definitely attracted to him and wondered what it would feel like to kiss him, or anyone, but she couldn't forget what Rose had said the previous night, and so she opted to enjoy being with him and wait. She wasn't sure how he knew so quickly that he liked her enough to wait for a kiss. All she knew was that she didn't want to move; she wanted to sit there all day with him watching the water flow by.

Cai squinted slightly as he looked at her. "You have such interesting blue eyes."

"I've always wondered if I got it from my mom or my dad's side, or maybe both."

"How much do you know about them?"

"Not much really—which is sad. I'd love to learn more about

them, but I have no idea how to find out anything. It seems they were strangely unconnected when it came to extended family and any known connections were already deceased."

"If I've learned anything from my father's profession, it's that there is always something to learn if you can just ask the right people. I'm willing to help if you want."

"I'd love that."

They sat at the water's edge for another hour talking before they retraced the secret trail back to the Greenbelt. They walked to where his car was parked, he used his remote to unlock the doors, and helped her into the truck. "I think we need some ice cream. Ever been to Chip's Creamery?"

"Once, and it was good."

"Good. They have one in BoDo on Eighth Street." BoDo was the nickname of Downtown Boise.

The drive was only a few minutes since it was a Saturday. He parked the truck four blocks away and they walked north on Eighth Street and entered the little ice cream shop. One of the two girls working behind the counter asked for their order.

Elliana peered down through the glass case to examine all the flavors and then asked the brunette with a pixie haircut if she could sample the mint ice cream. After a taste, she ordered mint ice cream with fudge cookies.

The brunette grabbed an ice cream scoop in each hand and worked a layer of mint ice cream into a perfect ball before transferring it to the frosty metal counter that ran the length of the ice cream case. She set two fudge cookies on top of the ice cream, skillfully crushed the cookies, mixed the cookie crumbles into the ice cream, and handed Elliana the frozen masterpiece in a cone with a long-handled white spoon.

Elliana tasted her ice cream as she stood at the cash register while Cai picked his flavor and mix-ins. The girl that was serving him was very pretty with long, straight black hair and almond eyes. She leaned forward suggestively as she manipulated the cheesecake ice cream into a round scoop. The brazen girl!

"One of my favorite flavors," the girl said. "I meant the ice cream. Although...." She trailed off as she appeared to be looking him up and down.

The little minx! Elliana's ears warmed at the overt flirtation of the black-haired girl. She tried not to act like she was paying all that much attention, and she turned to look past them at the front of the store as self-doubt and insecurity somersaulted into her head. Maybe it was too obvious that she and Cai weren't in a serious relationship. Maybe the black-haired girl thought she was prettier than Elliana and stood a chance at intercepting her date, which maybe was true because the ice cream girl was pretty in the way that most guys seemed to like.

As the black-haired girl mixed the ice cream with strawberries and graham crackers, she continued to flirt. In fact, Elliana could have sworn that she overheard the ice cream girl ask Cai what he was doing later. Elliana rolled her eyes as another wave of insecurity passed through her. She tried not to imagine jabbing the girl in the eyes with an ice cream spoon like she was tempted to do.

She softened when she heard his answer: "I'm star-gazing with my incredible date. Isn't she beautiful?"

The ice cream mistress nodded in defeat. "Yeah."

Cai winked at Elliana as he walked toward the cash register, flipping open his leather billfold. After he paid for the ice cream, they walked outside.

"That girl hit on me," Cai said.

Thankfully he brought it up and sounded offended. "Yeah, that's awkward. It's not like I wasn't standing right there."

"Well, I'm sorry about that."

"It's not your fault you're...cute." She immediately felt silly because that's not what she intended to say.

He perched his arm around her shoulder for a quick squeeze and said, "Oh, am I?"

She knew he was teasing, so she elbowed him and then motioned toward an empty bench in the sun. They sat down across the street from a bistro with an outdoor seating area and watched the passersby: some in a hurry, some seeming to relish the walk downtown on a sunny spring day, some trying hard not to be noticed.

Cai pointed his spoon toward a couple sitting at a table and said, "That couple. Think they're in love?"

"I'm not sure. Do you?" Maybe this conversation would help her with her quest.

"No. Look at the way he watches everyone walk by, especially the females. He definitely has eyes for other women."

Elliana motioned toward a girl gazing at a guy. "Right. What about that couple over there?"

"Nah. They probably like each other, but I don't think they're in love."

"I don't know, look at the way she's looking at him."

Cai shook his head. "True, but he's only looking at her like he wants to make out with her, but I don't think they're in love. At least not mutually."

"Fine. There has got to be a couple in-love somewhere around here."

They both scanned their neighbors on Eighth Street. Many "friends" dotted the sidewalk, but lovers seemed hard to come by for several minutes, and Elliana was determined to find some.

From down the street to the left, an elderly couple approached. Tufts of white hair stuck out from underneath the brown cowboy hat that the man was wearing, and he took short steps so his wife could keep up. The woman had gray hair pulled into a bun, shaded by a straw sun hat with a lavender rose. The two strolled leisurely, arm in arm.

If Elliana weren't such a scaredy cat, she thought it would be nice to meet them, but small talk with strangers filled her with dread because she usually said something stupid. Rose had said that she should be opened minded and seek, and maybe this was one of those times. Probably not. But getting out of her comfort zone would be good practice for one of those times that would matter more. She gestured toward the aging lovers and said, "Those two."

Cai watched them for a moment. "Yep. When they look at each other, it's like they're looking past the wrinkles and age spots and loving the other's soul."

"So cute. I hope I'm still that in love when I'm that age." Elliana raised the last spoon of ice cream to her lips. "I mean, once I fall in love." That was the second graceless thing she'd said in ten minutes.

"Me, too." He let her comment slide. "What do you think their secret is?"

"I don't know. Dare you to ask them." She didn't have the guts to stop them, but maybe Cai did, and she really did want to know. She needed all the help she could get on romance, love, and understanding the human heart.

They threw their empty ice cream containers into the trash and started walking down the street toward the elderly couple.

As the suggestion turned into a real plan, her anxiety became more real, and she hoped he was bluffing. "You're not really going to ask them, are you?"

He shrugged. "They look nice enough."

When they stood a few paces away, Cai politely stopped them and asked if they might share their secret to a long, happy marriage—a topic that was probably related to understanding the human heart, her quest, and acting on hope.

The old man got a twinkle in his eye. "Choose wisely."

"He's right. We got to know each other well before we decided to get married, and we went into it agreeing that divorce was not an option, so we've always been deeply committed to each other and to getting along. I look past the worn-out boots he refuses to throw away, and he looks past my wanting everything painted purple. Those things don't matter a lick. What matters is that he knows I love him by how I treat him."

The grandpa rubbed his pot belly and smiled, insinuating he was well fed, then narrowed his eyes. "Kids, don't marry someone with the plan on changing them to fit your taste because you'll be disappointed. You can't love someone and treat them badly."

"And you can't live separate lives either. If you love each other, you'll find things you like to do together." The old woman's head bobbled with the symptoms of early Parkinson's disease. "Right now we are headed on our weekly date to Bernie's Used Books, like we've done each Saturday for the past many years to buy a book to read the next week. You should stop in sometime—it's full of treasures."

"I think we will." Elliana liked idea of a used book store. "How long have you guys been married?"

Simultaneously the couple replied, "Fifty-three years."

"I hope one day to be that successful in love," Cai said.

"Falling in love and staying in love is hard work but worth every effort. I see too many kids doing it wrong these days—they marry someone that brings out their worst traits and then wonder why they don't get along and why they aren't happy." The man looked at Cai. "The most important part is to find a woman that makes you a better man—then always treat her right, and you'll be on your way."

Cai and Elliana thanked them for their time, and the old man said, "Glad to have spoken with you two youngens. Best of luck to you." He tipped his hat, his wife waved goodbye, and they ambled down Eighth Street, arm in arm.

Elliana spun to face Cai. "How are you so brave that you'll just stop some random people on the street and talk to them?"

"I don't think it has to do with bravery as much as it has to do with realizing that you can learn something from everyone you meet."

She recalled almost those exact same words coming out of Orly's beaked mouth a few days before. It made her wonder if there had been a need to talk to that particular couple, or if it was indeed just practice. Maybe being willing and open to talk to anyone was just a general rule that successful people lived by. Either way, she was glad they stopped the older couple.

Cai's cell phone buzzed in his pocket with an incoming text. "My sisters are wondering when we will be home. Shall we go?"

Elliana nodded, and they turned around to walk the few blocks back to his truck and nearly ran over an anxious toddler of about four years who had gotten away from her mother and was twirling in circles. Her springy blond curls bounced as she ricocheted off of Cai's leg and fell back onto the pavement. Her smile turned downward into a pout.

They stooped down to see how badly the girl was hurt and to help her up. A worried mother scampered toward the toddler while holding an infant in her arms. "Ellie, baby! Are you okay?" She shifted the infant to her other hip. The child stuck out pouty lips and her reddened palms; her mother bent down to kiss both of the child's palms before getting a firm hold on little Ellie's hand.

"Ellie, you have a very pretty name," Cai said to the toddler. "My friend here goes by Ellie, too. Isn't that neat?"

The blond girl nodded her head and gazed up at Elliana and then at Cai. With her tiny, pudgy hand guarding her mouth, she whispered, "She's a pwetty pwincess. Is she youw gulfwiend?"

He whispered back, "I don't know, I haven't asked her yet, but I hope so." He stood back up and apologized to the mother again.

The mother of the two children graciously took the blame for the incident for allowing the four-year old to get away from her, thanked them for their kindness, and shuffled away.

As they walked the few blocks back to where he'd parked, she thought about what she learned from the little girl, and part of it was seeing how adorably Cai interacted with the fallen toddler.

Elliana spotted golden letters on a small window sign across the street that read "Bernie's Used Books," sandwiched between a women's apparel store and a nail salon. She had never noticed that narrow little shop being there before, but today it stood out. Through the arched windows she could see endless shelves of books which tugged at her mind like a fish on a hook—but books normally did that to her because she had book-hoarding tendencies. "There's that used book store that old couple was talking about."

"Let's go." He pulled open the heavy wooden door, and the scent of sweet, almost fruity-smelling paper wafted outside.

Inside was a complicated maze of bookshelves that stretched to the ceiling and lined every wall. The aisles were only wide enough for one person in most places. They walked past the cashier who was shrouded by several tall stacks of books. The rest of the books were definitely not in alphabetical order, but they seemed loosely organized by genre. They glanced at titles briefly as they continued their walk toward the back of the store, passing Art and Biography sections, until they came to a room of children's books.

The two spent a few minutes looking through the children's books until Elliana felt the line tugging her deeper into the store. Near the back wall was another little room crammed with books with a *Fantasy* sign above the door. They walked into the room to see that it was also crammed with more columns of bookshelves.

Cai removed a thin paperback from the top shelf near the door. "*The Alchemist* is one of my favorite books. Ever read it?"

She hadn't and suggested that they could read each other's favorite books. Since he was game, they scanned the shelves for any of her favorite books, which included a retelling of a Grimm's fairytale, and if they couldn't find that, anything Jane Austen. When they couldn't find *Goose Girl* they figured they might not be in the right area and moved on to the Young Adult section in the corner, right next to Romance.

They perused the Young Adult and Romance titles for several minutes, but the sections didn't seem to have very clear boundaries. Elliana decided that there was a book there for her, an idea she chose to believe because of the couple mentioning the used book store and then feeling hooked and reeled into the store. Browsing the books was more of an adventure when she decided it was no coincidence she had ended up there.

Because he was taller, Cai scanned the top two shelves and asked what color the cover was to her favorite book.

"I think it's peach or orange or mango."

Cai laughed. "Those are fruits." He scanned the second column of bookshelves and pulled an orange book off the shelf whose title had been worn off the spine. It turned out to be re-bound collection of short stories he had never heard of.

Elliana found a peach book whose spine was so damaged that she couldn't read the title. Upon examining the front cover, she quickly returned it to the shelf and said, "Ew! That was no Jane Austen. Nasty book burned my eyes."

"My grandma's friend is always reading those trashy novels. It was probably hers." He laughed.

Several minutes elapsed without luck, and Elliana thought she would have just let him borrow her copy at home if that's what this was all about, but something told her to keep at it and find her treasure, which was fine because Cai wasn't pressing her for time. At this point in the search it was more likely to find a Jane Austen novel, so she made that her focus.

Cai squeezed past her to look a few shelves over and crouched down slightly. An old brown book was sticking out. "Ellie, here's *Persuasion* by Jane Austen."

"Oh good, that'll work."

As he removed the book from the shelf, a smaller book tumbled to the floor that had been stuck to the side of the Jane Austen novel. She watched him pick up the fallen book which had a black binding and textured maroon cover that was stamped with gold letters: *My Diary*.

"Why would anyone give their diary to a used book store? That's bizarre. Whose secrets are these anyway?" Cai flipped open the front cover and read, "'This belongs to Madeline R. Upright.' Whoever that is."

"Shut up!" She gripped his arm.

He blinked rapidly. "What? What did I do?"

"Sorry. What did you just say? The name?" she said, slurring her words together because her mind was working faster than her mouth.

"Madeline R. Upright. Who is she?"

Realizing she was breathing too quickly and acting too strangely, she told herself to calm the freak down. It was too incredible. Maybe there were two Madeline Uprights? But probably not with the same middle initial. There had to be some explanation for it. Maybe it was a cruel joke. Maybe the name was spelled differently. Or maybe the explanation was that it was meant to be, one of those chances placed in her path—like she was meant to find her diary as part of her quest. Rather than remaining safely on the shore of skepticism, and against her better judgment and usual aversion to risk, she let herself believe, and hope washed through her body, nearly choking her. "Cai, that was my first mom's name. Can I please see that?"

He handed her the book. "Do you think it's really hers?"

"Just hoping." Elliana grasped the book in her shaking hands and hugged it to her chest for few seconds before opening it. She drew in her breath, looked up at Cai, and then read the first entry.

Today is the best day of my entire life. Dylan and I finally got to bring home our baby girl, after waiting so very long. We signed the papers this morning and everything is final!! She's one week old today, and she is the sweetest little baby, my baby, our baby. We named her Elliana, because the heavens sent us this little miracle. Birthright Adoption Agency called us barely a week ago to let us know that we had been chosen for this little baby girl. Talk about short notice!

She stopped reading, and between shallow breaths said, "This has to be my first mom's diary—my first dad's name was Dylan—but I didn't know I was adopted twice." Abbie probably was too. She blinked quickly to hide her tears.

"You okay?"

She nodded and sighed. "Yeah, it's just really strange and kind of raises more questions than it answers. All this time I thought she—Madeline—was my birth mom. Now I have two sets of adoptive parents and a mystery birth mom."

"It might be hard news, but how impossible is it that we found that here? It's like it was meant to be."

He was right. This couldn't be coincidence—this was part of the answer she sought, her treasure. It was difficult to close the book because a part of her wanted to sit right down on the crowded floor and read the entire thing right then, even if it took all day and all night. But she was on a date, so she flipped to the back cover to see the price: 295 dollars! That seemed a little steep, but there was no question in her mind that she needed to buy that journal. She didn't have that much in cash, but she could write a check, or worst-case scenario borrow from Cai. No. She couldn't do that—she didn't want to make Cai ever think she used him for his money. She stood with the book in her hand, staring at nothing, trying to figure out how to pay for the book, when Cai interrupted her thought process.

"I think there's a Birthright Adoption Agency in my dad's building, on the third floor, not far from here. Want to go see if anyone's there?"

"Sure, but I have to buy this diary first." She decided she would try to haggle with the cashier, put it on hold, and use her savings if she had to.

They walked to the counter to pay for the book, where a middle-aged man sat reading Tolstoy with his wire spectacles balancing on the very tip of his nose.

The man stood up and set his thick book down. "You're interested in that old diary?" He peered at her above the rim of his glasses.

"Very. Can you come down on the price at all?"

The man studied her and tapped his finger on his lips, in a friendly way, like he wanted to know more.

"This belonged to my mother that died when I was three."

The man paused. "That was given to me many years ago by an anonymous donor. It seemed a treasure for someone, so I held on to it and priced it high so that only the person who was meant to have it would consider buying it. It's yours."

Wrinkles gathered on her forehead. Did that mean it was free or that he'd lower the price?

The man's serious expression grew soft in a way that made his eyes smile. "No charge. It's my gift to you."

Elliana hugged the book to her chest, almost as if she wished she could hug her first mother through the solidness of the diary, and she told him that she could never repay him for his kindness and generosity. He suggested she somehow pay it forward, and she agreed.

Elliana walked silently next to Cai. They crossed the street to his truck, and wonder and gratitude overwhelmed her because this was one answer she had hoped for most of her life. Cai helped her into the cab and then hopped in through the driver's side. His father's office was right across from the Stadium on the river. "I'm not sure if they'll be open on a Saturday, but it won't hurt to try."

≈

Within ten minutes they parked the truck in the empty parking lot in front of the tall building with mirrored windows. They found the elevator and Cai punched the button for the third floor and asked how she was feeling.

"A little nervous. I guess I've always been interested in knowing more, but something has always held me back. Maybe I didn't want my real parents to feel betrayed or hurt that I wanted to know more about my first parents—who I now know are not my birth parents—but I sure have wondered. More than I have ever let on to anybody."

When the elevator doors opened, they walked down the hall until they reached the office of Birthright Adoption Agency. A woman was just locking the door behind her when they approached.

"Excuse me, it looks like you're closing. When will you reopen?" Cai asked.

The startled woman looked up and said, "Oh, sorry. I didn't realize anyone was here. We open at eight on Monday. We aren't usually open on Saturdays—I just had to grab some papers before I head to the hospital." She took them in with her eyes. "You two look a little young to be adopting."

"We're not married...yet, even though I think she is quite smitten with me," he replied, using his hand to shield his mouth as if he were sharing a secret, but speaking loud enough for anyone to hear.

The woman didn't laugh, but Elliana did. "I believe I was adopted through your agency as a baby and we were coming to see if you had any records on me."

"What's your name?"

"Elliana...Upright. My parents were Dylan and Madeline Upright."

"You're Elliana Upright? That was one of my first adoption cases! I was so sorry to hear about the car accident."

"I was only three when they died, so I was hoping you could tell me more about them."

"I'd love to talk with you, but unfortunately I am already late for a placement. Can you come by on Monday?" she said, handing Elliana a business card. "Ask for Janet Higby."

They thanked Janet and watched her walk toward the elevator. Elliana elbowed Cai in the side, calling him a rascal.

"I couldn't help it. It was the perfect set up," he said. "Are you ready to meet my sisters? They are probably reorganizing their closets or the entire kitchen out of impatience."

She nodded but had no idea why they were so anxious to meet her.

CHAPTER THIRTEEN

Timing

HIS TRUCK REVVED up the hill and turned right on the street that wound around the east side of the foothills. Elliana's eyes grew bigger with each house they passed. Most looked like they contained at least three stories and had expensive stone fences and wrought iron gates. Some homes reflected European style, some Spanish, and others traditional—but all were palatial.

Toward the end of the lane, he pulled into the hedged semi-circle drive of a stately brick home with a French Country influence. The gabled roof wore reddish-brown shingles and sported several chimneys. A grand stone-covered archway stood over the front porch that was surrounded by immaculate desert landscaping. She wasn't a good judge of home values, but it was a mansion compared to the home she grew up in, and it made Marlee's house look small.

"Cai, your home is beautiful." She stifled the worries that her manners wouldn't measure up, or that she might commit some social faux pas, and took a deep breath. She felt nervous meeting his sisters because she cared a lot that they liked her.

"It's my mom's dream home. Just wait until you see the inside, and the backyard."

He parked the car in front of the last door of the four-car garage. They ambled up the large steps leading to the front porch and Cai pushed open the heavy oak door to expose a warm and inviting entry way and a staircase with a dark banister. He led Elliana past the parlor to the far center of the home where the kitchen was.

"Paige, Lauren! I'm ho-ome!" Cai called out.

Within a few seconds, footsteps raced above and then down the hardwood steps. Two girls appeared at the kitchen entrance and stopped short. The younger-looking sister had a chubby babyface framed by dark blond hair—she didn't look more than fourteen or fifteen, but she was supposed to be a senior. The older sister had lighter hair and shared an obvious resemblance to the younger sister.

"Elliana! We're so excited to meet you. I'm Paige, and I'm the youngest."

"Nice to meet you, Paige." Elliana turned her eyes toward Lauren, but she was met with silence which made her uncomfortable.

When Lauren failed to speak up and just stared with a confused smile at the guest, Paige said, "This is our sister, Lauren. She's apparently daydreaming or something." Paige turned to Lauren, nudged her and said, "Lauren, you're being rude!"

Lauren finally shook herself out of her reverie and said, "Sorry. You look so familiar to me, and I was just trying to figure out…. I didn't mean to be rude, please forgive me."

Elliana assured her it was fine and smiled.

Lauren looked at Cai and asked, "Did she say 'yes'?"

Cai nodded, clearly amused with what was about to unfold.

Elliana had no idea what any of them were bubbling about.

Paige said, "Okay, come with us! Cai, you stay here."

Paige and Lauren each grabbed one of Elliana's hands and lured her up the grand staircase, down a hall, and into a room filled with a sewing machine, a cutting table, rubber stamps, ink pads, hot glue guns, and endless spools of ribbon.

Lauren walked to the door in the far corner and opened it up to expose a walk-in cedar closet, about the size of her own bedroom, filled with formal evening wear organized by color—shades of every color of the rainbow. She had never seen anything like it in her life. It was almost like a miniature bridal boutique.

"These are all of our dresses; most of them have only been worn once or twice. Pick whichever one you want to wear to Spring Formal. You can try them all on if you want to."

Elliana walked slowly around the closet, admiring the shiny taffetas and smooth velvets. There had to be at least forty dresses. "Why do you have so many dresses?"

"We've had to go to a lot of formal dinners for our dad's work and such, and some are from school dances," Paige said. "And our mom and grandma love to sew. What colors do you like?"

"I like pink, red and blue."

Lauren walked over to the pinks. "Let's start here."

Cai appeared in the doorway, leaning against the jamb, smiling, and Lauren shoved him out of the closet and out of the craft room and locked the door.

She returned and held up a hot pink satin gown that had a mermaid silhouette punctuated with a flare. "Try this one and we'll wait outside in the craft room. Come out when you're ready."

Elliana waited for the door to shut before she began

undressing. If she were being honest with herself, she had no idea what she should be feeling. Not really uncomfortable, not really nervous, but something. Maybe enlivened.

It was a little awkward getting undressed in the cedar closet and then modeling the dresses to two people she had just barely met, but she decided to have fun with it because trying on formal gowns was one of those hoops that girls often liked to jump through. And it was a much better option than dress shopping with Marlee.

She stepped into the dress and fed her arms through the capped sleeves, and then rapped on the closet door holding the back of her dress closed. "I need someone to finish zipping me up."

Paige came to her rescue and Elliana sucked in her stomach, but it was no use—the dress was too tight.

"No biggie. Go pick out a red dress." Paige joined her sister again in the craft room.

A few minutes later, Elliana came out wearing a burgundy ball gown with capped sleeves, a princess neckline, a corset-style bodice, and a sparkly tulle skirt. She felt elegant.

The two judges thought it looked great.

Elliana curtsied and picked up her skirt so she wouldn't trip over it and closed the door behind her. She tiptoed over to the blues. There was a turquoise dress that looked so pretty on the hanger, and a baby blue one as well, but her fingers lingered on a navy-blue gown with midnight undertones.

She could hear them chattering as she changed dresses. With a side zipper, this dress was fairly easy to put on and fit well. She opened the door and twisted back and forth, and the sisters said she looked lovely.

Elliana's cheeks warmed. She put her arms down at her sides

and straightened her posture as she glanced in the full-length mirror on the front of the closet door, turning to see the back of the gown as well. She admired the beautifully beaded bodice and full skirt with draping puckers, feeling radiant. It was crazy, how a dress could transform a girl and make her yearn to go to a dance.

Lauren and Paige gave each other high fives.

⁇

Ten minutes later, girl-noise entered the family room.

Cai looked up from a thin hardbound book he'd been reading. "Did she find a dress?"

"She sure did. You're going to love it," Paige said.

"Perfect." He set the book down. "Now how about we go outside."

The patio ran the full length of the house and was decorated with large potted plants, three tables with umbrellas and chairs, and an outdoor kitchen and BBQ that was easily the size of her own kitchen. Beyond the patio was an in-ground pool in the shape of a bean that appeared to still be winterized.

"Your backyard is amazing. You might have a hard time getting me to go home."

"I can handle that."

At the far end, they sat on a redwood bench up against a half cement wall. They talked easily, sharing a pasta salad lunch with his sisters. Elliana felt more connected to Cai and his sisters as they ate and wondered what it would have been like to have more siblings, a thought which gnawed slowly at her heart, reminding her of what she learned reading her first mom's diary. She kind of zoned out of the conversation for a brief minute and daydreamed about her birth mom, if she looked anything like her, feeling a little melancholy that couldn't share any genetic traits with her first mom, Madeline.

Noticing Elliana had been a bit withdrawn in the conversation for several minutes, Cai re-engaged her and she suppressed any longing to read her first mom's diary until she got home.

Paige and Lauren impressed Elliana with their knowledge about things she knew nothing about, like politics, local musicians, and the latest scientific discoveries, but they weren't condescending and didn't make her feel stupid. They were excellent conversationalists, a trait which must run in the family. Paige had more of a light-hearted nature and often interjected witty statements that made them all laugh. Though Lauren was friendly, she seemed more serious and more passionate; her comments showed that she felt deeply about injustices, almost to the point that Elliana wished she could be more passionate about a few things. Maybe it was just a natural outcome of experience, or being in college, or having a lawyer as a father and having to attend fund-raisers and important events.

After spending the afternoon with his sisters, Elliana believed both girls were good people, but knew she needed to be careful around Lauren so that nothing she said or did was misread because she didn't want to find herself on the other end of Lauren's passion and sense of injustice.

Toward evening, Elliana and Cai meandered around the neighborhood, through the community walking path in the hills behind his home. Even after having spent several hours together, they didn't run out of things to talk about and were able connect on a deeper level. She enjoyed his personality and the way she felt around him. They returned to his backyard and reclined in pool loungers on his back patio watching the sunset.

As the sky changed from tangerine to purple, the air chilled.

The first time Cai noticed Elliana rubbing the goose bumps on her arms, he excused himself. He reappeared a minute later with a huge quilt and a royal blue Boise State hooded sweatshirt. Elliana pulled the sweatshirt over her head carefully, to avoid messing up her hair, and tugged the soft fabric down around her waist.

"BSU looks good on you, Ellie."

Her cheeks flushed.

They laid the quilt in the grass and sat cross-legged, gazing at the stars. It took longer than they anticipated to find the star that was probably hers—what really helped was using a free star-gazing app. Her star was barely a twinkle in the sky, not very close to any other stars, and not incredibly bright, but to her all glitter was beautiful. She scanned the sky for Orion and the Pleiades, but Electra was already beyond the horizon, hidden by the vast range of the still white-capped Rocky Mountains.

Elliana hummed "Twinkle, twinkle, little star" and wiggled her toes to the tune. "You know, that was my favorite song as a little girl. I remember wanting my mother to sing that to me every night after we looked at the Big Dipper."

"Tina or your first mom?"

Her eyes moved upward as she thought about the answer. "I think I remember my first-mom, Madeline, singing that song to me when I was just little. That's kind of funny; I have so few memories of her because I was so young when she died. She had a beautiful voice from what I can remember and would sing to me and stroke my forehead and hair to help me fall asleep."

"You might find yourself remembering a lot more now that you have her journal."

She hoped he was right. "My sister is going to freak out

when she finds out we found my first-mom's journal today. It's one of those stories that's pretty much impossible. Who does that really happen to?"

"Only you."

Elliana laughed at the thought that her life was so uncommon, and then remembered how she was scared to tell anyone about the Seeking Realm because it was too unbelievable—but that didn't mean it wasn't real.

They stared at the beautiful, twinkling night sky for a few minutes and then Cai rolled on to his side, facing her. He moved his foot against hers playfully. She didn't retract her toes in hopes she wouldn't emit nervous insecurity, so she was surprised when a moment later he reached his hand in his side pocket, pressed a dull, greenish-gray stone into her palm and asked her what she was thinking.

She lifted her hand to look at the stone, examining to see what it was, wondering why he had chosen to give her such an ugly little rock. "I thought it was supposed to be a penny for my thoughts."

"It is. But your thoughts are worth more to me than just a penny, and that rock's an uncut alexandrite, which is pretty valuable. My grandmother gave it to me when I was a little boy obsessed with rocks—well, I guess I'm still obsessed with rocks. So anyways, what're you thinking?"

She glanced down at the rock that didn't look anything like a valuable gem. "Honestly?"

"Honestly."

"How can you know your heart's in it already? I mean, how do you know you're not going to change your mind next week or next month?"

"Ellie, I've met a lot of girls, and it doesn't take me long at this point to tell whether or not I want a relationship to continue, and I want this one to continue. That's what I meant. I was of course attracted to you when I first saw you in that intersection, and then sitting there in the Confucius restaurant with your family, but when we talked that night, it was your personality and wit that really drew me in. I like you, and I want to keep seeing you."

"I get it." She rubbed the gem between her fingers. "It almost feels too good to be true. I mean, I've never had a guy treat me so well. But I've never had a guy that was more than a friend either."

"I mean everything I say—I hope you know I'm not a schmoozer."

Elliana smiled and felt lucky.

"My dad still calls my mom his bride and tells her she's beautiful every day, and they are still happily married. I'm just following an expert. And don't ever settle for less than being treated well." He tapped her foot with his toe. "Is that all you were thinking?"

No. She was thinking how vulnerable he just made himself by telling her he liked her. It had taken her two years to confess her crush to Burke, and that didn't turn out the way she had hoped, maybe because she waited too long to be vulnerable. Or maybe she was really meant to be with Cai. Her heart beat faster when she told him she enjoyed being with him.

About thirty minutes before her curfew, she returned the rock to Cai, they folded the quilt and headed back inside the house. His sisters had zipped the navy-blue formal gown in a garment bag and put it in the truck and stood nearby talking to Elliana.

She thanked them again for letting her borrow the dress.

"I'm excited to go to Spring Formal now. And just as excited to see this one in a tux." Elliana pointed to Cai.

"You won't be able to take your eyes off me. I'll be wearing my finest manly tights. All the girls will be swooning." He bowed like royalty.

His sisters strictly forbade him to wear tights.

Elliana didn't feel one bit guilty that she was still wearing the borrowed Boise State sweatshirt as they winded down the foothills of Boise and on to the main road that led westward to Star.

"Thanks for spending the day with me," Cai said.

"It was so much fun. I like your sisters. And so many good things happened today, too. My first-mom's journal is The Find of a Lifetime!" Elliana reached down to pat the brown paper bag with the treasured dairy, but neither the bag nor the book was on the seat. "Oh, no! It's not here. I thought I left it on this seat when we got to your house. I don't remember taking it in."

She tried not to act as panicked as she felt, but this journal was irreplaceable and held clues to her past that she felt driven to discover. She had only read a small portion of the first page—there were so many answers yet to uncover, and she had planned to pretty much read the whole thing that night. Maybe the diary was misplaced in Cai's house somewhere, but that wouldn't make any sense because she was sure she had left it right there on the seat. It also didn't make sense that someone would have taken it.

"Maybe it fell when my sisters were putting the dress in my truck," Cai said.

"Maybe." She reached forward to check under the seat but didn't find anything. "I don't see it anywhere. It's too dark to see much though." She spoke hurriedly, betraying the panic within.

"I'll pull over and help you look. Grab the flashlight in the jockey box." He put on his right turn signal and pulled toward the shoulder, pressing the brakes, allowing a semi-trailer truck to whiz past. Within seconds, the semi jerked to the left, jolted, and came to a screeching halt on the shoulder.

Elliana peered into the darkness. "Did that semi hit something?"

"Let's go see if everything is okay." He flew out the door the second his truck stopped. Elliana followed.

He could see the driver through the window, but she was motionless as if frozen by shock. He tapped on the window and asked, "Ma'am, is everything alright?"

The driver stirred. She nodded, opened her door, and forced her wobbly legs to step down from the cab. Cai walked with her around her truck to survey the damage.

Smack dab in the middle of the heavy-duty grill guard was evidence of a winning battle against an animal, with tufts of brown fur sticking to the round metal bars. The grill guard had absorbed the impact, leaving the grill and most of the bumper in good shape, although it was blood spattered and tragic looking enough to turn a girl's stomach. On the ground several yards away lay a bloodied, mangled, mature bull elk—large enough that her elk hunter uncle would be depressed to have lost the chance.

"You sure you're okay?" The adrenaline surge caused Cai to breathe heavily, and the female truck driver's face was still white with fear.

"I reckon I'm alright. Just a bit stiff and skittish. Though I'm certain I'll be right sore come morning." She continued to assess the damage and smoothed loose strands of hair behind her ears. "We made eye contact, me and that elk. I'm pretty shook up—my hands won't steady themselves. That darn elk just darted onto the road, and there was no way I could have avoided him."

"Definitely not." Cai looked at Elliana and back at the woman. "But that should have been us. We pulled over to look for something in my truck."

"If you kids had hit that elk, it would have probably come straight through your windshield, and you could have easily been killed or at least maimed. I had that grill guard installed just last week after one of my trucking buddies wrecked his truck hitting a buffalo coming through Yellowstone—and thank heavens I did. As much as I hate to kill an animal, I'm glad it was me and not you young kids."

A cold shudder slithered up Elliana's spine as she thought about the tragedy they avoided because Cai decided to pull over at just the right moment to help her look for her mother's journal. She felt a coldness, a dark fear, in the air, cozying up to her, whispering that it should have been her. She shivered again and moved closer to Cai. It struck her that her mother's now-missing journal had just saved her life somehow, like her first-mom was protecting her from beyond the grave.

CHAPTER FOURTEEN

Demise

MADELINE WAS AN INCREDIBLE woman. A part of Elliana felt complete from reading more about her first mom, a comfort, a reassurance of how much she was loved.

Discovering her origins was supposed to help with her task, but this new insight only opened up another vast question about her origins, and she would try to get as much information from Janet Higby as she could and then try to lay the matter to rest for the sake of her own happiness. If this search became unhealthy and spiraled her down an emotional path that would distract her from living and loving life, she hoped she'd be strong enough to stop.

After she retrieved Madeline's journal from behind the seat in Cai's truck, which probably fell there while driving uphill to his house Saturday afternoon, she had stayed up most of the night reading it, but found herself creating a thousand different scenarios about why she was given up for adoption in the first place.

What really made Elliana feel safe in her quest was that her whole family offered to show their support by going with her Monday morning to talk to Janet. The time between Sunday afternoon and Monday morning passed slowly enough to bring out Elliana's impatience.

When Monday morning finally arrived, the receptionist directed Elliana and her family to wait in an area near Janet Higby's chair since she was running late. They talked amongst themselves, about nothing important really at first. Then her dad, probably trying to help calm her nerves, asked her if she had made a decision about college.

She had two choices: go on a new adventure in a new state and meet all new people, or play it safe and stay in Boise close to home. If she chose Boise, that could mean she was a wimp who was scared to take chances, and she didn't really want to feel that way about her choice. But she wasn't sure if going to school in Washington State was right for her either. "I don't know, Daddy."

"Your mom and I want to help with your education. We'll make it work. Let me ask you this: Where would you most like to go if tuition weren't an issue?"

Elliana doubted her parents had the finances to help much with her schooling. "Maybe Boise State?" She said it more like a question than an answer. The truth is that she hadn't really allowed herself to get excited about any other school because of the unknowns. It felt as if her vow to live on the edge was on trial.

Her parents looked at each other and then her dad asked, "Does this have anything to do with a certain BSU student?"

Yes. "Only a little bit. The pros are that I'm pretty familiar with the area and the campus, it's a good school, with free tuition, and I love their football team."

"I don't want to try and tell you where you should go to school," her mom said, "but if you're basing your decision upon a boy, I'm telling you right now to rethink it. What if your relationship with Cai fizzles and you end up feeling like you settled for something you didn't really want?"

Elliana had considered Boise State before she had even met Cai. It was the safe choice and wouldn't require expensive student loans if she kept her academic scholarship. Although her parents didn't share their financial stresses with her, she knew they were nearing retirement age and didn't want to burden them with expensive college tuition, or any tuition at all, especially since Abbie had always been the more expensive of the two. She didn't want her aging parents to have to work to put her through college.

University of Washington had offered a scholarship as well. It wasn't too far away, and she thought it might be a fun adventure to live in Seattle. They had vacationed there once and she had fallen in love with the bay.

As she thought it over, she was evenly split between the two universities. Each one offered something that she wanted. If she stayed close to home, she would still have her friends and family close by—well the friends that weren't going out of state. If she went to Seattle, she could start over. Be adventurous for once. Find new friends—not the kind that would stab her in the back—and experience life in a different way and in a different climate.

However appealing going to school in Seattle was, she was still hanging on to Boise State, and she couldn't deny that it helped that it was where a cute boy was also enrolled. It was foolish to choose a school based upon a possible relationship, but BSU would make a great back up plan. Plan A would be Seattle. Plan B Boise.

She told her family that she was leaning more toward the

University of Washington and shared her reasoning.

Her mom looked pleased and her dad agreed that it was a good school.

Abbie was more enthusiastic. "Now I can go visit her at college and meet her college friends and hang out with college boys." She wore a smug look. She often said things like that just for the reaction.

Her dad ignored it. "Yeah, we can all go up together to visit her. That's a great idea."

Abbie rolled her eyes. "By myself."

"Of course you'll be allowed to visit your sister...in your pajamas with messy hair and no makeup." Now her dad wore the smug look. He glanced at the clock above Janet's desk which read 8:40 and told his family that if Janet didn't show up in the next five minutes, they'd have to come back another time.

Elliana was obviously disappointed about that because she was so anxious and excited to discover her origins and learn about her birth parents. Saying *birth parents* still felt really foreign on her tongue, and those words stumbled on the way out—it was a new concept that she hadn't yet gotten used to. Mystery *birth parents*.

Elliana had read the entire journal to her sister and parents on Sunday and discovered that Abbie actually wasn't adopted by the Uprights like she had been. Rather, Abbie was a miracle baby born to Madeline after doctors had told her she would probably never be able to have children. In a way it had planted a tiny seed of insecurity in Elliana, not knowing who her birth parents were—like Abbie did—and why they gave her up. She reminded herself that she had a wonderful, loving family, and discovering Abbie's parentage didn't change things with Abbie—they were sisters through and through.

Elliana tried to tell herself that knowing who her birth parents were wasn't really that big a deal, but the news got her mind wondering. Was she born to a teenage mom? Maybe her parents hadn't wanted her, and hopefully they eventually regretted giving her up. It wasn't a comfortable thought and she didn't want to think any more about it; she wouldn't have let it matter so much if Wayne and Rose hadn't given her the quest to discover her origins.

A very out-of-breath Janet Higby burst through the door, stopping briefly to talk to the receptionist. Elliana overheard her saying that her car wouldn't start, and long story short, her neighbor helped her re-tighten the battery cable and get it running. The receptionist let her know a family was waiting to see her, and she pointed in their direction.

Janet turned to look toward her desk and then gave a look of panic as she made her way through the office to her desk. Her cheeks and nose were rosy and wind-bitten. As she set down her attaché and jacket, she said, "I'm so sorry to have kept you waiting. It's been a rough morning. What can I do for you?"

Then Janet recognized Elliana. "Oh, you're here about the Uprights, correct?"

"Yes, Madeline and Dylan Upright. This is my sister Abbie, Madeline's other daughter, and my parents Harrison and Tina Reinhart."

"Nice to meet you all," she said, pulling her chair out from her desk and parking her plump posterior into the cushioned seat. "What exactly do you want to know?"

"Anything you can tell me about the Uprights, and also about my birth parents."

Janet asked them to wait a minute and walked toward a long wall mostly obscured by dozens of tall filing cabinets. Near the far end, she pulled out a long drawer, sifted deftly through the file tabs with her long acrylic nails, and removed a thin file.

She walked back and placed it on her desk, flipping open the cover, and explained that it was a closed adoption, which meant she was unable to release any information about the birth mother, but that sometimes courts could grant permission to unseal the adoption. Janet offered to do some research and get back to her.

As for the Uprights, Janet told them they were a young couple who were unable to have children themselves because of some problems Madeline had. She mostly remembered meeting them at the office when she placed Elliana, swaddled in a pink flannel receiving blanket, into their arms. The Uprights were brimming with joy. The file had their birthdates and an address in Battle Mountain, Nevada, which matched their driver's licenses. Madeline's journal had more information than the file did.

This adoption agency had a policy that two separate agents handle closed cases, so one agent got Elliana from her mother, and Janet was the one who delivered the baby to the Uprights. The other agent on the case was Sherman Hocking, but he had died six years earlier. Elliana exhaled, her shoulders drooped, and her hope plummeted at the news of the dead end.

Janet looked Elliana in the eyes. "I will tell you that your birth mom gave you up for adoption so you could have your best chance. She did it because she wanted a better life for you. You can be sure of that."

Those were good words to hear, but they left many questions unanswered.

"Is there any other information in the file that you can give out?" her dad asked.

Janet turned the pages and stopped when she came to a scrap piece of yellow paper which read:

H. Adams 156-830.

"This is random. I have no idea who wrote this down or who placed it in the file, but it looks like it links to another file in our numeric filing system. Give me just another minute to find this other file."

She walked in the opposite direction she had before, turning left at a corner and disappearing from view.

Abbie broke the silence. "I wonder what it all means. Who is this H. Adams and what does he or she have to do with my sister?"

Elliana felt overwhelmed. "This is all too real. I'm almost afraid to find out anything because it could change things—maybe even complicate them."

"I don't think it will hurt anything to know," her dad reassured her. "You can do as you choose with the information you get. It might actually help make sense of things. You never know."

The rustling of Janet's skirt announced her arrival before they saw her. "This is weird. Here's the file it links to, and there's just another slip of yellow paper that looks like it was torn from the one in your file, but it doesn't say much. Here, see for yourself."

Houston, TX
1999

"So, all we have is H. Adams and Houston, Texas, and

1999?" Elliana asked. "1999 is the year I was born, so maybe this H. Adams is my birth mother."

"It goes against policy to put that information in a closed file, but I can't say that it's impossible. I've never heard of this in all my years working here. We don't keep random scraps of paper in files, so it is obvious to me that someone is purposefully leaving you clues."

"She'll probably take what she can get, right, Ellie?" Her dad set his hand on Elliana's shoulder.

"I'm always game for a little research," Elliana said.

"Let me make you some copies." Janet reached for the yellow scraps of paper. "And I'll let you know if I can find any non-identifying information on your birth mother that I'm allowed to share."

ꝯ

By the time Abbie and Elliana had arrived at school, it was nearly fourth period. She had missed calculus (with Burke), Spanish, and Study Hall. She sat through Mr. Nash's English class completely unable to follow what he was saying because her mind was still dissecting the mysterious clues she had received from her adoption file.

Halfway through fifth period art class, Elliana sat painting at her easel when she felt her cell phone vibrate in her back pocket. It was Janet Higby. She silenced the vibrating call immediately.

She glanced around the room and found Mrs. Pratt bent over helping another student to create the perfect shade of sky blue. Her teacher could be so absent-minded sometimes, and a bit unpredictable; Elliana was feeling a bit unpredictable herself. She had to know if Janet discovered anything, and since she was in good with her teacher, she slinked out of the classroom without a pass and ducked into the closest bathroom to return the call—the first time she'd ever done something like that in school. If she could get answers, maybe her mind would calm down and she could get something out of school that week.

Before sneaking back in a few minutes later, Elliana peeked around the door and made sure Mrs. Pratt was oblivious. She was in the corner at her desk, so Elliana slipped into the room and resumed her painting. Granger sat across from her and said in a low voice, "Where'd you go?"

"I got a call from a lady who is doing some research for me. Did Mrs. Pratt ever realize I was gone?"

"Yeah, because some girl ratted you out." Granger pointed to a petite dark-headed girl bending over her canvas. It was Veronica Curry's little sister. Figures. The Curry girl looked up and caught Elliana's gaze, casting her a wicked smile and raising an eyebrow.

"Where have you been?"

Elliana turned around to find her art teacher standing right behind her. "I had to go to the bathroom."

"Why didn't you ask for a pass?"

"It was an emergency, and I didn't want to bother you." That much was true.

"Well I heard you were answering your phone, which is against school policy, so I need you to go to the principal's office."

Elliana looked around the room, shocked that she was getting sent to Mr. Carmichael's office for the first time in four years of high school, a month shy of graduation. She began to gather her things and realized she didn't know the standard protocol for being sent to the principal's office. Was she supposed to leave her stuff at her table or take it with her?

"Clean out your brushes first. And I'm going to come check on you in a few minutes to make sure you went to the office."

If she had to clean her brushes, she guessed that meant she should probably take her backpack with her to the office. Elliana wondered why her teacher seemed colder than usual. She had been Mrs. Pratt's best student for years. Dang that Curry girl for ratting her out like that!

After she rinsed her paintbrushes and placed her canvas to dry on her assigned shelf, she slung her backpack over her right shoulder and headed into the hallway, mouthing to Granger, "Wish me luck!"

He gave her a thumbs-up and then used his forefinger to draw an imaginary incision across the base of his neck.

Her stomach filled with lead. The hallway was empty, not a teacher in sight. She felt sick to her stomach about having to talk to Mr. Carmichael because she made a phone call about important family matters. She knew she would lose her cell phone for rest of the week. That was not an option.

She walked past the English and Languages wing, turned left at the corner, and took a deep breath as she stepped into the office, still unsure of what to do or say. The most trouble she'd ever gotten into was a demerit in middle school for squeaking her clarinet during band—as if she could have done that on purpose. Now she would mar her near-perfect high school record by getting sent to the office at the end of her senior year.

The administrative assistant looked surprised to see Elliana standing there. "What brings you here, Elliana?"

"Hi, Mrs. White." She decided to use the wording of her art teacher to her advantage. "My teacher wanted me to come to the office and wait... until she comes to get me."

"That's fine, sweetie. Take a seat on the bench if you'd

like." Mrs. White readjusted her turquoise reading glasses and continued her work.

Elliana dropped her backpack on the bench and slumped down, and at that exact instant, she felt thoroughly rotten. Why did she say that? She left an important part of the story out, which was dishonest, and it wasn't like her. She wavered between feeling lucky and feeling yucky. She decided to see how far this lucky feeling would carry her, feeling justified that she hadn't necessarily told any outright lies—Mrs. Pratt never said she had to talk to the Principal, just go to the office. Her teacher should have been more clear and specific. Elliana had been a good, well-behaved student, and this wasn't necessary—she was not a problem child. Getting into trouble would definitely ruin her week.

The longer she sat, the more excuses she conjured up. She sat on the honey oak bench for ten long minutes, staring through the mailboxes into the mail room, watching the office aide stuffing bright orange papers in each of the boxes on the other side, but mostly thinking about what a scoundrel she was—hopefully a lucky one. Though it wasn't cold, she started to shiver from the stress and burden of her guilt.

She had no idea what to say if Mr. Carmichael saw her sitting on the office bench and called her back. He knew she was a good kid. Just last month Elliana was out of her class with her teacher's permission but didn't have a hall pass to prove it. When she saw Mr. Carmichael walking toward her, she yelled, "Hey, Mr. Carmichael! I'm out of class without a pass. Try and catch me!"

She had turned to run but heard him call out after her: "I know Elliana Reinhart would never leave class without a pass." And the chase was over before it even began. At first, she was slightly disappointed that he didn't fall for her joke, but it boosted her to know that she had a good reputation.

Had. Maybe this trick would ruin her reputation as a good, honest student if she got caught in her deception. She pressed down on her legs to keep them from jouncing so obviously. It would be so easy for Mrs. Pratt to waltz in, all casual like, and ask if Elliana had seen the principal yet—loud enough for Mrs. White to hear. That would be awkward. And it would be even more awkward to recant her original reason for coming to the office.

It was more important to have her phone to receive the vastly important, possibly life-changing phone call from Janet Higby—who might have information about her origins, which was pretty much an official task from the Seeking Realm, which therefore trumped this ridiculous earthly business of getting in trouble over a phone call that was part of her higher purpose to save a dying star from enemy control.

Just as she was admitting to herself that her logic possibly resembled a block of Swiss cheese, Mrs. Pratt and her gray-blond hair were visible through the office windows by the door. Elliana looked up from a book she was pretending to read and waved at her.

Her art teacher walked into the doorway, seemed pleased with the situation, and nodded before leaving again.

Elliana looked over to Mrs. White, who nodded at her.

That's my cue! She picked up her backpack and exited with a wave to Mrs. White. She stepped softly and steered herself like she was following her teacher, but once she was out of view from the office, she turned abruptly and went the opposite direction towards PE.

She was lucky enough to have dodged the bullet that time,

but figured she'd better never do anything like that again. Ever. She hated the anxious churning in her stomach and didn't understand why some students were not deterred by being sent to the principal's office. With graduation approaching, and with stress still ruffling her insides, Elliana decided she would do whatever it took to stay out of the principal's office for the rest of high school.

The bell rang loudly overhead and the halls instantly teemed with noisy teenagers rushing to their lockers and onto their next classes.

Why would her birth mother's file have disappeared? Janet was baffled by it as well. She couldn't figure why someone would take the time to leave her clues on yellow scraps of paper and remove the files she wanted so desperately. Elliana supposed it was possible that it wasn't the same person who had done both. Janet had suggested it wasn't unfeasible that the file had gotten lost or misplaced in the move ten years ago from the old house where the adoption agency used to be located.

Elliana sat in a wooden chair at the kitchen table with her family after school, running her fingers through her hair, wondering what all of this meant, wondering if she would ever be able to discover her origins, let alone save a dying star—a roller-coaster of quests that seemed bleaker than it had yesterday. Or maybe this stumbling block was part of her quest.

Her family took turns studying the copies of the clues. "How many people with the name H. Adams do you think there are in Houston, Texas?" Elliana asked.

"Probably a lot—Adams is a very common surname. That's if our H. Adams is still there after all these years." Her dad rubbed his five o'clock shadow along his jaw.

"Your birth mother's file was missing—like completely gone?" her mom asked.

"Yeah. Janet said she checked my file, and because it was a closed adoption, the agency replaces the mother's name with a numeric ID. She looked in the ID resource and there was no such number. Which means she has no idea how to track down my birth mother. She said it was back in the day when not all the records were kept on the computer, so this sometimes happens."

"Do you think that your birth mother lives in Houston, Texas?" Abbie asked.

"Maybe, but why would she place me for adoption in Idaho if she was from Texas?"

"And the Uprights were from Nevada," Abbie said.

Her father nodded. "I think some adoption agencies do out-of-state placements, just depending on which family the birth mother chooses. I don't think it's uncommon at all."

Elliana shook her head as if her mind were growing tired from thinking and feeling. "It still doesn't make a whole lot of sense—no record of my birth mother."

"I wonder if Janet checked the files for the name H. Adams as well?" Abbie wondered aloud.

"We could always call and ask," her mom said. "I'm not sure why we didn't think to ask while we were in her office—it seems like she should have done that right off."

Elliana dialed the phone. It was 4:30 p.m. and very likely that the office was closing soon, if not already closed.

The phone rang and rang and eventually want to voicemail. "Hi, Janet. This is Elliana Reinhart. I just wondered if you could look for any sort of file on H. Adams? Can you please call me back when you get a minute? Thanks, bye."

After school on Tuesday, Cai came over to hang out at Elliana's house. She told him everything they found out from the adoption agency, and even included her rebel story about getting sent to the principal's office.

"You'd get along so well with my friend, Christopher."

"Why? Is he a scoundrel like me?"

"He is Boise's King of Snarky. He can be philosophical, brutish, and hilarious. You'd like him." Cai leaned back on the couch. "I'm having a pre-finals soiree on Friday with some friends. You should come."

"A soiree?"

"It's a party. Basically, it's a marketing ploy to call it a soiree. It sounds better. That's what Christopher and I call my parties because there's no boozing or table dancing—though not as tame as a nursing-home shindig, and with better food, though I wouldn't really know."

"So, you want me, a senior in high school, to hang out with a bunch of college students?"

"It'll be fun. I think you'll like my friends."

"Especially this Christopher dude?"

"He's one of my best friends." Cai told her how they had met almost three years ago in the same Intro to Geoscience class. "I really want you to meet him and his girlfriend. They're getting married in June after he graduates, and I'm the best man."

"How many people will be at this soiree?"

"Not more than ten or twelve. Don't worry—you're very charming and witty. They'll love you."

She shrugged her shoulders. "Yeah, but I've never hung out with college kids before, much less college kids who are about to graduate. What if I say something stupid, or if they make fun of me for still being in high school?" She didn't sound like a rebel-girl now.

"Just use your sense of humor, and they'll respect you."

"Or I could pretend to be a real idiot and embarrass you."

"I'm sure you couldn't pull off stupid even if you tried," Cai said.

"I guess you're right. I did get four questions right while watching Jeopardy last night. Four!" Elliana held up three fingers.

He laughed. "That's what I'm talking about."

It was now Wednesday, nearly two full days after Elliana had left the first message for Janet and had still not heard back from her. The nerve! This was something that was very important to her, something she had waited long enough to find out. She had even visited Rose to get advice and was encouraged to keep at it. She was trying to be patient and had left a total of three messages; this time she decided not to call Janet's direct line.

She looked at Janet's business card and dialed the main number, which was answered within the first two rings. "Birthright Adoption Agency. Gretchen speaking. How may I help you?"

Gretchen's friendly voice put Elliana at ease. "Hi, Gretchen. This is Elliana Reinhart. I haven't been able to get ahold of Janet. Is she on vacation?"

The voice on the other line hesitated. "No. I've been meaning to call you back. I was supposed to tell you that Janet never did find the file you asked about. She could probably give you more details, but—"

"Can you have her call me when she gets in, please?"

"Actually, that's what I was supposed to talk to you about.

Janet's in the hospital in the ICU, and if she lives, the doctors expect her to have permanent brain damage."

"What? That's terrible! What happened?" Elliana felt bile rise up in her throat—the closer she thought she was getting to finding answers, the further away she seemed to get from those answers.

Gretchen's voice cracked as she explained the malady. Elliana could hear the emotion in Gretchen's voice and thought she needed to let her get back to her work, even though she wanted to ask her a thousand questions. "I'm so sorry to hear about Janet. I hope she makes it."

"I appreciate that. Good luck to you."

Elliana's expression was probably unreadable, but the eavesdroppers at the table were able to piece together from the conversation that something terrible had befallen Janet Higby.

Abbie waved her hand in front of Elliana's face and said, "Hello! What happened? Tell us what happened!"

"The only two people that seem to know anything about my adoption are either dead or on the verge of dying. And I'm sad for Janet's family and friends, but I'm also feeling a little selfish right now. I really wanted to find out who my birth mother is. The file is missing and Janet is in the ICU from a diabetic coma that wasn't treated in time, and if she makes it, she'll probably have permanent brain damage."

"It's tragic for sure, but we have to think positively. At least we were able to garner what information we could." Her mom forced a smile and rubbed the top of Elliana's hand. "All things happen for a reason."

There were those words again. "I'm trying to believe that. I'm sorry I'm being a brat about this, but now that I know I have a different birth mother, I really feel like I need to find out more." She felt like kicking or punching something; she felt even worse that she was being so selfish about Janet's condition.

"It's okay," her mom replied. "And maybe there is someone in the office that can research H. Adams. But we should probably wait until next week before we ask. Give them time to process what's happening to their co-worker. And in the meantime, let's hope for a miracle for Janet."

CHAPTER FIFTEEN

Friction

ALL THOSE ENDLESS, tedious hours of writing her English paper, and it was gone! The writing itself had taken twenty hours, and that didn't include finding the initial research. Maybe her laptop had malfunctioned and lost the data, but she had saved it and now the file was nowhere to be found. Every time she clicked on the "English Paper May4" title, it gave her an error. If only she had made a back-up copy like she had been planning, but she reasoned that it was a new laptop and shouldn't crash. She had searched the computer and its folders for nearly thirty minutes and had reached her breaking point. Her light brown hair tumbled over her shoulders and shook as she sobbed with her head on her desk.

The essay was due tomorrow, May 4, and it was already 8:07 p.m. It was one of the more difficult papers she had written, slow in coming, but she had finished it after school and then hung out with a few friends on the trampoline in her backyard for about an hour. And when she returned later to print it, the file had disappeared like a contact lens in a city pool.

Hearing her sobs, her dad knocked softly on the door and asked if he could come in.

She looked up with swollen, reddened eyes. "Daddy, what am I going to do? My paper is due tomorrow and I can't find the file anywhere. I don't know how I'm going to rewrite the whole thing by tomorrow morning."

He walked towards her, and she stood up and buried her face in his chest with her hands covering her eyes. Her frame shook with emotion.

"Did your laptop crash?"

"I don't know. But I guess it could have because it was off when I came up here to print it. I thought I only put it to sleep." She sniffled.

Her dad offered to help search her hard drive and the cloud for any trace of the document, even a temporary file. He figured that it would be relatively easy to find with it being such a new laptop and not having very many documents on the hard drive. He did numerous searches under every possible name, and then resorted to opening every folder and file he could find. Unfortunately, after digging through folders and files on her new laptop for thirty minutes, he could only find a temporary file with part of the introductory paragraph and told his daughter that she'd be better off not wasting any more time looking and should rewrite the paper.

English was her hardest subject and her grade was important to her. If only she didn't have to be a perfectionist about it. She tended towards slow writing because she revised and edited as she went, but most of the content was familiar in her mind.

To help center herself, she sat on the floor with her paja-ma-clad legs outstretched and leaned forward until her hamstrings burned and her nose was nearly buried between her knees. She pushed to the point of pain and then counted to twenty with each stretch. A few minutes of stretches and exercises loosened her tense muscles and dried her tears.

She grabbed her English notebook and a few tattered and highlighted articles and sat cross-legged on her bed with her laptop. Thankfully most of her thesis statement was scrawled in her notebook, and most of the quotes she had used were marked with post-it tabs in the books or in printed articles spread out on her bed. She saved the document as "English Paper May4," and began typing the first paragraph.

Ten minutes later, Abbie and her mom appeared at her bedroom door with an orange soda, a small bag of chewy candy, and some pistachios. "Dad told us what happened, and Mom and I thought you could use some snacks."

"Thanks, guys," she said with less gusto than she had intended. "I appreciate it. Really."

Her mom hugged Elliana and gave her a kiss on the forehead. She placed her hand on her daughter's shoulder for a moment, and then left the room. Abbie gave her a quick back rub before bidding her goodnight and good luck.

If only her mind would cooperate. Surely brains didn't purge data like computers. It had to be in there somewhere. The words came, but not fast enough. Her thoughts jumbled and bounced off each other in a most awkward fashion, and though a partial calm had settled over her, she still felt overwhelmed by the daunting task of rewriting the paper. Her mind fought against itself as she tried to choose her wording. Frustration was mounting and she couldn't think straight enough to make much progress—at this pace it would take at least ten hours to finish, ten hours she couldn't spare.

She figured peace and clarity of mind were worth a precious few seconds and sneaked out the back door to one of the aspen trees. Using the shortcut that Rose had taught her, she took one step into the darkness, opened her eyes and felt immediate peace in the forest that led to her Garden. She hadn't been in a few days and missed it.

The warm pages emerged from the printer by 3:30 in the morning. She quickly stacked and stapled the pages, slid it into her English folder in her backpack, and slept fitfully, with images of fire-breathing dogs stealing her homework.

Elliana felt a huge sense of relief when she placed her five-page sleep-sacrifice on the English teacher's desk. To her, after the long night she had had, it felt like crossing the finish line of a triathlon. A yawn escaped her mouth as she took her seat.

Jared walked toward her on his way back to his desk. "Hey, Reinhart. What's your paper on?"

"The benefits of adoption."

"Cool."

"What's your paper on?"

Jared shifted to let a student pass. "Evolution of music. I was up all night finishing it."

"Me, too! I lost my file and had to rewrite the entire thing last night. I'm glad it's over."

"That sucks, but you'll still get a higher grade than me." He grinned and she couldn't help but admire his great smile without braces.

"Class, take your seats." Mr. Nash rubbed his hands together. "If your paper isn't on my desk in thirty seconds, it's late."

A few students scrambled to the front of the classroom to add their papers to the growing stack.

Mr. Nash introduced his lecture, turned on the projector, and dimmed the lights.

Good. She could use a nap. She rested her head atop her folded arms; her desire for sleep overpowered her fear that she might drool or snore.

~

Elliana was nervous and wanted time to slow down. But Friday evening refused to arrive fashionably late—and she worried her lack of sleep would make her dull. In a few minutes, she would head to Cai's house for his so-called soiree.

She sniffed at her wrists and her shirt, and cherry blossom scent filled her nose. She ran her fingers through her curled hair and added a touch more hairspray, and after applying one more layer of shiny lip gloss, she decided she was ready. She wiped the sweat from her palms onto the jeans that Marlee had given her a few weeks earlier. She hated that she cared so much about how she looked, but she wanted to impress Cai and fit in so he wouldn't change his mind about her.

Rose had told Elliana earlier that week that she would become like the people she surrounded herself with, so she shouldn't shy away from joining a new peer group that could inspire and motivate her in her educational pursuits.

When she arrived on his doorstep, she quickly rubbed her palms on the backside of her jeans one last time and rang the doorbell. Her heart felt like it was beating too loudly, announcing her anxiousness. She heard footsteps approaching the door and took a deep breath. *I can do this.*

When Cai opened the door and flashed the smile that made her palms sweat once again, she almost felt relieved. She could manage to mingle with an older crowd if she was with him. She liked being with him, even if it meant trying to fit in with an older, more educated crowd of strangers.

"Hi, Ellie. Come on in." Cai stepped to the side to let her in before closing the door again. "I'm so glad you're here."

She heard a male's voice from the kitchen say, "Ah, she's here. The lady of the hour." The voice got louder as his footsteps approached.

A tall blond guy appeared around the corner with a dark-brown-haired girl close on his heels.

"Ellie, this is Christopher and his fiancée Sheena."

The brown-eyed, native-skinned girl smiled. "It's nice to meet you, Ellie."

Christopher looked at her, stuck out his right hand and said. "You must be the Starlight Lover. Pleased to finally meet you." He kept a straight face, but from what she gathered from Cai though, Christopher was a teaser, and he obviously knew about The Deal. She could play his game.

"It's nice to meet you both." Elliana looked Christopher in the eyes and said, "It seems I'm at a disadvantage. You know more about me than I know about you. Cai never mentioned you." She watched Christopher for a reaction and a smile crept from her lips. She could see Cai grinning in approval.

Christopher turned toward Cai and said, "Ah, you were right, Cai. She might be still in high school, but she'll do." This time, he smirked at Elliana. "I can tell we're going to get along just fine, Starlight."

"Starlight?" Elliana muttered to herself as if no one else were in the room. Sounds like she already had a nickname that she wasn't sure she liked.

Sheena leaned forward to offer some helpful advice. "It's okay, Elliana. You can call him Frick. That's his last name—soon to be my last name. He just loves it."

"Frick? I assume you'll be hyphenating your last name when you get married?" Elliana joked.

"Actually, Sheena Frick is going to look great on my résumé. Much better than Sheena Heffer. H-E-F-F-E-R."

"You're kidding, right?" Elliana feared offending her new acquaintance but couldn't suppress a childish giggle especially since Sheena did not resemble a cow in the least.

"Nope. Although being Sheena Heffer has been quite the thrill ride with plenty of overweight-bovine jokes, Christopher pretty much knows I'm marrying him just for his last name. Right, babe?"

Christopher smiled, shaking his head slightly. "She's marrying me for my lack of money and my rugged good looks. Don't let her fool you, Starlight."

Sheena kissed Christopher on the cheek before pulling him down the hallway to the great room.

Cai walked Elliana to the great room, where they sat down next to each other on the couch and resumed their banter.

"Frick, when are you two getting married?" Elliana asked.

"June second."

That was less than a month away. Cai was going, and Elliana secretly hoped that he would take her.

Christopher told the story of how he met Sheena. He saw her sitting by herself in the library looking lonely, beckoning him with her brown eyes, while Sheena interjected corrections on how things really happened, like how she was trying to study and some kid kept bugging her by throwing bits of paper onto her table to get her attention.

A group of people showed up thirty minutes later: Becca, Tin, and Daniel. They had brought three pizzas to add to the veggie tray, sodas, and chips that Cai had provided.

Becca grabbed two slices of pepperoni pizza and sat down by Elliana. "Cai tells us you are trying to decide whether or not to come to BSU. How can we sway you?"

"Actually, I have already made up my mind on where I'll be going to college."

Cai cast her a questioning look. She just smiled back at him and waited for the question. Christopher was the first to jump.

"Do tell, Starlight. Will you be gracing BSU with your shining presence?"

"Nope, University of Washington. I decided a few days ago. The scholarship was a big factor." If Elliana read him right, Cai seemed disappointed. She suddenly felt like a jerk for not telling Cai about her college decision before she announced it to a group of strangers.

"You chose a scholarship over me?" Christopher said with mock indignation.

Elliana grinned at him. "You are the main reason I'm not staying here."

Christopher turned his poker face toward Cai. "You didn't tell me your girlfriend was so cruel."

"It's all good, Frick. You could use a dose of your own medicine." Cai turned to Sheena. "Right?"

Sheena was loyal. "I have no idea what you're talking about. Christopher is pure sunshine."

"Speaking of sunshine reminds me of starlight," Christopher said, "which makes me wonder when you're finally going to get on with it and smooch my good friend here."

Elliana had been sipping some ginger ale from her glass and burst out laughing, spewing pop onto the interrogator and a couch pillow. Seeing Christopher covered in a sticky mist, everyone else started laughing. Christopher kept a straight face, but Sheena was laughing herself nearly to tears, even though she had caught some of the airborne soda on her left arm.

"Heathen!" Christopher grabbed a napkin and wiped the soda from his face and clothing.

Between suppressed chuckles, Elliana apologized to Christopher. "I'm. So. Sorry." She had to regain her composure before she continued. "You totally caught me off-guard. You should never make me laugh while I'm drinking."

"I really hope you are not carrying any communicable diseases. But there's a way you can make it up to me."

Elliana said, "I already apologized."

"You sabotaged my dashing thrift store outfit with your unsavory display of affection."

This only made Elliana laugh harder. Everyone in the room was still laughing, too.

"Fine," Elliana conceded, feeling a tinge badly for spraying him with a mouthful of pop. "Perhaps my dousing you was unpleasant. What do you want?"

Christopher grew a mischievous smile. "If you two haven't kissed by June second, Cai gets to kiss you at my wedding." He shrugged his shoulders when he saw her shocked face. "What? I'm just looking out for my best man."

"You don't have to promise him anything, Ellie," Cai said. "Besides, we wouldn't want to steal the spotlight on their wedding day."

Sheena looked excited about the proposition, almost like she was about to get a brand-new puppy. Why she would be interested in Cai and Elliana's kissing was beyond her. People were silly. Christopher puckered his lips and made a few obnoxious kissing noises before falling silent in expectation of an answer. "So?"

June 2 was four weeks away, which should give her plenty of time to know whether or not she wanted to kiss Cai. But then again, she wasn't sure she wanted a public first kiss with the scrutinizing eyes of people who were more experienced than she was. No. She wanted a kiss that was part of a special moment, not forced up on her because of some arbitrary deal. She wanted a kiss to be the result of true emotion from heartfelt feelings—surely that was part of her task to understand the human heart.

And what's with everyone trying to make her make deals? She cast a nervous glance at Cai, who shook his head at Elliana, letting her know she didn't have to comply with Christopher's irrational demands.

"Only if I catch the bouquet." She would make darn sure that bouquet had no chance of falling within a nine hundred-foot radius of her hands. In fact, she mentally scheduled a bathroom break during that charade.

Christopher and Sheena gave each other a fist bump like they were the force bringing Elliana and Cai together.

Eventually the geo-nerds got to talking about rocks and how Idaho had some of the highest levels of geothermal activity in all of the United States. Elliana asked, "Do you guys happen to know of any secret hot springs then? I've been to the ones that charge you an arm and a leg, but never to one right out in nature."

The college students looked around at each other like they were unsure about sharing a very important secret with a non-geo-nerd.

Cai nodded. "The Dive-In Hot Springs are about an hour away. By far the best, and mostly undiscovered. We call them Dive-In Hot Springs because the one pool is so deep you could probably dive into it, though Frick is always too chicken to try."

"When are you taking me?" Elliana asked.

Cai probably remembered he was taking her to Spring Formal in a week. "How about two weeks from Saturday? Who else wants to come?"

Sheena looked at Christopher. "Let's totally go. That sounds like way more fun than going to my aunt's annual barbeque. We'll see them all at the wedding anyways."

"Sheena, I have a better idea. Let's totally go. That sounds like way more fun than going to your aunt's barbeque. We'll see them all at the wedding anyways." He didn't even smirk.

Sheena elbowed him. "We're in."

Elliana was summoned to the principal's office during second period the following Wednesday. For a second, she was glad to be missing class because they were supposed to watch a low-budget version of *Don Quixote* in AP Spanish—a guaranteed headache. Then she remembered how she weaseled her way out of meeting with the principal the week before, and she got a sinking feeling. With her backpack on her shoulders, she walked into the office and approached the desk. "Hey, Mrs. White. I got a note that said to come to Mr. Carmichael's office."

Mrs. White glanced up from what she was working on and said, "Oh, yes. Take a seat on the bench, sweetie. He'll be with you in a few minutes."

Elliana lowered herself onto the bench for the second time in less than two weeks, the same bench she vowed to avoid—although this time she wasn't sure exactly what had brought her there. Looking around the room in anticipation, she watched a few teachers come in and get their mail from their boxes opposite the bench she was seated on.

Her mind began to run through all the different reasons

one could get called to the principal's office: skipping school, mouthing off to staff, damaging someone's property, being dishonest, but she hadn't done any of that within the past few days, except for what she'd pulled on Mrs. Pratt. Perhaps this really was about last week. Maybe the principal found out that she was sent to the office and tricked Mrs. White into letting her leave. Regret was pushing any idea of innocence out of her mind. If asked, she would admit what she had done: she left class to answer her phone, and then got so scared about getting sent to the principal's office and losing her phone that she told a half-truth.

Her parents entered the office. What were they doing here? Something was wrong. If the occasion were good news, her parents would be smiling more. Her chest tightened. Before she could inquire about their unexpected appearance in the school's office or their tense expressions, Mr. Carmichael's voice boomed, "Hello, Reinharts. Follow me, please."

Mr. Carmichael led the way, and they walked past the front desk, turned the corner to the right, and entered the office at the end of the hall.

He motioned for the Reinharts to take a seat in front of his desk, closed his door, and positioned himself stiffly in his chair. His body language spoke of discipline. A rock grew in Elliana's throat.

"I'll get right to it. I'm sure you're all wondering. This is one of the least favorite parts of my job, Mr. and Mrs. Reinhart, but because of academic dishonesty, your daughter has failed her English course and will be suspended for three days and will likely need to take summer school to make up the English credit. Mr. Reinhart, I'm sure given your line of work that you fully understand our zero-tolerance policy on plagiarism at any level at this school. I have been in this position for nearly a decade, and I haven't ever gone easy on this offense, otherwise it would damage the credibility of this charter school in addition to handicapping a student's future success."

Stunned silence sucked the energy out of the room like a commercial vacuum. Because she didn't really understand why he thought she had plagiarized, she wasn't sure how to defend herself. A dense fog of confusion settled over her. In her head, she replayed typing her bibliography, using quotation marks, using in-text citations for borrowed material, and writing the paper line by line in the early hours of the morning before her paper was due. She had done nothing amiss, she was sure. More than feeling angry, she felt incredulous. When she was called to his office, she assumed she was going to have to come clean about her sly-dogging the office over a week ago—but this plagiarism accusation came out of nowhere and she wasn't prepared.

He looked at Elliana. "This also means you will not be able to participate in school activities, more specifically Spring Formal and graduation."

Her dad looked at her with his mouth agape, and her mom started fidgeting. Feeling the cold lump grow steadily larger in her throat, like a snowball grows as it rolls, and feeling the frosty fingers of indignation claw at her from the inside, Elliana's thoughts began flurrying away to an awful realization that her life's dreams were ending for something she didn't do. She was being suspended, banned from Spring Formal, and purposefully excluded from graduation. Did that mean no diploma?

This was no time to play it safe.

She determined to speak her mind for once because this was

pure absurdity. "Mr. Carmichael. I have no idea what you're talking about. I can assure you that I don't plagiarize—it goes against everything I am."

"I doubted Mr. Nash's accusation until I saw the paper myself. How can you refute this proof?" Mr. Carmichael pushed a copy of her essay toward the three pairs of expectant eyes. "This entire English paper was downloaded straight from the internet. I met with Mr. Nash and the Vice Principal this morning, and we are all in agreement that this is blatant plagiarism at the highest level of infraction, and rather than expel you, because of your good conduct up until now, we all agreed that you should be suspended—effective immediately."

Her dad was the first to grab the stapled paper. "I can't believe my daughter would do such a thing. Ellie, you didn't do this, did you?"

Of course he would doubt her because of how distraught she was that night. She was desperate and almost irrational with emotion when he entered her bedroom. But did he really believe she was capable of cheating? She knew better than to steal a paper off the internet, especially since Mr. Nash had mentioned last fall that he was using a new program that checked for plagiarized papers. Even if English wasn't her best subject, she wouldn't resort to plagiarism to pass, even more so because she would never purposefully tarnish her father's respected name. She retrieved the paper from her dad's hands, searching his face.

It was one thing to have the principal not believe her, but the fact that her father was falling for this outrageous set-up fanned the flames that melted the cold knot in her throat. "This is bullcrap! This isn't even my paper! My paper was on adoption, and this paper is on wind energy! Where did you get this? The only text I recognize in this whole paper is my name, the date, and the class in the upper corner. That's it!" She tossed the paper back onto the desk.

"Miss Reinhart, I understand that you are angry at being caught, but there is little room for you to disprove the evidence. Unless of course you have a copy of this supposed paper on adoption that you claim to have written."

Her mom shifted in her seat. "You do you have it, right Ellie? You did you rewrite it that night, right?"

"Yes, mom, of course I rewrote it and put it on Mr. Nash's desk. But since I turned in the hardcopy, I don't have a copy handy to prove it." That her mom questioned her only made her angrier, so Elliana tried to control her temper. Her innocence would be easy enough to prove. "I wouldn't have been up until three thirty in the morning if I was just printing off someone else's paper."

She turned to Mr. Carmichael. "Besides, I'm not stupid enough to print something directly from the internet. Have I ever had to sit in this office before to be disciplined?" She felt a little guilty about last week's incident but knew that she had to make a point and rely on her perceived strong character. "No. Never. I am not that kind of a person. I am honest and I work hard in school. Ask anyone who knows me." Finally, the reality hit and she felt a surge of desperation. Tears spilled down her cheeks, melting her mascara.

"I must admit this is the last thing I expected from you. I wouldn't have been surprised if certain individuals in the school did this, but you? Where is this paper you claim you wrote last week?"

Elliana wiped at her eyes. "On my laptop."

"Mr. and Mrs. Reinhart, would one of you do your daughter

a favor and retrieve her laptop so that we can settle this once and for all?"

Her dad's hands shook as he reached for the door handle. Elliana felt her heart breaking and worried the stress would give her dad high blood pressure problems.

She was glad her mom stayed. Her mom reached over and held her hand. "We'll get this figured out. Everything will be okay. I believe you."

She felt so relieved that her mom believed her. Elliana leaned her head on her mom's shoulder with two words replaying over and over in her head: *failed, suspended.* What would she be able to do after this? She was sure that when her dad brought her laptop and she opened the file, that he'd reverse the punishments. He'd have to.

Elliana picked up the plagiarized paper and started reading it again. It was so perfectly written with advanced academic language that it was obviously not written by a high school student. Whoever had done this wanted to make sure she got caught. She could feel that someone out there disliked her deeply, or maybe even hated her. She was tempted to blame it all on that demonic Veronica Curry or her snotty little sister, but she had zero evidence. She wouldn't put it past either one of them, but that theory put too much stock in their intelligence.

The twenty minutes Elliana had to wait felt like an hour. The clock seemed to tick more slowly with each passing second. *Tick.* The chair underneath her grew more uncomfortable by the minute, like it was made of grated metal. *Tock.* The air was hot and stuffy, bordering on stale. But the worst of it was Mr. Carmichael's expressions, ranging from disappointment to frustration to pity. *Tick.* She hated to be pitied. And she hated to be in his office under these false circumstances, but she allowed herself to hope for redemption because she knew she had proof of her innocence on her laptop. *Tock.*

At long last her dad arrived with her laptop. He handed it to Elliana just as the bell rang for third period. She flipped open the cover with anxious hands and booted it up. She double-clicked through the folders:

Cloud > School > English > Adoption Paper >

But there was no "English Paper May4." The folder was empty. Her tears spilled down her face once again. "It's not here. It's been deleted again. This happened the night before it was due as well. I had it saved in this folder, and when I went to print it, the file was gone. No trace of it. And then I stayed up all that night rewriting the dang thing. I swear I handed in my own work, not that stupid paper on wind energy, of all things."

"This doesn't look good for you, Miss Reinhart." Mr. Carmichael shook his head as he spoke. "Your story is pretty far-fetched, and believe me, I've heard them all."

Elliana looked up at the ceiling, trying to think of a solution, feeling panicked, overwhelmed, cursed, hated. She opened her word processing program and checked the recent documents in the pulldown menu. She clicked on the "English Paper May4" title and received an error: "File not found."

"See, right here, it says the name of my paper, but the file is missing." None of this made any sense, and she was baffled by the impossibility of her file vanishing a second time.

"For all I know that could have been the name of your plagiarized paper and you deleted it so you wouldn't get caught. Do you have that file backed up anywhere else?"

Her heart beat wildly and she shook her head, feeling like an idiot for being so anxious to get to bed that she didn't back up her file.

"I'm sure that I need not remind you of the privilege of attending this outstanding charter school which has a very long waiting list. Truthfully, we all feel terribly that such a good student as yourself would be lured into plagiarizing. It is unfortunate that you will not be able to walk with your peers at graduation, but you can do summer school or get your GED. And naturally, most of your scholarship offers will be rescinded upon receiving a letter from me. We are extremely disappointed in your breach of honesty."

No Spring Formal, no diploma, and now no scholarship or degree from a respectable university? Her life was over. Everything she had ever worked hard for was over. It felt like her life was continuously being turned upside down lately, and the past thirty minutes it entered a death spiral.

"I'm afraid I have no other option but to suspend you. You need to go home with your parents."

Her parents protested, but without evidence of her innocence, the principal's decision would stand.

People would believe the lie now. She couldn't stand that she would be the hot topic at lunch. A sob erupted from her throat. Elliana grabbed her backpack, grabbed the laptop, put it in her bag and stomped out. Her parents followed solemnly after her, casting the principal bewildered, yet pleading gazes.

Mr. Carmichael didn't even flinch. He stood and crossed his arms and watched the Reinharts exit his office. The warring emotions within her body made her physically ill, and she felt helpless, breathless, like she was smothered by an avalanche without a shovel or a hand to help.

CHAPTER SIXTEEN

Trash Talk

ELLIANA LEFT HER CAR in the parking lot for her sister to drive home, having sent a note to Abbie with the keys saying that she had gone home early.

The car ride home with her parents was tense. Elliana pleaded with her parents to believe her. "I know I was hysterical that night, and I'm sure I seemed desperate, but I didn't do what he's accusing me of. I promise you. I really did rewrite that paper."

"We believe you," her dad said. "You're too smart to throw away your future by cheating on a paper. It just doesn't sound like something you'd do."

"I'm so glad you believe me, Daddy. I thought you fell for it like Mr. Carmichael did."

"No, definitely not. I am just having a hard time processing this whole situation. How would that paper have your name on it?" He looked at her through the rear-view mirror. "Who would do this to you? Do you have enemies?"

"No one I'd consider an enemy. I don't think Marlee's too fond of me right now, but she's the only person I can think of. She's done some selfish, catty things, but I have a really hard time believing she would go out of her way to sabotage my high school and college career. That's not like her."

"I'm wondering who had access to your laptop, because this whole scheme was very well planned out," her mom said.

Elliana closed her eyes while reviewing the past week. "I had some friends over last Thursday. Burke, Marlee, Keisha, and some others, but they are all my friends. And none of them used my laptop. I had my laptop with me at school on Monday, but no one used it but me."

"Here's what I'm thinking," her dad said. "Whoever deleted your file on Thursday had to have access to it again after to delete your rewritten paper. Unless you were hacked."

Her mom asked who would have had any sort of access to her laptop.

"I don't know. I'm drawing a blank, Mom. I just don't know."

"We'll get it figured out, sweetie." Her mom turned around to look at her. "Don't give up hope."

She had been depressed when Marlee betrayed her, and here she was again, down in the dumps, feeling like her life had been crushed like an empty soda can. She would be remembered as the loser who cheated and didn't graduate on time.

Once they arrived home, she grabbed her backpack and walked sullenly up the stairs to her room, not looking back at her parents.

The minutes ticked by slower than they had ever before. Only ten minutes had passed and Elliana felt like she was going crazy. She lay on her stomach on her bed, feeling angry and stuck.

She glanced toward the window to find Orly on the window sill. If she tried to go downstairs, her parents might see her and start talking to her, and she wasn't ready for that. She had time for an experiment. Carefully, she looked around the room to see if anything could be used as a portal—something Orly could land on. She decided to let the bird in to see where she would land.

Quietly, she opened the window just a few inches, and Orly flew right in and landed on a bed post at the foot of her bed. She held the post with her right hand, closed her eyes and whispered, "Port to Seeking Realm."

Within seconds she was walking through the forest with Wayne, amazed at what she had just figured out.

"Sorry you've had a hard day, sweetie," he said before dismounting and giving her a warm embrace.

She gave a wan smile. "Thanks."

He walked her all the way to the cottage this time and gave Rose a kiss on the cheek before mounting Serenada and returning to his post.

When she saw Rose, Elliana meant to voice her troubles, but they came out more like a long complaint. Rose was gracious and hugged her and empathized with her.

"I'm thinking someone must really hate me, otherwise they wouldn't have taken the time to get me in trouble and ruin my life with a lie. I don't know what to do about it. It's not true, and so I keep thinking there must be a way to prove my innocence, but no ideas are coming to my head."

"Let's go tend the garden while we brainstorm." Rose led the way toward a patch of flowers with curly petals. She started singing a lulling song as she touched the leaves and petals. "Come, dear, and handle the plants and think hopeful thoughts. Gardening is good for the soul."

As she touched the petals, the flowers opened wider and glowed even more brightly than they had before. Hopeful thoughts. But hopeful thoughts weren't coming to her mind yet.

"Rose, I wish something miraculous would happen. I have no way to get out of this mess by myself. But there has to be a way. If only I knew what to do."

They worked out an answer and Rose cautioned, "Now you know you have an enemy, so be watchful."

Elliana nodded. "How do you know so much?"

Rose's eyes twinkled. "I'm a young Redwood, dear. I've learned the lessons from history."

Elliana gave Rose a hug and ran off toward the tree portal with a beautiful bird perched on the lowest branch. She chatted with Wayne a minute and then said goodbye.

As soon as she reappeared in her room, Orly fluttered back to her perch on the sill. Elliana smiled at her bird, closed the window, and ran downstairs.

"Mom! Dad! I have an idea!"

By the time she arrived back at the high school with her parents, it was fifth period. Mr. Carmichael was barely friendly, but he went willingly with the Reinharts.

In the room where she had English, another teacher was in the middle of her eleventh grade English class. With a short "excuse me," Mr. Carmichael walked straight to the garbage can, pulled out the large gray trash bag and walked right back out like it was no big deal. Elliana tried to stay hidden from the view of the juniors who stared at the exiting principal.

From there, they walked toward the teacher's lounge. Mr. Nash was there, sitting on an old green sofa sipping coffee smugly from a mug.

"Mr. Nash. Could you please help us out?" Mr. Carmichael

asked.

Mr. Nash agreed after giving Elliana a disapproving look.

"We'd like to search the garbage in your office to see if Miss Reinhart's original paper wasn't disposed of in there."

"Original paper?"

"Yes, she claims she wrote a paper on adoption and that someone switched it with a plagiarized paper to get her in trouble."

They walked the short distance to his office in the language wing and followed Mr. Nash inside. It was cramped and extremely cluttered. His metal desk was covered with stacks and stacks of books at least three feet high, scrawled post-it notes, a styrofoam cup, crumpled napkins, a bag of opened sunflower seeds, an array of red pens, and a stack of CDs. There was barely enough room for a computer monitor and keyboard. The trash underneath the desk only contained some candy bar wrappers, crumpled up receipts, and a completed book of crossword puzzles.

The principal thanked Mr. Nash, and they moved on down the hallway and turned left at the first garbage can. It was rather full, but it was usually emptied on a regular basis. Mr. Carmichael pulled the entire bag from the receptacle anyways, handed it to Elliana's dad, and continued walking toward the bathrooms that were further down the hall. Elliana and her mom grabbed the bag from the girls' bathroom, while her dad and the principal got the bag from the boys' stinky bathroom.

Elliana's desire for exoneration mostly outweighed the embarrassment of carrying trash bags with her parents down the hall to the janitor's room. They brought the bags inside and began to sort through the trash on the cold, industrial floor. Rummaging through people's discarded things was pretty disgusting, and they still hadn't found Elliana's missing paper.

Elliana willed herself not to cry and stared at the garbage all over the floor, expecting to find her paper, hoping they had only overlooked it.

"There you are!" Mr. Nash appeared in the doorway. "You'll never believe what I found," He paused for what felt like a minute to catch his breath and held up a stapled paper. "She was telling the truth."

Elliana rushed toward her teacher and had to stop herself from hugging him.

"I was in my office after you left, embarrassed by the mess, so I started to tidy up. I was throwing away a styrofoam cup, but I missed and it rolled under my desk. And what do you think it landed on? This paper! I would have never seen it. Whoever threw her paper away must have missed the garbage can like I did!"

Elliana let out a long long long sigh, and then hugged her parents until it was hard to breathe and tears streamed down her cheeks. Surely, she would be vindicated.

Mr. Carmichael took the paper from the teacher and began reading it just as the bell sounded. Indeed, it was the paper on the benefits of adoption. After reading the first paragraph, he said the words she had been waiting for: "You are off the hook, Miss Reinhart. You are fully reinstated. I'm so relieved. I didn't want to believe you were capable of plagiarizing."

"You're relieved? Hello! I'm relieved! I thought I wasn't going to graduate or get to go to college or accomplish any of my dreams. I thought my life was over! I'm so glad Mr. Nash dropped that cup!" Whoever sabotaged her didn't realize their sloppy aim in a messy office would save her skin.

Mr. Carmichael apologized and vowed to investigate and

find the conniver behind this scam, and the Reinharts shared their theories and memories of the past week to try and offer some sort of starting point for the principal and Mr. Nash.

"Rest assured, we will investigate this situation." Mr. Carmichael extended his hand to the Reinharts. "Again, I'm so sorry for the panic you all must have felt, but equally glad we figured it out. Off to class, Miss Reinhart. Sixth period started fifteen minutes ago." This time he was smiling.

She was glad she never had to talk to Mr. Carmichael the day Mrs. Pratt sent her to the office—it would have made her look worse, and he might not have been so willing to help. She instantly forgave herself for that stunt last week. That was the last time she would have to meet with the principal—what a comforting thought. It could only get better now.

It probably wouldn't sound good if she said she hoped she'd never see him again, but that's exactly what she was thinking.

❧

At lunch, Burke and Keisha wondered aloud why Elliana wasn't at lunch and mentioned to the table that she never showed up to third period study hall.

"Ellie wasn't in fourth period English either, man," Jared said.

"But I saw her this morning in Calculus." Burke was mostly puzzled because if anything big had happened, she usually told him about it.

"She wasn't in fifth period art either," Granger added.

"That doesn't make any sense," Keisha said. "Ellie doesn't skip class... ever. And she didn't look sick."

A girl who was sitting at a neighboring table, leaned over to Keisha and whispered, "I saw Ellie's parents walk into the principal's office during second period. Ellie was in there too."

The friends gave each other puzzled looks and shrugged their shoulders, not having any clue what the principal would want with Elliana that also needed her parents' presence. Burke wondered if it might be some kind of award.

Granger cleared his throat. "You know she got sent to the principal's office last week during art class for sneaking out into the hallway in the middle of class to answer her phone."

"Yeah, she told me that," Burke said, "but she didn't actually talk to the principal. She sort of tricked Mrs. White into thinking she was just waiting there for her teacher and then left."

Granger's jaw dropped. "How'd she do that?"

Burke retold the story, and all the kids laughed that Elliana, of all people, would have lived so dangerously and taken the risk.

"She's a quick one, that Ellie." Granger nodded in respect of her feat. "She has my utmost respect for pulling that off."

"Maybe that's why she's in trouble," Burke said.

Keisha asked, "But why would they call her parents in for that?"

"Good question. We'll have to ask her if we ever find her." Just as the words escaped Burke's mouth, in walked his brown-haired friend.

&

"Ellie Reinhart! You have some explaining to do! We've been worried sick," Keisha scolded in a motherly tone as her friend neared the table.

"Tell me about it! I was even more worried sick. You're never going to believe this." Elliana pulled out a chair and sat down between Keisha and Burke. "I got suspended this morning!" She let that sink in as she scooted her chair forward.

Her friends' jaws dropped in unison.

"What the—?" Burke said.

The friends listened intently to Elliana's version of the day's events. As she relayed the story, she consciously studied each person's reaction to the news to detect any guilt, even though she didn't think her friends would do anything like that to her—but they were the only ones with access to her laptop. Everyone at her table was stupefied that someone would turn in a stolen, plagiarized paper with her name on it, and that this same someone would cover his or her tracks so well.

"Weren't you scared?" Keisha asked.

"Of course. I was terrified, but on the other hand I knew I didn't do what he was accusing me of. I tried not to freak out too badly, but I did get a little snippy with Mr. Carmichael."

"Good for you!" Burke said. "He should know better than to believe Ellie Reinhart would plagiarize an English paper."

Marlee seemed genuinely surprised by the story but said nothing, though her wide eyes seemed to betray her surprise.

"Why would anyone do that to you?" Granger's eyebrows bunched angrily in the center. "Mean people suck. Who do you think did it?"

"I don't know, but it sure makes me feel like hud. I'm just glad it's over, and I need some serious fun this weekend." She planned on having a blast at Spring Formal. Being told that she wasn't allowed to go to Spring Formal only made her want to go all the more.

"Hey guys, I just remembered that I left my backpack at home after I got suspended. Anyone have any lunch money I can borrow?" Elliana said.

Marlee reached into her pocket and put a five-dollar bill in her friend's hand and whispered, "Don't worry about paying me back."

"Thanks, Marlee."

That eighteen-karat heart was still in there somewhere. Or she was really good at hiding guilt.

CHAPTER SEVENTEEN

Formalities

Because of the emotional roller coaster Elliana had been forced to ride by some anonymous saboteur, she craved Cai's company. He had been busy all week, so she hadn't seen him since the previous weekend, when she met Christopher Frick and Sheena Heffer. (As childish as it was, just the thought of their names made her smile.)

Cai hadn't called or texted at all until Friday afternoon. That felt rotten, but they had firm plans for Spring Formal and to go to the hot spring the following weekend, so she pushed any feelings of disappointment away.

Cai was supposed to pick her up and drive them to dinner at his house and then to Spring Formal at the Stueckle Sky Center in Boise State's Broncos Stadium.

Abbie curled Elliana's hair, added a wide braid on the side, and then coated the hairdo with a layer of glitter hairspray.

She stood in front of the mirror, turning from side to side. Two tendrils hung a little lower than her rhinestone earrings. Long waves cascaded down the middle of her back. She smoothed her hands down the front of the borrowed midnight blue satin dress, admiring the bead work on the bodice as well as the puckered skirt. Elliana felt like a princess. A sweaty, nervous princess. She sprayed another mist of perfume on her arms and neck and hoped her deodorant would last all night.

Abbie stood back to look at her sister. "My work here is done."

Elliana gave Abbie a big squeeze.

The doorbell rang. Although she wanted to run down the stairs to meet him, Elliana figured she'd need to walk carefully in her four-inch heels to avoid tumbling down the steps and ripping her borrowed dress or breaking her ankle. She watched her feet carefully, and halfway down the steps, she caught Cai's eyes.

He was looking at her face, smiling. "Wow, you look... stunning."

"Thanks." Elliana reached the bottom. She looked him up and down, admiring how handsome he looked in his black tuxedo and navy cummerbund. "You look sharp, yourself."

Cai slid a red rose corsage around her wrist. She pinned a matching flower to his lapel, taking extra care not to prick her finger since her hands were unsteady. When she successfully affixed the corsage, they posed for pictures. He draped his arm around her waist, and her mom and sister snapped a few hundred pictures. Elliana didn't mind.

"You take good care of my princess, Cai." Her dad cast Cai a stern look. "No funny business. And if I need to be more specific, I'd be glad to spell it out."

Cai said, "Not necessary, sir. I'll take good care of her. And definitely no funny business. I'm taking it as a good sign that you weren't cleaning your shotgun when I arrived."

"Hah, yes!" Her dad slapped Cai on the back. "She told you about that one. Just have her back by 3 am in the same or better

condition and my gun will stay locked in the safe."

"Yes, sir."

Elliana had to laugh at that statement—as if 3 am was a permissible curfew at her house. Normally, he'd balk at her coming home one minute past eleven-thirty, especially if she was on a date. But After-Formal would be at the local rec center, and she had permission to stay out late.

He placed her hand on his arm and walked her to the freshly-waxed black Mercedes that he had borrowed from his dad for the occasion. He opened her door to help her in, keeping her satin skirt away from the door as he closed it.

It was odd how nervous she felt now that she was in a fancy dress and he was in a tuxedo. Somehow the formal attire in a fancy car seemed to call for formal conversation.

"What's on the menu?" she asked.

"Chicken cordon bleu with veggies, salad, and a loaded baked potato."

"Did you know that chicken cordon bleu is my favorite?"

"Not until I asked your mom. It's one of my favorites, too."

She smiled at him. "It sounds wonderful. I know you were super busy and stressed out with finals this week. Thanks for going to all this trouble for my Spring Formal."

"Getting to see you looking like this could never be classified as trouble. Besides, I finished my last final at noon; it's time to celebrate."

"I need some fun, too. I had a pretty rough week." She updated him on the whole getting-expelled-and-then-getting-re-instated fiasco, and how she wanted to call him to tell him but didn't want to stress him out during finals.

"You should have called."

"I know. I just don't want to be the annoying girl that calls every ten minutes."

He just laughed. "You could never be annoying. I like talking to you."

When they arrived at Cai's home, she met his parents for the first time.

"Ellie, it's so great to finally meet you," his mom said. "And I hope you don't mind if I call you Ellie."

"Not at all. It's great to meet you, Mrs. Wittington."

Mr. Wittington was warm and not as scary as she imagined. He shook her hand and gave her a side hug. "I've heard a lot of nice things about you, and it's a pleasure to have you in our home. You are welcome here any time. Seriously."

"Thank you, Mr. Wittington. It's nice to meet you. You both have such a beautiful home."

After friendly conversation, Cai escorted her into the formal dining room lit by several white taper candles. The table was bedecked in a blue brocade table cloth, white folded napkins, and all the proper place settings. He pulled out her chair and helped her scoot her chair closer to the table.

Paige brought out two bowls of green salad. "Dinner is served, your majesties."

Lauren brought in two large dinner plates, and after placing the plates on the table, both sisters left the room.

"Bon appétit," Cai said. "Or as my parents just learned from Flemish Belgium, 'Eet smakelijk.'"

The first bite was mouth-watering—he could cook. The whole setting was so much more her style than a restaurant filled with loud, competing conversations and backstabbers.

They arrived at the Stueckle Sky Center at the Broncos Stadium fashionably late, and only a few couples had moved onto the dance floor. Most were sitting on benches or leaning against the wall with their group. When the first slow song came on, Cai asked her to dance. Most of the other couples danced with their arms around each other, but Cai clasped her right hand with his left hand, and then put his right hand around her back, pulling her close.

"You smell really good," she said, "just like when I walked past you at Confucius."

"Oh really? You smelled me at the restaurant?"

"Why do you think I ran you over?"

"You ran me over because you're an inattentive driver, cutie pie."

"Actually, I ran you over because I was slightly twitterpated."

"I like this story. Tell me more," Cai said.

"Well, after I tried to kill you for having the audacity to read my journal, we walked to a park and you became twitterpated as well, telling me far-fetched stories of the skies, and baiting me with a deal."

"It worked, didn't it?"

Elliana looked up and smiled. "Don't you think it's a pretty unique story? Our story?"

"Best story ever. Like some other force had to bring us together because you were too scared to walk over to my table, confess your attraction, and ask me out." He suppressed a smirk.

"Oh please! You were there with two pretty girls, and for all I knew, you were taken! Besides, I don't ask strange boys out. And you could have just asked me out yourself instead of diving under my tire in some sort of maniacal attempt for attention."

He laughed out loud. "I was hoping for some excuse to talk

to you, but I wasn't about to make a move with your parents sitting there. I just kept hoping that you would give me a reason to come talk to you. It's not like it would have been proper to follow you to the bathroom and strike up a conversation. My sister noticed that I was looking over at your table, so when she saw you left your journal on the seat, she told me it was meant to be."

"That's the way I look at it, too. Or maybe it's because I rubbed Buddha's belly—my dad thinks it's good luck."

"You're good luck. For me." He pulled her closer, resting his cheek on her head and told her how glad he was that they met and how beautiful she looked in the blue dress.

Elliana spent every slow song with Cai. During one song in particular, he whirled her out and then reeled her back, spinning her in a circle back into his arms.

After a few dozen dances, they sat sipping their drinks, looking out onto Boise State's smurf turf aglow with field lights. A new song started playing that caught her attention—it was the last song from the CD Burke gave her. Although he only listed ten songs, she discovered there was a hidden eleventh track...a love song. That same song, "Second Chances," was now playing loudly over the speakers, nudging her thoughts away from Cai and toward Burke, wondering what he meant by including that song on the CD at all. At first, she had dismissed it as friendship. But the more she thought about it and listened to the words, the more she wondered if perhaps it meant more.

Just then Burke appeared to formally ask Cai permission to dance with his date.

Cai consented and slowly relinquished Elliana's hand.

Burke turned toward Elliana and extended his hand. "Will you dance with me?"

They headed to the dance floor. Burke placed his hands on the curve of her waist and pulled her closer than she had expected, but still comfortable; she rested her hands behind his neck. He didn't say anything but inclined his head toward hers.

"You put this song on my CD. I can't believe they are playing it."

"I requested it."

"Oh." Her heart got thumpy.

"You look gorgeous, Ellie."

"Thanks." She gulped as quietly as she could.

He didn't say anything for several long seconds. "I think the hardest part of seeing you in that dress is also seeing you on the arm of another guy. I've been kicking myself for not noticing you that way, and tonight is my punishment."

These were almost the exact words she had been dreaming of hearing for months, even years. And now she was hearing them while at Spring Formal with a different, but wonderful, guy, making it all too surreal to process. Why did he have to wait until this moment?

She avoided his gaze. "I...I don't know what to say."

"I guess I want to know if I've completely lost my chance with you."

She opened her mouth to respond, but then closed it. She thought of Cai, and how much she cared for him, and how reluctant she was to hurt him by choosing Burke right there. She would be devastated if that happened to her.

"You don't have to say anything. Just nod yes or no."

Their eyes met and they almost stopped moving to the music; this conversation was getting awkward fast. If it had happened two months ago she would have welcomed it, but tonight it didn't feel right. She shrugged her satiny shoulders. "You know I have pretty strong feelings for Cai, right?"

"I figured as much. It's not hard to tell."

"I really don't want to hurt Cai so I can't promise you anything right now. He really is an awesome guy. I want to see if things are going to work out with him first."

"And if it doesn't, then you'll give me a chance?"

She nodded.

He squeezed her tight. "Thanks. My mom has been reminding me for weeks that I'm an idiot for letting you get away."

"She was right."

"I know. My heart has been beating out of my chest ever since you walked in here looking like that, and I knew I had to talk to you and see if you had any feelings for me. The more time I spend with Marlee, the more I realize that you're the one I want."

They swayed to the music, and it dawned on her that she would not only be hurting Cai with this decision, but she would be hurting Marlee too—if Marlee's feelings for Burke were real rather than for show. The choice would be easier if things hadn't gotten more complicated during the past three weeks.

She glanced around to find Marlee dancing with Cai. Marlee looked pretty tonight. She was wearing an expensive, flashy red sequin gown that hugged her figure and had a long slit up the front that extended to her mid-thigh. Her up-do was the product of a professional hairdresser, and she had been hanging on Burke like a wet towel. At the moment, she was throwing her head back in quiet laughter, completely oblivious that her date had just declared his affections to the best friend she betrayed. Karma.

After the specially-requested song had ended, Burke walked Elliana back to her date. Marlee quickly latched on to Burke's arm and played like she was attending a royal ball in her honor, proud yet pleasant. Spring Formal King and Queen would be announced soon.

Elliana told Cai who she thought would win, and she was pretty sure that she wasn't in the running. She figured Marlee would really love to win, and it might even make her normal again, or it could make things worse, and if Marlee did win, Elliana would be gracious.

What she cared most about was who would be voted King.

They sat talking for another ten minutes before Mr. Carmichael's voice echoed from the speakers. "It is now time to present your Spring Formal King and Queen. The envelope please."

Mrs. White hurried over to hand him a large white envelope, and Elliana found herself crossing her fingers.

"When I call your name, please come forward and join me on the stand. In third place, we have Quintin Charles and Keisha Fox." The crowd cheered as the two walked to the stand, and Elliana hollered. "In second place, we have Burke Bradford and Hollie Phillips." Elliana and Cai clapped their hands, and Elliana hooted. "And your Spring Formal King and Queen are...Bobby McCleod and Marlee Mooney!"

The room burst with applause, and Elliana hooted and hollered. This was a turning point for her because she felt like she finally atoned for that half-comment to Bobby in seventh grade, and Granger's sociability was partly to thank. She was proud of her classmates for taking the high road and voting for someone who needed the boost, who needed to be shown that there was still good in the world. She forgave herself for seventh grade.

Elliana wanted to give her best to Marlee and have one last dance before they left. The lights dimmed slightly and the DJ began playing a slow country love song as the three couples began their royal dance on the floor. Marlee looked happy with her title even though Burke wasn't the King. When the crowd joined in, Cai took Elliana's hand and pulled her close as they stepped and swayed to the music.

After the song ended, Elliana pushed away her insecurities, hurried over to Marlee with a warm embrace, saying, "I'm so happy for you, Marlee! Congrats!"

Elliana was glad to feel Marlee hug her back and hear her whisper, "Thanks, Ellie." And just like that the hug was over. She gave Bobby a quick hug and a "You deserved it," as her classmates began swarming. Because there were many people who wanted to talk to the Royal court, Elliana couldn't find Burke, Keisha, or Quintin in the crowd, so she retreated with Cai to a small couch in the corner and kicked off her heels. The balls of her feet throbbed from pressure.

She tugged on his sleeve. "Marlee hugged me back. Maybe things will be okay with us now."

"Maybe so." Cai was deep in thought.

They left the dance fifteen minutes later to change clothes and head over to the rec center for After-Formal.

Cai dropped Elliana off ten minutes before curfew, staying in good favor with her father, leaving her with a gentle kiss on her hand.

∾

"She really said that? You know it's not true, right?" Another sucker punch from Marlee. Was this ever going to end?

"I don't believe it for a second, but I wanted you to know what she was saying," Cai said. "I know it's a lie. You didn't even know who I was before we started dating, mostly because I didn't want you to. I was careful because I didn't want who I was to affect how you felt about me. And I know you weren't exactly on good terms with her when we met either—it's not like you'd be spilling your guts to her about me. It's an obvious fabrication."

"Why does she do this to me?" Elliana was hurt and exasperated by another betrayal. Elliana sat on the couch next to Cai in his family room blinking away her tears.

While dancing with Cai at Spring Formal the night before, Marlee played the she-devil, trying to poison Cai against her.

"Who knows why she said that, Ellie. Maybe it was jealousy because you were dancing with Burke, or because you were the most dazzling girl at the dance last night. The truth is that you might never know what happened with her or why she has turned on you."

"I know, but going behind my back, telling you I'm a 'gold-digger,' and that I only like 'rich boys,' is just crap!" Granted, Cai's family was affluent, and Burke's family was well-off, but their money had nothing to do with her liking them. "Besides, your dad is the wealthy one. It's not like I can get my gold-diggin' claws on his money by going out with you." She formed her hands into eagle talons.

"You sort of can," Cai said with a perplexed look. "You didn't read that article in the paper earlier this year?"

She looked sheepish. "I don't read the paper."

"Leo Wittington's Oldest Trust Baby Comes of Age." He waived his palms in the air and waited for a reaction but was only met with a confused and blank stare. "If you have no clue what I'm talking about, it's just further proof that she is inventing lies. My dad won a huge case several years back—one of the biggest he's ever won—and he was on the local news for a week. When asked what my dad planned to do with his share, he said he would donate a portion of the surplus to a fund for kids with kidney disease and the rest he was putting into three trust funds for his kids. When I turned twenty-one several months ago, I got access to my trust fund. It was big news in Boise, and the newspaper ran an article about how much I was worth, but I declined to do an interview. I hope they don't drag my sisters through the same thing when they turn twenty-one. I think the news angle was to show whether my dad really did what he said he'd do with the money.

"After that story hit, I had all these new 'friends' coming out of the woodwork," he said, using his fingers to imitate quotation marks. "Everyone wanted to be buddy-buddy with me, and it was especially bad with the girls, which is why I didn't want you to know. I wanted you to like me for me, and not because of money."

Elliana cocked her head to the side. "But you've worn the same outfit more than once, and you drive a Chevy truck."

"First of all, yes, the trust fund is a nice chunk, but it's not millions like everyone was assuming, and I'm using it to pay for college and pilot school. Second of all, my dad encourages me to donate to charity, and my mom tries to keep me humble by telling me stories about how money has ruined good people. When I was in middle school, a few of the kids guessed that my dad made a lot of money. They called me the 'son of an ambulance chaser.' I wanted to become invisible. Flaunting money only invites trouble, and driving a Jag or a Lambo would attract the wrong people. I've love the way my truck drives, but to be honest, I've also put a lot of upgrades into it, more than you probably realize.

"I had a girlfriend when I turned twenty-one and before the newspaper ink had even dried, she suddenly wanted me to help her pay for rent, to co-sign on a car, to buy her jewelry, et cetera. I got out of that relationship as fast as I could. The last reason I want people to like me is for my inheritance."

"You're so good at acting normal that I didn't even know you had any yourself."

"I'm not acting. It's who I am." He played with a curled strand of her hair.

"That's what I meant. You're so down-to-earth. And fun, and smart, and sweet. Are you sure you're real?" She reached over to pinch his arm.

He put his arm around her and gave her a squeeze. "I'm real. Real enough to make mistakes and get hurt and fall too fast."

"Good. No secrets, then." As soon as the words escaped her mouth, she was seized with guilt for the secret she'd been keeping. Perhaps it wasn't so much a secret as it was information. She needed to tell him, but how could she broach the subject? Her mind was skipping like a stone tossed on choppy ocean water.

A few moments later, he placed his uncut gem in her palm, folded her hand over it, and said, "Tell me what's on your mind. Are you still mad about what Marlee said?"

"I'm not going to let her get under my skin, but that's not what I was thinking about. How'd you know that I had something on my mind?"

"Your forehead wrinkle."

"Oh, I didn't realize it did that." She rubbed her forehead as if to smooth it out and then looked at her hands as she fidgeted with the rock. "I'm not sure even how to say this, but I think you should know. When I was dancing with Burke last night, he caught me off guard by asking if he had completely lost his chance with me. I told him that I had strong feelings for you, and that he might have a chance only if things don't work out between you and me. I would have told you sooner, but I didn't want that to be the most prominent memory of Spring Formal. I wanted our memories to be about us."

"How much do you still like him?" He looked curious but not mad.

"I don't know. My feelings for him were definitely starting to fade the past few weeks, but during that dance, I realized that I wasn't completely over him yet. Horrible timing, huh?"

Cai asked her what she wanted to do, and she told him she didn't want to break up—she wanted to see how things worked out with each other first.

He put his arm around her shoulder. "I definitely don't want to break up or lose you, so please understand that. But what if we don't date exclusively so you are free to try things out with Burke?"

Elliana shook her head in confusion and felt her stomach sinking. "Burke said he would wait. Does your suggestion have anything to do with what Marlee told you?"

"Not at all, I promise."

"Are you breaking up with me?"

He retracted his arm from behind her and turned towards her, holding both of her hands in his. "No, never. That is not my intention because you are the only girl I want to be with. But I don't want you to wonder what would have happened with Burke if the timing had been better. I want you to choose me because there is no one else in the world you'd rather be with. If your heart is torn between two people, you can't ever give it fully to either one of us. I want you to be certain of who you want, whether it's Burke or me or someone else."

It made sense, but it felt achy. "Doesn't that scare you? It really scares me—not knowing what will or won't happen."

"Of course it scares me a little, but I've got a feeling everything will work out the way it's supposed to, and we'll all be better because of it."

Elliana looked down. "I don't want to hurt anyone or inflict any unnecessary pain on myself or anyone else either."

Cai gently lifted her chin so that she was looking directly into his eyes. "A little bit of pain in the beginning might save you from a heck of a lot more pain in the end. I don't want you to have any regrets about who you're with. I'm willing to let you see other people so that you never have the nagging wonder of what could have been. My goal is a healthy relationship."

Her lips began to tremble, and she looked across the room at a painting of a horse to buy herself a moment to control her emotions.

He leaned away from her and put his hands behind his head and closed his eyes, like he was lost in thought. When he shifted away from her, she felt a stabbing pain in her chest from fearing she could lose him. Perhaps permanently.

She could lean forward and kiss him while his eyes were still closed. Wouldn't she know from the kiss whether or not she should take a step back from her relationship with Cai? With that thought, the urge to kiss him surpassed any previous urge. She touched her fingertips to her lips as she contemplated what it would feel like if her lips met his. Then she remembered Rose had said that she would inevitably choose the one she kissed in order to keep her heart sincere. That wouldn't be so bad to choose Cai though, would it? He was everything she'd ever wanted so far: handsome, funny, kind, gentle, dreamy, intelligent. But she would be toying with her heart, and if she was meant to be with Burke, she might regret not knowing that sometime down the road.

She lamented that she could lose Cai in the process of trying things out with Burke, only to find out things would never work out between her and Burke. She would surely regret that more. Her mind felt bogged down, stuck, sad.

The timing was terrible—for endless months she had wanted Burke to see her as a girlfriend, and now when she was so close to closing that door he had to waltz back in, all charming and handsome, and ask for redemption with his pleading blue eyes.

Cai's eyes were still closed, like he was uncomfortable.

"Are you okay?" she asked.

"Yeah. Just thinking."

"How would it all work if we weren't dating exclusively? Does that mean we would still go out occasionally?"

He opened his eyes and made eye contact with her. "Of course, as long as you want to, Ellie. I would love to still be able to talk to you on the phone and take you out, but it's all up to you."

"Why are you making me make the decision?"

"Because I don't want you to resent me some day if I manipulated you."

Maybe he was noncommittal. Maybe he wanted to try things out with someone else. Right now, all she could think about was how much easier it would be if he would just come right out and say he was not giving her up, not for anything. She almost wanted him to put up a fight, but he didn't.

"Are you going to let me go that easily?" she asked softly.

"No. Who said I'm letting you go at all? I'm just giving you more choice."

"I know, but it feels more final than that. Like we are breaking up."

"That's not what I meant when I said it was all up to you. I meant that I will still call you, and I will still ask you out, and still try to make you think about me all day long instead of him, but you have every right to tell me no."

Her heart calmed only slightly. "Okay. I like the sound of that. So you'll call me tomorrow?" She leaned her head on his chest and felt the weight of his arm settle on her shoulder.

He squeezed her tight. "Of course. I'm not going down without a fight, baby. Not over you."

When she tried to return the alexandrite stone later that evening, he refused it and said, "Hang on to it. It will give you reason to think about me."

CHAPTER EIGHTEEN

Payback

THE CONVERSATION AFTER SCHOOL on Monday was just as awkward as the one she had with Burke at Spring Formal a few days earlier. But it got the job done because Burke had invited Elliana over to his house to watch a movie on Wednesday evening.

After finishing her calculus and Spanish homework on Wednesday, Elliana drove to Burke's house. She didn't even have to ring the doorbell because Burke was waiting.

"Ellie," he said, giving her a hug.

"Sorry I'm a little late. Calculus was rough." She followed Burke through the entry way full of shoes and backpacks and into the kitchen where she saw his mom.

"Hi, Mrs. Bradford."

"Ellie, it's good to see you. It's been a while." His mom patted her on the back.

Burke's younger brothers and sister came running in from outside and greeted Elliana. His sister Kylie, who was ten years old and the youngest, gave Elliana a tight hug around the waist.

"Don't worry, Ellie, my mom is bribing them with ice cream sandwiches and popcorn to leave us alone."

Elliana smiled but didn't say anything, not wanting to hurt anyone's feelings nor to show her interest in being alone with Burke to watch a movie. "What are we watching?"

"An old movie that's supposed to be really funny."

They walked downstairs to the movie room. Last year Burke's dad converted the oldest brother's bedroom in the basement into a theater room with two rows of stadium seating in the back, a couch in the front row, a projector, and a silver screen large enough to take up almost the entire short wall. She sat on a couch next to Burke in their movie room with their shoulders touching as they watched a movie and snacked from the same bowl of salty pretzels and buttery popcorn.

Elliana had a gift for making a mess when she ate. She dropped popcorn half a dozen times on the couch, and this last time, a few pieces of popcorn fell smack dab between her leg and his. She reached down to recover the popcorn, grazing Burke's outer thigh.

"Ellie, are you coming on to me? If you wanted a reason to goose me, you could have just asked."

She elbowed him in the side, and then leaned away slightly to get at the popcorn that had rolled underneath her at this point. Perhaps to get her back for the jab in the ribs, Burke started tickling her side. She turned towards him in an effort to push him away, but ended up curling forward laughing hysterically and yelling for him to stop, issuing a false threat of losing bladder control if he didn't.

He paused for a minute giving her a skeptical look and then said, "I doubt that. You wouldn't dare ruin my dad's leather couch."

"Shut up, I'm going to blame it all on you," she said between laughs. With a burst of strength, she lunged forward with both hands, trying to disarm him, but he grabbed her wrists. "What are you going to do now, ninja?"

Being restrained just made her squirm all the harder as she tried to wriggle free, and she playfully threw her knee toward Burke, which sent the bowl of popcorn and pretzels flying off the couch all over the floor. At this point, she was laying down on the couch with her feet still on the ground, and he was on his knees hovering over her, still holding her wrists, laughing. He lowered his face and puckered his lips, threatening to drop spit on her.

She could only move her head side to side and yell, "No, don't spit on me, please."

He paused. "I won't, I promise." He was staring at her now. She stared back at him; he was no longer wearing a laughing smile, but a charming one. "Have you kissed Cai yet?" he asked all of a sudden, pulling her upright and letting go of her wrists, but holding on to one of her hands instead.

Her eyes grew wide with the question, not sure whether to say, "Why do you care?" or "None of your business," or just admitting, "No, not yet." Or maybe even lie and say, "Yeah, we make out all the time." What would he think if she had kissed him? But the only reason she was willing to date both of them non-exclusively was because she hadn't kissed either of them.

"Why do you ask?" she said.

"Just curious. Have you?"

"No, not yet. Although I'm surprised he didn't try a few times." She figured it would be easier to turn the conversation on Burke because what she wanted to know was whether or not he had kissed Marlee, or the other way around, so she asked, "Have you kissed anyone since you and Zaylee broke up in January?"

He nodded. "Sort of."

"What do you mean sort of? How do you sort of kiss someone?"

"Marlee kissed me. I guess I kissed back for a split second but ended it and told her I wasn't interested in that kind of relationship with her."

"When did that happen?" she said, pretending not to care a rat's tail about the matter, though it made her mad.

"At Spring Formal. Before you and I danced."

"Did you like it?" She wondered if this line of conversation was more comfortable than about her and Burke starting a relationship.

He gave her a look that said, If I liked it that much I would have kept kissing her. "No. I just wanted it to be someone else." He paused. "Like you."

She couldn't prevent her heart from skipping a beat and wondered how they were going to talk without it getting weird, like it inevitably had the last few times they talked about themselves as a couple. All she could think to do was smile. No words formed on her tongue. Maybe if she used humor it would lighten things a bit. "Now why in the world would you want to kiss me?"

"Because you're pretty, and it could be fun...." His eyes were clearly darting back and forth between her eyes and her lips, which made her nervous.

"But I don't kiss on the first date, and technically this is our first date," she said.

"First date? We've held hands before, and we've danced really closely, and you've been over to my house roughly four thousand times. So we've been on four thousand dates, and you've totally been trying to kiss me ever since the movie started."

"Nice try. You were never interested in me those times."

"What about kissing on a second date?"

"Let me put it this way: Cai and I have been on six dates at least, and we still haven't kissed. Well, he's kissed my hand."

Before she could even process what was happening, Burke lifted the hand he was holding to his mouth and kissed it. "Like that?"

It was a sweet kiss on her skin and it made her smile. "Weasel."

"What's with him not kissing you if he really likes you?"

"Because remember we made that deal about our first kiss? He left it all up to me to decide when I was ready."

"Well isn't Mr. Amazing gallant," Burke said. "Are you ready to kiss him?"

"Sometimes I think I am, and then the likes of you barge in and invite me over for a movie, and then that," she said, pointing to the mess of food all over the carpet, "and kissing my hand."

"How are we going to know if there's a spark between us if we don't kiss? It's not like we don't know each other well enough, or that we need to spend more time together to build our friendship." He lowered his voice ever so slightly. "I think we're at a point where we need to test the waters."

He had a good point. They knew each other well because they had spent so much time together over the past several years. He was her best friend, and she told him most everything that had gone on in her life, and maybe it was in the interest of time to see if there was anything more between them than just being friends. But then she remembered what Rose had taught her in The Garden. What if she kissed Burke and then lost her feelings for Cai? She really didn't want that to happen. Cai was special, and he made her feel like nobody else did. Even sitting there talking with Burke felt different—a different kind of really good feeling. No, she couldn't kiss Burke yet. He'd have to wait, too.

She winked. "Good things come to those who wait."

He smiled in defeat, intertwined his fingers with hers, and leaned back on the couch. "Okay, sugar lips, let's finish the movie."

Elliana smacked her lips and said, "Yep, cotton candy lip gloss today."

They had missed a chunk of the movie, but they didn't skip back to the where they had left off. The main character was just discovering that her scoundrel of a neighbor was stealing water from her parent's home to water his own lawn and garden.

"I forgot to tell you," Burke said, "that I've seen Mr. Wolfe across the street doing the same thing to the widow that lives next door to him."

"That doesn't surprise me. Mr. Wolfe is a weasel."

"I thought I was a weasel. I refuse to be compared to lurky Mr. Wolfe."

Wolfe was one of those neighbors who had to have the most chaotic clustering of flowers, the greenest grass, and a violent assortment of miniature wooden windmills, gnomes, mushrooms, cherub statues, and bird baths. He was a bit on the nosy side, and was overly-friendly at times, especially to teenage girls and pretty women, despite the fact that he was not worth looking at once. Worse yet, he gardened in short-shorts, which had traumatized her more than once. How his fuddy-duddy wife put up with antics like his was incomprehensible.

The widow next to Mr. Wolfe was a very sweet elderly

woman who had a beautiful garden with flowers that never died nor wilted. Her late husband had always planted a garden and tended them throughout the years, and now that he was gone, she kept her garden bright by planting plastic flowers around her yard that she could admire year-round.

Burke popped a pretzel in his mouth. "I see him hook up his garden hose to the faucet by her garage and water his lawn and flowers, early in the morning. Probably because of water rationing."

"Are you kidding me? Poor Widow Jones. I can't believe he would steal city water from an old woman who's probably living on social security."

"Are you thinking what I'm thinking?"

Elliana's smile grew wide with curious anticipation. "Yes, what are we going to do?"

"We need to put something in his hose to teach him a lesson."

"Like a snake." She paused to think. "Wait, I'm not touching a snake. And I guess it would be hard to make the snake stay in the hose, although I think he totally deserves a slithery surprise."

"We need to think of something that won't do permanent damage, but that will stop him from ever stealing her water again." They both fell silent as ideas began to sprout in their heads.

"We could just tell him that we know what he's doing and that we're going to tell Widow Jones," Elliana said.

"What is she going to do about it? She's a little old lady, and he steals water from her because she's mostly helpless. Even if she called the cops, that wouldn't guarantee he'd stop. He'd just be more careful."

By the end of the evening they had devised a two-step plan: a note tonight, and payback tomorrow after dark. They shook on it. Tonight they would clean up the popcorn and pretzels on the carpet, and then tuck a note under the wiper blade on Mr. Wolfe's windshield that said, "We're on to you, Mr. Wolfe."

Burke walked her to her car that night and gave her a bear hug, swinging her around in a circle, and asked, "What are you doing Friday night?"

ৼ

Burke and Elliana giggled and laughed all through lunch on Thursday with the prospect of carrying through on their sinister payback plan. Marlee seemed to snarl at their sudden secretiveness. He told Marlee he wasn't interested in "that kind of a relationship," but it probably looked like Burke was headed towards that kind of relationship with Elliana.

As the bell rang signaling that lunch period was over, Keisha sidled up to Elliana on the way out and asked how things were with Burke.

"Really good. I went over to his house yesterday and we watched a movie. It was so much fun. And he held my hand."

Keisha's eyebrows danced momentarily. "What does Cai think about all of this?"

"He doesn't want to know the details of my dates with Burke, but Cai and I have plans on Saturday to go to a hot spring."

Keisha asked, "Who do you like more?"

"Don't know. That's all I thought about last night. It's different with both of them: one is electric, and the other is comfortable and fun, but still exciting."

"I overheard Marlee telling Burke that you get your kicks from leading guys on, so watch your back."

That hurt. "Yeah, me and my long list of boyfriends. Pages

and pages. Two guys finally show a little interest in me and all
of a sudden I'm some sort of flirtatious tease who uses guys."
It was apparent that Marlee wasn't going to let this go. Such a
waste of energy. And it honestly bugged her that she was being
labeled as a user, when the real problem was the many guys
who used girls like dollar-store toys.

In the middle of doing her English homework after school,
Cai called, and Elliana answered on the first ring.

They talked for a few minutes before Cai asked if she still
wanted to go to the hot spring on Saturday, to which she said,
yes, of course, but she had forgotten about Abbie's district track
meet scheduled on Saturday morning, so she wouldn't be free
until noon.

"Don't worry about it. I can come pick you up from the track
meet, and then we'll drive up to the hot spring from there."

She remembered that Burke would be at the track meet as
well, which had the potential to be really weird, but she wanted
to see Cai, and she reasoned to herself that Cai would only be
picking her up, not staying the whole time. "Okay, want to pick
me up at noon? Abbie should be done racing by then."

"Sure. Can't wait to see you. I've been thinking about you all
week, and now I don't even have finals or homework to distract
me."

After slipping her finished homework into her backpack, she
ran upstairs to change into dark clothes.

When she arrived at Burke's house, it was still light outside,
so they sat in the front room and watched out the window for
any sign of the Wolfes. His wife, nicknamed Fuddy-Duddy by
Burke's dad, was in the front yard trimming the grass along

the edge of the garden with scissors. Their long-haired black cat stepped carefully along the stone edging toward Fuddy-Duddy, making a spectacle of itself by rubbing up against her legs, curling its tail upward and licking her face. Cats were so presumptuous.

A few minutes later, Elliana followed Burke into his three-car garage to fill up the reservoir attachment with football field chalk paint. They would put it between the two hoses that Widow Jones had on the outside garage wall. If Mr. Wolfe decided to steal water from that hose, he would end up painting his lawn and garden white.

"Should we test it to make sure it works?" Elliana asked.

"I guess we could. That way we know if we have added enough chalk paint. Let's try it out in the backyard."

In his fully fenced backyard, Burke hooked the chalk-paint-filled reservoir up to the hose and turned the water on. He sprayed the lawn on the side of the house that was rarely used, spelling out "B+E" and then turned off the water. The chalk paint seemed to work just fine. He removed the reservoir and reattached the hose to the faucet.

Elliana turned the faucet back on. "We should rinse the hose out to make sure there isn't any more paint left in it. We don't want to prank your parents."

It only took a few seconds before the water began running clear, and only a few seconds later she got hit in the leg with a blast of cold water. Elliana looked up at Burke. "You rat! You're asking for it!"

Burke was laughing until he got hit in the head with a handful of mulch. He dropped the hose to knock the mulch out of his hair, which gave Elliana just enough time to seize the hose and aim it at his chest. She knew he would be quick in his revenge, it took all of five seconds for Burke to retrieve the hose.

"Don't spray me!" She ran toward the sliding door, which Burke's mom happened to be opening at that moment.

"Burke, don't you dare spray Ellie!" His mom eyed Elliana's wet pant leg and Burke's dripping shirt.

Elliana stuck out her tongue at Burke, looking pleased at the timely intervention. The whole neighborhood probably heard her scream. Burke dropped the hose and moved toward the faucet to turn it off, which satisfied his mother, who went back inside. Elliana had planned to tackle him by jumping on his back as he was facing the faucet. She crept toward him, and Burke surprised her by spinning around and giving her a bear hug. Water from his shirt seeped onto hers.

"There. Payback." He let go and took a step back.

Elliana tugged at the front of her black long-sleeved t-shirt which was wet and clingy. "You're not going to win me over with your brotherly or Wolfey love."

He grabbed one of her hands. "Sorry. I couldn't help it. You're just so huggable." Maybe it wasn't the way he said the words as much as it was the look he gave her—one of those puppy dog looks that was hard to stay mad at.

"Fine, but I'm going to need a new black shirt if we're going through with our plan."

"You can borrow one of mine." He pulled her hand and brought her closer. "And since you're already soaked, I can steal another hug, and it won't be one of those offensive brotherly hugs, or the creepy Mr. Wolfe hugs." He bent towards her, since he was at least a head taller, and wrapped his arms around her, pulling her close for a brief, firm hug, his face getting danger-ously close to hers which caused her stomach to tighten in an attempt to keep the butterflies calmed. But he leaned his head and rested his cheek on hers, and whispered in her ear, "You are so cute and irresistible when you're trying to be mad, which isn't good motivation for me to not kiss you."

She pulled away and gave him a look to behave himself.

They kicked off their wet shoes by the back door and went inside. Burke ran to his room to find a shirt for Elliana. Kylie flitted over to her, dressed in a flowered nightgown, to give her a hug, but Elliana warned her, "Your big brother got my shirt wet, so you might not want to hug me just yet."

Kylie hugged her anyway but was careful not to get wet. "I got an A+ on my spelling test today! I was the only one!"

"Good job, Kylie!"

The ten-year old Kylie leaned up on her tiptoes and whispered, "I think my brother likes you. I heard him talking to my mom last night."

Elliana smiled as Kylie skipped away.

It only took Burke a minute to come bounding down the steps offering her one of his black t-shirts that said "I've Seen Sasquatch" across the back with a picture of a deranged-looking gorilla man on the front. "It's even my favorite shirt, just to prove how sorry I am."

"Oh, please. You're not all that sorry."

He smiled and told her to change in the bathroom. She had seen him wear this t-shirt many times, and its smooth cottony texture felt good against her cold skin. It smelled just like him—sporty and wonderful. She looked in the mirror to see how big the shirt was on her. Not terribly big, because Burke was more toned than built.

When she emerged from the bathroom with her wet shirt folded up, he said, "My favorite shirt on my favorite girl."

They sat down next to each other on the couch in the family room, Elliana being careful not to get the couch wet from her pant leg. "So Kylie tells me you've been talking to your mom about me."

"The little eavesdropper. What did she say?"

"Just that she thinks you like me."

"I don't know where she got that impression," he said with a look that meant otherwise.

"What changed your mind?"

"Guys can be pretty dense. I remember that Zaylee tended to get jealous of you when we were going out, but I assured her that we were best friends, and nothing more. And that's how I felt at the time. I guess that's how I kept thinking because I'm terrible at taking hints. It didn't really cross my mind until that night Marlee asked me to Spring Formal, and you and I had that talk when I drove you home."

"I was so worried you would think I was wacko and never talk to me again."

"It actually kind of woke me up," Burke said. "Sorry I was so dense."

"Do you remember when we got called down in March to get our yearbook picture taken for 'Cutest Couple that Never Was'?"

Burke nodded. "I was actually surprised by that."

"Why?"

"I don't know. I guess because other people thought we would make a cute couple and I hadn't thought of us like that."

"Why did you hold my hand during that scary movie?" Elliana asked.

"Because you were scared and... I didn't want you to be."

"Oh. And it was just your average, run-of-the-mill friendly

hand-holding session? No butterflies?"

"It was comfortable, and was fun, but I don't remember butterflies."

"Okay." She readjusted her shirt. "Do you get butterflies now, like when you hug me or hold my hand?"

He held her hand for a moment or two and then brought it up to his heart so she could feel the powerful thud within his chest.

Her lips drew into a satisfied smile. "What's the difference now?"

"I was thinking about that last night. I've tackled you, tickled you, and tried to drop spit on you before—"

"Yeah, way too many times."

"But when I did it last night, it wasn't the same. All I could think about was…, well, you know what I felt like doing. The only way I can explain it is that you've been my best friend for years, and during that whole time you never had a boyfriend. You were always there. I wonder if it took you getting a boyfriend to make me wise up and realize you weren't always going to be hanging around as my single best friend."

"What's your status with Marlee? She gives me unfriendly looks at lunch, like I'm treading on her territory."

"I've flat out told her that I'm not interested in her romantically and that I want to see what happens with us. She's just clingy. Don't worry about her. She invites herself over and invites me over still, but we don't have a thing. I just think she's going through a hard time and needs someone to hang out with. She's not herself lately."

"You can say that again."

"She's not herself lately."

Elliana elbowed him in the side. "Wiseacre."

Pretty soon it was dark. They walked outside to get the reservoir attachment and crept stealthily down the side yard, through the gate, and stood under the tree by the front of his house. The only lights on at the Wolfe's were in the TV room on the opposite of the side of the house from where they planned to be. No lights at all were on in Widow Jones's house. They moved like a bullet's shadow into her yard, to the side of Widow Jones's garage, mustering as much self-control to keep from laughing and alerting the whole neighborhood that Mr. Wolfe was going to be painting his roses white.

Burke untwisted the two hoses connected to each other, attached the reservoir in between the hoses, and then tried to hide the portion with the reservoir in a nearby bush as best he could. Mr. Wolfe attached his hose to the end of the widow's, so he most likely wouldn't even realize anything had changed.

By the time the two had set foot on Burke's lawn, they were laughing hysterically and completely out of breath. Adrenaline surged through their bodies like electricity through circuits, and they fell down on the front lawn under the large maple tree and lay on their backs, laughing until their sides ached.

"I can't wait to see his face...when he realizes...there are consequences...to stealing water from widows." Burke was still laughing which made it hard to talk. He told her that Mr. Wolfe usually waters around six in the morning, so he would watch before school and let her know how it went.

"Are you sure Widow Jones won't be using her water in the meantime? What if she gets chalked?" She would feel awful if the prank backfired on Widow Jones—she wouldn't be able to live with herself and would have to confess.

Burke reassured her that Widow Jones had a sprinkler system for the lawn, and her flowers didn't need water, obviously, and he promised to remove the reservoir as soon as the prank had been played.

Elliana held up two crossed fingers.

Burke stood up and pulled Elliana by the hand, and they went in the front door.

"What have you two been up to?" his dad asked as he walked from the den. He looked like an older version of Burke but with dark hair and a goatee.

"Just spying on the Wolfe's," Burke said.

His dad just laughed and walked into the kitchen. "It's a school night, kids."

"We know." Burke turned to Elliana. "Just come over tomorrow about six and I'll get a movie. I'm inviting the usual suspects, too."

"See you tomorrow." She pulled her keys from her pocket and called down the hall. "Goodnight, Mr. Bradford."

"Goodnight, Ellie."

Burke walked her to her car and called her the cutest Sasquatch believer, then gave her a hug similar to the one in the backyard that soaked her shirt.

CHAPTER NINETEEN

Mixed Messages

FRIDAY WAS THE FIRST DAY in a long time that she didn't have homework. Her weekend seemed promising: Friday night in Burke's theater room watching a movie with her friends, Saturday morning at the track meet, and Saturday afternoon with Cai at the hot spring.

She spruced up her hairdo, re-curling some of the ends, freshened up her makeup, and looked at her watch, which read 5:02. She would still have to wait nearly another hour and was bored—or maybe just a little too excited for movie night. Abbie was at a track team dinner with her parents, so Elliana was itching for something to do, someone to hang out with. She picked up her cell phone and texted Burke.

I know the party starts at 6, but can I come early? :)

Burke's phone buzzed with an incoming text message. He had set it down on the couch to help his mother put away the groceries, some of which were for his movie night. Marlee's curiosity drove her to pick up his phone. A text message from Ellie.

Upon reading the message, she began to seethe for the third time that day. The first time was when she saw Elliana and Burke talking in the hallway by his locker, a little too closely; Burke was playing with her hand, looking at Elliana the way he should have been looking at her.

The second time was when she saw a black shirt folded on the entryway table at Burke's house, and when she'd asked Burke whose it was, he'd smiled and said, "Ellie's. She left it here last night."

She had kissed Burke two weeks before Spring Formal, and he had kissed back. And he had kissed back about a week ago. She thought she was finally getting somewhere with Burke, but then he'd pushed her away when she tried to kiss him at Spring Formal last weekend.

She turned around to look in the kitchen where she saw Burke was still bringing in bags of groceries from the SUV in the garage. She picked up the cell phone and hit reply, making sure to mimic Burke's complete-sentence texting style.

Sorry, Ellie. I have to cancel. Family thing came up.

Marlee felt a slight twinge of guilt before she hit send, but it vanished as quickly as it took their last kiss to end. The reply came immediately.

Ok. So sad. I wanted to see you. Call me later.

Marlee could let it go at that and not respond to Elliana's last text, or she could send that adorable little Elliana packing.

I hate to do this with a text. But I don't think it's going to work out between us. Sorry.

Elliana sucked in her breath as if she had gotten sacked in the stomach. He was breaking it off with a stupid text message? And especially after spending Wednesday and Thursday together. Why had she been so stupid to think that Burke liked her as much as she had liked him? Maybe she should have let him kiss her. Or maybe she never would have been his type. At least the mystery was over, even though it was so unlike Burke to text her a message like that. Maybe he would call later and explain things.

She threw her phone at the recliner across the room, flopped onto the couch, rolled onto her stomach, and buried her head in the cushions. A few tears flowed onto her forearms before she decided she wasn't going to cry. Her heart couldn't be entirely broken by him because she had given at least half of it to Cai.

She ran upstairs and grabbed the alexandrite from her nightstand and put it in her pocket, then picked up the phone and dialed Cai.

"Ellie? I didn't expect to hear from you tonight. What's up?"

"Change of plans. Are you busy?" Her voice quivered slightly.

"Not just yet. I'm supposed to be heading out the door in an hour. You okay?"

"Yeah, I just want to get the heck out of here tonight. I'm home alone."

"Well, I don't want your father to engrave my name on any of his bullets, so I'm not going over there if you're home alone." He heard her chuckle on the other end of the phone. "Why don't you come to the movies with us?"

"Who's us?"

"Me, Christopher, Tin and a few other people."

"Am I going to be the only girl?" When she heard Sheena was coming to, she agreed to join them, and Cai offered to pick her up in 45 minutes and grab a bite to eat since neither had eaten dinner yet. "Cai, my phone is about to die, so I'll see you in a few."

Her battery was useless the past few months, and she'd have to bring a charging cord with her because her phone was so old that none of her friends had the right cord in their cars. But Cai would have his cell phone with him if she needed to make a call. She walked into the kitchen and connected her phone to her charger, left it in the charging basket, and then patted the gem in her pocket.

୭

By 6:01 Burke had already started wondering where Elliana was. She was never late. Keisha, Hollie, Quintin, Marlee, Granger, Bobby, and a few others had already arrived at his house. Well, Marlee hadn't just arrived; she had shown up early, uninvited, because she "needed to talk." But having to help with the groceries and getting the food all organized, they hadn't really been able to chat.

By 6:05 he asked out loud, "Does anyone know where Ellie is?"

"Oh, yeah, I forgot to tell you. She called about an hour ago and said she couldn't make it because she had a family thing," Marlee said as if it was useless information.

"She called you?" he said, reaching for his cell phone on the couch to check his missed call log, which didn't have Elliana's name listed.

"Yup," she said, smacking her gum. "I'll tell you the rest later."

Burke gave her an odd look, wondering since when Marlee and Elliana had been on phone-call terms since the fiasco at Eagle Island. "Okay. Let's head downstairs, guys. Dibs on the middle row." He wasn't going to be stuck with Marlee on the couch where she could hang all over him like a female version of Mr. Wolfe.

Despite how hard he tried to get Keisha and Quintin to sit next to him, by the time he got the movie running, Marlee was sitting in the seat right next to his. Keisha shrugged her shoulders at him in sympathy. He turned off the lights and took his seat.

Every time Marlee bumped him while reaching for popcorn or her drink, it just made him wonder where Elliana was. What kind of family thing did she have? Maybe she went to the track meet dinner with Abbie. He looked at his watch and decided that he'd call her. He walked into the hallway.

Her phone went straight to voicemail each time he called, which meant either she was on the other line or her phone was dead. So he tried calling her home phone, but that just rang and rang and rang. He called her cell phone again and left a message. "Hey, Ellie. It's Burke. Just calling to see how you're doing. I hope everything's okay."

Just to be thorough, he clicked into his text inbox to see if he hadn't accidentally missed a text from her. Nope. Why on earth Elliana would call Marlee to cancel was beyond him. He stood at the theater room door and motioned for Marlee.

She offered a sexy smile, smoothed out her shirt when she stood up, and followed him out of the room. "Want me all to yourself?"

He shook his head. "Actually, I was wondering what else Ellie said. She won't answer her phone."

"Oh, yeah. She said she had a family thing, and...."

"And...what?"

"And she said to tell you that things weren't going to work out between you, and that I could have you." The seductive look on her face was unmistakable.

"Marlee, I've already told you. Even if nothing happens with Ellie, nothing will be happening between us."

She glared at him. "Why don't you like me?"

"I do like you—as a friend, but not in the sense of a romantic relationship."

"What makes her so much better than me?"

"First of all, Ellie and I have been best friends for years—you should know what a great friend she can be. Second of all, since the night you asked me to Spring Formal and Ellie found out you betrayed her, she has never spoken an ill word about you. Yes, she was hurt, but she didn't tell the whole school what really happened. She could have turned everyone against you. You, on the other hand, try almost on a daily basis to talk smack about her, but I won't listen to it. She's a true friend. I admit you're beautiful, but I have a hard time trusting you. That's the big difference."

She broke down into tears, wrapped her arms around his neck and cried. "You have no idea how much I need a friend right now, how much I need you."

He knew she had been fragile lately, but her brazen behavior eroded his patience. He didn't mean to speak so harshly to her, to make her cry, so he patted her back without hugging her.

"Can we go somewhere to talk?" she said between sniffles, carefully wiping the tears from her eyes without smudging her makeup.

"Right now?"

She nodded.

He walked to the couch in the basement's family room. He sat at one end of the couch, which was a mistake, because she sat so close to him that he had no room to scoot away. "What's up?"

"I think my parents are getting a divorce." Marlee sniveled.

This sob session wasn't really what he had planned. "What happened?"

"My parents fight all the time. A little over a month ago I heard my mom accuse my dad of not loving her, and he said maybe he didn't anymore and maybe he never did. They got in a huge fight and he disappeared for three days. My mom cries all the time now, and my dad is always on edge, ready to rip someone's head off."

"I'm sorry, Marlee." He tried to assure her that everything would work out somehow, that it wasn't her fault, and that there is never a good reason to mistreat someone you love. "Just keep hoping for the best, but don't be fooled into believing that your parents don't love you if they end up getting divorced." He grabbed a box of tissues from the end table and handed it to her.

This must be the reason Marlee had been acting strangely out of character for the past month. And now that he thought about it, it was exactly four weeks ago that she had asked him to Spring Formal. Maybe her parent's fighting had a lot to do with her betraying Elliana, although it was no excuse.

Marlee cried on his shoulder for a few more minutes and then abruptly asked, "Has Jared ever said anything about me?"

"No. Why?"

"About liking me or why he doesn't like me? Anything at all?"

Burke shook his head several times. "Why? Do you still like him?"

She shook her head. "Nevermind. I was just curious. It's no big deal. We can finish watching the movie. Please don't tell anyone what I told you, please. Promise me?" She wiped at her eyes with a mascara-stained tissue.

Burke nodded and asked Marlee if she had confided in anyone else, and she said she didn't want anyone else to know.

"What about Ellie? She's still your friend, you know."

"I know." Marlee looked down at her feet. "She's loyal to a fault. The truth is that I don't hate her. But I'm not ready to tell Miss Perfect anything."

"Don't you look pretty tonight, Ellie." Cai took her hand and helped her up into his red truck and walked to the driver's side.

"Thanks." Elliana scooted next to Cai on the bench seat. "And thanks for coming to get me."

He looked at her as he backed out of the driveway. "How did you find yourself all alone tonight?"

"We were all supposed to watch a movie over at Burke's," she said, watching for his reaction, "but I got a text from him that said it was cancelled and that things weren't going to work out between us."

Cai grimaced. "He sent that in a text?"

"Yeah, but before you jump to any conclusions, I have to tell you that I can't believe he would do that. He's the type of person who would rather talk in person or on the phone than text. So that's why I'm having a hard time believing...."

Cai cleared his throat and put the truck in drive. "Have you guys been hanging out...together?"

"Are you sure you want to hear this?"

"No, not really, but I'm trying to help. I just don't want any of the kissy-kissy details," he said with a gruff laugh.

Elliana assured him they hadn't kissed and he seemed relieved. It was definitely weird to share the details of her date with Burke, but she told him anyway. "I hung out with him Wednesday and Thursday. And he acted like he liked me. Even in the hall today he was sweet to me."

"Nothing happened in between then and now?"

"Nothing that I can think of." She played nervously with her purse strap and then wished he'd hold her hand.

"Well, as much as I'd love to tell you Burke's a tactless, insensitive jerk who doesn't deserve you, his breakup text seems a little fishy to me. I think you should talk to him."

"You're probably right." Elliana didn't want to spend her Friday night with Cai lamenting over Burke, so she said, "Okay, we're done talking about Burke tonight. I'm all yours."

She felt her face flush at her comment and was surprised when he reached over and held her hand. He gave her a look to make sure it was okay with her; Elliana nodded and smiled, hoping her face wasn't as red as it felt. Her heart quickened, forcing her to take shallow breaths, and she forgot her stress. They held hands all the way to their destination.

They pulled into the parking lot to the Hamburger Hut to grab a bite to eat. Although the little burger joint was small, a line trailed almost to the door, signaling a long wait.

They stood at the end of the line, and Cai held her hand. "Don't look now, but my ex-girlfriend is over there in the corner booth. I hope she doesn't see us because she's the type that would come over and chat."

Of course Elliana had to look, but she tried to be nonchalant about it. The girl was tall, actually really tall, and slender with long straight brown hair and chunky blond highlights. Elliana could only see her from behind, but she looked pretty enough. "What's her name again?"

"Candie, sweet as sugar. Well, that's what she tells pretty much everyone she meets. It gets old."

"This is the one that...?"

"Yeah. That's the real gold-digger over there." He leaned backward against the wall, pulled Elliana toward him to block his view, and changed the subject. "Are you excited for the hot springs tomorrow?"

"Yes! I'm not going to get scalded or burned beyond recognition, am I?"

"No." He told her she'd probably read too many signs in Yellowstone, and not to worry because he's been going for several years, and the lower two pools were perfectly safe.

"Christopher isn't going to wear a speedo, is he? He totally strikes me as that type."

Cai burst out laughing, which perked up the ears of his ex-girlfriend who started walking towards them.

"Oh, great. She's seen me now."

Candie's long legs strutted over to greet him. Elliana didn't turn around until the last moment and did not expect to see someone as beautiful as the woman standing in front of her, thanks in part to her lash extensions. Candie pushed in between them to give Cai a great big hug, the kind Mr. Wolfe would relish. Cai let go of Elliana's hand and hugged back.

Ew.

"Candie, this is Elliana, my girlfriend."

The five-inch red heels that Candie was wearing made her about six feet tall, which meant she towered over Elliana. She looked down and smiled. "Well isn't she a cute little thang."

It's not like Elliana could say that she's heard so many wonderful things about this woman, so she was grasping for words as she stood there smiling. "Nice to meet you, Candie."

"You guys should come over and sit in our booth. We have room. It would be so much fun to catch up." Although she had said "you guys," she didn't take her eyes off of Cai.

Elliana couldn't blame anyone for not falling into a trance at the sight of Candie, and she felt instantly jealous while watching Cai smile and act friendly towards his ex.

When their order was ready, after looking around and not seeing an empty table, Cai said they'd stop by Candie's booth. Elliana turned away and closed her eyes to prevent anyone from seeing her eyeballs rolling around like angry marbles.

Candie beamed when they approached.

Though it was an awkward social situation—which she couldn't seem to avoid lately—Elliana was pleasant toward Cai's ex. Candie asked how they met and then talked about her glamorous life, and that's how she learned that Candie's and Cai's fathers were buddies and their families were friends. Candie was nice enough underneath her materialism, though Elliana kept getting a weird vibe from her, especially when she kept repeating, "When Cai and I were together...."

Elliana didn't want to complicate the already complicated situation with Cai, so she smiled and nodded and never let on how out of place she felt.

Ten minutes after Cai and Elliana sat down, Candie stood up and readjusted her clothing before grabbing her tray. "It was so good to run into you. Don't be a stranger, hun." Candie strutted away, never looking back.

Cai put his arm around Elliana. "Sorry about that. I was

kind of using her for her booth."

Elliana gave a questioning look.

"She might have a pretty face, but I'm over her. I promise."

Elliana hated that she laughed when she felt uncomfortable and said lies like, "Okay. No biggie." But who was she to complain when she had been out with Burke the past two days?

Elliana woke up an hour earlier than usual that Saturday morning, probably because she knew she'd see Burke. She had gotten his message after she had gotten home from her date with Cai, but it had been too late to call back, and she wished his voicemail did more to dispel her confusion from his last text message. He asked her to call him back. Was he just wondering if she was okay now that he had toyed with her and then broken things off? Too many things were going weird.

Taking a walk usually helped her think things through, so she grabbed her purple running shoes. She may not have been a cross-country runner like her sister, but she enjoyed walking, especially now that she had a companion who fluttered alongside her. Keeping a swift pace, she realized that as good as walking was for thinking, she never received answers as well as she did when she was in her Garden. When she got to a secluded spot at the end of her street, she ported to the Seeking Realm.

Wayne asked her about her day and walked her to the cottage. Then she and Rose walked through the Garden as she recounted the two evenings she spent with Burke, the break-up text message, and then the wonderful evening with Cai. The glinting foliage seemed to cheer her and buoy her spirits, and Rose was an excellent listener.

She asked Rose for advice on whether to let it go and focus

on Cai, or to pursue things with Burke. Rose asked her if she had chosen one with her heart yet. That was a hard question. She thought she had until the previous weekend when Burke waltzed in and revived her waning affections. Both were wonderful guys, but both of their relationships were different.

Rose shared her wisdom that some people are better matches for another. And then there are matches that make all the difference—the ones that bring out the best in the other, the ones that guard the other's soul.

Elliana had to admit that she and Burke pulled a prank on his creepy neighbor, and though it was for a good cause, it didn't exactly count for bringing out the best in her. She said, "I can be myself around him. He makes me feel like having fun, and I really enjoy being with him."

"What about when you're with Cai?"

"It's different, that's for sure. We don't play pranks, but we still laugh a lot. He makes me feel like a love-sick girl at times, especially when he held my hand last night."

Rose patted Elliana's knee. "Try talking to Burke to see what he's really feeling—if he has decided that you two aren't right for each other, you have your answer. If he still likes you, you may need to spend more time with each one before you make your decision. I sense you aren't quite ready yet to choose between the two, but I will give you a clue to help you on your quest: Who you choose has everything to do with saving a dying star."

That was a lot of pressure to choose right. Elliana repeated in her head several times the last thing Rose had said, but it still wasn't clear why her choice would have that impact.

Rose explained that choosing wisely for the sake of healthy, long-term relationships was foundational to Electra's revival and staving off dark power. Elliana was learning more about the human heart and her origins, and now she needed to learn to trust her own heart because her example could influence others to choose well and practice pure love, and she could be a catalyst for saving Electra from the Shadow Realm.

After saying goodbye, she ported back to the Earth Realm and quickly walked home, followed by her common-looking bird, which made her wonder how many extraordinary people were disguised by ordinary exteriors.

Because Cai would be picking her up from the track meet at noon, Elliana rode with Abbie and her parents. When she had talked to Burke at school on Friday, he had planned to meet her at 9:30 am. It was only nine o'clock, so she sat by her parents and watched and waited and watched and waited.

From where she was sitting, she could see Abbie with her pony-tail bobbing around as she warmed up, jumping and stretching to keep her muscles loose. She watched Granger walk up to her sister. Abbie quickly stood up and her whole demeanor changed—like she got nervous and was trying to impress him. Elliana sat watching the two interact, a bit of flirting coming from both, wondering how she hadn't noticed this peculiar attraction before.

"Hey, Mom. Look over there at Abbie. Do you see anything worth mentioning?"

Her mom watched Abbie for a second or two. "That boy is flirting with my Abbie." After a pause, "And my Abbie's flirting with that boy."

This, of course, got her dad's attention and he looked to his daughter, but spent more time watching Granger. "I think that boy likes Abbie."

"It's Granger, that new kid, the one who runs as fast as a bolt of lightning."

"That's the same boy who dropped her off after track practice this week," her mom said. "I didn't notice it before, but it's very obvious to me now."

"Abbie's never mentioned him to me—nothing about liking him or anything. But I can't blame him for liking her because Abbie's pretty cute," Elliana said.

"Well, he's too old for her," her dad said, "and my Abbie's too young. I may have to break his arms."

"I doubt you'll have to." Elliana laughed at her dad's over-protectiveness. "Why hasn't Abbs said anything to us? Oh wait, maybe she's afraid dad will maim any guy that shows any romantic interest in his little baby girl."

Her dad smiled, appreciating her humor. "You're my baby girl, too, you know. I don't really like the idea of you having so many dates either."

"I have to make up for lost time."

Her mom asked, "Who's winning?"

"What do you mean, Mom? The races won't start for another fifteen minutes." Elliana knew full well what her mom was getting at, but she also enjoyed teasing her mother.

"You know what I'm talking about."

Elliana shifted on the bleacher and felt the alexandrite in her pocket. "Yesterday afternoon it would have been a tie, but after last night Cai might be pulling ahead. We'll see if anything changes if Burke shows up." Not if. When. Surely he was still coming. She glanced behind the stands toward the parking lot, looking for his Tahoe, squinting from the sun glaring off the cars in the parking lot. It was still fifteen minutes before he was supposed to arrive. The weather was steadily getting warmer, and sitting in the bleachers helped her work on her farmer's tan—which was sure to look attractive when wearing a bathing suit later on.

Her thoughts jumped between the two young men in her life for the next fifteen minutes, until Burke showed his handsome face, slid down beside her on the bench, and held her hand with both of his. Her heart pounded.

"Hey, Ellie." Burke squeezed her hand and then greeted Elliana's parents.

His holding her hand made his last text even more confusing. "We need to talk," she whispered in his ear. She could wait until Abbie's first race was over and then go on a walk with Burke to see what was up. Or, she could open her phone, click on her inbox, and show Burke the text that had puzzled her for more than half a day—which is just what she did.

≈

Burke flinched. "I don't understand. Who sent this?"

"It came from your phone, silly."

"I promise you I never sent those texts. Cross my heart." Reading those messages made him a little bit angry. Maybe one of his siblings sent them, but he couldn't imagine any of them running off Elliana because they all loved her.

"Didn't you ever get my text?" She scrolled through the messages to show him the one she had originally sent.

He took the phone from her. "I don't have any messages from you in my phone from yesterday. I checked several times when you didn't show up. Take a look." He handed his cell phone to her.

"If you didn't send those messages, then who did?"

Burke thought for a minute before realizing that he had left his phone on the couch when he was unloading groceries.

Marlee. It had to have been Marlee—she was the only one at

his house that early.

But if he told Elliana who the culprit was, it would worsen their already rocky friendship, and what Marlee needed most right now was a friend, someone to lean on. She made that clear the night before. "I don't know why anyone would send that, Ellie. But none of it's true." He squeezed her hand again. "I promise. I'm always happier when I'm with you."

Elliana sighed.

His mind had been hijacked by the revelation that Marlee was trying to sabotage his relationship with Elliana, that he almost forgot what he had been wanting to tell her since 6:30 that morning.

"Ellie, oh my gosh, I've been dying to tell you the update on Mr. Wolfe. You're going to be so sad you missed it." Burke shared what he had seen that morning looking out his bedroom window. Apparently, Mr. Wolfe was so busy looking over his shoulder making sure no one was watching him, that he sprayed most of his flowers and a wide strip of his lawn before he noticed things were turning white. He had tried rinsing the white grass with the hose water, making a mess of his yard with stolen water, and finally let go of the nozzle and he hurried over to disconnect his hose. Burke thoroughly enjoyed watching Mr. Wolfe stare at his precious lawn in horror.

"I wish you could have seen it," Burke said. "It was absolutely hilarious. I laughed until I cried, and so did my brothers. Of course, we were pretty noisy when we came downstairs and my dad asked what we thought was so funny. We didn't tell him, but I'm sure he'll put two and two together by the time I get home."

❧

Elliana really hoped that her name wouldn't come up during

any conversations about the absurdity of Mr. Wolfe, the lawn lover, somehow whitewashing his own lawn. She didn't really feel badly about doing it because the man was clearly a thief, but she wasn't proud of it either. "Don't tell him I was involved. I like being up on a pedestal in your parents' minds."

"I won't tell them. Promise."

They watched Abbie run her races with a lime green cast on her arm, pulling ahead at the last second, winning both times. The Reinharts had no shame when it came to jumping and shouting in celebration, especially considering the risk Abbie was taking by running before her arm was healed. The Reinharts weren't the only ones praising their daughter; Granger looked impressed as well, making sure to congratulate her after each win with a high five and a hug.

When Elliana pointed it out, Burke agreed with her conclusion, even though neither of them had heard a peep in school about Granger and Abbie liking each other. "We could invite them to our next movie night and spy on them."

Hot Spots

AFTER AN HOUR on the road, half of it uphill, they parked at the end of the dirt road that led to the trailhead. His was the first vehicle there—the rest would be along shortly, no doubt. After Cai opened her door, Elliana jumped down and admired mother nature. The majestic lodge pole pines scraped the sky and creaked with the gentle breeze. To the north, behind some tall bushes, stood an unpainted wooden post free from markings. Pointing to the post, Cai said that his professor put it there about twenty years ago and the hot spring was a two-mile hike in.

Elliana swung her backpack over her shoulders and started up the path, gripping the shoulder straps of her bag.

The trail wasn't all that bad. Only a few spots would get steep, on the switchbacks, and Cai assured her that he would help her through the rough terrain. They ambled along admiring the loveliness of the forest and the scent of pine. As beautiful as the woods were, they were bare and dull compared to her Garden. The company was pretty good though.

The air was chilly in the shade at such a high elevation and almost felt like a fall morning. The sun winked through the tops of the trees as they walked along the mostly unbeaten path, stepping over fallen timber, and crunching the pine-needle flooring. The forest birds chirped back and forth, and Orly was easy to spot. At one point, Orly blended in with all the forest bird activity that she hardly noticed her bird at all.

The path wasn't always worn enough to know where to follow with the new growth from spring, but pressure-treated posts helped guide the way. At one point, Cai stopped abruptly to scan the scenery, not immediately sure whether the path veered to the right or left, so he looked for another hidden post.

She squinted her eyes, then pointed to the left behind a tree. As they walked in that direction, he held her hand again, causing her heart to pound and her stomach to lighten. The path led around the side of the mountain with a switchback in view, a drop-off to the left, and the mountain wall to the right. It wasn't steep enough to lose footing, and the path was about eight feet wide. Looking upward they could see the blue sky unobscured by trees because the mountain side rose up steeply. A lone cloud floated lazily near the sun.

They heard a rustling noise up the mountain. Maybe rustling wasn't the right word. It was unnerving, a noise that didn't belong. Within two heartbeats, it got louder and more unnatural.

"What was that?" Elliana blurted, stopping to look up. They were standing close together, both trying to focus their eyes on the source of the noise. Cai tilted his head and walked a step further up the path.

The sound grew louder and faster; something was approaching. Elliana first thought it might have been a deer or mountain goat scaling the side of the mountain, but there was nothing to see. A few more rapid heartbeats thudded in their chests, growing louder like the sound which resembled something heavy falling and bouncing down the rocky mountain side.

A large, car-tire-sized angular rock barreled down the mountain wall toward them, bouncing to the right, and then the left, and then the right, and then the left, like they were in the crosshairs of its taunting but deliberate aim. The rock suddenly hit a jutting out and caught air briefly before making contact again. It seemed to only have one, maybe two more bounces left before it made its lethal impact.

Elliana's legs glued themselves to the ground and her eyes widened as she followed the path of the falling rock. If she was a magnet for disaster, she could move to the left and the last bounce could project the falling rock right to where she had moved. It would surely strike somewhere within a small radius where she and Cai stood. As ludicrous as it was for a deer to stare at headlights belonging to a vehicle that could take its life, she found herself paralyzed by the same instinct to stare toward the rock and the impending collision.

She locked her gaze on the falling object, knowing that unless the jagged rock was somehow diverted in the next second, she would be a dead woman in one and a half seconds.

Suddenly, Cai yanked on her hand, grabbed her around the waist, leapt backward, and pulled hard on Elliana—all so quickly that she was unaware of where she was going to land, unsure of where the rock would strike. A deafening thud sounded in her ears just as they fell on the pine-cone laden ground with Elliana landing mostly on top of Cai. She waited, smashing her eyelids together, bracing herself for the sting of death to steal her destiny.

The shower of pebbles and debris pricked and bit her delicate skin. The cracking and pounding sounds continued, growing fainter. She didn't feel the throbbing pain yet. Perhaps her body was in shock. She could feel the quick and thunderous thud of her heartbeat pounding against her ribs—or maybe that was Cai's heartbeat she was feeling in her chest. Thud ud, thud ud, thud ud! It was then that she knew that sound, that sensation, was life rattling in her rib cage, shouting and screaming her survival. When she opened her eyes, she met Cai's paled gaze. "It missed us?"

"I guess so." He didn't say anything else right away but hugged her with one arm tight enough that she knew she wasn't dead or numb. "I thought we both were goners. It almost hit us. Did you get hurt?"

"My wrist." Only then did she realize that her wrist was aching because her hand was bent in an unnatural position. She pulled her hand back and maneuvered her wrist around in a few circles before deciding it was only cramped. "I'll be fine. What about you? You okay?"

He blinked a few times. "Okay, I guess. Just in shock. I can't get the visual out of my head of that huge rock headed right for us, big enough to have killed one of us at the rate it was falling. All I do know is that we just avoided death by some miracle."

"I couldn't move. I felt like my feet were knee-deep in mud. You saved me." As she spoke the last sentence, a wave of relief passed through her body with the realization of what had just happened. She buried her head in his neck and, to her surprise, began to sob so hard she shook.

"I'm just glad you're okay." He smoothed his hands down the back of her hair and then rubbed her back.

She was too relieved to not cry, and the tears trickled down her face. "Sorry I'm crying. I was just so scared and now I'm—"

"It's okay. I don't mind if you cry." His lips brushed against her forehead and his arms held her tight.

She wiped her eyes with her sleeve and raised her head to look at him, the man who had just saved both of their lives with his quick thinking and superhuman strength, and felt a warmth tingling within her chest. Perhaps it could be described as a *heartfelt* warmth. Or perhaps it was just a surge of gratitude at having avoided a fatal catastrophe in the mountains. She searched his eyes, but she wasn't sure if he was feeling the same thing—although she was becoming more convinced as she stared at him.

Instead of kissing her though, he shifted her to the side. Setting his feet underneath him, he helped Elliana to her feet. Maybe he didn't have that amazingly warm, tingly feeling that she had.

He held both of her hands. "Do you have any idea how badly I want to kiss you right now?"

"No," she lied. Her heart resumed pounding so loudly she thought he'd be able to hear it.

"Let's just say it's an overwhelming urge, and I'm still trying to fight it."

She gulped rather loudly. "Why fight it?"

He pulled on her hands and drew her close. "Because I promised you that it would be when you're ready."

"I think I'm ready."

"Are you sure it's not just the adrenaline?" Cai lowered his lips just a hair toward hers.

She shrugged and bit her bottom lip. "Don't you think I'd get an adrenaline rush either way?"

He lowered his lips even closer. "If I kissed you right now, it's too early for the stars to be out, and so we'd have no idea if our first kiss will make the star glow brighter."

"Yeah, but you told me that we can't even see the Pleiades before my curfew until October or something." Rocking forward on her toes, she gradually reached her lips toward his.

"Cai! Starlight!" Suddenly they were accosted by Christopher Frick and Sheena who stood about twenty yards away, Christopher looking much too pleased with his timing. "Go on. Kiss." He actually refrained from making kissing noises.

"You kind of ruined the moment, Frick." Elliana glared at Christopher. "Besides, I thought you wanted us to wait for your wedding."

"You're right, Starlight. You keep your puckered, glossy little lips off Cai for another week." He raised his eyebrows up and down. Sheena just rolled her eyes.

Cai laughed and then winked at Elliana, mouthing the word "later."

&

They finished the rest of the hike to the hot spring without incident. Three warm, clear pools were nestled in the rock of the mountain close to the rushing river. The first pool was small and flowed down into the lower two pools. The second pool was the deepest—the one that looked like you could dive in—with a smooth rock ledge on one side. The last pool was wider, but rather shallow, and had crystal blue water.

"That first pot is hot enough to scald you," Christopher said casually, "but these other two are quite nice. I, myself, will be taking a dip in the deep pool." He set his almost empty backpack on a flat rock, swiftly yanked off his shirt, and dropped his drawers revealing a pair of bright orange swim trunks. He wasted no time in jumping in the deep end of the hot pot, coming to the surface looking satisfied. "Ahh, this feels nice. Come on in, Sheena."

Sheena pulled her long, native hair into a high pony tail, stripped down to her red one-piece, and jumped in.

Cai walked Elliana to the edge of the second pool and told her to test the water of the second and third pools with her toes. The second pool was bearably hot.

"I think I want this one," Elliana said pointing to the middle pool. She set her backpack next to Cai's, which was just a step away from where he was shedding a layer of clothing. She felt the chilling bite of the crisp air on her back as she lifted off her long-sleeve t-shirt. She unfastened her button-fly jeans and felt her leg muscles tense from the cold as she stepped out of them. After adjusting her turquoise and lime one-piece that tied behind her neck, she slid into the hot blue water. It felt amazing.

Cai entered the water just after her.

As he was sliding into the water, she noticed a horizontal scar on his lower back. "What's that scar from?"

"Oh, I donated a kidney to Paige when I was a freshman in high school."

She melted that he would do that for his sister—and was amazed that he was a match. When asked why his sister needed a kidney, Cai shared that Paige had a rare kidney disease caused by her liver not making the right enzymes. Anti-rejection drugs explained Paige's babyface.

Sitting in the hot pool for forty minutes was enough to feel cooked. Elliana had been perched on the ledge, dangling her legs into the water for the last ten minutes. "Cai, do you want to go on a little hike with me?"

Christopher perked right up. "Where to, Starlight?"

"I want to look for lions, tigers, and bears for my high school science project," she said flatly. "You're not invited."

Cai laughed. "Sure, I could stand some cool air for a little bit." He hopped out of the pool and grabbed a towel from his backpack, patting his back, legs, and arms dry.

"Remember what I said, you two," Christopher said pointing to his lips.

Cai replied, "Yeah, yeah, we'll bring you back a unicorn, Frick. I know you've wanted one since the third grade."

"Whatever."

Sheena burst into laughter.

Cai and Elliana headed away from the river and up the mountain slope, talking as they walked. She asked why Christopher was making such a big deal about them kissing.

Cai said that Christopher only teased people he liked, and he figured out it was a hot button because he got a reaction from her. "He likes you and thinks you're funny. I do, too."

When the path got steep, their words became staggered as they had to pause and catch their breath. Eventually, they neared the top. They plopped down to lean against a fallen log in the sunshine.

"I still can't believe we avoided that rock," Elliana said.

Cai grabbed her hand and rubbed it with his thumb. "I know. That was so bizarre. I didn't mention it to Christopher or Sheena because he might just make fun of it, or make us think we're crazy."

"I'm sure he would. Maybe they're better off not knowing." Barely dodging the falling rock was an intense emotional experience, almost special. No one else would fully understand the horror of nearly being smashed or the joy at having been left alive.

"He's a great guy, but a ruthless teaser—as you well know."

Elliana nodded. "It'll be our little secret. But it makes me wonder why the craziest things happen when I'm with you—I morph into a damsel in distress!"

"I was thinking the same thing earlier. First you nearly flatten me with your car. Then we narrowly avoid an elk marching through our windshield, and now a falling rock."

"Are you just a magnet for bad luck? Or is it me?"

Cai grew serious. "Neither, actually. I think something's trying to keep us apart. Like we should be together, because you're good for me, and I hope I'm good for you, too."

"I like that theory." Her eyes brightened. "You are good for me. I'm always happy when I'm around you. Even if you have to save my life a few times."

Cai leaned close. "Any time."

Normally he had a wonderful woodsy smell, but now he smelled of sulfur. She smelled her own arm and was dismayed to discover that she was just as rank. "We stink."

Cai laughed. "Yeah, but hot springs are so much fun that I'm willing to smell like a rotten egg for a few hours."

A few minutes later they walked to the edge of the mountain to admire the view that stretched on for miles. Cai lowered his gaze and a wrinkle grew between his eyebrows. He pointed to a freshly disturbed patch of ground near the edge. "What does that look like to you?"

A wrinkle crept across her forehead. "Like a little crater, like someone pushed a rock out of it, off the edge." Leaning forward a little bit, Elliana could see the path where they almost died.

Neither spoke a word.

It was impossible. It was completely absurd. It was downright preposterous.

The two glanced at each other and then back down at the hollow in the ground. But there were no human tracks around—just some from animals.

After hiking back down the mountain, Cai and Elliana walked over to the hot spring pools. Cai sat down on the ledge. Christopher and Sheena were drying off next to where Elliana stood.

She looked down. "AHHH!" A black hairy spider with dots on its back ran toward Elliana's foot, so she dug her shoe into the rocky ground in an effort to smash it, but when she moved her foot, the spider got up and darted away again. It seemed to leap. It was incredibly fast, so Elliana jumped and landed her left foot on the spider, which she pressed as firmly to the ground as she could, but it scurried away again when she released the pressure.

Christopher joined the game, jumping and stomping in the direction of the nasty spider that seemed intent on getting away with all eight legs intact. He smashed his shoe down on the spider and twisted his foot about twenty times before lifting. At last it was dead, with all of its insides stuck to the bottom of Christopher's hiking shoe.

She exhaled loudly. "Thanks, Frick. It's like the dang thing was invincible."

Christopher wiped his shoe off on in the nearby brush. "I was thinking the same thing."

"Then you should have let it bite you," Elliana taunted.

"Why?" he asked.

"You know, Spiderman? It could have given you special powers."

The whole group laughed.

"But I'm already pretty powerful, so maybe you should have let it bite you," Christopher said to Elliana as he flexed his bicep.

"No way," she said with a look of horror on her face. "I loathe spiders! I don't have any problem murdering them."

"What did spiders ever do to you, Starlight?"

"I don't know, SpiderFrick. I've always hated them, for as long as I can remember."

Elliana talked for hours with Rose that night, getting her all caught up. A lot had happened since she had last been there. In her Garden, it was always easy to share her heart. She told Rose about nearly getting killed by a falling rock on the way to the hot springs, and how Cai had saved her by pulling her to the ground with him. She even told Rose that she wanted him to kiss her, but he stood up right at the moment she thought he would kiss her, and then their next moment was interrupted by Christopher and Sheena. "Why wouldn't he kiss me if the moment felt so right?

Rose smiled her wise, knowing smile and patted Elliana's hand. "Elliana, dear, that shows what's in his heart towards you. No gentleman would ever kiss a girl while lying down."

"Why?"

"It shows a lack of respect because it puts her in a compromising position. It's too easy to take advantage of someone, and it lets emotions get out of control."

"Oh. I get it."

"Cai has deep respect for you, Elliana. He is being a true gentleman and helping to protect your virtue. Never let someone kiss you while lying down."

"Okay, that sounds like great advice." Elliana's heart warmed at the realization that he hadn't kissed her during that tense moment out of respect, and she reached up and toyed with her sapphire pendant. "Rose, I think after today that I know who my heart is starting to choose."

"Good." Rose's smile flattened. "Now it's time to talk about your friends and enemies."

CHAPTER TWENTY-ONE

Publicity

"Why me?" Elliana said a little less politely than usual. "I'm not the class president, and I'm certainly not the valedictorian or salutatorian. There's got to be someone better."

Mr. Krump waited until she was finished speaking. "You're the one we need. And I apologize that we have only given you one week's notice."

Elliana's sigh came out as a huff. This was not the way her last full week of high school was supposed to go—it was Thursday, and a week from Friday was graduation. Now the last week would be pure torture.

"Mr. Carmichael specifically said he wanted you to speak at graduation. He said the graduating class could learn a lot from you, especially after recent events."

"But what about the valedictorian?"

"He's speaking first. You'll be right after him."

He had to have known this was going to be a hard sell. Apparently, administration heard rumors that the graduates planned a walk-out if the second speaker stayed on the program because she was going to misuse the platform to shame a political view held by many. During a staff meeting, when they talked about finding a replacement speaker, Elliana's name came up more than once. Mr. Carmichael made an executive decision and had given the task to Mr. Krump because he had a better relationship with her.

Mr. Krump didn't waver. "You know as well as I do that the valedictorian doesn't have a good rapport with your classmates. The faculty are very worried about how good his speech will be, and we can't write it for him. But we can follow it up with a great speech, your speech."

"I don't mean to be so difficult, Mr. Krump, but first of all, I'm not much of a public speaker, which is why I have never run for class presidency—only a student council rep—to avoid giving any type of speech during elections because I am scared to death of public speaking! I made a fool of myself in the fifth-grade spelling bee. I clammed up and couldn't talk. And I still can't. Second of all, who cares what I have to say?"

"The leader of the school does. I do. Your friends do. Your classmates do."

"I can't say yes. Anyone who knows me knows I avoid public speaking at all costs—it's not a skill I was born with."

Mr. Krump rubbed his chin like he was trying to erase a frown. "If you don't, you're letting them win."

"Not necessarily. Everyone has haters, that doesn't mean I have to give a speech to them."

"In a way you're right," Mr. Krump said. "But in a way, I'm right. Your classmates need to hear what you have to say—most all of them would listen to you and would be better off for it."

"If, IF, I said yes, how long would my speech have to be?"

"Five, six minutes tops." Mr. Krump couldn't hide the smile that was forming. "The principal said he was impressed with how you handled yourself with the whole plagiarism incident.

We could all learn a lot from you. You have wisdom to share, and so Mr. Carmichael believes you're the right one to address your fellow graduates." He lowered his voice and informed her she could also enter her speech in the local academic scholarship contest.

"Fine. I'll do it. But don't complain if I ruin graduation." She swallowed hard and felt nauseated.

"No one is worried about that, I assure you."

"I am." She leaned her head back in frustration before rising.

Mr. Krump stood and walked her to the door. "I know you can do this. You'll do great."

"Thanks, Mr. Krump. I hope for my reputation's sake you're right."

If only she could assure herself. The trials of the past few weeks had allowed self-doubt to creep into her thoughts, but mostly, she had no idea what to say. Graduation speeches are a pretty big thing and they're supposed to be profound and articulate. She had nothing to say that would change anyone's life—unless she wanted to get committed for declaring there is another Realm she has access to.

She shuffled down the hallway and off to study hall in the cafeteria to have a panic attack or puke or something unpleasant. She handed her late slip to the monitor and took a seat by her friends at the table near the window.

Burke gave her a questioning look, but Keisha cut to the chase. "What's up? You look stressed."

"I was just coerced into speaking at graduation." She quickly gulped down the fear that rose with the spoken acknowledgment.

Keisha clapped her hands in excitement. "I know I should offer my condolences, but I'm actually excited for you."

"Excited to watch my public demise? I tried to get out of it because I have zero desire to stand up in front of my entire class and their loved ones and make a permanent fool of myself."

"I'd much rather listen to you than anyone else on the program," Burke said. "You'll do great!"

"What're you going to say?" Granger asked.

"Something that ensures no one asks me to speak again."

"Ellie, don't even worry. You're going to rock this. You just have a way with people, and I personally think they picked the right person." Granger double-fist bumped her. "I'll be the guy cheering wildly from the stands."

He had no idea how hard this was going to be for her. Fifth grade all over again. Mute. Mortified.

On Tuesday, three days before graduation, Elliana sobbed uncontrollably on Keisha's shoulder in the girls' bathroom for nearly twenty minutes during lunch. Although her hunger pangs had been strong moments before, they were no match for the pains unleashed by the computer-generated meme that she had ripped off her locker with the downward swipe of her hand, which was now crumpled into a tight ball. It had a picture of her taken from afar with white block letters saying:

Two timeing
stuck up
duck faced loser

"What have I ever done to make someone hate me so much?" Elliana stifled a sob, her breathing ragged and worn with raw emotions.

Keisha rubbed her back. "Nothing, Ellie. None of it's true,

just remember that. It's all lies. And whoever did it doesn't even know how to spell *two-timing* or use hyphens correctly."

"I want to believe that, but with everything that's gone wrong lately, it makes me feel so terrible! I have never felt so hated in my entire life." Really, she was beginning to hate her high school experience for the first time since she was a freshman, and it wasn't supposed to end this badly.

"I know, Ellie. Whoever did it probably hates themself and thinks this will make them feel better. I'm sure it's just some moron that is jealous of your wickedly smart brain and pretty face."

Elliana feigned a smile, knowing her friend was trying to cheer her up. "I'm afraid to know how long it was posted on my locker. It wasn't there before fourth period. Who knows how many people saw it. I'm so humiliated."

"No one who knows the real Ellie will think any less of you. I'm sure."

"I'm so ready to give up. I can't do this anymore. Let's go to the principal's office so I can bow out of that stupid graduation speech—I need some moral support, not more public humiliation. I never wanted to do it in the first place, and there's no way I'm giving it now." She had struggled with the speech all weekend and furiously deleted everything she wrote.

"Of course." Keisha handed her friend another rolled wad of toilet paper to blot away her smeared mascara and makeup.

The rough texture of the industrial toilet paper stung the tender, swollen skin under her eyes. "Let's go now while the halls are mostly empty."

Elliana allowed herself a few more sniffles before looking in the mirror, trying to force an expression that disguised her obvious sadness. Keisha put her arm around Elliana and walked her down the hall.

Mrs. White looked concerned when she saw the duo enter the office and immediately sent them back to see the principal.

As they entered his office, Elliana opened her mouth to speak, but no words came out. Keisha grabbed the crumpled note from her friend's fist, smoothed it out, and handed it to the principal. "Mr. Carmichael, read what we just found on Ellie's locker."

Elliana forced herself to show more courage than she currently had. She steeled her emotions and promised herself that she could be mad and angry and frustrated, but she was not going to cry anymore, especially not in front of the principal.

He finished reading the note and looked at Elliana.

"I'm not speaking at graduation. I'm not."

"Girls, take a seat. Let's talk about this."

Keisha sat in a chair to the right, but Elliana remained standing.

"Tell me what happened. When did you find this?"

After a silent pause, Elliana sat in a chair and explained how she had found the note taped to her locker just before lunch. The anger in her voice was evident, although she tried not to direct it at Mr. Carmichael.

"Someone in this school hates me. Maybe more than one person. And I'm done. I can't handle the haters any more. It's too much."

He studied her face. "I know this must hurt, even if it's all lies, but the Elliana I know never quits. She tackles challenges head-on."

"I'm not that person anymore."

"Sure you are. You're just trying to protect her, but she's still in there."

Elliana glared at him. "Are you seriously going to make me give the speech anyways?"

"I'm not going to force you to do anything. But I think you should. I think the school needs to hear from you. I think you need to deliver an awesome speech that makes the haters look misinformed and ridiculous. Show them what you're made of."

Keisha reached over and rested her hand on Elliana's arm which helped comfort her.

"I don't want to," Elliana repeated.

Mr. Carmichael pointed to a framed quote hanging on the wall next to his door. Reluctantly, Elliana silently read the quote by Nelson Mandela: "I learned that courage was not the absence of fear, but the triumph over it. The brave man is not he who does not feel afraid, but he who conquers that fear."

She refused to be convinced.

He shifted forward in his seat and clasped his hands together, extending his forefingers at Elliana. "I still think you're the girl for the job. Why don't you think about it for a day and let me know your decision in the morning? The programs have already been printed, and it's going to be pretty short notice if I have to find someone else, but I don't think it's going to end that way. I think you're going to show your classmates that you're bigger than some cowardly, cruel note."

"I'll think about it," Elliana said as if she was thinking about whether to jump into a barrel of spiders. She stood up ready to leave and motioned toward the note that lay on his desk and said, "You can have that."

"I'll ask the faculty if they hear anything about it. Do you girls need a pass?"

"No, we're just missing lunch," both girls replied.

"Okay then." He nodded at the girls and smiled as they

turned to leave. "And Elliana?"

Both girls turned back around.

"You have way more fans than you have foes. I know that for a fact. Wouldn't you agree, Miss Fox?"

"Yes, sir," Keisha said.

"So show 'em! Let them rally around you in support."

Keisha put her arm around Elliana and walked her out of the office.

They dawdled in the hallway until Elliana's face wasn't so blotchy and red. One benefit to being a half an hour late to lunch is that there was no line, and so they paid for their food and found their usual table.

"What took you guys so long?" Burke stared at Elliana's face.

Elliana whispered to Keisha, "You can tell them, but I don't want to talk about it or I'm going to start crying."

With seven sets of curious eyes on her, Keisha told the table what had happened with the note and the visit to Mr. Carmichael's office.

Burke cursed and threated to kill whoever did it.

Elliana just shrugged her shoulders and tried to look braver than she felt. Burke reached under the table and held her hand, and she felt just a little bit stronger.

The whole table was dumbfounded that anyone would do that to her and couldn't even name one person that would do such a thing. Even Marlee, who sat in between Jared and Quintin, looked as if she felt sorry for her, which hopefully meant that she had nothing to do with it because she was definitely a suspect.

"It's all crap. Sounds to me like someone is trying to get to you," Granger said, "right before your speech."

Burke nodded. "How's it coming, by the way?"

"It's not. I told Mr. Carmichael that I don't want to do it, and I'm supposed to give him my final answer tomorrow morning. And if I bow out, I'll recommend one of you guys fill in for me."

This made the table laugh and lightened the mood. She pointed at Granger and said, "Maybe you should write my speech! You always seem to know what to say."

"Too bad I'm a junior." Granger laughed, then reassured her that he would help her if she needed him to.

"Too bad I'm going to knock it out of the park by myself then."

"That's our Ellie," Jared said, flashing his dapper smile.

Burke put his arm around her chair and cheered her up. He said the poster wasn't on her locker a few minutes before lunch started. Perhaps very few people had actually seen it.

Talking about the humiliating note on her locker on the ride home from school with Abbie caused her emotions to resurface. When they got home, Abbie sat in the front room with a gloomy look on her face watching Elliana sob into her mother's neck. Her mother hugged her tightly and said she was so sorry that it had happened. She told her daughter how wonderful she was, talented and beautiful, and that she believed in her. It was what Elliana needed to hear, but she still hurt.

"I wonder who did it?" Abbie said, almost to herself.

"It was computer-generated so there's really no way to know. But Mr. Carmichael is going to ask the teachers if they've heard anything."

"If it was that hater, Veronica, I'll claw her eyes out. The more I think about it, the more I think a gang of one is behind the sabotage lately. Someone is mighty jealous of you or they wouldn't go to all the trouble." Abbie liked to talk tough, but she was soft-hearted about her family and tended toward over-protection. Elliana appreciated her well-meaning threat of violence.

A triple scoop of ice cream might help soothe her soul, so she picked up her phone. She hadn't thought much about who she would call, but she found herself calling Cai.

"Hi, Ellie."

"Hey. Are you busy?"

"Well I'm at work and I have to finish grading some papers. Why?"

"Because I had another rough day and I need some ice cream and someone to talk to, and I figured that someone ought to be you."

"Sure. I'm always game for gorging on ice cream and seeing your beautiful face. I can be ready to leave in about thirty minutes."

"Okay, I'll pick you up." She hoped half an hour was enough time for the puffiness in her face to fade.

After she got off the phone with Cai, she disappeared to her Garden for a few minutes to talk to Wayne and Rose and to get another pep talk.

Elliana dipped her feet in the gentle stream, eying the glowing rocks, feeling the negativity pulled out from her toes. "Rose, it seems like everything in my life is going wrong. Something bad is always happening lately. I don't think I can take another disappointment or betrayal. I just can't."

"Sometimes our life gets difficult, not for reasons of our choosing, but because opposition is a part of life, and it prepares us for something great. Do you remember how you were warned on your first visit here that things might get difficult?"

Elliana nodded.

"Trials come to everyone, regardless. That is life. But I promise you that you will have more help and support and strength to overcome if you continue to visit the Seeking Realm often. Continue to be a Seeker."

Elliana nodded again.

Rose sighed and wished Elliana would seek for lost truths by asking the right questions.

CHAPTER TWENTY-TWO

Fury

"Yeah, but I'm sick of everything being so hard. Why does it have to be so hard?"

Rose said, "Remember what I told you about the Shadow Realm competing with the Seeking Realm for power? Because you are making the Seeking Realm more powerful by working on your quest, the Shadow Realm is unleashing more fury to try to discourage and distract you from accomplishing your aim."

"Well, it's working," Elliana mumbled.

"Think of it this way: something wonderful is in store for you, and you'll appreciate it more when it happens because of all the frustrating and painful things you have just experienced. It wouldn't feel as wonderful if you hadn't felt so much pain. Opposition carves out room for elation. Remember, anytime you feel like life is ganging up on you and giving you misery, tell yourself that something fabulous is about to happen, dear."

She mustered some strength to repeat it. "Something fabulous is about to happen."

"That's a girl. Just keep telling yourself that. One day you will look back and see how this helped you, even though it doesn't make any sense to you now. You will learn to be careful who you surround yourself with—some people are good for you, and others are not really friends but poison. Poison is a tactic of the Shadow Realm to discourage you so they can gain control. Don't let them win."

Rose reminded Elliana that something good truly was around the corner, and then advised, "Be strong. There's more trouble coming at you, so be prepared to face it."

Rose seemed to know what Elliana needed to hear, even though it wasn't necessarily what she wanted to hear, but their conversations always made her feel a little stronger.

A few minutes later, Elliana drove to Boise State to pick up Cai. When she saw him exit the science building, she breathed a heavy sigh. She had been a little nervous to see him after spending half the day crying, but he had just hugged her and told her she looked beautiful and kissed her on the head. Any girl could get used to that.

She drove to the Hamburger Hut for a milkshake where she told him all about her sucky day and how she was still expected to give the blasted graduation speech.

When a tear trickled down her cheek, Cai caught it with his thumb and wiped it away. "One thing my dad taught me is if it doesn't kill me, it's only going to make me stronger. Remind yourself that you are bigger than this, Ellie. You are more than stupid lies. And you will be stronger because of it."

She nodded her head. "You're right. I knew I called the right person."

"You know what one of my favorite quotes is?" Cai asked.

"What?"

"When you do the things you fear the most, the death of

fear is certain."

She thought about it for a few seconds and repeated, "The death of fear?"

"It seems silly now, but I used to be scared to death of heights, because when I was about eight years old, I climbed on my grandmother's roof with some cousins and fell off and broke my leg in two places. I spent all summer lying around, watching my sisters run and play, feeling badly for myself. By the time I got my cast off, I was scared to death of breaking my leg again—because to me it was a prison sentence. I remember my mom took us to the park, and my sisters ran faster than me because I didn't want to hurt my leg. Anyways, there was this really cool slide that came out of the first story of a three-story rocket ship on the playground—then there were ladders to get to the two other levels. It used to be my favorite place to play. But when I climbed to the first level, I could not make myself go down the slide. I'd become terrified of heights."

"Really?"

"Yeah, I cried like a sissy. My mom had to climb up the ladder and help me climb back down. Ellie, I was so scared that I couldn't even go down a stupid playground slide!"

"Well you fly planes now, so what happened?"

"Nothing happened for a few years. I was still scared of heights, but we went to this water park with a long twisty slide, and I wanted so badly to go down the slide into the water like my sisters. My dad told me that quote about fear, and so I decided that I wasn't going to be afraid of heights anymore. Of course, it wasn't that easy. I learned to go down slides again, starting with the shortest ones. Then I stood at the end of a diving board until I had enough courage to jump off. And eventually, I went down the twisty slide at the water park."

"I never would have guessed," she said.

Cai shrugged. "Most people don't know that story about me, but I know from experience that when you face your fears, you start living again. Fear sucks life from you, but facing it gives you control."

It would be easy for anyone to assume he'd had an easy life, but she kept learning that he's had weaknesses he's had to work on and has had his fair share of opposition, too.

He was really growing on her: he was easy to get along with, inspired her to try harder, and seemed to get better looking the more time she spent with him.

A few hours later, she sat down on her bed to write her graduation speech, but her thoughts were jumping around like popcorn in a hot pan—each idea seemed like a good idea until the next idea popped. Pretty soon her mind was overwhelmed with all the possible things she could say, and there was only one thing to do.

She ported.

Rose sat next to her near the Ambrosia Tree, and Elliana savored a few plucked fruits.

"What message do you think your classmates most need to hear?" Rose asked.

"That's the problem: I can think of about twenty and none of them pop out as THE best idea."

"Then you need to change the way you're brainstorming. Try this: what is one virtue or trait that you think your generation needs the most right now?"

Elliana stared at nothing while she thought. "It's a toss-up between developing a good work ethic and having the guts to do difficult things—like sticking up for a friend or a belief, or even learning to say no. Sometimes I watch the people at school, and it's like they live to mimic what's popular. They are obsessed with things and social media and with being just like somebody else—somebodies that are lame excuses for heroes."

"What will it take to stand against popular culture?" Rose folded her hands in her lap.

"Courage, I guess, to be better. Too many kids are like mindless mirrors with no internal drive or compass. It's like they have traded their power to think for the chance to be popular. And it's not that they aren't smart enough to think for themselves—because I think most of them are, although they are too self-absorbed to think about the bigger picture—but I think it's more of an issue of not being brave enough to listen to the good voice. Everyone is so worried what everyone else will think, and so everyone just goes along with the loudmouths even when the loudmouths are wrong. Maybe those people are just waiting for someone to give them permission to be who they should be, without fear."

Rose smiled like she had known the answer all along and was just waiting for Elliana to arrive there herself. "Sounds like you have your topic."

Elliana ported home to grab a note pad and pen and ported back to the Seeking Realm to write her speech in a place that constantly inspired her and gave her courage and answers. Her mind was filled with a sudden stream of thoughts that quickly morphed into a speech—like she had been given the words to speak. Mr. Carmichael and Cai had both said things that got her thinking. When she wrote, the right words came powerfully to her mind, which made writing her speech feel less like pulling thistles barehanded.

After two hours of writing and rewriting, she had a speech

that she felt was good and hoped her nerves would calm the freak down. She ported home to type her speech.

She'd told Mr. Carmichael she'd speak at graduation. The hardest part of speech still lay ahead: the actual delivery in front of a huge audience. Her stomach flipped at the thought—her mind always seemed to go completely blank when she had to give any sort of presentation. When her mouth was speaking to a formal group, her mind was incapable of thinking, so she rehearsed giving her speech aloud seven times.

Once she was confident with the fluidity of words, she practiced on her family. Her dad helped her reword a few sentences and use rhetorical devices for greater impact and patted her on the back for using anaphora all by herself. Her mom reminded her to smile, "Because smiling puts people at ease, including yourself." Elliana practiced again three more times while smiling in the mirror.

She headed to her room feeling pretty great until Keisha forwarded a picture message she had received: a snapshot of the poster on Elliana's locker, and a message that said:

> So sorry. I guess this is going around. Just wanted to warn you. Hugs!

Tears streamed down her cheeks.
A text from Granger beeped a minute later.

> Sorry, sweetheart. Remember, it's bunk. Stay strong and I'll see your pretty face tomorrow. If I find out who did it, I'll crush them to smithereens. Promise.

Burke called and made a similar threat. It was sweet, though it would be virtually impossible to know who had started the viral text, which seemed to be spreading like flames on a dry wheat field. Perhaps it was payback for the cruel words had said to Bobby those many years ago. Her pain reminded her to add something to her speech.

Elliana regained strength from focusing on the positive and her true friends and her Garden. Someone, perhaps from the Shadow Realm, was trying to get her to back down from giving her speech at graduation, but it was too late because her mind was made up at that point. She looked in the mirror. "Haters, you can't keep me down. Something fabulous is about to happen."

≈

On Wednesday, people who she hadn't talked to recently walked up to her and said things like, "People are idiots. Forget them." Or "We're on your side. You'll do great." Considering how horrible she felt less than twenty-four hours earlier, she was glad to have some of the pain eased by kind words. She hoped her speech had the same effect.

She could think of at least thirty seniors that were struggling because of family problems, motivation problems, or addictions. She hoped her speech would inspire those who felt like giving up, those who felt like a stick tossed into a burning fire, to rise up and try again, just like she would rise up and speak even after the viral bully text.

She still had to face her fear and speak publicly. If her speech was a flop, she wouldn't have to face her classmates in high school ever again AND she would still graduate. Either way, it was success.

≈

Friday was a half-day of school. Elliana met her friends for breakfast at the Sunrise Café. In all, 23 students met up to celebrate their last day of high school; Elliana and Burke sat together. Keisha pointed out that Elliana was way more talkative than usual. Elliana realized it was a subconscious strategy to drown out the noise in her head. Each time a negative thought appeared, Elliana just talked over it so she didn't have to listen to it. With her speech in seven hours, nervousness gnawed at her stomach.

When they arrived at the high school, Burke walked Elliana to her locker, which was covered in notes, hearts and flowers and a big sign in the middle that read: "Ellie Rocks! Congrats!"

"Did you do this?"

He just shook his head and acted like he had nothing to do with it.

"I love my friends." She turned the dial of her combination. When her locker door opened, a mylar helium balloon popped out, bearing the message, "Good Luck."

Burke reached up to grab it by the string and handed it to Elliana. "Looks like your friends love you back."

She had given her combination to only three people: Burke, Marlee, and Keisha, and instead of trying to figure out the mystery, she decided to just take it at face value and enjoy it. "I don't know who to thank, but if you know who did it, please tell the good-luck leprechauns that it made my day."

Granger rounded the corner and handed her a pink long-stemmed carnation and gave her a quick hug. She had enough fans.

↯

Elliana fidgeted with her sapphire necklace, feeling her pulse in her throat, hoping that she wasn't going to lose what little was in her stomach. She had been so nervous that day that she had hardly eaten more than a few bites of French toast with strawberries.

She saw the valedictorian's hands tremble as he approached the podium. Heavy dread sunk in her gut as she sat under the stage lights, awaiting her time to speak.

CHAPTER TWENTY-THREE

Fearsome

AT THE END of the valedictorian's speech, the auditorium filled with applause—Elliana didn't know if it was because it had been a good speech or that the audience was glad it was over. She hadn't really been listening—she had been reviewing her notes and mentally instructing herself on what she needed to do. She took several deep breaths and glanced toward her family and Cai. He smiled.

Mr. Carmichael approached the podium. "Now we'll hear from one of our finest students who has exhibited admirable character through her ups and downs here at Copernicus Charter High School. I present to you, Miss Elliana Reinhart."

An uneasy, rushing feeling consumed her body like millions of microscopic helium balloons rising up her throat as her name was spoken and as she started walking to the podium to address the thousands in the audience. Her nerves shook her bones like old windows in a thunder storm, and she gulped several times. Fear nearly suffocated her courage, but she knew the only way out of this task was through it, so she focused on how many times she had rehearsed the speech and how important she felt the message was. Reaching the podium, she drew in her breath, fixed her view a few feet above everyone's heads, and exhaled slowly. Just before she began, she remembered to smile.

"The past four years have been amazing, fun, and thrilling... and also difficult, frustrating, and painful.

"And because of that, the past four years have taught me more than just math, science, writing, history and painting. The past four years have taught me about life—lessons which I will take with me into my future about who I am and who I am not.

"I am more than my relationship status, my Facebook status, my socioeconomic status, or my GPA.

"I am more than my dress size or the size of the house I live in.

"I am more than my physical abilities, the brand of clothing I wear, or the amount of money in my wallet.

"I am more than the number of friends I have. And I am more than the number of enemies I have. I am not my mistakes, because I have the courage to pick myself up after I fall and try again.

"We all are more than our mistakes and more than our parent's mistakes. We are more than our IQs or the awards we've won—or never received.

"We are more than our face, our race, or our popularity.

"We are more than how many people like our social media post or how many people sit with us at lunch.

"We are more than the number of times we've scored a goal, hit a ball, or cleared the bar.

"We are not the wrong things we've done. We are not our failures, our faults, nor our fumbles. Once we forgive ourselves and others, and give ourselves permission to move forward, we transform into limitless potential—and we are destined for greatness.

"Standing here before you today, minutes away from graduation, hours away from beginning a new chapter in our book of life, days away from seeking our destinies, we might think we know each other, and we might think we know ourselves, because of the past. But the past is ignorant of the future. We all have the power to readjust our course and determine our own destiny.

"We are all companions on this crowded road to self-discovery and self-mastery. It is a long road of learning, of triumphs and of failures, but most importantly of growing and of becoming who we are meant to become: hope for the hopeless, friends for the forlorn, and shining stars in the darkness. Our mistakes are stepping stones on the path to success. Like a phoenix, we can rise out of the ashes of yesterday's experiences and soar to new heights today, and we can do that on a daily basis if only we give ourselves permission to rise up.

"It is time to say goodbye to two roadblocks to success: fears and perceived injustices. These roadblocks are excuses that enable us to remain mediocre when greatness is most probable. All it takes is the courage to believe.

"We are the world's future, each of us, for we make up the world. Truly the world can't be the world without you, me, or anyone else. It needs the experiences of every single person. It doesn't take much for a person or incident to become a part of us, because they give us the opportunity to think and grow. And so it is that we all leave our marks, good and bad, whether we are conscious of it at that time or not.

"Now I ask you: What mark will you leave on the world?

"Have the courage to never be a bully in any form but use your words to build others up. Have the courage to say 'I'm sorry' and to believe that the world is still a good place. Have the courage to stand firm against the crowd and to stand for something you believe in. Have the courage to be accountable for your decisions, to forgive, and to put the past behind you. And have the courage to aim high and try something difficult. We can't all be the sun, but we can each be a star, and whatever your aim might be, remember all it takes is the courage to stand tall.

"So as we move forward into the future, we must always remember who we are and who we are not. We must remember that we are NOT our failures or mistakes, but we are our infinite potential. We are the change agents for today and for tomorrow. All it takes is the courage to act.

"Let us seize every opportunity to make our world a better place, whether by inventing a new technology, finding a new cure, discovering a new species, drafting an innovative blueprint, or writing a ground-breaking book. Anything is possible if we resist the tug of mediocrity, ignore negative peer pressure, and aim for the very greatest possibilities. As Ghandi put it, 'we must become the good we wish to see in the world.'

"When we have the courage to believe and stand tall and act, we are endowed with the power to change ourselves and make a positive difference in the world, to love and be loved, to forgive and forget, and to break the status quo and set a new standard of greatness. Because We. Are. Courageous! Congratulations Class of 20--!

"Thank you."

As the last two words left her lips, a dull ache radiated down her quadriceps from holding her knees rigid during her speech. She sighed silently as she smiled, and then took a step back to shake her knees loose. It was over. Not only had she given the speech, but she didn't stutter or stumble. More importantly, she knew that she finally believed everything she had just said.

The audience erupted with applause and whistling. Green-and-silver-graduation-gown-clad students burst from their seats on the stage, clapping, hooting, and hollering, followed by their loved ones in the audience. Her eyes scanned the crowd again, landing on her salt-and-pepper-haired parents, her sister, and Cai—her rocks. She wished Wayne and Rose could have been there, too.

This opportunity held the answer to her future. The amazing feeling of accomplishment after giving her speech was worth the stress of conquering the self-doubt she had entertained in previous days. Finding her voice was one of the most powerful, meaningful events in her life, and she understood how her mistakes and trials built her and prepared her and filled her with enough passion and compassion to give her speech on courage.

Now she could see her self-doubt for what it was: a villain in her book of life, a robber of accomplishment, and a thief of happiness. Giving that speech gave her self-doubt an eviction notice.

CHAPTER TWENTY-FOUR

To Wed

ELLIANA ENJOYED AFTER-GRAD and spending some time with her classmates—even though a few of them could be obnoxious and annoying—probably because she knew it was the last time they would be together before they moved on in life. Towards the end, Burke asked her if she wanted to go play mini-golf for the chance to challenge "The Master." After nine holes under bright lights at midnight, Burke was still "The Master," but Elliana was the comic relief with her horrible posture and putting.

After returning the putters and ball, Burke grabbed Elliana's hand and pulled her closer. "You're killing me, Ellie."

"Sorry, I've never really been good at golf."

"No, your terrible golfing was hilarious, not murderous."

Elliana pretended to be offended and tried to push him away, but he held on to her hand.

"So how am I doing in the other competition?" He chewed on his lip. "And you know what I'm referring to."

"Oh. That. To be honest, you were doing pretty good until you insulted my fine putting skills. That cuts real deep like."

"For real, Ellie. I gotta know."

She turned serious. "You're still in the running. I don't know if I know much more than that because it gets confusing sometimes. I know I love spending time with you, and I still look forward to it. But I still don't know."

"Okay, that's good to know. It's better than the bad news anyway. Do I at least get a hug for winning the mini-golf tournament?" Burke got the playful look back in his eyes.

This time when they hugged, he surprised her by being gentle. This wasn't a best-friend hug that made her eyes bulge out of her head. Their cheeks touched.

"How am I doing now?" he asked.

"You're a weasel," Elliana whispered. "Or maybe a teddy bear."

"A guy's gotta try, right? Can I interest you in some ice cream with gummy fish? It's all on the house tonight."

"Better idea than my playing mini-golf." She pulled back slightly.

He smiled and his gaze lingered on her eyes, just a moment on her lips, back up to her eyes, and then they were interrupted.

"Hey, what are you guys doing?" Marlee was staring at Burke.

"Going to get ice cream." Burke pulled Elliana by the hand toward the concession stand.

"It didn't look like you were going to get ice cream," Marlee said. Her expression didn't really match the next two words out of her mouth: "Just kidding. But I need to talk to you, Burke. Like right now."

"Sorry, Marlee. We're getting ice cream. Maybe later," he replied.

"It can't wait. This is really important."

"Really, Marlee. It's going to have to wait. Ellie and I are going to get ice cream."

"Fine." Marlee tossed her auburn hair over her shoulder and huffed off in the opposite direction.

Elliana felt a surge of frustration or perhaps jealousy. She was glad Burke had not left her to cater to Marlee's demands, because that would have made her final decision easier. She was not desperate enough now to be in a relationship where she took the back seat. She wanted a guy who only wanted to be with her and showed it. Burke passed that test.

Burke shrugged his shoulders and shook his head. "Come on, sugar lips, let's get you hopped up on red dye." The two started towards the concessions booth inside the main building and then sat on a bench outside eating their ice cream and laughing. When the ice cream was gone, the sassy garnet-haired girl marched by without a word.

"I think Marlee's signaling you," Elliana said.

"I'm not on call tonight. She'll have to wait."

And that statement immediately took her mind to Cai, who was the one waiting that night, sort of. Elliana felt torn and happy at the same time, and she determined to figure this matter out, both for her sanity and for the sanity of her romantic interests. Tomorrow was Christopher and Sheena's wedding. She had really hoped to have known by now. After all, if Frick had anything to do with it, he'd have the relationship decided tomorrow AND sealed with a kiss.

&

The golden yellow sun hung low in the pinkish sky. Cai's backyard was aglow with a combination of white Christmas lights, lanterns, and lamps. Strands of starry, white Christmas lights hung from the gazebo and wrapped around every post and pole in sight.

"Hey, Frick!" Elliana stuck out her hand all professional-like.

She wasn't on hugging terms with him yet, but she gave his wife-to-be a quick hug. "Sheena, you look absolutely gorgeous! You make a beautiful bride."

"Speaking of the bride," Cai said to Christopher, lowering his voice, "I think she needs one last kiss before she becomes Mrs. Frick."

Elliana's heart panicked briefly until she saw the humor in Cai's eyes and the intensified glare in Christopher's eyes. "Go for it," Elliana said to Cai.

"Seriously, Wittington. You can't get a kiss out of Starlight, so you're going after my hottie? Fine, get it over with, you sorry sap. It might be the only kiss you get for a while, unless Starlight has anything to confess?" Christopher eyed Elliana to read her expression. "Just as I thought."

Cai hugged Sheena, careful not to snag her dress with his cuff links or mess up her hair, and kissed her on the cheek. "You look beautiful, Sheena. I'm not sure whether to say 'Congrats' or 'I'm sorry' though."

Christopher rolled his eyes. "Very funny, Mr. Charming. That's enough. Get your own.... On second thought, do what you'd like because I have plans to embarrass you and Starlight tonight."

Cai gave Sheena another squeeze and then took Elliana's hand.

Elliana asked Sheena, "How are you guys feeling? Nervous, excited, scared?"

Christopher gazed at his bride. "Pure excitement. I've waited for this day for a long time."

A few minutes later, the guests took their seats in front of the brightly-lit gazebo. Elliana couldn't help but notice that Christopher's vows were a lot more serious and loving than she would have expected, and even made her emotional. Tears and smiles punctuated Sheena's vows. The couple said "I Do," exchanged rings, and shared their first kiss as husband and wife. When Cai squeezed her hand, Elliana's heart swelled a little.

In true Christopher-style, he turned toward the guests, raised his and Sheena's hands like they had just won a boxing match, and yelled, "Let's get this party started!"

A poppy beat erupted from the speakers and then merged to a slow song for the newly married couple to share their first dance. Sheena held her train in her right hand, placed her left hand on the back of her husband's neck, and they swayed softly to the melody. Christopher and Sheena danced cheek to cheek. Towards the end of the song, Christopher reached up and wiped away a tear running down his wife's cheek.

Not only was Elliana surprised, but she was a little touched as well. She leaned in to Cai. "When did Christopher became such a tender turkey?"

Cai said, "I guess when he fell in love. I hear love will do that to a guy."

꙳

During a slow song near the end of the reception, after Elliana had purposefully missed catching the bouquet, the newlyweds sidled up next to Cai and Elliana. "Have you kissed him yet, Starlight? My man needs a kiss," said the groom.

"Yep, sorry you missed it," Elliana retorted, winking at Cai while they still swayed to the music. "Actually, I'm surprised you missed it with all the fireworks and stuff."

"Those fireworks were for Sheena and I. Nice try. Time to pucker up." Christopher made some annoying smooching sounds.

Elliana leaned in and whispered something in Cai's ear, making Christopher's ears perk up. Cai whispered back.

"We're waiting," Christopher said as he and Sheena danced a little closer to them.

Elliana stopped dancing, grabbed Cai's face with both hands, and inclined her face closer to Cai's by standing on her toes. She hesitated a moment and heard Christopher making more smooching sounds. She slowly moved forward, inching her lips toward his, and then quickly planted a kiss on Cai's blushing cheek before resuming the dance.

"Sorry, Frick. We already got you a wedding present—you don't get two," Elliana said.

Cai suppressed a belly laugh. Christopher muttered some juvenile insult, but Sheena told Elliana to ignore her husband as they danced away.

"Don't worry, I can wait," Cai said. "Really. I'm just glad to get to spend time with you all dressed up."

Almost unwillingly, and to her dismay, her thoughts jumped back to that single dance with Burke at Spring Formal when he said he wanted a chance. Again, her heart felt torn. She wanted to know more than anything how to figure it all out.

CHAPTER TWENTY-FIVE

Soul Sister

THE WEEKS THAT HAD PASSED since graduation had completely changed her life.

No, Mr. Carmichael never caught the cowardly bully who shared the cruel meme of Elliana, so she never got the satisfaction of shanking him or her in the spleen, but at least she was done with high school drama. Not only was she feeling more self-confident after her graduation speech won her a two-thousand-dollar scholarship, and feeling more adventurous after spending a week camping with Keisha, but one of her wildest daydreams had come true about discovering her origins. It happened in such a way that the reunion had to be providence.

Elliana walked to the mirror and examined the features on the face that always stared back. Her slender fingers traced her brow line, her jaw and chin, and the slope of her nose. She couldn't count how many times those features followed her every move—and she contrasted it to the new face that looked almost identical. That new face belonged to Hannah.

After their miraculous meeting, Elliana brought Hannah and her father to her home and talked like old friends. They stayed for dinner but eventually had to get some sleep. When the Reinharts walked both Hannah and her dad out to their rental car, Elliana felt an emotional pang surge for a moment until she reminded herself that she would see them again soon, and the pang subsided.

Her mind reviewed how it had all happened—it was impossibly unpredictable. Cai had left messages and texted, and Elliana felt badly that she hadn't yet had the chance to give him the scoop. She couldn't wait to tell Cai and dialed his number even though it was getting late.

"I have big news. Like enormous. But I want to tell you in person. Can you come over?"

Cai was grabbing a late snack and was only fifteen minutes away, so Elliana told him to come over but wouldn't give him anymore hints. "I'll be waiting outside," she said.

When Cai arrived, Elliana ran to his truck, practically jumping on him out of excitement. He hugged her back.

"Okay, spill it."

"Listen to this! I, me, Elliana, the twice-adopted kid—I have a sister! Like a real biological sister! And that's not all! She's my twin! Can you believe it?"

"What? No, yes, well tell me more and I'll see if I can believe it. How did you find out?"

"It's the craziest story that almost seems like it was meant to be. No, for sure it was meant to be. I really believe that. Anyways, this guy from Texas came to Idaho looking for investment properties." She hesitated a moment, looked around at her neighbor's houses, and said, "Wait, let's go sit on my front porch. My neighbors might think I'm on drugs or something the way I'm bouncing around out here in the driveway."

"I don't think I've ever seen you this excited, Ellie. Not even when you pretended to run me over to try and get my number."

"Very funny," she said as she sat down on the front step, facing Cai. "It's like a dream come true—a dream that I didn't realize was a dream until it came true! So anyways, Marlee's dad is a realtor and was showing this Texan some land and they decided to get lunch at Hamburger Hut. Burke happened to be grabbing a bite to eat there, too. He saw a girl he thought was me.

"Trying to get my attention, he said my name, but she didn't respond. So he hugged her from behind and whispered in her ear, 'Sugar lips, you're terrible at pretending to ignore me. Give it up.'"

Cai's eyes widened. "He calls you sugar lips?"

Elliana realized Cai thought Burke called her sugar lips because he thought they probably kissed. Her heart sunk a little. "Cai, I promise I haven't kissed him—he calls me that just to tease me."

"Okay, go on," Cai said.

Elliana wasted no time. "The girl turned around, slapped him hard, and drawled, 'I really don't know you. Get your gropey hands off me if you want to keep them attached.'

"Burke said, 'Ellie, don't be ridiculous.' It's probably a good thing Mr. Mooney and Hannah's dad were in line ordering when Burke was detaining her with questions. Mr. Mooney later told Burke that he himself had made the same mistake when he first met her and her father that morning and had thought it was proof that everyone in the world has a doppelganger.

"Anyways, Burke told me that the resemblance was too close, so he started asking her personal questions, like: 'How old are you? Nineteen?' She said all twangy-like, *'None of your business.'* He asked, 'Is your birthday in April?' *'Again, none of*

your business. Has anyone told you that you're annoying and tacky?'
'The twenty-seventh?' *'This conversation is way too creepy. I'm*
sure you know my security number by now as well.' He ignored her
comment and asked where she lived. *'Texas. Can't you tell from*
my accent?' 'Houston?' *'How do you know that? I'm fixin' to call the*
cops!'

"Burke said that's when his mind started doing flips because
we were the same age, shared the same birth date, and she
was from Houston, Texas. Her first name started with an H.
He said he only needed to ask one more question to be sure.
'Is your last name Adams?' *'Are you a freaking stalker? Watch it,*
because my daddy's packin' right now, and he knows how to hide
corpses.'

"He backed up a few feet. But that's when he believed he had
found my blood-twin. He called me right away and told me to
meet him at Hamburger Hut but wouldn't tell me why—just
that he wanted me to meet someone. And he told her the same
thing because he didn't want to ruin the surprise for either of
us.

"I walked into Hamburger Hut and it was the weirdest thing.
The only way I can describe it is that it was like looking in the
mirror. Her jaw dropped; my jaw dropped; we stared at each
other, looking the other up and down to take in the similarity,
wondering.

"Finally, Burke interrupted our staring contest and said,
'Ellie, meet Hannah with a Capital H, who is nineteen, born
on April 27, 1999, lives in Houston, Texas, and whose last
name is Adams.'

"I burst into tears and bear-hugged that girl like she was
my deceased mother reincarnated. She sorta hugged me back,
but it didn't click initially, so I let go and told her that I had

been looking for an H. Adams with the year 1999 and city of Houston, Texas, because that information was in my adoption file. I told her she was my sister—my twin sister. There was no mistaking. It just had to be, given the evidence.

"She grabbed me and started hugging me and sobbing on my neck. It was like we instantly loved each other! Or actually, like we had already loved each other. Can you believe that?"

Cai was shaking his head and all he could say was, "Amazing. When do I get to meet her?"

"She was only staying for the weekend, but she convinced her dad to fly her out here again in a month. You can meet her, but only if you promise not to have a crush on her or sneak up on her from behind...because she looks just like me, literally. Just with different clothes and a different purse. And she slaps people."

"Don't worry. I don't just like you for your looks; I'm smitten by your personality and your heart."

"That's sweet."

"Not just sweet. True," Cai said.

Elliana smiled. "By the way, Hannah thinks Burke is a creep, and I'm hoping she'll eventually lower his high ranking on the creep-factor scale because of how everything turned out. He said she got pretty snarky when answering his probing questions and she rolled her eyes a lot. Hannah told me that Burke reminded her of this smooth-talking jerk from back home. 'I know his type. You only let a guy like that hurt you once,' Hannah had said. She also said, 'I have to respect him, but I don't have to like him.' Maybe we don't have identical personalities, and we certainly don't talk the same, but it's uncanny how much she looks like me."

Rattled

SHE STILL HADN'T KISSED anyone six weeks later, but Elliana had spent considerable time with each love interest to try and gain more perspective (when she wasn't calling and texting Hannah). Near the middle of July, she felt her heart decide.

Visiting her Garden was vital in finalizing this decision of choosing between two someones who meant the world to her. Her heart seemed to have decided which guy she liked most, but she also wanted to think about it in a place devoid of pressures so it could make sense in her mind as well. For days she thought, and pondered, and analyzed.

Burke was her best friend. She was loyal to him because he was loyal to her. He had only become interested in her romantically after she confessed her feelings and then started dating Cai. She had, of course, strong physical attraction to Burke; however, sometimes having it reciprocated felt a little awkward—a happy awkward, if there were such thing. She loved spending time with Burke, and especially making him laugh—or the other way around. But....

But she loved spending time with Cai, too. Meeting Cai seemed meant to be. She especially loved the story of how they met. Cai was good to her and supported her in her decisions and *deals*, without pressuring her to do something she wasn't ready for. Cai was fun to be around, and she was beginning to trust him like a best friend. The attraction was strong on her end, and she had to believe it was strong on his end as well. Or why would he continue pursuing her? Even though he gave her space to try things out with Burke, he had really good reasoning, and it didn't feel like a cop-out break-up line.

In making those hard comparisons, one thing stood out to her the most. One of the young men really made her want to be a better person. One had an inspiring, uplifting, confidence-building effect on her. She felt it nearly every time she was with him.

The words seemed to flow into her mind as she dipped her toes in the babbling brook: *Choose the one that makes you a better person.* And now her mind understood her heart's choice.

That night as she lay in bed, she pondered how this might all play out. She had to inform each where they stood in her heart. It was only fair, but it wasn't going to be easy. Securing her relationship with Cai would probably be exhilarating. How would she tell him? Was she ready to kiss him? Those thoughts made her heart quicken and her palms sweat a bit.

She planned to first tell the one she chose and see how that process went before telling the other that, though she adored him, she had chosen someone else. The thought of telling Burke that he wasn't the one for her pained her heart. She loved him as a friend, and she certainly never intended to hurt anyone. This fork in the road could cool their friendship. Maybe it would be too awkward to be around each other after The Talk. They had been close friends for a lot longer than they had been love interests, so she tried to convince herself that all would not be ruined. Instinctively, she gently pressed her right hand over her heart and hoped for the best for Burke—hoping also to soothe the stinging pain while feeling warmth of emotion for Cai.

She tossed and turned and flopped all night.

ᴥ

The next morning, Elliana showered and put on one of her very favorite outfits and was confident that day was going to be amazing. The excitement over seeing Cai felt like pop rocks in her heart. Rather than giving anything away, she decided to surprise him by showing up on his doorstep—but not too early. She'd give him time to be ready for the day.

She broke the speed limit on the winding two-lane backroad near the foothills leading towards Cai's neighborhood. She felt sure and had formulated in her head what she was going to say. Again, she pressed her hand against her heart, and fidgeted with her necklace, but with little calming influence.

As she pulled into his driveway, Elliana breathed deeply. She couldn't help but smile all the way to the doorstep. She ran her fingers through her hair and smacked her lip gloss one last time before ringing the doorbell, but there was no answer. She glanced around and noticed that one of the cars was gone. She rang the doorbell a second time for good measure.

Paige greeted her wearing a heavy expression. "Hey, Ellie. Cai just tried to call you."

Elliana reached for her back pocket, but it was empty. She cursed herself for being so twitterpated and distracted that she left her phone charging on the kitchen counter. "Dang, I forgot my phone at home."

"Cai's not here, he's at the hospital, but I'll tell you what's going on."

Elliana's throat went dry.

"My grandma developed a pulmonary embolism early this morning. I'd be at the hospital with my family too, but I have a weakened immune system from anti-rejection drugs, so I stayed home. Cai's been keeping me updated."

"What's her prognosis?"

"Her doctor thinks she can make a full recovery, but it will take a long time and a lot of rehabilitation. They are giving her something to help dissolve the clot, and if that works, we hope my grandma can come home in a few days, but for now she's resting and sedated." Paige frowned.

"I'm sorry about your grandma, Paige. Let Cai know that I stopped by."

"Sure, and just so you know, he wants to see you tonight. But don't tell him I told you."

They said goodbye, and Elliana smiled, and then felt guilty for feeling so giddy given his grandma's poor health, especially knowing the hard recovery from her dad's stroke years before.

As she retraced the road out of his development, she wondered what she could do so that the day wasn't totally boring and disappointing. She needed to kill time until she got to see Cai that evening. Chinese food sounded good and so did the scenic route and a hike in one of her favorite secluded spots.

&

A two-hour hike was enough to bake her car. It was already 105 degrees outside. Before her air conditioning started cooling her down, less than two minutes from the trail head parking lot, she heard a whooshing and flapping sound. She glanced quickly around at the empty road and wondered what could be making the noise and felt the driver's side sink toward the ground. She pressed her foot on the brake pedal, put on her hazards, and pulled onto the gravel shoulder. Even though two cars had been parked at the trail head, she didn't run into a single soul on her hike. And the road was still empty.

She couldn't curse her luck, because Elliana still believed this was going to be an incredible day, flat tire or not. Of course she didn't have her stupid phone—that would have been too easy— but her father had taught her how to change a flat tire when she got her license three years prior. If she couldn't get the tire changed in thirty minutes, she would try to flag down a driver, even if she had to walk to a different road.

The sun was already bright and scorching as she rounded her car to lift the spare tire out of the trunk. With some effort, she hefted the spare and placed it on the ground by the back-left deflated tire. She rubbed her forehead with her wrist and felt the sun's heat on her arms. By the time this ordeal was over, she figured she might be a little sweaty, but there was no need to turn the car into a sauna with Southwest Idaho's blistering summer heat. Elliana walked to the passenger side of her car and opened both doors to allow the car to breathe.

She could not get the lug nuts to budge while exerting all her strength turning lefty-loosey. The only thing left to do was to stand on the wrench. Still nothing.

She almost gave up because she wasn't strong enough to loosen the lug nuts by herself. But before she would try to flag down someone to help, she used her weight one more time. There was no one in sight and so she didn't need to worry about looking like a crazy fool on the side of the road. She placed her shoe on the wrench, gripped the roof of her car, hopped three or four times, and the wrench gave way. She put the wrench on an opposite lug nut and hopped on it until it loosened. She jacked up the car and finished removing the lug nuts, and the spare went on pretty easily.

Elliana carried the flat tire, which was unfortunately a lot more difficult to handle than the spare, and heaved it into the trunk, careful to not scratch the bumper, and was rewarded with black smudges on her arms and shirt. She put the jack and wrench in their assigned cubby.

Changing the flat tire all by herself took her twenty-five minutes. She hurried to the passenger side of her car and closed the two doors, and then hopped into the hot driver's seat. The leather seat seared her hamstrings.

She resumed her drive to Confucius, made sure the A/C was cranked up, and even sped a little to help it out. But she had an abnormal, nagging feeling that wasn't caused from sweating and sticking to her leather seat.

A year ago, a gigantic bee had gotten trapped in her car and buzzed wildly in front of her face, almost causing her to drive off the road and wreck her car when swatting it away. Luckily, she had been able to roll the window down and get rid of it. That same uneasy feeling was welling up inside her just then. She had no reason to feel panicked or troubled, but she was definitely unsettled.

Trying to reassure herself that she was making something out of nothing, and that everything would be fine once she got there, she scolded herself for being such a pansy. When taking a deep breath did relatively little to settle her wildly twisting insides, she could sense she was not alone. She felt a cold, almost dark, presence. Shivers raced from one end of her body to the other, and her stomach clenched like a fist. Suddenly it was difficult to draw breath.

She had heard of people having panic attacks and wondered

if that's what she was experiencing—although she had no reason to panic, even if a difficult conversation lay ahead. She breathed deeply to calm her body, but somehow, she still felt wrong.

A distinct noise came from the passenger side of the car, somewhere, signaling danger. The sound completely drained the blood from her face. An unmistakable rattle echoed against her ears, her stomach heaved in fear, goosebumps exploded in her skin, and hot and cold blood flooded her system.

Screaming was probably not the best course of action, but it was her first instinct; however, sound did not accompany her expelled air. Her throat was dry, raspy, constricted. If she dared look around the car, it would confirm what she already knew: she would die and nobody would know to try and save her.

As much as she hated spiders, she loathed snakes even more. Rattle snakes were common in some arid parts of the state, and she feared them like she feared losing her appendages. Now she was the bee trapped in a car with no possible escape. She couldn't roll down the window and flutter out like a winged insect, and she certainly couldn't open the door and roll onto the road while driving fifty-five miles per hour. Stopping the car abruptly would probably irritate the rattler and make it more likely to strike. She kept her eyes on the road and lifted her foot off the gas pedal.

Against the passenger door, she saw the evil, flat head of the snake, tasting the air with its split tongue, hissing loudly. The snake serpentined slowly from the floor onto the passenger's seat, and twirled its earthy-colored scaled skin gracefully into striking position. Its head reared with aggression and hissed again. The car slowed and Elliana pleaded in her mind, thinking of her Garden and Wayne: *Please help me, please, please.*

I don't know what to do.

If the circumstance had not been so dire, she likely would have asked herself why there was a disgusting snake in her car. But she didn't have the luxury of wonder; she had to focus on survival. She hadn't watched enough nature shows to know how to wrestle a snake and not die.

Her instinct was to stop the car gradually and put it into park without any sudden movements. Her foot pressed the brake pedal, and she steered toward the right shoulder.

Time. Slowed. Down. Each heart beat felt separated by an entire minute's worth of fear and panic. If the snake did bite her, she had no cell phone to call for help, and who knows how long it would take for a passerby on that lonely road to rescue her. The regret of not having told anyone where she was going sat like a boulder on her chest.

The car crawled until it stilled. Elliana took her right arm from the steering wheel and moved it carefully to the gear shift between the driver and passenger seat—treacherously close to the snake. Her hand inched to the right, silently depressed the button on the side of the gear shift to change gears, and she lamented that *Park* was a lightyear away from *Drive*. She thought of Cai and how she wanted so badly to see him. She wished he were there to save her, or at least hold her hand while she died. Dying alone in her car with a snake was absurd.

After what felt like minutes, she was fully parked with her hand resting on the gear shift only a mere foot or two from the rattler. Almost imperceptibly, she began to withdraw her hand. The snake hissed and rattled.

It was unlikely that she could coax the scaly bastard out of an open window, but she'd open them just in case. Elliana held her breath and reached to press the buttons to roll down the front two windows because they were closer than the door handle. Maybe it would slither out the passenger window instead of lunging at her neck. But it seemed more likely that she needed to get out of the car fast—just not fast enough to become dinner.

She slowly raised her left hand to reach for the door handle, and the rattler leered and pulled its head back ready to strike. Its eyes were menacing, dark, evil. Each shallow breath she took was almost painful.

She stared at the snake's brown eyes. Maybe eye contact with a snake made it feel threatened, but she feared that it if she looked away, it would strike. Almost in slow motion, as if the snake heard her last thought, it rattled its tail, tasted the air with its tongue, and opened its mouth wider in a mock smile ready to strike. She was about two feet away from where the snake lay constantly rattling, and its coiled body looked long enough to reach her.

From the corner of her left eye, she saw movement that gave her heart hope.

Orly.

Unfortunately, there was nothing close by to use as a portal. Her heart sank and dread consumed her.

Again, she pleaded in her mind for some sort of inspiration, some way out of this impossible situation. She knew of an escape, and not just any escape, but THE best escape on the planet, but she was nowhere near a tree or a post. The snake's head lurched forward—it was striking, headed towards her right shoulder. At the very same instant as the snake began to strike, Orly flitted inside the driver's side window and landed her tiny, prickly feet on Elliana's left shoulder. And at the very same instant that Orly perched on her shoulder, without thinking, the words "Port to Seeking Realm" rushed out of her mouth as one word.

She was gone. Gone in an instant before the fangs sank into her flesh! Gone from the front seat of her snake-infested car.

CHAPTER TWENTY-SEVEN

Revealed

SHE FELL BACKWARDS into the Seeking Realm, because she ported from a sitting position, and landed on her rump. But she was safe. Orly had turned Elliana's shoulder, her body into a portal! Her mind flashed to the time she had ported from her bedroom after getting accused of plagiarism—at the time it felt like unnecessary suffering, but she had learned knowledge about accessing the Seeking Realm, which had just saved her life. Instead of standing up, she leaned back and let her head fall to the soft earth and watched the glowing winged insects flutter above in the canopy. Of all the good emotions she had ever felt, feeling safe was one of the very best. There were no words to express how it felt to be lying on the guarded ground of the Seeking Realm.

An escape from her snake situation had seemed most impossible. Perhaps impossible things are always possible, and impossibility is just a rat that lives in the human mind.

She gazed upwards at the beautiful, green canopy and admired the sun flare through the leaves. Now that she was safe, the luxury of wonder returned. She wondered how in Hades a snake had gotten into her car and why. Why did she not hear its rattle until it was too late? None of it made any sense, but it happened.

Everything seemed to be going wrong. Not seeing Cai. Not getting to tell him she chose him. The flat tire. The stupid snake. Now she understood why Seekers had gotten discouraged and quit their task of saving Electra. She tried so hard to be good and to be strong, but life was getting downright ridiculous. There had to be a reason. She'd ask Wayne.

But Wayne wasn't there. Odd. She'd have to ask Rose.

She sat upright and padded to the cottage to talk to Rose, who was actually not in the cottage, but planting a small dormant tree. "Rose, I need to talk!" Rose probably already knew, but Elliana would tell her anyways. After all, she felt that surviving such a ridiculously crazy situation awarded her with the story rights. It would be an exciting tale to tell once she got home, unless she had to explain how she escaped. That detail made Rose her only audience.

Elliana's frustrations of the day poured off her tongue as they walked the short distance to the bench by her Great Rain tree. After she told the part where Orly landed on her shoulder and she ported to her Garden, she asked Rose, "Why did that stupid snake end up in my car in the first place, and why do things keep going wrong?"

Rose smiled at Elliana and nodded to validate her emotions. "That is a great question with a long answer. I can help you understand the many tactics of the Shadow Realm, but first let me tell you a story."

Elliana nodded—she was humble at this point, humbler than she had been in a very long time.

"Once there was young man who lived in a village of the foothills of a faraway country. He tilled the ground and raised animals to make a living through trading with the villagers of the countryside. He was a smart man who studied diligently and read books to enliven his mind. He was also a caring man who took time to help others in need.

"One morning, he walked outside of his home and found a young squirrel scavenging for food. The squirrel spoke to him and asked, 'Please sir, I've lost my mother. I don't want to be alone.' The man replied, 'Come, Squirrel and I will take you to a family of squirrels that lives in a tree that I pass every morning on the way to the marketplace. Follow me.'

"The man grabbed his cart of vegetables and eggs and started on the path towards the marketplace, with the squirrel scurrying right beside him. Eventually they came to a tree which the man pointed to, and the squirrel squeaked a 'thank you' and ran off to meet the others.

"The next week a fuzzy gray cat was sitting on his doorstep when he emerged from his home to make his daily trip to the marketplace. The cat mewed, 'Please sir, my owners no longer want me and I am all alone. I would love to find a farmer who would take care of me, and I could keep his fields mice-free.' The man replied, 'Come, Cat. I know just the farmer. He is a widower and his children have left home; he would love the company. I'll show you the way.' The man grabbed his cart and walked the road for a mile when he pointed to farm and said, 'The farmer lives there.' The cat rubbed his head affectionately on the man's pant leg and then pounced his way to the farmer's house.

"Two weeks later, a red fox pawed at his doorstep. When the man opened his door, it said, 'Please sir, the villagers dug up the ground that I lived in. I have no home.' The man thought of helping the squirrel find a new family, of taking the cat to a lonely farmer's lot, and now a fox. He wasn't sure he liked foxes all that much, so he said, 'Red Fox, I know the likes of you. You'll eat my chickens if they get free from their run. Why should I help you?' The fox lowered its snout humbly and replied, 'Sir, I promise I won't ever hunt on your property if you help me this once. I just need to find a good hole to keep me warm and safe for winter.' That deal sounded good to the man, so he grabbed his cart and headed away from the marketplace a great distance to a thicket that looked safe enough for a fox. He pointed to the thicket and said, 'There. You can dig your hole there. And now you will keep your promise to never hurt one of my animals.' The fox jumped joyfully. 'Yes, sir. Thank you.'

"That night the man lay in bed thinking about all the needy animals that had been appearing on his doorstep. He was glad to help the critters, and now that he helped the red fox, he felt certain his chickens would be safer. He had no regrets.

"The next month after his morning chores, the man stepped out of his house and grabbed his cart and headed towards the marketplace. As soon as he reached the main road, he saw a tawny dingo resting in the road. It raised its head and said, 'Please, sir. I didn't dare come to your home so that you would know that I mean no harm to you and your animals. I have traveled a long distance because my pack turned on me, and I need help finding a home and food.' The man rubbed his chin, thought a minute, and then replied, 'If I help you find a good home, what will you do for me?' The wild dingo wiggled its tail like a faithful, loyal dog, and said, 'I will keep all other dingoes away from your farm and I will never harm your animals.' That seemed like a fair trade to the man. 'It's a deal. You will keep your promise, and I will find you a den close to lizards and rodents so that you won't be hungry.'

"The man left his cart by the roadside to walk the dingo away from the village, in the opposite direction of the market-place, for he didn't want the dingo near the common ways of the village. He walked toward the mountain, and the dingo padding beside him. The path became rocky and ascended up the foothill. An hour later the dingo complained, 'Please, sir. I grow so very hungry.' The man kept walking, and the dingo followed more slowly behind him. After another hour the dingo pleaded, 'Please, sir. My body aches with hunger.' The man kept walking, and the dingo followed more slowly behind him. After a few minutes, the dingo begged again, 'Please, sir. I need food.'

"The man wearied of the dingo's neediness. They were near a wild berry bush, a perfect spot at the foot of the large mountain. He said, 'I will pick you some berries to stave off your hunger, and you can live and hunt here, and you will keep your promise.' The dingo collapsed on the dirt and said, 'Thank you.'

"The man walked to the bush and put a handful of picked berries in the fold of his shirt and returned to lay the fruits in front of the dingo. Immediately the dingo attacked the man and began chewing his arm. The man screamed in agony, 'Dirty beggar, I helped you! You broke your promise!' The dingo replied with clenched teeth, 'I never promised not to harm *you*. I'm a starving dingo and you are a feast, fool!' The man cursed at the dingo for his disloyalty, but that didn't stop the dingo from killing the man in a secluded place far from the help of his village."

Elliana was confused. "That's a sad story, but I'm not sure how it answers my question."

"Each of the animals that begged for help was the same."

Elliana wrinkled her forehead. "They all needed help?"

Rose guided her thinking with a question. "Why did the dingo attack the man if the man was giving him food?"

"Because it was being an animal and being driven by instincts?"

Rose continued to ask questions to get Elliana to think critically about the story. "Do you think the man would have helped the wild dingo if he hadn't already helped the squirrel, the cat, and the fox without incident?"

"Probably not. He was more willing to help the wild dingo because things turned out okay when he helped the other animals."

"Good. Why do you think people turn and do bad things?"

"Because they choose to listen to the bad inside them instead of the good."

"Yes. We can say that wild dingo was following negative enticements instead of good." Then Rose asked what the good man's fatal mistake was.

Elliana pondered on those last few sentences, thinking about the weakness of human nature—how easy it is to let negative emotions get the best of a person, to be driven by them. Negative emotions like envy and anger made things rocky between her and Marlee, and it tempted her to give Marlee a dose of her own poison. She answered, "Believing the wild dingo actually meant to help him when it promised to keep other dingoes away from the man's farm, and believing the dingo wouldn't harm him, even though it was in his nature to be ruthless and bloodthirsty. The dingo acted like he would help the man by making a tricky promise, which lured the man from safety."

"Yes, that is the fatal flaw of each man or woman who falls. They believe the lies that nothing bad will happen, not to them, even though reason would tell them otherwise. Following the negative enticements always starts out gradually, until we embrace them and what follows after. The squirrel, cat, and fox represent the gradual luring we each face, from innocence to vice, until eventually we are trapped by that thing we originally would not have embraced. That's the Parable of the Wild Dingo."

Elliana understood the parable better but didn't understand what any of that had to do with the snake getting into her car. Rose re-emphasized that the story had another message: each animal in the story was the same.

After a few incorrect answers, Elliana landed on the right conclusion. "So you're saying the squirrel, the cat, the fox, and the dingo represent the same thing, or that they were a disguise or were being controlled or something?"

"Yes. The squirrel, the cat, the fox, and the dingo were being ruled, manipulated, influenced by the same being—a Shadow—who gains trust by appearing innocent at first and shifts his methods gradually until his evil can be accepted without any resistance. Although many consider the parable a folktale, it speaks of reality. All Shadows live to tempt and trap. All Shadows are members of the Shadow Realm, whose purpose is to collect dark power to take control of Electra and thereby control Earth's friends."

Rose explained that members of the Shadow Realm each sought power at any and all cost, gaining power through greasing the gears of evil by trading dirty favors—which is why Shadows call themselves Grifters. Shadows had to pay their dues before they had the power to command an animal, and only if they had a big enough credit of power, and all Shadows learn first to command animals because they are easier to control than humans. Rose spoke her next few words more slowly for impact: "A commandeered animal's eyes will resemble the Shadow who manipulates it."

Elliana's eyes widened and she clenched her jaw as she remembered the snake's eyes. "That rattle snake that tried to bite me, it was commandeered by a Shadow?"

Rose nodded.

"But why me?"

"For a few reasons. Shadows focus on the biggest threats to gaining control of Electra. Your Guardian allowed it today to show you how much courage you have. Remember, the Seeking Realm doesn't remove opposition or trials, but it can strengthen you to face them. Today you needed to know that you can be courageous, especially in the face of fear and danger, and that you will always have help when you need it most. You needed that experience to instruct you how to accomplish the tasks to fulfill your Soul Purpose."

"But what if I would have died?" The portal wasn't even guarded when Elliana got there.

"Wayne guards you day and night. No unnecessary harm would have come to you because, first, we knew you would port because Wayne was in your mind, guiding you," Rose said. "Second, your Guardian would have intervened to prevent disaster because you are seeking to fulfill your purpose, which is why he wasn't there by the Tree Portal when you arrived—he was guarding you from the Earth Realm side, so you wouldn't have been able to see him. But you should also know that intervention is never guaranteed if you choose to walk a different path."

Elliana was relieved and grateful to know she had a faithful Guardian—that's what Wayne meant when he said he was the

Guardian of the Portal—which explained a lot of her miracles. Her mind drifted to that awful accident years ago. "Was my Guardian there when my parents died?" Elliana brushed her fingertips across some budding flowers.

Rose nodded. "That's why you lived. The Seeking Realm needed you to make a difference. Shadows thought they were ruining the plan, but really they just made you stronger."

As much as Elliana wanted to doubt, her mind could not doubt truth while in the Seeking Realm; rather, it seemed to cling to it. The wisdom she had just gained strengthened her. She wondered aloud if the same Shadow had troubled her more than once.

Rose explained that the moment she set foot in her Garden back in April she became a crucial target of the Shadow Realm who sought to thwart her power and foil her efforts, which explained the poisonous snake in her car. If the Shadow Realm could discourage her enough to give up, she would fail and Electra would continue to dim.

Rose asked her to think back to the time when she first discovered the Seeking Realm, to think about anyone new in her life around that time. Elliana sifted memories in her mind—and then it clicked. There was someone new.

It all made sense. In fact, all of the stupid, frustrating, maddening, horrible things that had happened since finding the Seeking Realm now made sense. Elliana shook her head in wonder and huffed loudly. She knew who the low-down, dirty Shadow was, and she felt stupid for ever having trusted him. That wretch had groomed her by acting like a trusted friend. She wondered how their next encounter would go and whether she would sock him in the jaw or shank him with whatever she had in her purse.

"Rose, why would a Shadow waste his time on me? Why don't they pick on someone else? I'm a nobody."

"Not to them. They pay the most attention to the ones with the most potential for good, to Seekers. They see you can be the source of a positive difference, which will lead to a positive change, which makes you a significant threat to their quest for dark power—there is no middle ground for them, so they target all those who spread light and pure love. The members of the Shadow Realm have two purposes: to gain control and to inflict misery. Power and pain. You stand in their way. If they can control the tie between Earth and Electra by destroying love and goodness, the Shadow Realm will obtain unchecked power over all Earth Friends. Light on Electra is what keeps Earth good and beautiful—it's what nurtures love. If Electra dies, everything you love also dies because love dies, and hearts will turn numb and dark." Rose paused. "Your quest has the power to limit and destroy the power of the Shadow Realm."

Realization flooded Elliana's body. "That's why it is so important to save Electra. But I still don't understand what I'm supposed to do."

"You will. It will be given to you in steps. You searched for your origins and found your sister. Next, understand the human heart, its emotions, and how to care for and heal it." Rose promised Elliana that she would teach her how to defeat the Shadows if Elliana continued to visit frequently, because it would take a great foundation of understanding, and a lot of learning on top of that. Sporadic, short visits wouldn't impart the knowledge she needed for her quest—she had to drink deeply and frequently from the living nectar of the Seeking Realm to succeed. "Truth is earned by seeking it and by living what you've already gained."

There was still so much to learn, and time kept a steady pace no one could alter.

Elliana asked Rose if it would be safe to port back to her car. Rose assured Elliana that Wayne had made it safe; his crystal sword severed the dark power of the Shadow over the snake. A Guardian would always have more power than any Shadow because light power always trumps dark power.

She walked to the Portal where she had landed, wondering at the marvelous mysteries she had just unveiled in the special realm where believing came easy. Instead of perching in the tree like usual, Orly swooped down and rested on Elliana's shoulder, tickling her skin with her curly, furry feathers. Elliana hadn't asked Rose about the dormant tree she saw her planting, but she knew she'd be back again soon.

She whispered a few words and found herself sitting in the blazing hot driver's seat of her car with Orly on her shoulder and no rattler in sight.

This day was not turning out at all how she had planned, but that was not going to stop her.

Her stomach purred like an attention-seeking cat, reminding her that she wanted egg rolls and sweet and sour chicken from Confucius to share with Abbie. And while she was in the sharing mood, Elliana had secrets to tell Abbie as well.

Several minutes later, she pulled into the Confucius parking lot and spotted Marlee's car near the entrance. Her head dropped involuntarily. Elliana would have gone somewhere else, but she had just survived the worst, and she really had a hankering for her favorite Chinese food. Of course, if she had her cell phone, she could have called ahead to put in her order and avoided the situation. Marlee was probably sitting in

a booth, so Elliana wouldn't have to interact with her.

She wasn't that lucky.

Elliana came face-to-face with Marlee at the counter. If Marlee did say something snarky, Elliana would have wished she didn't run into her, but her heart whispered that Marlee needed a friend, so she would try to be pleasant. She determined to be friendly and hoped Marlee would return the favor. "Hi, Marlee. How are you?"

"Super, as usual. Just grabbing some food for the gang, you know."

Whatever gang she was referring to, Elliana did not know. "How has your summer been? I haven't really seen you since—"

"Since I was voted Spring Formal Queen?" Marlee interrupted and followed with an obnoxious laugh.

Since graduation, but no use in correcting her. "You looked so pretty. Congrats, again."

"You weren't jealous?" Marlee smiled like what she had said was kind.

Elliana thought this whole conversation was a little too passive-aggressive and looked for a way to shut it down. "Jealous of what?"

Marlee jerked her head slightly to show that her comment had stung a little bit. Marlee's tone turned sarcastic. "I was kidding. Learn how to take a joke, gosh. You're always so serious up there on your high horse."

A waitress approached the counter and handed a white sack of food to Marlee, who promptly left with a curt "Later."

"Bye." Elliana felt defeated, gritted her teeth, and felt her skin prickle with anger. Marlee was difficult to get along with lately, so she hoped that would be the last run-in for a long, long while. They rarely saw each other now that they had graduated, which was okay, and she had heard things wouldn't be the same after high school.

She paid for her meal with cash from her pocket and waited off to the side. Ten minutes later, the waitress brought out her order. The tart vinegar aroma from the sweet and sour chicken made her stomach rumble again, and she headed toward her car.

Elliana set the take-out containers in the snake-free passenger seat and then buckled her seatbelt. "Nothing like drowning my sorrows in Chinese food. Who needs her anyway!" Emotion prickled her skin from the inside again. "And now I'm a weirdo who talks to herself." She burst out laughing at her own ridiculousness and thought, *seriously, who wouldn't want to be my friend? I'm a riot.* She laughed and started her car.

Abbie appeared skeptical but concerned. She took another bite out of her egg roll.

Elliana nodded her head emphatically. "I'm serious. I know it sounds hokey. But everything bad that has happened lately only started happening once Granger Lamme showed up." She wasn't going to tell her sister about the rattler in her car because she wasn't ready to tell Abbie about her secret Garden yet. But she could still rat out Granger. "Think about it."

"Except for Marlee stabbing you in the back. That happened before."

"Okay, you're right about that, but the rest of it has to be him. He was at the track meet talking to Veronica right before she tripped you. He was over when I set up my laptop and on the same day my file went missing. He could have easily turned in that plagiarized paper with my name on it. He probably put that hateful sign on my locker. And I'm sure he caused my flat tire somehow, and probably the coma and probable death of Janet Higby, too!" She left out the elk, falling rock, and snake incidents on purpose.

Abbie bust out laughing and lost several grains of sticky rice, which fell onto the picnic table. "You realize how preposterous that sounds, right? Like the wackiest murder conspiracy theory ever. He's a kid with issues, I'll give you that, but probably not homicidal issues."

"Okay murder might be a stretch, especially since Janet technically isn't dead, but you can't deny the rest of it. I'm telling you to stay away from that guy. He's trouble." She had learned her Guardian was with her in that accident sixteen years ago, and she wondered if a Shadow had deliberately caused her first parent's deaths. She made a mental note to ask Rose.

Abbie pointed at her. "Alright, you win. I'll stay away from him—mostly because I'm already staying away from him." Apparently, Granger had quit calling a few weeks ago, but Abbie didn't really care because it's not like she liked him or anything. "Actually, he's rather aggressive. He kept trying to get fresh with me, so I slapped him good across the face and left a handprint. He hasn't called since."

Elliana's hands clenched. She had never seen Granger's dark side, only the personable, outgoing, friendly side. He was so very likable, and this new information made her angry. He was a skilled pretender, which meant there was no telling what he was capable of. "Abbie, you should have told me! I could have... done something!"

"I can take care of myself."

"I know you can, but I'm still allowed to be overprotective. I bet his last name isn't even Lamme." Abbie's maturity made Elliana think that she could tell her about the Garden. Maybe

Abbie wouldn't be jealous or as skeptical as she had thought. Maybe Abbie wouldn't think she was a mental case. She should tell her all about it soon, but she still had a lot to sort through in her mind, so not today.

When the conversation shifted to Cai, Abbie planned their wedding with the colors, food, and bridesmaids. Elliana went along with it because it was actually fun to think about the idea for a few minutes that she could be somebody's love, somebody's bride. But a lot still had to happen before any of that could. They hadn't even kissed yet. The next move was still hers.

Elliana hated to bother him at the hospital, so she waited for Cai to call. She answered on the second ring.

"Hey, Cai. I'm so sorry to hear about your grandma."

"Paige told me you stopped by. Sorry I wasn't home."

"I'm glad you're there with her—I know you two are very close. By the way, I'm really dying to see you." Elliana sucked in her breath to recall the words. "Oh my gosh, I'm an insensitive jerk. I'm going to stop talking."

"Nah, don't even worry about it. I'm dying to see you too." His voice carried his smile through the phone. "The doctors say she is stable and will be okay. I should be home by dinnertime, if you want to go out."

"Yes!" Elliana replied a little too quickly.

She heard him chuckle over the phone. "You're so cute, Ellie. It'll probably be around six o'clock, but I'll call you."

She wondered if he had any clue why she wanted to see him so badly.

CHAPTER TWENTY-EIGHT

Clarity

FOLLOWING HER MOM'S ADVICE, Elliana headed to the drug store to buy Cai's family a sympathy card. She picked up a card to read the inside when she thought she heard Marlee's voice a few aisles over and stiffened with regret for choosing that idiotic moment to go shopping. If she had only gone to a different store or left a little later. After their encounter at Confucius, Elliana planned to just be invisible and avoid all possible contact because the last thing she wanted to do was have another super pleasant social interaction. She would hurry and buy the card and sneak out unnoticed.

She read the inside messages of the cards until she found one that said: "Thinking of you during this difficult time." She plucked the matching envelope from behind the stack of cards when she heard Marlee's voice again, as well as a male's voice that sounded familiar. But whose? It wasn't Burke's. She strained her ears.

A low male voice said, "Baby, tonight is going to be amazing. I promise."

Marlee giggled. "Yeah? How do you know?"

"Because I can already tell that you and I are meant for each other. I've met a lot of girls, but none of them are as sexy and as hot as you."

That last line really caught Elliana's attention and so she walked to the cash register to get a peek at who Marlee was with, but she also tried not to care a rat's tail because of Marlee's obvious distaste for her. But that voice. It didn't sound like Jared the smooth-talker either. She strained her ears.

"That sounds like a line to me."

"I'm serious. Any guy who can't see how beautiful you are is a fool. I mean, look at those legs! H-O-T. Hot."

"There's more to me than just my legs, hon." Marlee laughed again flirtatiously.

"Baby, I know, and I can't wait to find out all about you."

So what if some guy is trying to hook up with Marlee? Why should she care? It was none of her business. But as much as she wanted not to care, there was something inside that was forcing her. She caught a glimpse of the male and realized that she was now in an even more complicated predicament. Curses.

Handing the card and envelope to the cashier, she fumbled through her purse to find four dollars. She dropped the four pennies she received in change into the dish on the counter, grabbed her bag, and turned to watch the couple of the evening walk out the door. Marlee and that wicked Granger Lamme.

Elliana froze near the exit. They hadn't seen her. She could avoid all the weirdness and not tell Marlee what a pretender Granger was, because, she reminded herself, that Marlee thought very little of her opinion, even if her opinion also happened to be a fact. She crouched low by the gumball machines to buy herself time to think without being conspicuous, letting her hair fall in front of her face. She inserted a quarter into a machine that dispensed small toys, turned the handle, and cupped her hand underneath to catch an opaque fluorescent orange capsule about the size of a ping pong ball.

She figured she would only make a fool of herself and be laughed to scorn by being presumptuous enough to rescue a girl who might not feel she needed rescuing—a girl who seemed to detest or even loathe her. Her nervous fingers pried off the cap to reveal her prize, and her stomach dropped. Inside she found a green rubber snake which reminded her exactly why Marlee needed rescuing: he was on an errand to create misery, and Marlee seemed to already have plenty.

Unfortunately, Elliana wasn't in the mood to be social with difficult people. She just wanted to be near Cai and far from the high school drama she kept trying to leave behind. Doubt and fear badgered her mind and almost weakened her courage until she remembered something Rose had said that first day in the Garden: "Doing the right thing only for the sake of curiosity or hope is still better than not doing it at all." And today she had said, "You needed to know that you can be courageous, and that you will always have help when you need it most."

Elliana pushed the exit door open and found Marlee and Granger standing dangerously close in front of his car about twenty feet away. She would play it cool.

"Hey, Marlee! Hey, Gray!" The timing seemed awkward, like Frick interrupting her and Cai's almost-first kiss.

Marlee looked startled by the call-out but acknowledged her. Granger said, "Hey, Ellie. Good to see you—it's been a while."

Clutching the toy snake in her hand, she walked over to where her two friends stood, hoping the right words would come out. Granger was definitely putting on an act to hide who he really was, and neither would likely take her seriously. He gave her a fist bump and smiled.

Elliana said, "What are you guys doing tonight? Do you want to come over to my house and eat pizza and watch a movie with Cai and me?" Her plans with Cai weren't really to stay in and watch a movie, but she needed to test Granger even if it meant changing her plans tonight.

"We're just hanging out, and Marlee's going to let me tell her she's pretty."

Elliana tried not to roll her eyes. "Why don't you guys come hang out at my house?"

"Not tonight, Ellie, but thanks for the offer. I already promised Marlee a special evening." Granger spoke evenly, not even bordering on being rude. "Maybe next week?"

He was really good. "Oh, I didn't realize you two were a thing, but I guess it's time you found someone else since Abbie shut down your aggressive advances."

Marlee scrunched her eyebrows slightly.

"What are you talking about? If Abbie said that, she's probably referring to someone else," Granger said, his voice controlled but amiable.

"Would I be lying if I said you were a snake with ulterior motives?" Elliana asked.

"Ellie, I have no idea what you're talking about." Granger laughed like they were friends, and it made Elliana feel like she was insane.

"What's gotten into you? You're acting like a spoiled baby," Marlee said. "You're just jealous and want to ruin my date."

"Marlee, I'm not jealous and you know full well I have a good reason for everything I do. If I wanted to ruin you, I would have done it several months ago after Eagle Island—no offense. I'm asking you to trust me and not go anywhere with Granger tonight."

"Well too bad. We're leaving." Marlee began to swing around.

Elliana grabbed Marlee's wrist before she could turn around, and said in a low voice, "He's not who he pretends to be. Normally I'd keep to myself, but I can't let you go with him. Please come with me."

Marlee yanked her hand away. "Ellie, just leave us alone. You're embarrassing yourself."

"It's true, Ellie. Did something happen today to make you lose it? You seem disturbed or *rattled* by something." His demeanor changed.

The way Granger jeered at Elliana told her she was right about him. His brown eyes seemed to taunt her, those same eyes from the car. Her grip tightened around the green snake in her hand, almost as if it would help choke the words out of the slippery Shadow. "Don't be a sore loser, Gray. It doesn't look good on you."

"Marlee looks good on me." Granger pulled Marlee close and kissed her cheek.

"Marlee can do much better than you."

Marlee looked confused and moved away from him slightly.

"What's your deal? Lighten up, Ellie!" Granger sneered.

His laugh was more to scorn her than to lighten the situation, which stung. This was going all wrong. She pleaded in her heart for inspiration like she had been given when the snake was about to strike. She needed to say the right thing in the right way before he struck again. Although she couldn't be sure what misery and pain Granger was pursuing, for she didn't understand exactly how the Shadow Realm operated, nor what they had to do to gain power, but Elliana knew he intended to endanger her life hours before which clarified in her mind he was up to no good and shouldn't be trusted.

"Okay, I will. But first answer one question, and then I will leave you alone. Granger, are you interested in a long-term relationship with Marlee?"

"Ellie, I can take care of myself!" Marlee's cheeks flushed from embarrassment, but she looked to Granger for his answer.

Those were the exact same words Abbie had said earlier in the day, also about Granger, and she had believed Abbie who was strong and stubborn, but she didn't believe those words when spoken by Marlee. Elliana's next words needed to be strategic or she could lose her narrow chance at preventing unnecessary misery.

"You heard her. She can take care of herself."

"I know you can, Marlee. But this guy is a user." She fixed her eyes on Granger with the expectation of a rebuttal. Awkward silence hung heavy in the air. Elliana began to think that maybe she should not have said anything because it seemed he wasn't going to give her the dignity of a response, but he probably wouldn't admit he commandeered the snake either. Her mind entered self-doubt mode as the silence passed; each uncomfortable second chiseled at her courage, whittling it away. She hated confrontations, and Marlee didn't seem to be appreciative of her intervention.

Feeling stupid came easy. It washed over her like the tide, pulling her into a pool of negative emotions. If Granger said nothing, she would be forced to leave, with her pride and courage wounded.

Just then she recalled what Rose said in the Garden about courage. She had a part to play. She stepped away from the negative tide pool that threatened to crush her spirit. She crossed her arms and intensified her glare; she would not back down—not tonight. "Well, let's have it, Granger. It's not like you to be weak and afraid."

Granger's face changed to that smooth-talking, flirtatious, overly-confident sports jock. He looked at Marlee and made a face that was kind of tempting and seductive—a look that any girl would think meant that he wanted her, a look that would be hard to resist because it would make her feel like the only girl in the world. With his arm around Marlee, he pulled her into his chest. "C'mon, babe. We don't have time to waste on this nosy little goody-goody. Let's go."

Marlee's back stiffened ever so slightly, giving Elliana the courage to continue. "If you don't have anything to hide, then just say it. Are you interested in a long-term relationship with my best friend?" She hadn't expected to say those words, but they felt right in the moment.

Marlee flinched and batted her eyes to clear away the tears. Seconds later, Marlee turned toward Granger, who was only inches away from her face.

Of all the snarky, cutting comments Marlee had dished out in the past few months, now would be the time for at least one! Elliana shifted her stance as a fierce hope that Marlee wouldn't choose to go with Granger pounded in her chest. Her mind was abuzz with so many thoughts that it was hard to stay focused. She willed courage to stay in her breast and took a slight step to the right to see both facial expressions.

Marlee's words finally broke the thick silence. "We're both just looking for a good time, aren't we?" Her eyes tightened and her lips puckered ever so slightly.

Elliana must have misread the emotion in Marlee's eyes, because now it was all but apparent that Marlee had every intention of going with him—the delivery-boy of misery—and Elliana would look the fool. The tide waters lapped again at her feet, ankles, shins, knees. But if she worried looking the fool, her courage would leave her, so she ordered herself to remain strong.

The next few seconds dragged on uncomfortably, like when her leg would fall asleep and she would wait for the painful, prickling pins and needles to finally leave.

Granger spoke in a low tone with a seductive look on his face. "I'm looking for good time. You're looking for a good time. The stars have aligned, and tonight's the night to have a little fun, right bae?"

Elliana really wanted to shank him now. First of all, he had absolutely no idea about stars. Second of all, he also apparently had no clue about how to treat a girl or what a girl really wants—which is to be cherished, not objectified, and definitely not to be used.

She looked now at Marlee, whose facial expression was still hard to read. Would Marlee stay with him?

Marlee leaned toward Granger with pouty lips, getting closer and closer. Her left hand caressed Granger's left check. Then her right palm flew to his face with a deafening fleshy slap that sent his face spinning. Marlee pushed against Granger's chest so hard that he stumbled backwards and had to regain his footing. "Tonight is NOT the night! And there will never be another minute that I want to spend with you!"

Elliana sighed with relief so loudly that the other two must have heard it. This was exactly the ending she had hoped for. "C'mon, Marlee, I'll drive you home."

She reached for Marlee's elbow and locked arms while Granger regained his footing. "You're going to regret this, Elliana Reinhart. I promise." He hissed the ending of the last word.

Elliana tossed the toy snake at his feet and felt sorry for him. The two girls shuffled towards Elliana's car without looking back.

"I meant what I said back there. You are my best friend, Marlee. And he really is a jerk."

By the time they had closed the car doors, Marlee's shoulders began to heave and shake. Elliana assumed it was a mixture of emotions, probably from the embarrassment of Granger's jerkiness.

Elliana drove towards Marlee's house while her best friend cried, and she reached her arm over and grabbed Marlee's hand to comfort her. Not a word was spoken, but they were communicating, and the emotional distance between them was closing.

Her car rolled to a stop in the driveway, and she turned toward Marlee. "Can we talk?"

Marlee worked on gaining her composure. "What about your movie night?"

"I made that up to gauge Granger's intentions, sorry. I'm actually supposed to meet Cai later."

They walked arm in arm into the house, up the stairs, down the hallway, and into Marlee's room. Elliana immediately spun around and bear-hugged Marlee for the first time in what felt like months.

Marlee squeezed back and they stood hugging for a long minute. She could feel Marlee's sobs start to ebb and asked, "What happened to us?"

They sat on the bed across from each other, cross-legged, like in the good days. Through sobs and tears, Marlee said, "I don't deserve your friendship. I've been horrible and unkind and a total witch. Even today I was such a brat to you at Confucius.

Why did you bother to stop tonight? Why would you want to help me after everything I've done?"

Elliana hoped this would be the heart-to-heart talk that she longed for to heal their friendship and their hearts. "Marlee, all the kindness you've shown me over the years far outweighs the recent stuff. I don't know what I did to cause a rift, but I want you to know I'm sorry for my part in this."

Marlee wiped her eyes with her fingers. "No, I'm so sorry. It's all my fault. You didn't do anything but be nice to me. Each time you were nice to me reminded me of what a horrible person I am."

"You're not a horrible person. You're human, but not horrible."

"I lost it after what Jared did—leading me on and then totally dissing me. He stomped on my heart when it was hurting the most—right after my parents got in a huge fight. I don't know why I did what I did. I don't have any excuse except that I was jealous of you and I panicked."

Elliana's eyebrows rose. "Why in the world would you be jealous of me?"

"A lot of reasons actually. I wish I were like you. You're smart. You have the perfect family; I doubt your parents ever fight. And mostly because of who you attract. I might get the hot, popular guys, but you're close to the good ones that are worth keeping."

That revelation shocked Elliana. Never had she imagined any of that. In fact, she often thought that Marlee had disdain for her because she just couldn't measure up. But jealous? Wow. "I'm sorry about Jared, about your parents fighting, about Granger. There are a lot of jerky guys out there, but there is someone out there for you. Don't ever settle for someone that doesn't adore you and doesn't want to commit to you. Some guy will make you feel loved and will make you want to be a better person—that's the guy for you. Trust me, he's out there. Just be patient. Or slightly reckless—I hear running a guy over with a car works." Elliana figured Marlee had heard her story through the rumor mill.

Both girls started laughing, and then Marlee snorted as she tried to laugh and sob at the same time, which made them laugh even harder. It was so comforting to laugh with her best friend again. She had missed girl talk with Marlee. They chatted and laughed and cried. Burying the hatchet was good for the soul.

An hour into their heart-to-heart, which was teaching Elliana how to heal a broken heart, Cai called to see if they were still on for their date and apologized for being a few hours late in calling. He encouraged her to spend as much time as she needed and to call him when she was done.

The longer the girls talked, the heavier Elliana's heart felt. Marlee's home life had seemed like it was ideal—her parents spoiled her, she had pretty much everything she wanted—but home was troubled. Marlee didn't tell a soul because she was too embarrassed, especially when she saw so much going right for Elliana in the same moment that Marlee's life and happiness were crumbling beneath her feet. She had been trying to seek out stability, someone to lean on, something to cling to, but she failed. The more she chased love, the more it eluded her. The more she needed love and friendship, the more she behaved badly and repelled friends.

A few times during their conversation, one or both of the girls were brought to tears. Life could be cruel to everyone; insecurities even plagued the kids who seemed to have it all. The only thing that made it all worth it was to have the love and support of people close to you. Marlee didn't have any of that now. Her family had gradually been growing apart. Her dad spent even more time working, traveling—doing pretty much anything else but paying attention to her or her mom. Marlee's mom seemed to be having a midlife crisis and spent most of her days with her friends, at the gym, or getting pampered at the salon. Marlee had been feeling alone for many long months, even before the fallout in April.

"Please, let's never let that happen again to our friendship. I need you, and you need me," Elliana said.

"I know. I'm sorry about the past few months. You have no idea how good my heart feels tonight. It hasn't felt like this in a long while! Talking with you was like finding a life raft when I was about to drown."

Elliana reached forward and hugged her friend. Neither one of them could be the one that let go.

Something amazing had happened—and only because Elliana faced her fear with courage.

Marlee walked Elliana outside so she could still see Cai before it got too late. When they stepped out the front door, they were both immediately awestruck by the nightscape. The sky was an intense midnight blue and purple, dotted with billions of twinkling stars. They walked down the driveway to get a better look and stood a few minutes admiring the master-piece. The Milky Way was brighter than she had ever seen it. It was almost as if a curtain to the sky was opened. Every part of the night sky was bejeweled with stellar glitter balls. She saw stars she never knew existed.

The view was so mesmerizing that neither could look away. As she stared at the majestic night sky, a light, sparkly, happy, soaring feeling swelled inside her. The longer she stared at the sky, the more she wanted to stargaze with Cai, and her heart thumped.

As anxious as she was to see Cai, which was pretty freaking anxious, she first wanted to tell Rose about how her courage to act had led to making amends, especially since it would literally only take a minute.

꩜

"Tonight was a Great Sky," Rose said. "Every time a Great Sky appears, a heart has been healed on Earth. Looking at the stars of the Great Sky cleanses the heart and soul and helps humans reconnect with their origins. It re-centers the heart. That was your Great Sky tonight, and its beauty has been captured here in your Garden for you to remember." Rose pointed to the newly blossomed tree to her right, the same one Rose was planting during her last visit. "Electra needs many more Great Sky healings to grow stronger."

Elliana sized up the tree packed with yellow-orange blooms. Then she remembered what she wanted to ask Rose. "Did a Shadow purposefully cause my first parents' deaths?"

Rose nodded. "Yes, and I'm sorry. It had to happen for you to end up in Star, Idaho—to find the Seeking Realm. The Shadows thought they won with that tragedy, but you're here now, and you're stronger than you would be otherwise. But loss is never easy."

After a few minutes of silent contemplation, Rose patted Elliana's hand gently and said she would give her some time by herself to ponder and rejuvenate.

꩜

At 10:00 p.m., when she finally saw Cai for the first time that day, it felt like a week had gone by. He walked up her driveway and they embraced without saying a word. She had about a thousand things to say, but he probably did too.

She handed him the envelope and told him to give it to his parents, and then she asked about his grandmother and family as they walked to her backyard.

Cai explained that it was too soon to know the extent of the damage, but things looked promising and his grandmother had an excellent team of doctors. After summarizing what he found out at the hospital, Cai told her that his mind was exhausted with worry and he just wanted to spend time with her and take a break from the stress.

"Just look at the stars tonight and I'm sure you'll feel better." Elliana grabbed an old quilt from a basket near the back door. They spread the quilt on the flattest part of the lawn they could find and lay down on their backs, hands behind their heads, elbows touching.

"There are no words for how amazing the sky is tonight." Cai sighed.

"I know. I think it's the most beautiful starscape I've ever seen. It kind of looks like how my heart feels."

Cai turned his head to look at her. "What does that mean?"

"The miracle is that I made up with Marlee, and my heart feels so clear and light—it might sound dumb, but I don't know how else to describe it. First, let me tell you more of the story."

She rolled onto her side told him about seeing Marlee at Confucius, at the drug store, and what they talked about afterwards. She told him that she didn't trust Granger. No sooner had the words escaped her lips, she felt torn because there was so much more of the story about Granger that would make her look less crazy. Or perhaps more crazy, depending upon whether he believed in other realms.

"Really, it wasn't only because of the way Granger was

talking to Marlee. There's more, but it won't make sense just now. Just trust me."

He grabbed her hand. "I'm glad you two made up today. I know that's been weighing on you." Cai took her hand and placed it over his heart. "You're right. Something about tonight's sky steadies me."

He shared some of his favorite memories with his grandmother: drinking her ice-cold lemonade on hot summer days; her reading the grandkids bedtime stories that sometimes verged on scary; rock hunting in the mountains; wading in the brook behind her house; spending every Christmas Eve at grandma's house in front of the fire, sipping hot cocoa with marshmallows, and sucking on wintergreen candies.

The two talked under the stars until curfew—sharing family stories and relishing their childhoods. The moment never seemed right to say she wanted to be in an exclusive relationship with him, but she couldn't be disappointed because it was a beautiful night and a happy ending to her long, dramatic day—a day that seemed bent on being the worst day ever, but ended with a Great Sky and holding hands with Cai.

CHAPTER TWENTY-NINE

Starling

ANTICIPATING THE TALK with Burke made Elliana's stomach sour. She asked him to meet her for a game of mini-golf, which Burke won with a score that was less than half of hers. It was a welcome defeat. After returning the putters, they bought waffle cones and sat next to each other on a nearby bench under the wide shadow of a red maple tree.

"Let's have it, Ellie. What's really on your mind?"

"Heavy stuff. Well, it's not so heavy now that you annihilated my mini-golf score. Again." She laughed, hoping it would lighten the words she had just spoken, but a thickness hung in the air that choked out their easy conversation.

"I think I know what you're going to say."

"Well I'd better say it anyways, just to be fair."

"You don't have to say anything. I can read you, and I don't want this to be any harder than it has to be. You're my best friend."

A tear rolled down her cheek. "You're such a good one, Burke."

"Please don't cry." He reached over to catch her tear on his fingertip. "I think I knew it would turn out this way—maybe because this is how it was meant to be. I'm glad Cai didn't turn out to be a serial killer. You guys make a good couple, and I can tell he makes you happy."

Elliana nodded. "It's not that you—"

"You don't have to explain anything. Let's just say we have no regrets and we are stronger now because of it."

"You're going to make some girl very happy."

He bounced his eyebrows. "Yeah, Veronica Curry! She totally wants me and promised to write to me while she's in juvey." He couldn't keep a straight face for the last part of his sarcastic remark. He burst into laughter the same moment that Elliana did. Veronica had just gotten busted for illegal activities, and one rumor had it that she told someone that Burke was her secret boyfriend.

Elliana laughed herself into near hysteria, which made it really hard to eat melting ice cream. The more she laughed, the more the liquid dessert ran down her chin. Burke mimicked her unladylike-ness and they both laughed until they cried. Having ice cream dribble down her chin would have been embarrassing with anybody else, but Elliana and Burke had that type of relationship. Their best-friendship had not been ruined.

For the next ten minutes, each time one would regain composure, the other would start laughing again.

"Burke, you'll be the famous hot-sexy-boyfriend amongst the lady prisoners. They'll all be writing you and sending you pictures and making pretty promises to have your babies."

"Too bad there's only one of me. Someday I'll be the famous husband who stood by his crazy woman while she was in juvey. And then I'll run for office." Burke puffed out his chest.

An older gentleman walked by the laughing teenagers and

muttered to his wife, "Kids today are out of control."

Elliana and Burke laughed even harder.

At the end of their best-friend date while standing on her front porch, Elliana said, "Thank you."

"Anytime. Now please help me plan my wedding—the colors will be orange and orange. And if that doesn't work out, there's always your twin sister. I saw the way she was checking me out. She totally wants to marry me."

They both laughed again.

Elliana threw her arms around Burke's neck and hugged him tight. "You're the best."

"Right back at you, future sister-in-law."

Elliana's body and mind were exhausted. She had ported to the Seeking Realm to talk to Rose and felt she needed to stay awhile and enjoy the respite. She sat down on a glowing rock by the singing brook, leaned down, and touched the water with her fingertips. She never remembered feeling so tired, so drowsy of all the times she had been to the Seeking Realm. Exhaustion pressed down upon her. She lay down next to the brook and used her arm as a pillow, the other arm dangled over the edge and played with the water.

Her eyelids struggled to remain open. She gave in to the exhaustion and closed her eyes for what seemed like a moment, when she heard a man's voice say, "Elliana."

She opened her eyes and stood where she had been lying down, but Wayne was not there. Maybe she had been dreaming.

"Elliana," his voice came again from further down the garden. She walked through her Garden towards the voice and plucked two handfuls of fruits from the Ambrosia tree. She took a bite from the first fruit, her eyes squinting with delight, and finished the others as she walked farther.

"Elliana, open the gate."

She walked towards the gate. Several bushes and flowering plants formed a barrier. Squeezing through the thick growth, she found a white stone wall that glistened in the sunlight. A few feet to her right she saw a wrought-iron gate with crystalline pickets. She drew a deep breath.

After lifting the latch, she pushed the gate open to expose a full view of the cobblestone-paved path that stretched out before her. Unable to take her eyes off what lay ahead, she let the gate swing closed and began walking the path. Stone walls rose up on each side and the path began to climb. Once she reached the highest point of the path, after what felt like an hour, she could see a golden city, glistening with light, surrounded by a strip of gardens and a walking path. A wider walkway led to the castle in the center.

She arrived at the garden's edge and was greeted by a man tending the tulip garden. He stood, smiled, and said, "Welcome to Teleos. I will take you to the King." She did not recognize the man, though he did seem familiar.

"The King?" she asked. She remembered Wayne told her she would meet the rulers of the Seeking Realm one day and it would help her with her quest.

"Yes, please follow me, dear. The inner court is not far from here. They are waiting for you." As they started walking, he introduced himself and explained what some of the magnificent trees and plants were named and how old they were. Soon they had reached the palace, and he opened the door to let her pass through.

There a woman introduced herself and offered to take her to the King. Because she couldn't feel fear in the Seeking Realm, it felt right. The entry opened up into an ample, glorious hall with columns, polished floors, and murals painted on the walls. At the end of the hall, about fifty paces forward, two enormous double doors towered over her. They walked forward to the doors in silence, and the doors opened slowly. Two thrones stood near the back, their occupants rising to greet her.

Elliana immediately fell to her knees and bowed, unsure of proper protocol when meeting a King of an entire Realm.

"Elliana, please come, my dear," the King called from his throne. The room was larger than a conference hall, but his voice carried smoothly.

She rose to her feet and commenced the walk to the thrones. She did not know what to say to this King or Queen in their grandeur, nor why she was being presented to them. Elliana could barely make out the Queen clasping her hands to her heart.

It couldn't be. She sucked in her breath and reached up and placed her hand over her heart.

No, it was impossible.

The King looked exactly like Wayne, and the Queen like Rose.

The King stood and smiled, almost winking. "Welcome. I am King Teleos of the Seeking Realm," and pointing to his wife, "this is my Queen. We are your great-great-great-grandparents."

Queen Rose dashed forward and embraced her. It was the kind of embrace that felt like coming home. "Elliana, my great-granddaughter," she whispered.

King Wayne wrapped his arms around them both. It was then that she understood who she was and why she had come: she was coming home, to her origins. Tears poured from Elliana's eyes, and all three sank to their knees while holding hands. "How?"

Wayne answered. "Your great-great-great-grandmother and I sent your mother into the Earth Realm over twenty years ago. Your birth mother, Irena, passed tragically when you and Hannah were born, but it was part of the plan. You and your twin sister were adopted into different families with a plan to be reunited when the time was right. You've become a different person because of your hardships; you've become a Seeker."

She looked into Wayne's gentle eyes and was overwhelmed by the warmth she felt.

The King reached his left hand forward and stroked her cheek. "You will be the light for others. For that and many other reasons I rejoice in you. We are pleased that you have grown so much in character through your quests and journey of self-knowledge."

"Your Majesties," Elliana said, trying to speak properly now that she knew Wayne and Rose were actually the King and Queen, and feeling a little awkward at having called them by their first names before. "Thank you for encouraging me and for believing in me."

"You can call us by our family names now: Great-Grandfather and Great-Grandmother—no need for great-great-great or third-great. Too wordy, as our Earth Friends say." The King smiled. "We are so overjoyed with your life, and with your finding the Seeking Realm. It was so simple, finding your Garden. Was it not?"

"Yes, Great-Grandfather." The titles felt more natural because of the loving relationship they had developed throughout her visits to the Seeking Realm. "Why didn't you tell me before, that we are related?"

The Queen squeezed her hand. "We needed you to be a

Seeker, and Seekers can't get all the answers right away or it would rob them of valuable learning experiences. You are in training, and it is part of the strategy to help you grow."

Elliana nodded. "I wish I had known about the Seeking Realm earlier."

The King sighed. "Sweet child, it is not your fault. The Shadows from the enemy realm have spread lies to hide this knowledge from Earth in an effort to gain power and steal your higher destiny from you and all Earth Friends. They have succeeded in many of their sabotage plans throughout time. However, you were born with the Spark of Ambrosia that told your soul you were more than just one of billions, that your destiny was more than just survival, that your life was more than what you could comprehend. This Spark drove you to discover your powerful heritage, your origins, which was all part of the plan."

She hesitated, and the King sensed her apprehension. "Feel free to ask your question."

"I don't mean this with any disrespect, Great-Grandfather and Great-Grandmother, but I am curious. How come I couldn't live here with you, where it is so peaceful and beautiful all the time?"

"Elliana, your Great-Grandfather and I grieved at parting with your mother, as did the city of Teleos, but you could not learn all of life's lessons in this realm. We knew you could be a Seeker and help Electra regain her lost light. The thought of having our great-granddaughter reared in the Earth Realm without us was agonizing, but we planned a way for you to return, to discover the Seeking Realm when you were strong enough to understand and apply the knowledge you would gain from it. And we knew that you would seek truth and find your Garden after your dream."

"Please know," the King said, "that we are confident you will succeed because you rise each time you fall. You are being true to your purpose."

Knowing she was just one person, she otherwise would have felt disbelief in her ability to do much at all. But in the presence of her great-grandfather, doubt was not possible. "What else must I do?" Her eyes were pleading, searching.

"The Seeking Realm needs you," the Queen said, "to live true to that Ambrosia Spark within you. Follow the good voice in your heart. Live up to your potential. Lift others with pure love. Spread light. Share the lost truths."

"Think about what you can do, what you have done already." The King stood up and reached down to help lift the Queen and Elliana to their feet. "Many are needed to be change agents, but so many don't have the courage to actually make a difference. You have a special influence on others, and many will be willing to listen to you because of your heart. Begin with teaching Hannah to become a Seeker."

The simple answer struck her immediately. Never before had it dawned on her that finding her voice could lend such power in teaching earth friends about pure love and the lost treasure of knowledge of the Seeking Realm. A strange but wonderful thought entered her mind, and she looked up at her parents again.

He nodded. "Yes." He paused momentarily, not as if he had to think about what next to say, but to allow her time to process the realization of this new task. "You know what to do, Elliana. The Earth Realm has been waiting for your voice, your words, and Hannah's, too. You two will make a powerful team."

Elliana paused pensively. "What should I say?"

The Queen answered, "Teach Earth that each person must become the hope the world needs, to seek higher knowledge, and to see with new eyes. Teach them the secret of saving Electra by teaching them of truth and love—pure love inspired by goodness, not by greed nor self-interest nor lust. Teach of the loving Matron that awaits them in their very own Garden of this Seeking Realm, and that their Garden gives light and life to Electra. When each Garden glows from goodness, Electra glows too, for the Gardens of the Seeking Realm are the only sources of Electra's light. One must visit her Garden to know how to create light, and the more Earth friends that visit their Gardens, the brighter the star, and the better the universe. We need more Seekers."

"Thank you, Great-grandfather and Great-grandmother." Elliana would be overwhelmed and doubtful in any other circumstance upon being told of the grand expectations she needed to fulfill. This was different. Her mind began to do something it had never done before: it zoomed and soared past the self-imposed limits, past the harsh self-criticisms, and past the rolling eyes of doubters. After everything she had experienced—especially the hardships and setbacks—she knew, standing there, as knowledge and power seemed to fill her mind, that she could perform this task. She could make a difference. "I will."

The King and Queen both embraced her and walked her to the double doors, each holding one of Elliana's hands. The King's and Queen's eyes glistened with emotion, and they embraced Elliana again. She didn't let go for a long while now that she knew they were her great-grandparents—her blood family, her origins—and that she would have to leave them shortly to return to the Earth Realm. After a tearful farewell,

Elliana retraced the same path until she was back in her Garden near the singing brook. She was tired again.

She awakened suddenly next to the brook, unable to tell if meeting her royal great-grandparents had really just happened or if it had been a dream. But at that moment, she knew it didn't matter if it was real or just a vision. There was no need to walk to the edge of the Garden and retrace the cobbled path to see if Teleos really existed in the Seeking Realm. There was no need to verify that the King and Queen had spoken to her and counseled her. She already knew them, and their love was written in her heart.

She knew. She knew. She knew.

A Risk

"THIS IS GOING TO SOUND CRAZY and perhaps delusional, but please hear us out and don't cast any judgments until we've told you everything." Elliana and Hannah looked at each member of the Reinhart family and held their gaze.

Elliana said, "I've discovered a secret to making the world a better place, and I need your support. But first I have a lot to teach you."

Hannah and Elliana took turns teaching the Reinhart family. They taught how Electra reflects the condition of love on earth, giving it feedback on how it needed to improve; its dimming light is a warning to the Earth Realm about the balance of power between the Seeking Realm and the Shadow Realm. But the knowledge had been lost about how to access this special realm that lifted Seeker's thoughts and reflected the light of their goodness.

Her family listened, and to her relief, they didn't think she was a nutcase, especially when Hannah verified she had been there, too.

Having two Seekers working as a team made the job of finding more Seekers easier, because two people were more readily believed than one. Elliana and Hannah did make a powerful duo. Elliana knew that she needed many Seekers in order to accomplish her Soul Purpose.

When Elliana thought about her Soul Purpose and love, she thought about Cai, and each time she thought about him her heart thumped loudly in reminder of what she still needed to tell him. She had a star-gazing date with Cai that evening in his backyard, and it was nearly dinner time.

Elliana stood up and said, "I want to take you all to the Seeking Realm now, but it will only work if you believe with your whole soul, so I need to know. Do you hope and believe? Are you ready to seek?"

When each nodded their assent, Hannah said, "Y'all are going to love it."

Elliana led them to the backyard and they stood around one of the aspen trees and pointed to Orly. "This is my magic bird, Orly, who creates portals. Before we do this, you need to repeat in your mind 'I believe.'" Elliana put her right hand on the tree trunk and had her family stand behind her and do the same, with Hannah as the caboose. "Okay, now use your left hand and touch the person in front of you—on the shoulder or back is fine. We take four steps with our eyes open, and three with our eyes closed. One, two, three, four. Five, six, seven."

The night was warm and the sky was clear. They sat on a blanket in the grass playing footsie, making up stories about the stars: how stars were Guardians, how stars were living things, how stars could feel, and how that meant they could dim and die, like Electra.

Elliana scooted closer to Cai and said, "There's something I want to tell you." She fished the alexandrite out of her pocket and held it in her hand.

Cai raised his eyebrows and bit his bottom lip.

Her heart pounded. "I've been thinking, you know, about us. And I like us. So I've made my choice."

He smirked like he wasn't going to reply until she made a more concrete statement. "And what is this choice exactly?"

"You're seriously going to make me say all the words, aren't you?" She thought about how her last conversation with Burke was way easier than she expected, and this one was harder.

He leaned toward her. "Just a few pretty words, Starlight. You owe me that much."

She looked down at the stone, and then coyly looked back at his face. "You are good for me. I always want to be with you, and I think about you when I'm not, and you make me want to be a better person, and so I chose you."

His smile widened and he looked her deep in the eyes. "I knew it the first day I met you. It's okay that you're a little slow."

"There you go, Romeo, ruining the moment."

"Nah, I'm not ruining the moment. I'm adding to it. I'm agreeing with you. I like us, too." He paused. "How's your heart?"

She understood the reference.

"My heart says a kiss can wait another year." She burst out laughing a second later, even though she had tried to keep a straight face.

He grabbed her hand and made her look at him. "There you go, Starlight, ruining the mood. Now you have to make it up to me with a dance."

"We don't have any music."

"I'll provide the music." He rose and pulled her to a standing position, drew her to his chest, put his arm around her back,

and started to sing an old love song.

> When I see your face and hold your hand,
> I think I'm in a perfect dream land.
> When you look into my eyes and smile,
> I want us both to stay awhile
> In this place where you belong with me.
>
> When I see your bright eyes look my way,
> Your smile takes my breath away.
> And all I know is I get lost in your beauty.
> Please say you'll stay awhile
> In this place where you belong with me.
>
> Sometimes I think it's all just a dream,
> But I open my eyes and you're right here beside me.
> Darling, you are the wings that lift me higher,
> My starry sky after the long day is over,
> Together with you I can take on the world,
> Fight any foe, because you are my world.
> Holding you is holding onto
> Everything good I'll ever know, I'll ever see.
> Please say you'll stay awhile
> In this place where you belong with me.

He lowered his head and rested his jaw on her forehead as he sang while they danced. His raspy, smoky voice strummed her heart strings, fueling a surge of warmth in her chest. Elliana closed her eyes, rested her check against his jaw, and relished the music and the moment.

At the end of his song, Cai swung her around. When he set

her down, he held her close.

"I didn't know you could sing. That was really sweet." Elliana said.

"I knew if I sang this song any earlier, you'd've been swooning all over me, and I had to know that you liked me for me and not just for my romantic swooning songs." Cai tugged the ends of her hair. "Actually, I was saving it for when you would finally tell me that this amazing feeling is mutual. It was a long wait, you know, but I wouldn't have it any other way. Waiting made it better."

"Did you know I would choose you? I think I knew."

"I didn't really know for sure, but I hoped as much as a guy could."

She gazed into his eyes with a confidence she wasn't used to. No words came out, so she looked at his very kissable lips, and back up into his blue-gray eyes.

His eyebrows questioned her.

Elliana's smile made her eyes squint slightly, and she nodded.

Cai inclined his head towards hers, and Elliana raised up slightly on tip toes. The anticipation was incredible and seemed to slow down time.

Their. Lips. Met.

It was a pure kiss, one of the sweetest ever recorded in history. It was the sugar of baby's breath, it was the touch of velvet, it was shivers down her neck, it was sparks in her heart, but best of all, it was heartfelt. She knew exactly why it was worth waiting for the right one at the right time, because kisses weren't currency. Kisses were gems you only gave to the one who guarded your heart.

She grabbed both of his hands in hers and whistled a chirp. "Close your eyes," Elliana said.

"You're going to kiss me again, aren't you?" Cai closed his eyes and smirked.

"I have a surprise for you, but you have to believe in the star of love and the power of heartfelt kisses. You know, your theory on why Electra went dim." Elliana rubbed her sapphire pendant to calm her nerves.

Cai opened his eyes. "You know I had a dream about that the night before we met?"

"I wouldn't doubt that. You can tell me all about it in a minute. Right now I'm taking you somewhere special with the help of my magical bird." Air brushed against her cheek from the fluttering of wings and she felt Orly's feet prickle her shoulder. "Close your eyes again and keep them closed until I tell you to open them." She leaned her cheek on Orly's fluffy wing and said, "Port to Seeking Realm."

She waited a few seconds before saying, "Open your eyes, slowly."

Cai's eyes widened and slowly scanned the scenery. "Did you just slip me a hallucinogen, or what just happened?"

The King sat atop his grand horse, smiling. "I see you've brought a fifth visitor, Elliana. Welcome to the Star-side of the Seeking Realm, Cai." The King introduced himself and answered several of Cai's questions.

"Please leave your shoes at the foot of the tree," Orly sang.

"Great-grandfather, where can we see Electra from my Garden?" Elliana asked.

The King told her to stand on the right side of the Ambrosia tree and look near the horizon. "I'll let you two find your way."

Elliana and Cai walked to the Ambrosia tree where she pointed to a group of stars, and said, "There's Electra. We can test out your theory now, if you want to."

The Garden and Electra's weak light flickered and then surged. The star could heal if everyone who knew the secret shared it with someone.

But they'd have to dare to hope and be drawn to believe it first.

T H E   E N D

Bonus Chapter Follows

ACKNOWLEDGMENTS

Thank you to my sister Katrina who gave me loads of feedback and supported for years my dream to write. Thanks to my dad who took a break from his normal diet of nonfiction to read a work of fiction for the first time in decades and then cheered me on.

Thank you to all of my beta readers, especially Monica Fox, Amanda Jeffress Klerapek, Amy Glidewell, Jenn Bowler, Becky Smith, my daughter Mia, my nephew Bransen, and my nieces Faith, Gabby, and Mari. I could not have done this without all the encouragement and feedback from my family and friends. Thank you all.

ABOUT THE AUTHOR

Alana Lee grew up in Cleveland, Ohio. She received both a B.S. in Sociology and a Master of Organizational Behavior from Brigham Young University.

Since 2012, she has taught composition courses at San Juan College in Farmington, NM, where she has amazing students who inspire her by all they've overcome.

She now calls a dusty, tumbleweed-covered New Mexican mesa with a perfect view of the Shiprock monadnock home, where she lives with her husband and three daughters.

When she's not teaching or sweeping up after her kids, she enjoys graphic design, calligraphy, and eating bags of Swedish fish.

I love to hear from my readers. Please feel free to contact me in any of the following ways:
thestarlightlegend@gmail.com
www.facebook.com/alana.lee.12
www.instagram.com/alanaleedesigns

For a list of Book Club Questions, please visit my blog:
StarlightLegend.blogspot.com

To sign up for my newsletter:
http://eepurl.com/dKE_Mo

Snapped

GRANGER PUNCHED HIS FIST clean through the wall in his bedroom in hopes that the thrill and the pain would prevent his mind from replaying the chastisement from hours before.

You lost your chance, Granger. You thought you were so good, and your ego got in the way, and you burned that one bad. Now you're back at the bottom until you can do something to prove you're not completely useless.

Useless was the same insult his father had said to him nearly every day of his life. Now it was coming from someone he cared the most about impressing: Larry.

I took a chance on you, kid, and how do you repay me? You botch the most important mission yet. You make me sick—get outta my face before I demote you to rat duty.

Commandeering rats was child's play, for amateurs, not for seasoned Grifters like him.

He had duped Elliana like a professional. Thanks to his charisma and warmth, he'd become her trusted friend within weeks. With a nearly invisible spy app that he coded himself, he had been able to hack her computer and delete any file he wanted. He'd almost even gotten away with turning in a plagiarized paper with her name on it.

Disassembling Janet's car battery had been simple enough, but injecting her with a megadose of insulin while pretending to check for a supposed gas leak was evidence that he was better than most twice his age. Larry had been impressed.

Veronica was an easy pawn who willingly tripped Abbie, created the cruel poster, and sent the text that went viral—Veronica had swooned like a dry leaf in the wind the second he turned his charm on her.

Larry'd been right though because Granger's ego did get in the way. He misjudged with the elk and it hit the wrong driver. Larry had been hot about it.

Dislodging the stone on the mountain was one of his favorite moments—from the planning stage to execution—though ultimately that mission failed as well. He relished the sound of her sad little sobbings afterward. Of course he shared Larry's disappointment. But Granger knew terror had left a mark and helped break her down, and he still had several weeks to finish the job Larry had given him. As Granger saw it, he had been right on schedule, and he convinced Larry to see it the same way.

Placing a tracking device in Elliana's car had been easy, too. Knowing where she was at all times was essential to the final mission. But Larry was right. Being the best Grifter in the unit had inflated his ego.

His worst foul-up still seared in his memory. He'd gotten too cocky. She was supposed to die. But even if the bite didn't kill her, surely she'd have given up being a Seeker if she was lucky enough to survive the rattlesnake bite. Rather than immediately guiding the rattler to lunge right at Elliana's jugular, he used the snake to taunt her and heighten her terror and really just torture the crap out of her as long as he could. He'd meant to go through with it, and the snake's fangs were literally only centimeters away, which would have taken nanoseconds to close the gap, but he failed and the snake ended up dead.

He'd have strangled it himself if that stupid Guardian didn't slice through its neck. So now he found himself punching holes through his bedroom walls while his uncle was at work.

As soon as he'd seen that blasted featherball fly to her rescue, he'd realized he had misjudged by no more than a second. One second was the reason that he was now useless.

Well that was the first reason. The second reason was that he failed even more miserably when Elliana confronted him and Marlee in the drug store parking lot—though he'd hid from Larry to avoid another beating. He'd gone after Marlee as another angle to eventually get at and destroy Elliana; he wanted to get close to Marlee and play on her jealousy and anger to learn more of Elliana's weaknesses, and ultimately turn Marlee into a Grifter like him.

He'd miscalculated that Elliana Reinhart—she was more persuasive than he thought she could be. After she stole Marlee from him and tossed the toy snake at his feet, he'd never been more embarrassed and humiliated and rabid in his life—he now had sixteen holes in the wall to prove it.

The seventeenth time he punched the wall, he hit a stud. SNAP!

His wrist seared like he was stabbed with hot fire pins, bathed in acid, and then hit with a sledgehammer. He groaned and fell to the floor. Pain and adrenaline flooded his body, so he bit his bottom lip to prevent his scream from making the neighbors suspicious and calling the cops; getting in trouble with the law was automatic suspension for Grifters. He had worked too hard and come too far to jeopardize his status in the Shadow Realm.

A bitter metallic taste filled his mouth as his teeth broke through the flesh of his lip. The deformed bend in his wrist told him he'd be in a cast for six weeks. Useless.

Unless he figured out another way to destroy that darling Seeker and prove himself worthy of a promotion.

Larry would answer to him someday. He'd make sure of it.

Things were about to get real.

Made in the USA
Middletown, DE
31 October 2018